MW00787029

GO AWAY

A spy, a drug dealer, a thief and a murderer walk into a bar..

KATHLEEN SUMMERS

Book Cover by Brandi Doane McCann

Other Books by Kathleen Summers

Invisible Rider

Contents

Chapter One

DON'T LOOK BACK

ANTONIO

It was an explosion that would change his life.

It was just coming up on dawn, still black dark, a warm north Florida June morning on the Atlantic Ocean. Antonio was fishing just offshore, south of Jacksonville. His boat rocked steadily in an easy, balmy breeze, and the water gently licked the boat's sides. He killed his engine so as not to scare the fish. He loved it out here at this time of day. Quiet, dark and cool. He could barely feel the air on his skin. He had the ocean to himself. He hadn't caught anything yet, but that didn't matter. It was the solitude he enjoyed. He had a lot on his mind and some decisions to make.

Lily, his second wife, never left his mind. He'd made many mistakes, and she'd been a big one. She often crept back into the apartment in the early morning, like a cat coming in from its night on the prowl. If there'd been a cat door, she would have crawled through it. She was often barely standing when she returned. He didn't know where she went at night and didn't care. He'd wanted it to end, for her to go, disappear, get out of his life forever. She smeared his living space with her rancid slovenliness and her disdain. She'd been gone for two weeks. No one asked after her at the building. No one noticed she was gone. She hadn't come home for days before. This would not be considered new behavior.

He hadn't reclaimed the bedroom. Couldn't face it just yet. He wondered who'd come looking for her. Her mother?

There was no point in reporting her missing. That would create suspicion. Antonio didn't need that.

The stillness of the lapping waves was suddenly shattered by a loud boom. Antonio stood, rubbed his unshaven chin, lazily scratched his ass, and looked to the dark sky, wondering if some jet had broken the sound barrier. Seeing no jet trail, he turned his eyes to the shore. On the horizon was a stream of fire shooting up into the blackness, way over near his condo. *Couldn't be my building*, he thought; *too far away*. His building was miles inland and backed onto an industrial park. He turned on the boat radio.

The radio reporter said, "Breaking news. There's been a large explosion in Mariposa Industrial Park, just outside Jacksonville. It's adjacent to the Vanilla Palms condominium. We'll report further as we receive updates. Now, back to this morning's news. Jennifer?" Jennifer had a chirpy voice and chatted about a local basketball game as if nothing critical had happened. Antonio sat by the radio. His boat continued to sway silently.

He thought, *maybe it's time*.

Three weeks prior, Antonio had come home to his kitchen. He considered it his, not hers. Lily had exploded something in the microwave. It was everywhere. She'd also dropped a glass bowl; its shards lay all over the kitchen floor. She was nowhere to be seen. He slammed the bedroom door open. He hated entering this room now. It was so disgusting. There she lay, sprawled on her belly on the bed, passed out, mouth open, drool dropping onto the makeup-stained pillow slip. She'd stripped off everything but her panties. The rest of her soiled clothes lay all over the room. He said quietly, "Wake up, you slovenly bitch and clean up the kitchen." Lily opened one eye, then both and slowly emerged from her stupor. She said, "Fuck off," then rolled back over. Antonio grabbed her arm, pulled her off the bed and dragged her to the kitchen. "Clean it up, now," he said again quietly. Antonio was not violent but hadn't been this angry in a long time. Lily stood there, still half-stoned, not giving a damn about her bare breasts. She screamed at him, "I despise you." He turned his back on her and said, "Just clean up your mess." He heard her open a kitchen drawer. She'd grabbed a knife and came tearing at him, screaming like a little banshee. He was a big man. She was a small woman. He turned around and grabbed her arm, and took the knife from her. He said, "I want you out of here, now. Pack up and leave. It's over."

So much had happened since then.

Further news reports on the boat radio reported the chemical explosion. Antonio thought *time to get moving*. The chaos around the event would give him some room to move. He had an escape plan. He was ready, but he had to move fast.

He thought *they'll soon realize Lily and I weren't there. We could be anywhere. Eventually, they'll know we've disappeared, but that could take weeks or months.*

He motored in about a mile offshore and turned off his boat, leaving his rod and life jacket on the boat floor. Lots of guys didn't wear their life jackets while they fished. Too hot and cumbersome. He left his cell and wallet in the waterproof bag in the front cabinet of the boat, under the dashboard. There was nothing incriminating on his cell anyway, let alone the laptop on his desk at home. He'd been careful about that.

He lifted the boat drain plug just enough to let water in and make it look like he'd just forgotten to secure it. The saltwater would take care of any blood splatter found, should the boat ever resurface. He wanted to make this look like he fell in and drowned. It was still dark. Despite his back injury, he was a strong swimmer but stuck to a slow breaststroke. He took his time and easily reached the short stretch of beach below the pier. The tide was out, and he climbed onto the rocky beach in the dark, careful not to cut his bare feet on anything. He climbed the step ladder up to the pier and stayed low, making his way to his car. He'd parked out of the lights and hopefully any cameras. There was no one around. He stripped off his wet clothes and changed into the loose shirt, shorts and sneakers he kept in the car. He'd left his gun in the locked glove compartment. He grabbed his two burner phones and the fake ID packages he had hidden in his trunk and slipped his money vest on under his shirt. He dropped his wet shirt into the ocean and his shorts and underwear into separate garbage cans along the way. He'd left his flip-flops floating by the boat. Proof of his drowning.

Seagulls circled and swooped, rising and falling and crying out over something dead and tasty they'd found. The air held the smell of the sea and centuries of fish guts. A lone gull lifted off the dock, did a slow turn over Antonio, and dove into the water. *Good fishing old friend*, Antonio called out to him in his thoughts. He turned and walked away through all the crates, barrels and nets fishing ports collect. He probably wouldn't be spending much time with the sea in the future. Antonio didn't look back.

No one walked in Florida, especially not at this hour. He was a bit conspicuous. He was counting on his heritage. Just another Mexican gardener walking to work, nothing unusual here. He'd be doing some walking today. He was a big guy with a bit of a gut and not a graceful walker. Because of his back injury, he carried his shoulders too high, and his stride was short and tight.

There was a seedy little strip mall up the road from the docks with a corner store open 24/7. It sold liquor, beer, smokes and everything else you might need in the middle of the night. The doorbell tingled as he entered, and a camera over the door stared at him. *Not good*, he thought. He kept his head down and his sunglasses and ballcap on, even though the sun was barely up. He walked the narrow aisles and chose a wide, low-brimmed hat, a fresh cotton shirt, underwear, scissors, and a razor. He also picked up some covid masks. Nobody used them anymore. Few people used them when they were really needed in this state. The clerk barely acknowledged him, just took his money. It was the end of his shift, and he was tired. It was a day Antonio was glad his ethnicity was making him not worth notice.

He put on the hat and covid mask and headed to the nearest McDonald's. Another camera greeted him. Big Brother was everywhere. He shaved off his mustache in the washroom stall using the toilet paper dispenser as a mirror. His upper lip was pale and untanned. He'd had that stash since his early 20s. Lily had teased him about it. "Who you trying to be, Burt Reynolds? It's so 80s, get rid of it." He'd ignored her until now. He cut his hair short and then shaved it off as well as he could in a toilet booth. All his ID showed him with a full head of dark hair and a mustache. If a picture was posted of him for some reason, that would be who they'd be looking for. He hated his new image in the white light of the washroom mirror.

He'd always thought he was good-looking. He'd have to get used to the new look, a bald, fifty-five-year-old, slightly overweight Mexican man.

Antonio had the rest of his money in a secure storage vault and had to get to that eventually. He first needed a temporary motel where the desk clerk wouldn't ask questions. He also needed new false ID and a dependable car. He couldn't risk a breakdown and police interference. The muggy June Florida morning was steaming up, taking the grass dew and watered lawn moisture into the ether. He was soaking under his money vest as he walked on.

He didn't learn about the dead people at the Vanilla Palms until later.

ESTELLE

Estelle spent her life resembling a hawk. Her nose was a large curved beak. Her chin was almost non-existent and receded into her neck. Her face was thin with no apparent cheekbones. All she needed was a field mouse in her beak, preferably dead, to complete the picture.

It took her over six weeks to arrange her face surgery. She used a burner phone that couldn't be traced. Now that she had the money she was having everything fixed: teeth, nose, chin, skin. She had to send several selfies to the surgeon, telling him she couldn't get to Atlanta to meet due to other responsibilities. At his request, she had x-rays done locally. She'd used one of her fake IDs for that.

While she waited, she continued her bookkeeping business and acted normally. She visited her friend Phil in Miami a few times a month. They had dinner together as usual. She slept on his couch. She said nothing. She'd shut down nights out with Janie, her bar buddy. Too dangerous. She was no longer interested in meeting some loser in a Jacksonville bar anymore. She couldn't risk running into any of Rudy's friends.

She'd never socialized with anyone in her building and barely acknowledged anyone at the mailbox. None of her clients knew where she lived. She had a PO box on her invoice. She mostly worked from home and communicated regularly but only dropped by their offices when necessary, which wasn't often. They kept their employee and financial records at their offices. She just issued them. She thought, *when payrolls go undone and money doesn't show up in bank accounts, they won't know where to come looking for me. Phil doesn't even know where I live.*

She was a big-time thief now, maybe worse. Time to disappear.

She'd staged her apartment, leaving her phone and computer behind and her gun in the dresser drawer beside her bed. Her purse with her credentials, credit cards and some cash hung on the door. Her toothbrush and makeup were all there, as was her underwear. She overturned a kitchen chair, spilled a coffee cup on the table and knocked some dishes onto the floor. Her car was still parked on the lot.

She knew Phil would come looking for her eventually, and she'd wanted to create suspicion about her absence. She wanted whomever came looking to think she'd been kidnapped, murdered or both, rather than just having left town and gone underground. Eventually, someone would report her absence to the police. They'd check her apartment and either assume she'd just left for parts unknown, people do that, or she killed herself or had been murdered. It's Florida. Things happen to single women. She was an adult, and no family member would be looking for her. Certainly not her mother. She hadn't spoken to her in years. Estelle didn't know if she was still alive and didn't care.

Estelle thought *I'll soon be forgotten, just another missing woman in the sea of missing women.*

There weren't any cameras in the condo halls, but one was in the front lobby. Estelle didn't know Claire had disabled that one. There wasn't one at the rear exit door to the parking lot, *a severe oversight on the condo's part*, Estelle thought, but it benefited her. She slid out that door in the middle of the night in a wig, glasses, and dark clothes, with her backpack and her wheeled valise full of money.

She didn't want to be traced to a cab, so she walked miles to the bus station in the dark. She was soaked with sweat when she finally got there. Her bus to Atlanta came in at 5:45 AM. She wore a Covid mask along with her disguise. She didn't look into any of the cameras and kept her head down. She had three fake IDs she'd purchased through the dark web over the years. She'd never needed them until now but always thought it wise to have some backup. When she arrived in Atlanta, she walked again, still not wanting to risk a cab. Cabs often had cameras. Her face was hidden, but Estelle had a distinctive little wiggle when she walked. Her bottom didn't go unnoticed as she walked along the streets. Men honked at her and yelled out their car windows. She was a woman alone, a mark for harassment.

The clinic was about ten miles away, but she'd worn sneakers, was fit, and managed the mileage with no problem. She'd registered here at the spa under one of her fake names. She arrived and climbed wide elegant stairs to a substantial polished wooden double door with the clinic's logo carved in a middle panel. The door opened to a lush lobby. Thick carpets, dark wood furniture, comfortable looking sofas covered with pricey chintz. She thought, *a good sign, they're making money.* The art on the walls looked original. She was wet with sweat and didn't look like their usual clientele. Discretion was their thing, though, and an elegant young woman dressed conservatively but expensively booked her in. Estelle mostly noticed her manicure. An exquisite, perfect chipless red. This woman was flawless. Her face was perfection. *A walking advertisement* thought Estelle.

There were no questions regarding the cash payment. Lots of their clients paid with cash. Nobody wanted a trail. When she finally closed the door behind her in her room, she lay back on the bed and closed her eyes. She'd got this far. Her surgery and recovery schedules were printed and waiting for her on her bedside table. She examined her face before stripping off and sliding into a hot shower. *Goodbye face*, she thought, *you did me no favors.*

Back in her room, recuperating after the surgery, Estelle was enveloped by elegant and cozy white duvets, crisp linens, soft white towels, bathrobes and slippers. Everything was white and pink and soft. She felt tender, spoiled and cared for. A nurse visited twice a day to check her face and bandages. The nurses varied, but they were always discreet and kind. It was expensive as hell but worth every penny. The tall floor-to-ceiling room windows looked into an inner private courtyard with a mossy, unskimmed pond, palms, and green tropical foliage. A little jungle. Long white sheers drifted in the breeze. No one went out there but the gardeners and the birds. She watched the birds flit in and out, free to fly wherever they chose. *Soon, I'll be like them,* she thought.

Her old face had almost come to a point. She'd had her receding jaw realigned and rebuilt so it sat perfectly under her pretty new nose. Her skin had been resurfaced, all sunspots gone. The cheekbone implants finished her look. Her face was unrecognizable. She was still wrapped in gauze and in a lot of pain, but the Tramadol dulled the worst of it. It was soup and puddings for her until her jaw healed. She'd be at the clinic for at least another month.

She turned on the TV to get the morning news and was stunned. There'd been an explosion in the industrial park behind her old condo, and everyone in Vanilla Palms was dead, probably by some chemical poisoning. She was horrified. She hadn't known any of her neighbors, but it was a lot of innocent people dead, and one of them could have been her. That was a problem. They wouldn't find her body and might be looking for her sooner than she would have liked.

She thought about her will, leaving her condo to Phil and wondered if her mother would surface, looking for a piece of the pie. They would need to make a serious effort to find her before the will could be paid out. Phil would have to wait five years, continue paying the cost of the condo and jump through major hoops. She thought *he'll probably just let it go. Just not worth the agro*. However, there might be a class action suit by the condo relatives against the chemical company. Then her mother might have her hand out. She'd have to read the news and first see Estelle's name as a missing person. She couldn't imagine her mother reading the news.

Estelle recounted her money every day. Five million bucks less the cost of the surgery. The price of a new life. She still had to get it to New York safely. She was heading north.

RANDY

Randy woke in a soaking sweat and sat straight up. He didn't remember where he was, but he'd had that dream again. He was coming into the light from the dark. On the floor was a body. His dream mind said *don't go in there*. He saw that half the man's head was blown away. The man's remaining eye looked straight at Randy.

It was 3:45 AM. The highway outside was quiet. Randy had been parked in an Econo Lodge in Houston, Texas, for weeks. The bloody scene he'd found at the wharf in Jacksonville was forever embedded in his mind. He looked around in the dark motel room and started to cry. He was terrified. Someone was looking for him. He was sure of it. Only one person knew he was supposed to be in the warehouse district or could have seen him there. That was the client Pauly he'd never met or seen. Randy didn't know if Pauly was dead or alive or just alive and talking.

Randy was sure his life was in danger. He had to get out of Jacksonville. His weed dealer, Miguel, said this day might come. Randy didn't believe him. Then the day came.

Randy used a small quiet e-bike for his weed sales at night. No sense announcing your arrival. He drove an old Chevy to his day job at the Jacksonville Amazon distribution center. A few years back, one of his warehouse buddies suggested he get some backup fake IDs cause "you never know." Randy had no idea what he might "never know." The buddy said, "Everybody does it." Schoolyard advice Randy had taken. Even to his inexperienced eye, the IDs looked fake.

For his escape, he needed a road bike. The e-bike wouldn't cut it on the freeway. He found a Yamaha at a local lot and paid cash. He had lots of that. Holding his breath he presented his fake IDs to both the insurance agent and the licensing agent, expecting them to look up and tell him there was a problem. It all sailed through, and he had wheels.

The night he left, he cleaned up his apartment. He'd left his regular cell and laptop behind and his car in the lot. He got rid of the burner cell in a public bin, first taking out the SIM card. He had two handguns and brought both of those along with the ammunition cartridges. He'd had all kinds of horrible visions of actually having to shoot the damn things. It didn't occur to him that those guns could identify him. Randy wasn't a deep thinker.

He'd called his boss and booked off, saying he had family business to deal with and didn't know how long he'd be gone. No one knew he'd left for good.

He'd decided to first go to Houston, thinking *it's a big city and no one will recognize me there*. He had no idea what to do next. He just wanted to get away fast. It was a long, hot bike ride to Houston, but he did it in fourteen hours. He booked a ground-level room and had his bike in his room with him. He couldn't risk losing that. The motel owner didn't like it, but the floor was tiled, and he showed him he'd protected it. He'd paid a month in advance in cash. The motel was standard fare. Posters of oil wells on the walls, a light turquoise duvet that had seen better days and caramel tile on the floor. It was clean and livable. He had his food delivered in and paced the room like an anxious caged bear. He didn't ride out often. He envisioned cartel guys around every corner.

He wasn't sleeping well. He didn't do inactivity easily. He missed the normalness of his old job, the guys, and even the adrenaline hit of his side gig selling weed. As if running away from his life wasn't enough of an adrenaline hit. He was already bored with the prospect of doing nothing but hiding for the rest of his life.

He flipped on the TV, hoping to catch some sports, and there was a reporter in front of his building, the Vanilla Palms. He sat on the bed in shock as he took in the news of the explosion and deaths. Aside from that, it would soon be obvious he wasn't there. He'd hoped he had more time to think things through. He knew the cartel trusted no one, and his disappearance would set alarm bells off. He recounted the money stashed in his locked bike saddlebags and his backpack. Still over five million bucks. He stayed when the housekeeper came in. She wasn't happy about that, especially with a motorcycle leaning against the wall. That money was his life. He couldn't leave it for a housekeeper to snoop out.

He stayed tuned to the TV, waiting for more news of the dead people in his old building. The story hovered for a few days. There hadn't been anything in the news about the murders in the warehouse area. A tornado blew through Iowa, wiped out a town, and the news cycle moved on.

It dawned on him that carrying guns registered to his old self wasn't smart. He rode out and dropped them in the mud of the Buffalo Bayou, down in Memorial Park.

He couldn't go home, see his mother again or call Mary. He already felt like a ghost. A sad one. He had to make a plan, but what?

CLAIRE

At 3:00 AM, Claire felt her camera watch vibrate on her wrist and woke up fast. Someone on Malek's floor was on the move. She watched the camera she'd installed across the hall from his apartment door. It was Malek, and he was in a hurry. He had two bags with him and a backpack. He took the stairs. Didn't want to risk getting caught in an elevator, she surmised. She switched to her front door camera, but he'd left through the rear door, disappearing for about a half hour. *Where are you, and what are you up to?* She thought. Malek suddenly reappeared in front of the building, jumped into an unmarked car, probably an Uber, and was gone. She wondered if he'd had something stashed outside. Claire thought *if he's in trouble, the CIA are on to him and will be showing up soon asking questions.* She couldn't risk being under the microscope of the CIA, even if they didn't have any suspicions about her. Yet.

Claire was a Russian spy working for a tech company in Miami, undercover, as spies do. Malek was an Algerian illegal, also undercover. He'd come into the country on a student visa and left school after the first term. He was in the hack and ransom game. Claire was the cat, and Malek was the mouse. She'd been pawing at him for years.

Claire envisioned a knock on her door, and a CIA agent in suit and tie would say, "Good morning," show his badge, and say, "We're doing a routine inquiry about one of the residents here, Michael Robertson. Do you know him?" Malek's fake name was bland, like hers. Still, there were probably a million Michael Robertsons in the States, so, a good choice. She probably knew more about him than they did. His real Algerian name was Malek Bouziane, and he had a racist pattern in his computer shutdowns and ransom requests. He targeted Jews.

She didn't need the CIA snooping around her life now. The Russian SVR was already trying to get her placed with the CIA. She had an interview coming up with them in weeks. She'd planned to leave before that happened. Malek's exit hurried that up. She had to move fast.

Claire was always packed for a quick getaway. She didn't have a cell, used burner phones, and didn't need her laptop. She had all the information she needed on a small hard drive tucked into a Faraway wallet. She slipped down to Malek's floor, retrieved her miniature camera off the upper wall across from his apartment, and then her lobby camera. Claire had disengaged the lobby security cameras long ago, and the security company didn't realize they'd been looking at a four-week loop from months ago. Thanks to her, the camera on the parking lot door never worked.

She pulled on a brown wig streaked with gray, attached a prosthetic nose and added plain glasses. She looked like she was in her late 50s now. She traveled light, grabbed her backpack and gun and slipped out the back door. It was a small special gun with varied lethal capabilities. No American gun registry knew she had it.

It was 4 AM when she headed up the road in the warm dark. She didn't really need a disguise. She was already invisible. Claire was just a tall, thin, middle-aged woman with a backpack, unmemorable even at that hour. People lived odd lives in this state. Underneath her plain clothes, she was strong and fit. Proficient in martial arts, she could take down most men, regardless of size, or get herself out of a hold. She hadn't ever had to use these skills. Murder was much more effective in her game. She was prepared for anything. Still, Claire walked like a stiff stick, arms straight at her sides, not at ease in her body. There was no swing to her gait. She walked up the road unnoticed.

Florida's transient and dispossessed denizens are served by an assortment of shabby little coffee shops. Claire picked one to hang out in while she made her plans for her next move. She checked it for cameras, and there were none evident. Strange in itself, but she kept her head down anyway. No one even looked up when she entered. Just another night hawk. She chose a booth; loose chairs and tables seemed too visible. Most of the people in here were in booths. Everybody wanted their own little corner of privacy. She swept the crumbs off the bench and noticed the tabletop was sticky with dropped food, spilled drinks, glass rings, and unwashed hands. A stained, balled-up napkin lived on by the napkin dispenser.

A fly landed on her table, and she watched it sit there and flick its wings, as house flies do. It dropped its proboscis into a blob of leftover jam. She hated flies; something about their having to vomit up a substance to make whatever they want to eat into a liquid so that it can suck it up with its personal straw. She imagined fly viscous covering every surface.

She decided not to mention it. Didn't want to bring attention to herself. The black waitress stood with her back to the customers, generous bum spilling over the counter's edge while she scrolled through her phone. She carried the weight of cheap, starchy food. Hard to eat well on Florida's minimum wage. She was watching videos of her kids, but no one there gave her the credence of having a personal life, let alone a struggling one. Most customers had their own problems at this hour, eyes buried in their phones, looking at something that relieved their boredom and their stress; sports, old texts, pictures, or porn.

A TV droned on above the counter. Basketball players spinning on a court somewhere, sneakers squeaking on the arena floor as they pivoted. Claire never understood American sports. She'd had no experience with sports in Russia. Not her interest. Other than the TV, the café was quiet. No one was talking to anyone. Clothing in Florida was not a giveaway to one's status. In the muggy heat of June, everyone was in shorts, t-shirts, flip-flops, or sneakers. These people all looked oily. Probably hadn't bathed in a while. Florida is a state of nomads, so that wasn't surprising. The waitress brought Claire her coffee and toast, left the bill, and walked away. Just another night at EZY Break. The toast had minimal butter, enough to be detected but not tasted. The bread was dry and stale.

Around 6 AM, the sound on the TV increased. A reporter stood in front of an inferno wearing an oxygen mask. Because of the mask, his voice was unclear in his microphone, but he sounded scared. A bold red headline ran repeatedly across the bottom of the screen. "Breaking News." The reporter was saying there was an explosion in the Industrial Park next to Claire's condo. He said, "The Vanilla Palms condominium is untouched, but it's believed every occupant succumbed to something lethal, probably a chemical released by the explosion in the truck depot. Someone came on camera and told the reporter and the cameraman to move back behind the security ropes. The screen returned to the news desk, but Claire stopped listening to the details. She knew who was responsible. Malek had murdered her three dearest friends, 'the girls', plus all the others.

Claire knew the Russian's SVR, the foreign intelligence agency for whom she worked, would wonder why her body was never found. They'd know she'd done a runner and they weren't forgiving. They would have figured that out soon enough. Time to go. First, she needed to get some money from her offshore accounts and get a car. She sipped her coffee, took a bite of her dry toast and watched her personal fly. It was still dining on the jam, wings twitching, undisturbed. Her mind was spinning with her escape plans.

Chapter Two

PROPERTY MANAGEMENT

At the Vanilla Palms condo, Antonio, Claire, Randy, and Estelle passed each other in the hallways, at the mailbox, and in the parking lot. They took no notice of each other. It wasn't a small town where people greeted each other. There were many owners from big cities where that didn't happen. There was an understanding you minded your business and kept to yourself. Some residents guessed who might have money or not. They'd notice clothes, accessories, and cars. Few would recognize any of their neighbors if they ran into them in a different circumstance. This did not apply to many of the older Jewish residents. There was a small community there, a family of friends.

Billy Knudson was their young property manager. Two of the other property managers had recently quit. He'd had two condos to manage, and now he had eleven, up and down half the eastern coast of Florida. That was eleven evening board meetings a month. The boards were mostly made up of busybody seniors, arguing until late in the night about the dog poop in the elevator or the Indian food smell in the apartment down the hall. It was painfully numbing for a kid like Billy. He'd sit there and think, *I've got to find something else to do. I hate this job.* Every time his phone rang, his stomach contracted. It was always a petty problem.

Billy was 6'4" and bordering on underweight. Since he'd moved out and away from his parent's bottomless fridge, he was always hungry, hoovering down pizza, burgers, and coke. Never anything healthy. You could almost see the tongues of flame in his furnace of a stomach as he added hamburger fuel. It was never enough. He didn't play sports and wasn't ever interested. He'd been dragged into a few golf games with his buddies, but it bored him. His long frame allowed sweeping tee shots, but they went wide and landed on the wrong greens. It was too much walking to retrieve lost golf balls he didn't care about.

Because of his length, his shirts often came away from his pants. He couldn't seem to achieve 'buttoned down.' He kept his dark hair short and started out with a clean shave. By 11 PM, his five o'clock shadow was heading for midnight, and he was beginning to look tired and a bit sleazy.

The past few months had been tough. The property management company Billy worked for had been sold and was under new management. His last boss was a fun guy, a partier, easy-going. He drove a high-end Lexus, dressed in expensive suits and lived well. He didn't really manage the team of property managers. Just let them do their own thing. As a result, management of the condos was lax, calls weren't returned, and board meetings didn't happen regularly. Except for one new building near Jacksonville, Vanilla Palms, the buildings were run down and needed repair. Nobody looked at the finances closely. That boss ran out of money and sold the business.

Billy's new boss, Zenith Bachmann, was Swiss, spoke with an accent and wasn't a fun guy. In his early 60s, he had a full head of grey hair, and was just a smidge on the portly side. Humor went over his head or was just ignored as silly. Billy wondered, "Who names a kid Zenith anyway?" It made him think of a lightning bolt, and Zenith was not that. Zenith had an unseen business partner. Billy figured it was a financial institution and probably not American. Zenith didn't share. He had 45 condominiums in his management portfolio. The condominium fee cash flow was good but not good enough to keep up with the many repairs required on these old buildings.

After the heartbreaking collapse of the Surfside condo in Miami and the loss of so many lives, Zenith brought in engineers to inspect every property he managed. He was big on safety, keeping the buildings in good repair, avoiding accidents, structural failures and legal problems.

He insisted on weekly reports from his property managers, recording owners' complaints with recommended resolutions. Meeting minutes were to be forwarded to him the following day. Thus, the drop off of property managers. They weren't interested in working that hard.

Most condo fees had to be raised out of necessity. Many of the older buildings Zenith took over needed extensive repairs and special assessments to pay for them. Insurance companies had clamped down. Owners were in shock or denial, neither emotion helping them. They knew they'd have to sell up, probably at a loss, and find somewhere else to live they could afford. Many were pensioners or people already living on the edge.

Florida is a state occupied by the rich and the rest. Rich is a broad category and includes a loose middle class who chose the right education and jobs, earned a decent living, and had real estate, investments and some spare cash. They might have a boat, big or small and could afford their health care premiums and property taxes. They might take a few trips. The premium rich lived the same lives but with lots more of everything.

Then there were the rest, again a broad category. They included the strugglers living off meager pensions or still working a few jobs into their 70s to pay the rent and feed themselves. They got by. Florida was still relatively cheap if you knew where to shop. At the bottom of the ladder were the permanently displaced and homeless, the mentally abandoned, and the addicted. There were also those who, through generations of poverty, depended on the government to get them to the next month. It was their normal.

Zenith's owners fell in the middle. Not rich, not completely strapped, but most of them incapable of paying more than they were already paying.

The Vanilla Palms condo was at the far north end of Billy's territory, just outside Jacksonville. Recently built, it was still in good shape. After weeks of delivering bad news to the various boards up and down the state and watching their faces freeze, this board meeting was a pleasure. Billy and one of the engineers, Jack Phelan, presented a healthy financial statement, good reserves and a safe structural report to the Vanilla Palms board.

For a change, they met in the morning. Morty, the President, liked to get out of the Florida heat for the summer and head north to Savannah every year. He and his wife were packed and ready to leave as soon as this meeting was done. Morty was feeling good about the condo's state of affairs and was looking forward to his getaway. He was 82, not in the best of health, but he could still drive and did.

Billy and Jack returned to their cars in the heat of the Florida June morning. Billy said, "Thanks for coming along. These owners never consider me old enough to manage their properties. Your being there gives me some authority. Jack laughed and said, "This one was a pleasure. The others were hard. Don't worry. You're doing a great job."

He told Billy, "I know you want to walk away; this is a huge responsibility. I've known Zenith for years; he's hard-nosed, but he's a well-respected businessman on the strip and will want to do right by the owners as much as possible. He's basically a good human being. You can learn a lot from him. Don't give up hope." Billy said, "Lots of our owners are living on just their pensions, and they won't be able to afford the remediation cost. They'll have to leave." Jack said, "Don't forget, there is still land value in their condos, and depending on what Zenith and his partner or the lenders come up with, the owners won't walk away penniless. They may have to sell and rent elsewhere but won't be homeless. Zenith could end up owning their condos and reselling them once the remediation is done. It could be a goldmine for him."

Billy looked at Jack and said, "That sounds devious." Jack said, "As Zenith would say, "it's just business.""

On the long drive home back to Miami, Billy stopped at a Burger King for stomach fuel. He sat in his car, wolfing down the food and stared into the glaring sunlight. *Reality's harsh*, he thought. When he returned to his apartment, he knocked off the minutes and got them over to Zenith. He was hoping to take the rest of the day off. He was still undecided about sticking with this job. He had few skills and needed to figure out what else he could do.

At 7 AM the following day, his phone repeatedly rang and vibrated. He'd had too many beers with his buddies the night before. His mouth was fuzzy, and his brain matched his mouth. He'd only been asleep for 4 hours. He rolled over, rose from his fog and reached for the phone, seeing the call was from Zenith. Billy thought, *christ, what does he want this early in the morning?*

Chapter Three

FOLLOW THE MONEY

F ive million in $100 dollar bills weighs about 110 pounds. A heavy burden for most.

ESTELLE

Estelle had been a petty thief most of her life. Shoplifting small things, food at first, just to survive, then cheap jewelry, makeup, and clothes if she thought she could get away with it. She was good at it and only got caught once. She'd never stolen from her mother. There wasn't much to steal, and it would have been noticed. She was opportunistic. In her early cashier and waitress jobs, if there was cash to be lifted and not detected, she took it. After a while, she didn't get much of a buzz from doing it; it just became a bad habit. As too many habits are.

She had a couple of friends. Janie was one of her clients and also her bar-hopping friend. She was petite, busty and attracted men. Her tops were tight, her skirts short, and her heels spiked. She got what she was fishing for with her look. Sleazeballs looking for a lay. Definitely not keepers. No one came on to Estelle, too ugly. She always went home alone. Estelle was used to it and didn't mind playing 'wingman' to Janie. At least she got out and caught a few decent bands. Janie was intrepid. After a bad round with a creep who only wanted a flash of sex, she'd be ready to do it all over again the next weekend. Jacksonville bars were filled with too many over-tanned cruisers, still wearing gold chains. They were not looking for wives or even girlfriends, just a hook-up.

Estelle's other friend was Phil. He ran a Humane Society branch with a few staff and a lot of volunteers. Estelle did his payroll and bookkeeping. Phil was gay but perennially single. She had never known him to have a boyfriend. She'd suggested dating apps, but he wasn't interested. He would say, "I'm content, don't need anyone, don't bug me about it." So, she didn't. Phil carried about 60 extra pounds, not all the way to obese, but big and soft. He wore his hair with a bit of a bang, which Estelle teased him about. "Your bangs need trimming," she'd say. He'd say, "Yeah, all my cereal bowls are dirty. I'll get on it." They got together every couple of weeks for drinks and sometimes dinner. She'd sleep on his couch. It was a long drive back up north to her condo. Phil was funny and could tell a good tale. His dog pound stories were hilarious and too often sad. She relaxed with him. She didn't have to win his approval or worry about her looks. He didn't care. They were simply good friends and had been for years.

One of Phil's animal fosterers was Mike, an old guy, mid 80s. Mike loved cats. He was an enigma to Phil. He dressed as if he had money. You can always tell by the shoes, Phil thought. He wore expensive shoes. Mike wasn't a big man, only about 5'7", but he looked like he was built when he was younger. His shoulders were broad, and his hands, deeply veined now, were still square and strong-looking. When he talked, he had a way of staring at you directly, almost through you. Even at his age, he resonated power. Phil liked the guy.

Whenever Phil had an old cat that no one would adopt, and he'd probably have to put down, he'd talk to Mike about fostering. Mike now had about six of Phil's old cats, all females. They never left Mike's once he got them home. He couldn't part with his girls once he had them. Phil didn't know if Mike had any money, but he always covered his food and vet bills. Phil thought Mike was a kind old guy, and that expense shouldn't be on him.

One day, Mike came in and hung around the cat cages for a while, wiggling his fingers at the kittens and cooing at the rest. He looked at Phil with a long, sad look and said, "We need to talk." Phil said, "Sure, let's go into my office, what's up?" Mike's eyes filled up. He said, "I got bad news from my doc; I'm dying and might only have a month left." Phil reached out and squeezed his hand. He said, "I'm so sorry, Mike. Is there anything I can do to help?" Mike said, "Well, I need to find homes for my six girls." Phil was not a liar and said, "That will be hard, Mike; they're all old and sick." Mike choked up and said, "Then I think you'll need to put them down." Then he really broke down. Phil said, "Why don't I come to your place? We'll take cute pictures, maybe with some costumes, and put them on our website." He'd never been to Mike's place and envisioned a cat hair mess, but he was willing to do it for this kind old man. Mike said, "No, I'll bring them here. It would be better if I brought them here. I like your idea of the website pictures. You never know."

So that's what they did. Mike brought them in one by one, cried his eyes out as he left each one and then came back again until they were all in cages. Phil got to work with costumes. One of his volunteers was a photographer, and they set up a web page just for Mike's cats. They called it "Mike's Girls," sharing his story of impending death. Nothing like pathos to move people. It was a miracle, but all six cats were adopted into good homes. Mike could die peacefully now.

Estelle picked up Phil's payroll and bookkeeping information from him twice a month, and then they often went out for dinner. One day, Phil had a family function to attend, so he left her a key and the alarm code. The building had a dark corner in the entranceway that couldn't be seen from the street, just inside the doorway. Estelle noticed a shape on the ground in that dark corner as she was about to key in the door code. People too often left wriggling bags of kittens, puppies, or whatever animal they didn't want to deal with. On a closer look, she saw a large suitcase. She approached it slowly. It wasn't moving. She popped open the top and almost fell over. Inside the suitcase, there was a lot of money. Stacks of banded hundred-dollar bills. She thought *I've got to get this off the street before it's stolen.* She moved her car in front of the door and wheeled the suitcase over, hoisting it onto her passenger seat with great effort. There was no note inside, nothing identifying where the money came from. She thought quickly. *Someone wanted Phil or the agency to have the money. Phil doesn't know about it, but the donor will probably let him know pretty damn quick he left a shitload of money on his doorstep.* She quickly counted the stacks of bills and came up with six million dollars. Without a thought, she separated out five million and stuffed it under all her car seats and the spare tire space in the trunk. She left a million in the suitcase and returned it to its spot. If Phil was advised of how much money was left, he might assume it was stolen. It was.

She then went into the office, picked up the flash drive Phil had left and drove home. She methodically moved all the money up to her apartment using a backpack. It took a few trips. She had a sleeping bag in her closet, never used, but now it had a use. She filled it with the money and rolled it back up in her closet.

Estelle then did Phil's payroll and month end, sent off the pay remittances to the bank and thought about what to do next. This was a lifetime of money if she was careful. She had no second thoughts or guilt. She wasn't familiar with that emotion.

She and Phil had dinner the next night, and she returned the thumb drive. She casually asked, "How was the family function?" Phil said, "Boring. Dull people, dull food, crappy wine. I did my duty." No mention of the suitcase full of money. She wondered *did he get it? Did someone else get there first?* She couldn't ask.

Although one staff member remained on site overnight, they came and went by the rear door and slept in the back with the animals. Other than that person, Phil was always first in and spotted the bag as he came in. He too hoped it wasn't filled with kittens or puppies. When he opened the bag and found the money, he didn't know what to think. He searched it and found a note tucked deep into an inside pocket. It simply said, "Thanks from me and the girls." It was signed with a simple 'M' with a big flourish. Phil counted the money. He thought *a million bucks. Wow. That will help.* He was curious whether Mike had intended the money to go to the agency or to him. He decided to wait and see if Mike got in touch with him, and then he'd know his intentions. Whatever, Phil had plans for some of the money. He needed a new car.

Phil checked on the animals and relieved the night staff girl. All seemed to be okay. The volunteers arrived, and the day started with feeding and exercising, telephone calls, and potential adopters. Around 11 AM, Phil stopped for coffee and sat at his office desk, peeling through Google News. A news item popped out at him. He had to reread. It said, "Breaking news.

Notorious mob boss Mike the Spike was found dead by his housekeeper. She told the police he'd been suffering from an advanced illness." The picture was of a man in his 50s, well dressed, fit, in charge, surrounded by big men in suits. There was no mistaking it. It was his cat-loving Mike.

The news article went on to say when Mike was apprehended years ago, legal files were lost and possibly tampered with. There were rumors of police malfeasance. He'd never been convicted. He'd disappeared and was thought to have been killed by his own. A decade later, he resurfaced, living in modest luxury, pretty women on his arm around town, living the good life. His housekeeper said she didn't know who he was, but he was very kind and generous to her. "I'll miss him," she said. He lived in an expensive house with a walk out to the ocean. There were no next of kin. The truth was, his housekeeper knew exactly who he was.

He'd signed his house over to her months before he even knew about his impending death. He was an old man. It was time to get things in order. Along with the house, he gave her millions. Enough money to maintain the house and herself for the rest of her life. She'd be hiring her own housekeeper. Yes, he was generous.

Her name was Josephine, but everyone called her Jo. She was 46. Long divorced, no kids, no close family. No one to explain her luck to.

She had lived full-time at the house for over 15 years. In her younger years, she could have passed for cute on a good day, never beautiful. She'd thickened up around the middle as she aged and still smoked. She could afford hair salons and manicurists now. She started wearing makeup. Jo had never looked better.

She'd handled all of Mike's needs, cooking, cleaning and house mainte-nance. She even arranged girls when he felt up to it. She ushered them in and back out when they were done. It never took long. Just another service. None of her business where he found his pleasure.

Mike and Jo became good friends over the years. He completely trusted her. She was more like a daughter than an employee. Every night, they'd have a drink on the lanai after supper. They both loved old movies and watched them in the screening room. He was well prepared for his death.

He'd told her where to store the money. He said, "Get it out of the house. Leave nothing for the Feds to grab." They stripped the house of his good art and sculptures and stored everything. They left nothing of value that could be taken. She told the detectives he'd given her enough money to manage the house and live. She said she'd still have to work. She wouldn't, but they did not know that and never followed up. She and Mike had refurnished the house with bland furniture and prints. "He lived frugally," Jo lied.

The night Mike dropped off the cash at Phil's, Jo was out, and he'd called a cab and loaded the suitcase in with him. He got the driver to drop him a few blocks away and wait. He didn't want him to see where he was leaving the bag. It was a struggle, but he managed to wheel the suitcase to Phil's indoor passageway and tuck it into a dark corner. It couldn't be seen from the street. He'd already cased this corner out and was surprised Phil didn't have a camera there. He thought *nobody wants to break into the dog pound. Nothing to steal in there.* After depositing the bag, he slowly made his way back to the cab. The cabbie just thought he was a weird old man, and the next day, skimmed over the news article about Mike the Spikes's death. He was young and hadn't been in the country long enough to care about some dead old mafia guy. He definitely didn't make the connection.

Phil didn't want to know where the name Mike the Spike came from. He thought, *guess I won't be hearing from him about the money. Ill-gotten gains, but no one could trace it now.* He hoped Mike had kept his donation private from the housekeeper. He didn't have to worry. She wasn't talking to anyone. Four people with secrets, one of them dead.

Estelle got up in the middle of the night and checked the sleeping bag full of money, recounting the bills. She started to make plans.

ANTONIO

In his mid-40s, Antonio worked as a heavy equipment operator for a large industrial food manufacturer, loading and unloading heavy packaged stock and supplies. He was very safety conscious, but many of the other operators didn't pay enough attention. They'd load the upper shelves too heavily and precariously. Antonio paid a high price for the carelessness of others. He watched the 10-foot rack fall toward him, shedding heavy boxes as it fell, nudged by another equipment operator. He thought. I'm going to die right here on the warehouse floor. His last memory was of a large box speeding toward his face. Then, nothing. When he woke in the hospital, his wife Mira and daughters were at his bedside, worried looks on their faces. The news wasn't good. The bones in his face and his spine were broken, along with both his legs and one arm. He was told he wouldn't walk again.

It took about eighteen months, but Antonio was stubborn and fought back. He proved them wrong and got back on his feet. He could walk but had no job, money, or future. He was addicted to his painkillers, yet the pain stayed. He'd promise himself *tomorrow will be better, and then I'll stop.* The pain remained, and tomorrow never came.

He and his wife Mira had been unhappy together for a long while. Now, Antonio was angry with the world and hard to live with. Nothing pleased him. Mira stopped speaking to him, and his daughters ignored him. He and Mira still slept together but were reduced to moving past each other in the same space, trying not to touch. Anything would irritate him, and he'd bark. After everything he'd done to her, Mira had had enough.

The company's insurance wouldn't cover the accident, saying it was self-inflicted through a lack of attention to safety protocols. Antonio didn't have any insurance of his own. He'd taken a hit of Percodan and was lying on the couch, watching TV, praying for an hour of sleep and relief. An ad about personal injury claims came up. He'd seen it and others like it before. This one was for a law firm named Prestwick and Smith. Supposedly, they handled cases like his. A seemingly uninjured person exclaimed, "They got me ten million. The insurance company was only offering a million."

Antonio took all that with a grain of salt; it was just an ad. However, he had nothing to lose and called. A female took his details and said someone would get back to him. The next day, a guy named Robert called him, asking for more details. Robert listened to Antonio and said, "We may be able to help. I'll switch you back to Clarisse, and you can schedule an appointment. Antonio thought, *why don't you check your calendar and just make the damned appointment now. Why all the back and forth? However,* Robert wasn't the lawyer, just the preliminary contact, and Antonio would be meeting with their team. *Christ!* Antonio thought. *I can barely walk without wincing, and I have to give a command performance.*

Before the accident, Antonio had been a sharp dresser. He liked to look good and got appreciative glances from women. He looked at himself now, carrying too much weight, living in shorts and sandals and a four-day worn t-shirt.

He prepared carefully for this meeting. He knew how much appearances count, especially if you're Mexican. He didn't want to be written off. He found their office building downtown and thought, *yep, they have the whole damned building in the middle of downtown Miami. That's expensive real estate. They must be doing something right.* He rode to the penthouse and introduced himself to the receptionist. She said, "Yes, we spoke on the phone, Antonio. I'm Clarisse. Can I get you a coffee or a cold drink?" Antonio declined. Didn't want to spill anything. He was nervous. He felt like he was applying for a job. Ten minutes passed, and he was thinking about the Percodan pills in his pocket. The chairs weren't comfortable or easy to get out of. A door burst open, and a short, tanned, expensively dressed guy came out and introduced himself as Peter Prestwick, one of the firm's owners. Antonio thought his entrance was more dramatic than it needed to be. *What a little show-off.* Peter said he'd be one of the team considering Antonio's case. Peter Prestwick didn't have a hair out of place. His nails were manicured, and his suit was tailored to his fit, exercised body. He was a pretty man. Antonio was glad he'd worn a sportscoat and looked the best he could, which wasn't bad. He couldn't compete with this guy, but he looked pretty good.

Peter led him into a large boardroom with floor-to-ceiling windows over-looking the city. The windows were distracting. Including Peter, three men and a woman were sitting at the end of the extended glass table. The woman was 50ish, good-looking, with long well-styled hair. She, too, was impeccably dressed and manicured. These people emanated money.

It was an interrogation. The team wanted the history of Antonio's entire employment with the company. Had he ever been written up or warned? Had he ever been offered a promotion? How did he get along with his boss and coworkers? Did anybody have it in for him? What were the working conditions like? How was he treated? Did he have any beefs with the company? Had he shared those with anyone? They were looking for anything that might hang their case. Antonio had been an exemplary employee and got along with everyone. Promotions weren't offered to heavy equipment Mexican operators with a high school education. Antonio felt confident he'd done nothing wrong.

After several hours, Antonio was sweating with pain. Barbara observed Antonio's growing discomfort and said, "Well, I need a break, Antonio. How about you? The washrooms are just outside the door and down the hall. He thought *she knew I was hurting and needed a painkiller*. Whatever, he was thankful for her kindness. In the washroom, he washed his face with cold water, took a Percodan and waited for the pill to kick in. It took 15 minutes, but relief finally came. He returned to the board room where they'd been discussing his case.

Barbara smiled at him and asked, "Better?" Antonio said, "Yes, thank you." They'd obviously had many clients in pain before.

She looked at the others and said to Antonio, "We're familiar with your former employer. They have a long list of safety infractions, and you are not the first to want to sue them for physical damages. We have yet to handle cases with them, but we know several other firms who have, some successfully, some, not so much. Much depends on your court reliability, and you look very good. She reached out to him, putting a hand on his arm and said, "I know you're struggling with pain. Not good for you, but we can use that."

She turned to him and said, "We've decided to take on your case." Antonio went right to the nugget and asked, "What do you think I might get?"

He was thinking a million would be very good. She said, "It's early days, but we'll ask for $20 million and might get $10. Your life has been ruined. You have two daughters to put through college. You and your family must pay to live for another 50 years or more." She watched Antonio's face and said, "Don't get excited; that's not your take-home pay. We charge 40% of whatever we win. A $10 million win would give you $6 million. How's that sound?" His heart was racing at this huge amount, but he also thought, *$4 million for you? Hmmm.*

They were confident he'd jump at it and confident they'd win big. Antonio was nobody's fool. He now realized he had a hot case that others might be just as interested in. He decided to shop it around. He surprised them and said, "It's a lot of money and a big fee. It will take a lot of your time and take a lot out of me. I want to think about it." They all exchanged glances and saw their $4 million fee slipping away. Antonio said, "I'll get back to you in three weeks. Thank you for giving me such close consideration." He stood, wincing and walked out with a bit of a limp. They knew he'd now be interviewing other firms.

There were dozens of personal injury firms in Miami, but only a few were big enough to handle his case. He researched their success rates and reviews and made appointments with all the good ones, telling them he was talking to other firms at the end of each meeting. He got good at reading the room. They all knew they were in a competition for this juicy, winnable case.

He went home and waited for the phone to ring. He wasn't surprised when they all got back to him with a lower fee. He also had another tricky negotiation request. He wanted whatever they won delivered to him in $100. bills. He didn't want any bank involved with his money and their fees and wanted as little to do with the IRS as possible, with their withdrawal limits.

They all pushed back on this, saying getting that much cash delivered would be difficult and unsafe. Antonio stuck to his guns. That had to be part of the deal. The first firm he'd met with returned with a 28% fee offer, and he chose them. Besides, Barbara had been kind to him.

It took several months for the case to be resolved, but in the end, Antonio walked away with well over $9 million in cash. He was a rich man, set for life, such as his life was.

On the day he got the payment, he arrived at their offices with a bag large enough to carry all the cash and a wheely. He rolled it out to his old Ford Focus. He drove it directly to a Safe Haven vault and stored it. Of course, he was armed. They talked about that at the office all week. They'd never seen anything like it.

He kept back $3 million. His wife Mira came home from work that night and found 1 million dollars in cash piled neatly on the dining room table. She looked at Antonio suspiciously. She knew he'd been meeting with lawyers about his accident claim, but they didn't talk, and he hadn't up- dated her. Looking at the money and not at him, she asked, "Where'd this come from?" He said, "It was part of the court winnings for my accident. I'm also giving each of the girls $500,000." He didn't tell her about the entire amount. He knew she was done with him. She said, "I don't want your money." He said, "Whatever, keep it, give it to the girls, donate it, I don't give a shit anymore." He'd left the girls' cash on their beds. He left the house and didn't return for a few days.

He did not share what he'd won with his wife or daughters. He lied by omission, not for the first time and certainly not the last.

Only he and those lawyers knew he had that money. The IRS was notified of the payout but couldn't control the cash.

Mira and the girls kept the cash. She was planning to leave him and knew she'd need the money. She wasn't a fool either.

RANDY

It was a Wednesday night, quiet for Jacksonville. Randy had agreed to meet a client in the wharf district for a large sale of weed, bigger than Randy usually sold. The client's name was Pauly. Randy never went beyond first names. He figured the guy was selling small amounts to his friends. *His business*, Randy thought. *I don't care what he does with it.* He packed it in his bike saddle bag and rode to the docks. He wasn't comfortable carrying around this much product. It could land him in jail if he was ever stopped. He and Pauly were supposed to meet at the piers at 10 pm. It would be dark and secluded enough for a quick handoff of dope and money.

The place made Randy nervous. Too many long, shadowy, empty corridors of buildings, sitting in fishy, smelly silence. At least, he thought they were empty. He slowly rode his e-bike down the dark lane, keeping his eyes peeled for Pauly's car. He'd rewired his bike lights to turn them off with one switch, including his break lights. He did this now. Just before he turned the corner, he heard what sounded like gunshots. Pop, pop, pop. He pulled his bike tight into the building wall, crouched, and waited. He wasn't sure for what. He just thought, *keep your head down and then get the hell out of here.* A car peeled past him, shimmying around the corner, almost losing traction. Then it raced off. Then, silence.

He'd never met this guy Pauly and knew nothing about him. Randy thought *he was referred by a reliable source at work, so he shouldn't be an undercover cop. Besides which, I'm a nobody. Cops are after bigger fish than me. The damn stuff I'm selling is legal in half the states of the country.* Randy was nervous. He sensed something was very wrong.

Just before Randy arrived on the scene, Pauly had parked his car a building away and was on foot, looking for Randy. He saw a light on in a warehouse and thought Randy might be there. Three rough-looking men were sitting at a long wooden table, snorting lines of coke. A large leather bag sat beside one of the men on the floor, brimming with white plastic bags. Pauly thought, *probably what they were snorting.* In that split second, Pauly realized this wasn't Randy, and he was witnessing a big drug deal. As the three men turned to look at him, two of them drew on him.

Pauly immediately knew he had to kill them all, or he'd be a dead man. He wasn't supposed to be there, and he sure as hell wasn't supposed to be witnessing what was going down. Pauly was a good shot. Lots of shooting range practice. He took all three out in a split second. Pop, pop, pop. They dropped. The men were so stoned and surprised to see Pauly at the door that their responses were slow. None of them got to pull their triggers. Pauly started to shake. He couldn't believe he'd just shot three men dead. At least, they sure looked dead from the doorway. He peered out into the dark to see if anyone was around. No sirens were howling in the distance. All was silent. No one knew he was supposed to be there but Randy. He was nowhere around. *Where the hell was Randy?* He had to get out of there and lose his gun. The large satchel of coke called to him for some reason he would never be able to explain to himself later. He grabbed it and raced to his car. He peeled off, desperately hoping his car hadn't been captured on any cameras. He didn't know that the cameras had all been shot out years ago, and nobody cared. He hadn't seen the bag of money. That was the scene Randy came upon.

Randy stayed low, crawled to the corner of the building, and looked around. There was a light on in one of the warehouse doors. He waited ten minutes and heard no conversation. No sound at all. He came at the building and doorway sideways and dropped to a crawl. He slowly peered around the edge of the door. Two men were slumped over a table, and one was on the floor. They were lying very still. No one was moaning. There was a lot of blood and what looked like brains splattered about. The guy on the floor lay on his belly, arm extended, still holding his gun. All three had been shot in the head. Not a healthy sight. Randy constantly checked over his shoulder to the door to see if anyone else was around. He was careful not to step in the blood or touch anything. He wondered if Pauly was one of the dead guys, or was hiding somewhere or just never showed up. Or was he the guy who sped away? Too many options to consider.

Tucked underneath the table on the other side was a large open leather bag with packets of what appeared to be money spilling out. On closer inspection, Randy discovered it was filled with stacks of banded hundred dollar bills. Randy thought *there's millions of dollars in this bag.* He thought *it was probably a drug deal, but who's got the drugs, and why did they leave the money behind?* There was no sound from the street. No police sirens screaming their way there. Down in these empty canyons, no one else must have heard the shots but him and the shooter, whoever that was. He wondered again *who was driving that car.* The dead guy lying on the floor had one eye still open, staring right at Randy. The other half of his head was gone. That was unnerving. Randy knew he should turn around and get the hell out of there.

Like Pauly, in a split second, he made a life-changing decision. He grabbed the bag of money. He had balls of steel that night.

With his shirt sleeve, he turned off the warehouse light. He kept thinking *don't touch anything, don't touch anything.* Randy needed to ditch Pauly's large weed bag to make room for the money in his bike saddle bags. At the wharf edge, he found a brick, added it to the bag of weed, tossed it in the water and watched it sink. He stuffed his saddlebags with the money and tossed the money satchel with a brick in it in the water as well. His fingerprints would be on it. He had to be sure the evidence was gone.

Randy thought *someone shot these guys, and someone knows about the money and will realize it's gone.* His heart raced as he considered all that and rode slowly home. He sure didn't want to be stopped by the police now. He decided his bike lock-up was the safest place for the money. Only the leasing company knew he had that space; it was paid up for a year, and there would be no reason for anyone to break in to steal an e-bike. If someone came looking for him tonight, they wouldn't find any cash on him.

Randy and Pauly never knowingly spoke again. They both had big secrets, with the cartel searching for their money and their drugs and the shooter. The police were just looking for the shooter, but not very hard.

The next day, Randy got a call from his weed supplier, Miguel. Miguel said in his low, accented voice, "Hey," Randy said, "Hey, Miguel. What's up?" Miguel said, "Did you hear about the shoot-up last night?" Randy held his breath and asked, "What shoot up?" Miguel said, "It's in the news. Down at the docks. Three guys dead." Randy was careful with the next question. "What happened? Did you know the guys?" Miguel did but lied and said, "No. Cops think it's a drug deal that went wrong, probably Mexican cartel." Randy thought *I didn't see any drugs. Who has the drugs?* Miguel said, "I'm getting out. These guys will kill you for any reason." Randy asked, "Do they think you did it?" Miguel said, "I didn't have anything to do with it, but they'll be looking at everybody." He paused, then said, "I gotta get out of town." Randy said, "Yeah, I get it. Thanks for letting me know. No prob." Miguel said, "I'm losing this cell, so you won't be able to contact me. Remember, you don't know me." Randy said, "I'm not about to share anything with anyone." Miguel said, "Good, keep it that way." Randy knew Miguel was dealing with bigger stuff than weed, and he was rattled. Randy said, "Take care, man." Miguel said, "Yeah, you too." They hung up.

That was the end of Randy's part-time drug dealing gig. He figured he'd never hear from Miguel again. He sure didn't want to read he'd been murdered. He thought *whoever drove off in that car probably had the drugs and shot those guys.* If it was his Pauly, he could place Randy there. If Pauly wasn't part of the cartel but just happened on the deal going down, killed the guys and grabbed the drugs, neither he nor Randy were safe.

A few weeks later, as Randy was leaving the corner store, a greasy-looking guy wearing a headband resembling a leather dog collar walked quickly toward him. Randy didn't like the look of him and thought he was about to be held up. His mind oddly flashed on the headband and thought, *what is it with headbands and punks, a fashion statement?* The guy walked up too close to him, grabbed Randy by the shirt collar, and pushed him back against his car. He asked, "You work for Miguel?" Randy remembered Miguel's words when he first hired him, "Say nothing." Randy was scared but said, "Never heard of him, get your hands off me." Randy tried to move sideways, but the guy jerked him back up against the car. He smiled at him and said, "Good answer, me amigo." His breath reeked of something foul, and his teeth were rotting in his mouth. He said, "He's missing. Do you know where he is?" Randy said again, "I told you, I don't know who you're talking about. You've got the wrong guy." In a slow, accented cadence, the man said, "Relaaax mi amigo. My name is Cojo, and I'm your supplier now. Do you need any product?" Randy said, "You've got the wrong person. I don't need anything from you. Get off me." Cojo shook Randy loose and pushed him back against his car again. He said, "You'll be calling me, your car's shit, you need money." He shoved a ratty card in Randy's shirt pocket. "When you're ready or if you hear from Miguel, that's my number." Randy said nothing. Cojo came up too close to Randy's face again and said, "Meanwhile, keep your fucking mouth shut, understand?" Randy said, "I have nothing to say to anyone about anything." The guy started walking back to his car and said over his shoulder. "Keep it that way. There are consequences if you don't keep your mouth shut." He quickly turned around and aimed a gun at Randy, closed one eye, and Randy could have sworn he watched his trigger finger start to move. Randy's knees buckled, and he felt hot piss running down his leg. He'd never understood how someone could 'piss themselves.' Now he knew. Cojo looked at Randy's piss-stained leg, laughed, got into his car, and drove off.

Randy thought he was going to die right there in that parking lot. He was terrified. Miguel had said these guys played hardball.

He thought *Cojo followed me here. He must know where I live. Shit!*

Several weeks later, Randy came home to find his apartment door ajar, the lock obviously jimmied. His apartment was completely tossed, with the furniture and bedding ripped open. He thought *they must know I've got the money. Maybe they think I've got the drugs, too. Did the client Pauly rat me out? Was I seen there? What does Miguel have to do with this?* He thought *they wouldn't have found anything, so maybe they're satisfied that I have nothing.* There had been little in the paper about the murders. A brief news article read, "Three men found dead, apparently murdered in the warehouse district. Drug cartel involvement is suspected; police are investigating." Randy thought *or maybe the break-in was just a coincidence, just another Florida break-in. Except they took nothing.* The following day, he found his car with the doors wide open, and the trunk popped. Someone had slit all his seats. He no longer thought the break-in was a coincidence. Someone was looking for something.

He reported the apartment break-in to the condo property manager and the president, but he didn't tell them about his car or the extent of the damage. He got the apartment door lock fixed, but he thought it would be better if he just got seat covers for the car for the time being. It was too expensive to get them reupholstered. He still thought like a poor guy not one with five million bucks stashed.

He looked at the knifed-up furniture. His mother had given it to him as a housewarming gift. He knew it was probably expensive. He put cheap slipcovers on all the ripped furniture and donated everything damaged. The donation center did the pickup. He ordered a new mattress, and they took the old one away. He went to a used furniture store, ordered a very simple sofa, and had it delivered. His apartment looked bare, but at least he had something to sit on.

He knew he had to get out of town and disappear. As Miguel said, these guys killed people like mice in traps. They didn't care.

Randy was in a panic. He didn't want to die.

CLAIRE

Claire Richmond didn't have to worry about money. She had more than enough. She paid her rent on time, paid income taxes and lived a quiet life. She kept her head down and went through her life unnoticed. Claire was a well-behaved Russian spy living an everyday life in America.

She worked for the Russian SVR but planned to change her identity and leave. She had no loyalty to anyone. She was a woman without a country. They were all corrupt. She'd had hope for the States, but no more. It was a political insane asylum. Claire was getting out.

Claire's day job with a Miami tech firm involved supplying high-end security to a variety of companies. She mostly worked from home, meeting with her boss to discuss assignments once a month. She was the fox among the chickens. It gave her access to everything, and she sent the contacts back to herself. She knew how to hide her tracks. She never did anything illicit in work mode. She'd been there for years. Top employee. They kept trying to promote her, and she'd turn them down. She'd tell them she was not interested in developing people, just software.

She'd steal and then be called in to stop it. It amused her. There was always a young hotshot in the office who was sure they could crack the code. Claire would cheerfully say, "Have at it. You probably have skills I don't." They could never crack her subterfuge.

She was a model citizen and employee. Except she wasn't. Claire Richmond didn't exist.

The way she rationalized it, she wasn't endangering lives or outing anyone's spies. She wasn't selling state secrets, just corporate business secrets. In her mind, it was a legitimate theft between countries. Every country was sniffing through every other country's tech.

For the Russians, her job was all about stealing technology; for her, it was the money, her ticket out.

Malek played a different game. He shut down computer systems and demanded ransom money to reinstate them. Most of his targets were companies primarily made up of Jews. Claire had been following him for years and fixing what he broken. He knew someone was on to him but did not know who. That didn't deter him. He kept on doing it.

Claire had numerous IDs attached to multiple offshore accounts packed with loads of money. She'd transferred this money from various large corporations over the years, and lots of small amounts they didn't even notice were gone. She never had to draw down too much at a time, so she wasn't setting anyone's alarm bells off. She'd been a very careful Russian spy, so careful they didn't even know about all of her other identities and certainly not her money.

Her birth name was Anastasia Datsyuk. Only the Russians and her parents knew this. Her parents were loyal Russians, proud of their daughter, even though they hadn't seen her since she'd left Russia years ago. They were okay with that. She was working for the country. Neither her superiors nor her parents knew she'd long abandoned the politics of Russia. She'd been okay with the authoritarianism up to a point; she was once part of the Russian establishment, and it hadn't affected her. Once outside the country, it became much more obvious. She'd watched Putin rise over the years. He was a crook and a dictator, and she was done with him. She didn't want to play in that arena anymore.

She'd been planning her escape for a while, and if she hadn't met the three old women at the condo, she would have been long gone. They'd adopted her like a granddaughter and stolen her heart. She didn't even know she had a heart. Now they're dead.

She would start a new life as someone else again. It was time to retire. First, she had to find Malek.

Chapter Four

THE JOURNEY

ANTONIO

It was blazing hot, and Antonio's back was screaming at him. The places where the pins had been inserted were irritated and aching. He had a bit of a limp when he was tired and he was tired now.

He was looking for a downscale motel where the clerk wouldn't look at him suspiciously. Arriving on foot early in the morning without luggage was suspicious. He spotted the Palace Inn Motel, looking suitably run down in the morning sun. An East Indian clerk was there alone and looked wary. He stiffened and didn't smile as Antonio approached the desk. It wasn't much of a lobby. The clerk's desk was chipped, and the carpet was a dingy green and stained. There was one bad print of a palm tree on the wall behind him with a tear in the corner. The lobby hadn't been updated since the 50s. A musty smell with an overlay of cheap pine room spray hung in the air. Antonio half expected to see a mouse corpse in the corner.

Antonio spoke first, saying, "Good morning. I'm looking for a room for a few weeks. The clerk said, "Yes, sir, we have a few rooms free." Antonio thought, *try the whole damn motel.* The clerk continued, "We have an end unit if that would be your preference?" Antonio asked, "And the cost?" The clerk calculated it and said, "$1,026 per week. Would you like to book it?" Antonio said, "Yes, and I'll pay cash if that's okay." The clerk said, "Certainly, sir." Antonio asked, "Where can I park my car?" He invented a car that contained his invisible luggage. He was banking that the clerk wouldn't bother looking. The clerk said, "There's a spot in front of your room." Antonio thought *just the beginning of my lies.*

The room was narrow and dark, and the bedspread was as stained as the toilet bowl and shower. Dusty gatherings of who knows what lived in the corners, and the room smelled like the lobby, eau de dead mouse. It was a grubby hotel room, but it would do for now. Antonio was starving but needed a shower and a change of clothes. His shirt was soaking wet with sweat. It would have to do until he could pick up some new clothes. He showered and shaved his face and head again. He was a hairy guy, and he thought, *this may be a twice-a-day job for as long as I keep this look.* His fake ID pictures were of the old 'him,' this morning's 'him,' with a mustache and a full head of black hair. He needed to update those and thought *I might need to stay here longer to arrange that. It took two weeks for my last set to arrive. I can't buy a car without a new driver's license.*

Cleaned up, he headed across the street to an Arby's and wolfed down a huge breakfast with the works. He took one pain pill with his coffee. He began to feel human again. He'd kept his sunglasses and hat on and wore a blue Covid mask. Nobody in Florida wore those anymore unless for health reasons. The waitress looked at him and shook her head, her politics dripping from her. He spotted a thrift store down the street and bought a few more cheap shirts, socks, underwear, and long pants.

He returned to his room and, using one of his burner phones, snapped some selfies of himself for his new driver's license picture. Then he contacted his fake ID supplier and ordered new documents with his new picture. He requested an ID from someone dead, someone who wouldn't be looking for it. The responder said, "We can do that, but dead IDs are more expensive." Antonio explained he needed to pay in cash and had no car. His fake ID dealer, all customer service, said, "No problem, where would you like to exchange the cash?" Antonio said he could leave the cash in an envelope at the front desk of the hotel to be picked up. The ID dealer thought that was too risky and suggested a seldom-used park bench nearby. Antonio would tape the envelope to the bottom of the bench to be picked up later. The invisible dealer said, "Don't worry, it's secure; we do this all the time." Antonio did this that night, and at two AM, he received a text on his burner that the cash had been received. A crook with a good business head. He knew Antonio would probably have to hit him up again eventually for a changed ID. That's the way it worked when someone wanted to disappear. His new ID package arrived within a week. Good service. He was now John Caldwell, a nice middle-of-the-road name. It didn't really match his Mexican face.

He'd decided to go to Seattle. It was a sizeable city to get lost in and far away from Miami. If someone thought he was still alive and was searching for him, they probably wouldn't imagine him going to Seattle. He'd been raised in a hot state, and he probably wouldn't go to a cold, wet state. His daughter was just over the border in Vancouver, not that he could contact her. He was supposed to be dead, drowned. It would just be nice to know she was close.

He prearranged car insurance at a local agency he could walk to. So far, his driver's license hadn't bounced when the insurance agent checked it. For the car, he looked on autoTEMPEST. He wanted an SUV long enough that he could sleep in. He found a gray 2018 Hyundai Tucson nearby with decent mileage. It was a car that wouldn't stand out. He took an Uber to see the car and asked the driver to wait. He was acutely aware that the seller would have a long time to look at his face during this transaction. A woman came to the door, introduced herself as Betty and walked out to the car parked in the driveway. He wore his mask and said, "I hope my mask doesn't offend you. I'm going through chemo, and it's unfortunately necessary." Betty was in her mid-60s and had short, gray, curly hair. She had a thick-waisted teapot body and wore matching pink sweatpants and a top. Antonio thought *she's probably more comfortable than I am right now.* Betty said, "Please, don't worry about it. I hope you're going to be okay." He just said, "Thanks." She didn't need any more information.

She said, "I'm not sure about you taking my car out for a test drive. I don't know you. Would you mind if I called a neighbor to join us?" Antonio said, "Not at all. That's the smart thing to do. I could be anybody." Betty made a call, and a guy from two houses over showed up. They all shook hands like old friends, and he took it out for a test drive with the two of them in the car. Everything worked, and he agreed to buy the car. He let the Uber driver go. They now had to go to the Jacksonville DMV to transfer ownership and get new plates. This was the heart-stopping interaction when his fake driver's license would fly or not. If not, he planned to walk out and away quickly, and hopefully, no one would follow him. He worried about standing in a lineup outside a public building with cameras on him. He hoped his bald head and mask would compensate for that.

Betty seemed to trust Antonio and agreed to ride in the car without the neighbor. The lineup was long and winding around the corner outside the DMV building. He got them both cold drinks and waited for the questions he knew would be coming. He told her his last car had broken down; he needed it to drive his grandchildren around. He was just a regular guy who needed a car. He evaded her other questions. He knew she'd remember him, but hopefully not much of his face.

After the Miami Surfside collapse, pictures of the victims were posted online, but in large groupings of small images. It would be hard to gather pictures of all the dead people who'd lived in Vanilla Palms. Most people lived private lives, and it would take some digging to come up with pictures of all of them. The only picture they would have of him was his driver's license.

He'd willed his condo to his two daughters, but he had to be dead before they could claim it. Someone could be after him for insurance fraud, although the cash would go to his daughters, not him. The cash he had stashed from his insurance claim would be nowhere to be found. That money was legally his and he'd kept it a secret, but he wondered if insurance companies talked to each other. He imagined his insurance company talking to the condo insurance company. Missing people aren't allowed secrets. Lots to worry about.

An awning over the licensing bureau building exterior provided some shade. After an hour and a half and a lot of silence, they were inside, and his body tightened. If the driver's license didn't fly, he had a problem. The agent barely looked up to check Antonio's image to the license image and Antonio walked out to his new old car. He peeled off the bills, paid Betty her asking price, switched the plates, and drove her home.

He'd decided to camp in his car for the drive up to Seattle. Better to stay out of the eye of hotels and cameras while he was on the move. There would be cameras at gas stations, but he could at least use a Covid mask, sunglasses, and hat. His first stop was a car window tinting business. He was told he was allowed a 24% tint in Washington on all windows. That would take four hours, and he waited it out in their lobby with his mask on. Antonio thought *I'm dead. I've got all the time in the world*. His next stop was a camping gear distributor, where he bought a sleeping bag, pillow, and a headlamp so he could read after dark in the car. He then bought some cardboard and cut the pieces to fit his windows to give him nighttime privacy. His last stop was the money storage unit. He packed his money under the car seats and in the spare tire space, moving the tire up to his trunk. $6 million in hundred dollar bills was a fair bit of weight to carry with his bad back.

Antonio was on his way. He drove west through Louisiana and Texas, then north to the Oklahoma border and picked up Route 66. He'd always wanted to do that drive. Why not now? Two days later, he was skirting LA and heading north. He found KOA grounds that allowed him to park in a camping spot. He didn't want to leave the car for long, so quickly soaped up in the washroom sink. He'd catch a shower when he got to Seattle. America isn't kind to brown men sleeping in cars on the side of the road and camping spots filled up early. Lots of vagabonds on the road. Antonio would book his spot and then find a parking lot or a mall to hang out. He didn't want a chat with a campsite neighbor. It stayed light until ten, so his time sleeping in a dark car was contained. He stayed low.

Antonio had already scouted Seattle, thinking he'd rent out by Lake Sammamish. There was good fishing there. He wasn't interested in fishing in the bays off the choppy, cold gray Pacific. He knew his days of warm ocean fishing were probably over. He came in on the 405, avoiding the Pike Street market area, turned off on I90, and started looking for a motel. He didn't go quite as down market this time and chose a Quality Inn. The white duvets, pillows and towels were welcoming after his time on the road. This would be his base while he looked for an apartment. It was pouring rain, gray, cold and miserable. *Welcome bloody home*, he thought.

ESTELLE

After the surgery, Estelle surfaced in her bed, feeling nothing. A nurse sat beside her and said, "If you feel sick, I have a pan right here." Estelle put her hand to her face. She was covered in gauze bandages. She groggily said to the nurse, "How did it go? Am I beautiful yet?" The nurse laughed and said, "Not yet, honey. You've got some healing to do first." Within an hour, the pain started, and she did feel sick. That first day was rough.

After ten weeks, her bandages were off, and her face was bruised, but the swelling had gone down. *Nothing that a bit of makeup won't hide*, Estelle bravely thought. She didn't recognize the woman looking back at her in the mirror. Her new nose was pretty and delicate. Her eyes stood out now. She had a lovely chin and cheekbones. Her teeth were realigned, capped and perfect. Her sun-damaged skin had been brushed, peeled, and was soft as a peach. She looked like she was in her mid-30s and felt like she'd invaded someone else's body. Her old face had defined her old life: her mother's early disappointment, nasty kids in school, lonely high school years, and few choices with men unless it meant free sex. She was looking forward to what the rest of her life would serve up.

After two months, it was time to leave her cushy world and get started on the next steps. She had to order a new ID to match her face and needed to move to an interim address to do that.

Her surgeon wanted to see her again in three months, but she didn't have that luxury. She had to get moving. She left with a referral to a plastic surgeon in New York in case something went wrong. She'd found a decent little motel near the clinic and booked a room for two weeks. An Uber took her there. She wasn't walking this time. Estelle still had to make changes and bought hair dye, scissors and some business casual clothes to get her through. She wanted to look respectable when she applied for apartments. She had to be ready for anything.

Estelle had been a drugstore blonde since she was thirteen. At the motel, she snipped her long blonde hair into somewhat of a pixie cut and then dyed it dark brown. She liked her new look and couldn't stop checking her image in the mirror. *Who's that girl?* She'd think. Like Antonio, she snapped headshots of herself and sent them over to the fake ID dealer she'd used before. All she really needed was a driver's license and an SSN number. She'd get the address changed once she found somewhere to live in Manhattan. She, too, was smart enough to specify IDs from dead people rather than stolen ones. The money exchange was different in Atlanta. She had to meet a guy in a mall outside a lingerie store. She wondered if passing money to a stranger in front of a display window full of bras and panties was considered less suspect. He didn't look evil, just an ordi-nary, pleasant-looking guy in his early 50s dressed in khakis, a well-ironed, short-sleeved cotton shirt, and sneakers. He looked like somebody's dad who'd just stepped away from a family barbecue for a brief errand. They exchanged their coded greeting; he took her money, smiled warmly, and wished her luck. There was almost some kindness in this interaction. It was an interesting illegal exchange in the so-called dark underworld. She wondered what his story was but would never know. As she walked away, she suddenly became aware of a fact. He was responding to a pretty woman who might have a problem, given she needed a fake ID. Running from an abusive husband? It was her looks that made him smile and be kind. She th ought *so that's what I missed with that last face, kindness.*

In a week, she had her new ID. She was now Sharon Branson from Iowa. She researched all the places she might have frequented growing up and built a back story. Like Antonio, Claire, and Randy, she used the 'home-schooled' story, mostly invisible to town people. She lived with her mother until she died. She had no apartment references, was self-employed, and had no work references. She hoped cold, hard cash would shut down any future questions from landlords.

Estelle's bus left Atlanta for New York at five AM. She'd packed up her rollaway suitcase and her backpack of cash and Ubered over to the bus terminal. She removed the battery from her burner phone and tossed the phone into a big dumpster before she left. She had another one she hadn't set up yet. That could wait until she needed it in New York. She'd booked a hotel in downtown Manhattan near the bus station. Even though she had a new look, she knew she was always on camera and kept on her sunglasses, a hat and a Covid mask. A few people still wore masks in the bus depot, so she didn't feel too out of place. Cameras and Big Brother were definitely everywhere. No one should recognize her new face, but she had to be careful.

The bus to the Port Authority Midtown bus terminal was packed. Everybody in Atlanta wanted to go to New York for some reason. She wasn't crazy about sharing a seat with someone looking at her for 21 hours and secured a window seat so she'd be slightly less visible. She hadn't been on a bus since she was in her teens, but it still had the same smell of humanity, sweat, and deodorizer. A woman carrying about 275 pounds sat down beside her with an 'oomph.' She settled her broad bum and width into her seat and part of Estelle's. Estelle nodded at her. She had her traveling story down if asked. She was visiting a friend in Brownsville, Brooklyn. She planned to do a bit of sightseeing in Manhattan first. That was why she was staying at the hotel near the bus station if observed. She was from the Midwest. Other than that, she'd keep her mouth shut and wouldn't be initiating any conversations.

Turned out it wasn't a problem. This woman was a talker, but it was okay; she only wanted to talk about herself. She introduced herself as "Birdie." She regaled Estelle with intimate stories of her family in Atlanta, her sisters and brothers and past and current boyfriends, and it seemed anything that popped into her mind. She didn't need a response. She looked at Estelle and asked, "Why are you still wearing that damn mask?" Estelle said, "I have a condition." Birdie said, "Oh, I'm so sorry, what's wrong?" Estelle said quietly, "I don't discuss my health." The woman said, "Why not? You can tell me, honey. We're stuck together for most of the day." Estelle said nothing. The woman was relentless. This was good gossip, a real illness right beside her. She said "Hope it's nothin' I can catch." Estelle said, "You're safe." Birdie pressed on, "So what's wrong with you?" Estelle touched her arm gently and said, "It's my business." She plugged her earbuds in, leaned back and closed her eyes. Birdie just ignored that and rattled on to herself. Estelle's fake disease was driving Birdie's imagination nuts.

The bus stopped every now and then for bathroom and food breaks, although Birdie had been eating constantly. An endless picnic kept coming out of her bottomless bag. A fried chicken breast, a bag of corn chips, a can of coke, an unpleasantly fragrant meat sandwich, candies to chew on and suck on. Her menu was extensive. She could have fed the bus. She offered Estelle some of everything that appeared. Estelle stayed polite and said, thanks, but I'll let you enjoy it." Birdie said, "You're thin as a stick; you need to eat more, girl." At the stops, Estelle disembarked, lined up for the bathroom and kept her head down. She'd stretch in the privacy of the washroom stall, but women were waiting. She'd always been fit and promised herself to get back into a workout routine when she got settled. Birdie dozed off after lunch, farting in her sleep and lightly snoring. It was a reprieve from her constant prattle. The passengers around her looked over with disgust, and Estelle looked back at them and shrugged. She thought *you ride the bus, you join humanity.*

Almost a full day passed, and at 12:35 AM, the bus rolled into the hot and crowded terminal. Birdie had plopped down on a bench, fanning herself. They didn't exchange goodbyes. Estelle waited for her luggage, thinking the rest of her life was in that suitcase of money. It was finally delivered to her, and she wheeled it off with her backpack on her back. She walked to the hotel; it was only a few blocks away, and there were lots of people around.

Manhattan streets were busy even that early in the morning. A cabbie honked loudly at her as she jaywalked across the street. She gave him the finger. She was in "a New York state of mind."

RANDY

The afternoon sun streamed in through the blinds of his motel window, lighting up the opposite wall with the Texas oil rig prints. He thought *they'll fade out within a year, but the hotel probably has a stack of them in their office storage cabinet.* His bike sat on some paper towels he'd cadged from the cleaners cart. The air conditioner droned on, sounding like an old plane taking off.

Randy had been content in his old life and certainly hadn't been thinking of disappearing. He definitely hadn't thought through being on the run with his life in danger. He almost, but only almost, wished he'd never found the money. He couldn't return it now. Nobody to return it to. He didn't know where he was going, but he wanted to get as far away from Florida as possible. He didn't have a passport, not even a fake one and wouldn't risk crossing a border with the money and a fake passport anyway. That would get him caught and eventually killed in jail. He'd been thinking about L.A., although he'd never been there and had no idea what it was like. He'd seen stories on T.V. about the wildfires that hit the California coast. Still, they never seemed to hit L.A. Hollywood was there, famous people wandering the streets. It could be cool. He'd need to find something to do. He was a fidgety guy. He'd been gone three weeks now. They'd know he was missing when they didn't find his body. There was a little news dribbling out about insurance payouts, but nothing definitive. The insurance company was apparently questioning whether it was a bomb. Randy didn't know how that might affect insurance payouts. There was always some 'terrorism' clause in insurance policies.

His parents would be wondering what happened to him. He wished he could call Mary and ask if she missed him at all. He'd have been disappointed to know she hadn't known he was missing and really didn't care.

Some people look like no one in particular. If you saw them at a bus stop or on the subway, you wouldn't remember anything about them. Asked to describe them, you couldn't. Randy was one of those guys. He had an oval face, a bit of a pudding nose, a weak chin and thin lips. Not for him, the square-jawed good looks of the high school quarterback. This face, combined with thinning hair, made Randy entirely forgettable. He thought *I could always shave my head and grow a small beard. That might change my look.* That night, he shaved his head and didn't shave his face the next morning.

After three days of beard growth, he was miraculously better looking. Baldness oddly suited him.

He turned over his two fake IDs in his hands. In one, he was Philip Irving from Iowa. In the other, he was Michael Kernaghan, from Nevada. That would be Irish. Being Jewish, he didn't look even vaguely Irish. He hadn't decided which of them he wanted to be in his new life. He worried these were stolen and the two men could be looking for their stolen IDs. He thought *I should have considered that long ago, but I never thought I'd need them.*

He decided he needed IDs from dead guys. He'd at least brought that contact number with him. He texted the number, and a guy named Raul texted him back immediately. 'We doze, we never close' apparently in that business. Raul gave him the cost and asked him what he was driving. He reminded Randy he'd also need a new bike license and matching insurance. He could get stopped and have to produce some paperwork. Randy told him he'd probably buy a car in L.A. Raul said, "These IDs will hold up when you transfer the car ownership and buy insurance. We haven't had any problems." Randy hadn't thought the whole car purchase thing through. It all made him nervous. So many ways to get caught.

Raul named a pizza restaurant several miles from the hotel for the money exchange. He told Randy there was a large empty oil can at the back of the building. "Leave the money under the oil can in an envelope. Come at night, there aren't any cameras. Pick up a plain envelope at a dollar store; don't use the hotel's." He said, "I'll text you confirming the pick-up and when your new IDs are ready." He told Randy to take several selfies, advising him what to do with lighting and positioning. He said, "Send all those over to us, and we'll do the rest." Randy did this, sent the pictures, and drove to the restaurant with the money. There was the promised oil can. He thought *it could move in a stiff wind and didn't look too stable. I'm not sure about this.* No one was around, and he taped the envelope with the cash under the can and hoped for the best. Later that night, Raul texted him, saying, "Package received, thanks."

Randy googled Hollywood on his phone, looking at the city map and the familiar street names. He looked at job listings and apartment listings. *I could pick up a job on a movie set,* he thought. He hadn't considered he had to stay away from the IRS and couldn't go on someone's payroll. He had so much to learn.

He practiced his backup story in his head: *I was living with my parents, and they died. I have never rented before, so I can't provide any references.* He didn't need a job, but he wanted to do something. One thing Randy wasn't was lazy.

He planned his route. He'd be slightly beyond El Paso the first night and should make L.A. the next night.

It would take him a few days of hard riding, but at least it was action. He waited to hear back from Raul so he could hit the road.

Within a week, Raul got back to him and told him his new IDs were ready. He suggested Randy research the towns these people were from, the grade schools and high schools they might have attended, and any teacher's names he could glean. He told Randy it was wise to have a good story to go with his identity. Randy rode out to the oil can and found his package. That night, he followed Raul's advice and did a bit of research on both dead men. They'd probably died in infancy, and no one would remember them going to the local grade school or high school. That's alright, Randy thought *I don't remember anybody I went to school with either*. He chose one of the IDs. He was now Jake Campbell from Flint, Michigan. A long way from home.

Randy hit the road the next day, heading to Hollywood, glad for an action plan. He loaded his bike and headed across the country on I-10 to Hollywood. He wouldn't miss that Texas hotel room. He'd been there way too long.

It took him just over two days as he passed through San Antonio, went up to Fort Bliss, Tucson, and onto Hollywood. He rode carefully, not wanting to draw any attention to himself. He couldn't take the chance of being stopped and having his saddlebags searched. He could hear a cop saying, with his gun drawn. "There's a lot of money here, son; where did it come from?" He chose cheap economy motels and worried about his bike being stolen. They wouldn't be looking at him too closely. Lots of strangers passing through. "Don't ask, don't tell." would be their business mantra. He had no idea what he would find at the other end of this journey. He was riding out into nowhere.

He turned off the I-5 to 1-70, dropped down into Hollywood and rode down Santa Monica Blvd. In his head, he could hear Sheryl Crow singing, *"All I wanna do is have a little fun before I die.... Until the sun comes up over Santa Monica Boulevard."*

CLAIRE

Clair had decided on Chicago as her next stop. She'd been there a few times on business and knew it well. It was a big city, multicultural and a good place to disappear into the background.

After her night in the coffee shop, she found a motel up the road and checked in for a week. She was carrying around $50,000 in hundred-dollar bills. A portable five pounds of money. She'd need the cash to buy a car here and pay a rent deposit in her new location.

She didn't need anybody to get her false IDs. She was the dark web. She could create her own IDs. She knew where to get the right paper. Passport covers were trickier, but she had a connection. She had the IDs of a dozen dead people with all the prerequisite SSN numbers, driver's licenses, and backstories. Some had her regular picture, and others had her older lady with a fake nose and wig picture.

She could tell if one of her IDs was on someone's watch list and always checked before using it. It had never happened, but she was always careful.

She didn't waste time and found a suitable car for sale near her. She donned her mask, wig and hat, cabbed to the seller's house, and took it for a test run. He'd trusted her to take it out for a test drive alone. She thought *I guess he doesn't think older women are car thieves*. It was a quiet little gray Kia, no flash. She'd set up a preliminary insurance policy and phoned in the info. The seller needed to tell her more about the car than she wanted to know, but she let him talk. She couldn't seem in a hurry. He'd bought it for his daughter, but she'd wanted something showier, ideally a convertible. He said, "Teenagers huh?" Like Claire would know. She just smiled and said, "Yeah."

After changing the plates and ownership at the DMV, she'd paid the seller cash. She drove away with him squinting at her in the sun in her rearview mirror, hand shading his eyes as he stared after her. She thought *he sure loved this little car*. He thought *she was a strange one. I could swear that was a wig*.

She picked up her insurance papers and then went to her storage locker. She had an additional $100,000 stored there. She had millions more in her offshore bank accounts, but for now, she just needed to pay a large deposit for rent and live on the cash for a while. She placed the money in the emergency bag in the trunk. She thought *not perfect, but at least not readily visible*. Claire headed up the road. *So long Florida, hello cold, snowy winters*, she thought.

She'd been living in Florida as 'Claire' for so many years she found it rather exhilarating to start a new life with a new identity. She was now Caroline Mitchell.

Claire had no sad feelings about leaving Florida or even her job. She felt a little bad she'd never be able to see her boss again. He was a good guy and would be disappointed when he discovered what she'd been up to. However, Claire wasn't one to feel remorse about much. No point in apologizing. The job was a means to an end. This escape.

Chapter Five

A SAD SITE

The repeating buzz and vibration of his phone pulled Billy slowly to the surface. He closed his gaping mouth and moistened his lips and tongue. Zenith's name and number were flashing on his screen. Billy thought *it's seven AM; this can't be good.* Before picking up, he remoistened his mouth, smacked his lips, and wondered several things in that brief second: *was Zenith questioning the minutes I sent over yesterday? What did I do wrong?* Then he thought *maybe he's going to fire me.* Billy hated his job, but he couldn't afford to be fired. His stomach was tight as he answered the phone, "Hi Zenith, what's up?"

There was a silent pause at the end of the line, and Billy wondered if he'd missed the call. Finally, Zenith spoke, "More like down Billy. There was a big explosion in the industrial park behind Vanilla Palms this morning, releasing something toxic. It appears everyone in the condo is dead. The fire department has the environmental people on their way. It's early, and it's unidentified, but some toxic fumes came out of the explosion, hit the condo, and then blew off. The police chief who called said it looked like they all died immediately. The whole area is sealed off. Billy said, "Fuck, are you serious?" Zenith never swore, and Billy regretted his curse immediately. He'd have to watch his mouth. Zenith answered, "Sadly, yes." Billy asked. "What happened?" Zenith said, "I'm sure we'll find out soon enough. One of the sites in the industrial park was handling dangerous goods. Something got out of hand and blew up. They told me there's nothing left of that site, complete destruction. I have a meeting with the police, the fire department, and the insurance company today on-site. If it was a bomb, that's another hurdle."

Billy choked up, panic in his chest, mind racing. Everyone dead? How can that be? I just met with the board yesterday morning. He was too young to be familiar with death. He envisioned all those dead people. He asked, "What do we do? Where are the people?" Zenith said, "They told me the bodies are being moved to a large air-conditioned hall near Jacksonville. I'm providing the police with our owners' records so they can contact the next of kin. I can only hope there were a lot of people away this time of year. It will take some time to track down contacts. If people had visitors, they'd be unidentified. If we can't find people who are away, that's a different problem.

Zenith stayed silent, waiting for Billy to calm himself and reminded him. "Billy, we're not the owners. We're the property management company. We're not at fault here. But I'm going to need your help. All hands on deck and all that." Billy said, "Sure, what can I do?" He didn't want to do anything. He wished he'd left this job a month ago.

Zenith was cool as a cucumber. He'd faced disasters before and had gone into a calm, reasoned battle mode in his head. He was in control. It was all about keeping your head. He just had to ensure Billy kept his. He said, "Billy, the press will be looking for insider information. I don't want you talking to them. The police will interrogate you about the residents, and then Thompson Insurance will interrogate you. That's their right, but do not talk to the press. They'll be all over the site, and both of us. Only answer your phone if it's me or our lawyer, Doug McPherson. You've met him. Put his number in your phone contact list, so you recognize his calls. The other boards you oversee will call you for information and gossip. Don't respond. I'll call all the board presidents later this morning. If the media tracks you down, you only say, "It's being investigated thoroughly." That's a ll.

He then said, "I'm going over to the site. I think you should stay out of this today. Are you okay with that?" Billy said, "Yeah," and thought *Okay? Hell, I'm relieved. I didn't want to go down to that pile of death. I knew a lot of those dead people.* Zenith said, "Take the day off. Don't answer your phone. Meet me at the office tomorrow morning at eight ."

For a change, Billy was not hungry. His phone rang all day. Some calls were from board members from other condos, but mostly unknown numbers. He thought *who's giving out my number, and do they know where I live?* Thanks to the condo president Morty, the media found him. He couldn't see the street from his windows, but strangers with cameras, microphones and vans began to gather outside his building. They stopped other people living in the building and asked if they knew Billy. They didn't. Billy didn't mix with anyone in the building.

Images of the exploded site and the now empty dead condo were on the news all day, with various talking news heads posing opinions. Billy was relieved to see Morty, the condo president, talking to the press. Billy wouldn't have been happy knowing Morty had given them his address. Morty had said he and his wife were heading north. They were lucky. They dodged the bullet. Morty was telling them he knew them all. He was barely keeping it together, but he was.

At nine AM, his mother phoned. He needed to tell her he was okay and not to talk to anyone, so he answered the phone. She said, "Billy, I've been so worried. Are you alright?" He said, "It's awful, Mom. I knew some of those people. They were good people." She asked, "What happened?" He said, "Mom, it's a disaster, but I can't discuss it now. Sorry. The media are all over it. My phone hasn't stopped ringing. Zenith, my boss, told me not to talk to anyone. That applies to you and Dad, too. Your friends and neighbors will be asking you questions." She said, "What should we say?" He said, "Just tell them you don't know anything. Don't answer your phone for a week or two. His mother said, "Really? That seems a bit severe. This wasn't your fault." She paused, then asked, "Was it?" Billy was amused at how little faith his mother had in him. He said, "No, Mom, I'm just the property manager; we had nothing to do with it. Don't worry." She said, "Well, that's what I'll say then." Billy realized controlling his parents' communication wa s going to be difficult. He said again, "Mom, please, just say you don't know anything for now. Please." She said, "I'll have to cancel my bridge game this week. He said, "Sorry, Mom, but that would be a good idea." He realized asking her not to talk to her friends about this was a lost cause. It was juicy gossip, and her son was right in the middle.

Zenith parked a block away from the site and walked over. The acrid smell in the air was overwhelming. Nothing was left standing at the truck depot, but the fire department was still there, hosing it down. A large fire continued to burn. It was a steaming pile of soot and chemicals. The condo stood across the street, ostensibly empty, lights still on, nobody home. It was a sad sight. Zenith identified himself to the cop guarding access and was allowed under the rope.

Zenith was meeting the Chief of Police, the Fire Chief and the insurance adjuster here. The insurance adjuster's name was Carolyn Sweeney, and she said she'd be wearing a beige pantsuit. He knew he'd spend a lot of time with this woman for possibly years ahead, and he wanted to establish trust early. She would have a challenging job, sorting out the payouts. He spotted a woman in a beige pantsuit, early 50s, with a short haircut and a touch of grey coming through at the temple. She was talking to a man in a uniform and had a frown on her face. Zenith approached her and asked, "Carolyn?" She smiled briefly, not warmly, and said, "You must be Zenith. Hello." She did not offer her hand. She said, "This is the Fire Chief, Jack Silvester." Zenith shook Jack Silvester's hand and introduced himself. Jack was a big guy, about six feet tall, with gray hair and a receding hairline. He was about Zenith's age, 60ish. Jack would be close to retirement, and this wasn't the best gig to go out on. Zenith asked him, "What do you know so far?" Jack assessed Zenith. Late middle age, a bit overweight, conservatively dressed, with a slight accent. He portrayed quiet intelligence and authority without pushiness. He had to judge people quickly in his job, and he immediately liked Zenith. Carolyn, not so much.

He said to both of them, "Until we remove this rubble, we won't be able to find the source of the explosion if there even was one. It could have just been a chemical interaction." Zenith glanced at Carolyn and asked Jack, "Does it look like a chemical explosion or something else?" Jack was wary of questions like these, particularly around insurance adjusters. They could jump to conclusions. He said, "I honestly can't answer that. As I said, we won't know until we remove the rubble." Carolyn pushed and said, "It must look like one or the other. You've had years of experience." Jack said, "Never anything like this. I've never seen an entire building of people killed by an invisible toxic gas. I'll let you know as soon as we have examined everything." She asked in a bit of a cutting way, "How long do you think that will take?" Jack gave Zenith a quick glance, looked at the site, and said, "Could be months. There's a lot of stuff to clear here, and we have to supervise that to ensure we don't miss anything." Carolyn asked, "What are the chances the site might get contaminated before you sift through everything?" Jack said, "Hurricane season starts in August. All bets are off if we get hit with one before we finish. That gives us a couple of months. Hopefully, we'll have an answer before then. Rain won't change anything, and the site will be guarded 24/7 until we finish."

Carolyn was obviously unhappy with this answer, but Jack was experienced with insurance adjusters and backed her down with a look. Zenith gave them his card and told Jack he'd be in touch. Carolyn didn't like Zenith's immediate, easy way with the fire chief and said, "All reports must come to me first." Jack winked at Zenith and said, "The lady's in charge." She knew she wasn't. Zenith said, "Have you seen the Chief of Police? I was supposed to meet him here as well. Jack said, "Enrico? Yes, he's right over here, I'll introduce you." He moved Zenith away from Carolyn. She was feeling sidelined by the old boys.

Enrico Gaza, the Chief of Police, shook Zenith's hand. Zenith asked, "Do you prefer Chief Gaza, or...?" the Chief said, "Please, Enrico, you're not one of my staff." He said, "Thanks for getting the contacts over to us so quickly. The coroners are providing us with a list of bodies found by apartment. That's a good start. Obviously, there'll be people missing, and once we've determined who was there, we can start sifting through the owners who weren't. If they haven't already come forward. Then, we start working on the list of real missing people. I've assigned a detective to the case, Joe Piccioni. He's young, but he's smart. Anything you can do to help him will be most appreciated." Zenith said, "That's great. I have a competent young man who can work with your detective. He was the assigned property manager of the building and knew a lot of the people. He should be a big help. Hopefully, we can get in touch with everyone quickly." He then asked, "Who would you like to be the official speaker to the press?" The Chief said, "That's our job, and I'm on air in ten minutes." Zenith said, "I'll leave you to it. We'll talk later today."

Zenith returned to Carolyn, "Why don't we step over here into some shade and chat about the next steps." Carolyn felt Zenith taking the lead and didn't like it. She said assertively, "I'll be managing this case and will tell you what we need." Zenith smiled pleasantly at her and said, "The police and the fire department are in charge here, not us. You and I will do everything we can to help." Your job starts when the lawsuits start coming in. I'll get a list of the occupants and next of kin over to you if they've been noted. I'll update you as I learn who's been identified, who's not and who's missing. Carolyn said, "There'll be angry relatives lining up for their piece of the pie, and you'll probably be the first contact. Are you ready for that?" Zenith said, "We have a good team, and I'm advised we've been assigned a detective by the police chief."

Just in case, Zenith had already contacted a defense lawyer he knew well. He'd prepared. She asked Zenith if he knew anything about the developers who'd built the condo. Did they do a risk assessment? Zenith told her, "We just took over the property management contract a while ago. I do know who the developer was. I'll put you in touch with him." He then said, "Did they do a risk assessment? I doubt it. It would have been cheap land near an industrial park. Lots of things are built near industrial parks. As far as they knew, no one was handling dangerous goods back there when the building was put up, and besides that, it's an industrial park. Where else would dangerous goods be handled? Nobody, including you, can use that as a known risk in a court case. She said with a cool clip, "Thank you for your legal opinion. Are you a lawyer as well?" Zenith smiled at her and said, "If I'm wrong, I'm wrong." He left it at that. That drove her nuts. He wouldn't even disagree with her.

She asked, "Do you have any current property valuations for these apartments?" Zenith said, "When the lawsuits come in, they'll be directed at the company handling the dangerous goods that killed these people." They'll be for loss of life, not property. The building itself wasn't harmed. The apartment values will be affected in the short term. They'd be difficult to sell. If whoever inherits them can hang on to them, they'll be worth more eventually. Inexpensive Florida apartments are scarce. We'll run into a problem if owners can't be found. The missing people still own those apartments, and they can't be sold on. We could place a lien against their apartments for unpaid property management fees and line up behind the utilities and the government for unpaid property taxes. It takes five years and a lot of paperwork to declare a missing person dead in this state. That's a long time."

Zenith continued, "If you need them, you should get the apartment valuations from a registered realtor."

Zenith said, "The detective assigned to us and our Vanilla Palms property manager will be working together to look for any missing people. I'll follow up with you as needed." He thought *I don't want a power battle with this woman*.

He said, "The media will be all over this, and I've instructed my staff to only direct inquiries to me. The police chief wants to be the official media communicator. We don't want the legalities of this situation misted with false information and conjecture." I suggest you advise your staff to do the same. She thought again, *he's in charge; I'm not*. He said to her confidently, "Don't worry, we'll get through it together." She wished he didn't sound like her dad.

Zenith would later learn that the mysterious chemical particles were microscopic and had apparently seeped into the apartments through the air conditioners. When the bodies were autopsied, it was learned everyone's lungs were rigid. They would have choked quickly and died. The coroner said, "One small mercy. It was quick." The Fire Chief believed the chemical blew through the building, moved on and dissipated in the sea air. An untraceable phantom bringing human destruction.

After two hours, there was nothing left of the depot but ash. The water sprayed by the fire department had already evaporated in the heat. There was no need for cadaver dogs; nothing to find, no one to find. The air was putrid with burnt chemicals and black smoke. There was no smell of death. Nobody rotting in the noonday sun. There were 92 bodies and not enough morgues or coroners to handle them. In addition to the coroners' vehicles and ambulances, they'd commandeered some personal vans to move the bodies to the gymnasium. They were all laid out there, waiting for their relatives and friends to identify them and take up the ancient veil of sadness and grief. The bodies had apartment number tags and names if they had them, attached to their toes before removal. They couldn't be sure of their names. They would all have to be identified and autopsies done.

All those dead bodies made everybody nervous. What if the chemical that killed them was still in the air? No one felt safe, including Zenith.

An aptly named skeleton crew of firemen looked at the rubble and knew how hard it would be to find a source in the steaming pile of rubble. The Fire and Explosive investigators arrived, and the cleanup started. Was it an accident or terrorism? If it was terrorism, what was the motive?

A policeman told Zenith, "We don't think anyone was in the truck terminal when it blew." Zenith thought *small mercies given the death toll next door.*

Hundreds of relatives, friends and the media started to gather around the security ropes up the street, well away from the condominium, hoping against hope someone would be found alive. Maybe their missing person stepped out for a walk, a smoke, milk, anything. People were weeping and holding each other or just standing alone and staring. They were too far away to see the bodies being carried out one by one in black body bags and driven away. Small blessings. The families still weren't allowed into the gym to begin identifying the bodies. The coroners needed to determine the cause of death. It might not necessarily be the gas. Once the bodies were identified, they'd be moved out quickly to funeral homes, crematoriums, whatever. The unidentified would have to be moved to freezers fairly quickly. It was June, even though the air conditioning was set to icy.

The next morning, Billy stood unseen at the top of his apartment lobby stairs and looked out the window. There were two vans with cameras on top and at least eight reporters milling about with mics and cameras. He thought *every junior reporter was sent to my building to see if they could get some news. The only good news is bad news, apparently.* Senior reporters would have been assigned to the disaster site at Vanilla Palms outside Jacksonville. He thought *they don't know what I look like. I'll walk past them a couple of blocks, call a cab and ride into the office that way.* A couple of reporters rushed him when he went out, asking him if he knew Bill Knudson. He said, "Nope, I just moved in, and I don't know anybody

here." They fell back and returned to the side of the road, and he walked o
n. *That was easy,* he thought. He turned the corner, walked several blocks,
noted the address, and called a cab. He hadn't slept and hadn't eaten and
felt like crap. He got the cab driver to stop at a McDonald's and choked
down three burgers like a starving dog.

Zenith's property management head office was in a ten-floor building on
the outskirts of Miami. The press were also parked outside here, but again,
they didn't know who they were looking for. The security guard gave Billy a
nod, and he rode the elevator up to their office suite. The reporters weren't
allowed in the building.

Zenith greeted him with a brief hug when he got to the office. This was
a different Zenith. He seemed to be genuinely worried about Billie. He'd
contacted him several times yesterday, updating him on what was happening. Billie didn't know how valued he was. He was diligent and honest, and
all his buildings' owners loved him.

Zenith knew Billy was close to burnout before this happened and didn't
want to lose him. Property managers weren't easy to recruit. It was a
thankless, tedious job requiring quite a bit of structural knowledge and the
moxie to deal with all kinds of unhappy people wanting their particular
problem fixed yesterday. It didn't pay well, and the hours stunk.

The detective assigned to them, Joe Piccioni, came up at eleven. Joe and
Billy could have been brothers. They were both tall, skinny young men
with dark hair. Joe was about five years older than Billy. They both had the
same offbeat sense of humor, which they managed to test even in this dark
situation. They hit it off immediately.

Zenith, Billy and Joe began to lay out a plan. They got the contact list over
to Carolyn, and Zenith ordered lunch. He sized up the two young men's
appetites and ordered a lot of food, including a stack of chocolate bars and
a case of pop.

Zenith said, "Billy if you're okay with it, it might be better if the two of you
work out of your apartment. Having you both come and go here every day
will draw attention. Joe isn't in uniform, so he won't stand out coming in
and out of your apartment. They'll think he's another tenant. The media

has the attention span of a gnat, so I predict they're mostly gone in a week or so."

He said, "After the police have confirmed who's been notified, I'll start contacting relatives and extend our condolences and what we're doing to find anyone missing." Zenith continued, "There are several ways to track down missing people, right Joe?" Joe grinned and said, "Yes, sir, and we'll use them all." Zenith said, "There'll be many angry people wanting to lash out, find someone to blame and sue. That's not us. That's Carolyn's job. She's a tough broad and wants to manage this. We'll let her. We'll send flowers where we can. Meanwhile, Billy, I'm relieving you of all your property management duties. You and Joe have a big, important job ahead of you. It will require all of your attention. Pull up all your records of any communication with the owners. Talk to Morty. He says he knew them all. Start creating individual files for each owner. Lay low. Don't answer the phone. Order food in, and I'll pay for it. Get some sleep. This will be challenging. Call me if you need to talk about anything. We'll get through this. We're the lucky ones.

Billy was oddly excited about this new assignment that had fallen in his lap. Some detective work with a real detective. No board meetings with tedious board members. No handing out bad news about condominiums needing expensive repair. Well, it was different bad news. "We can't find your loved one." He thought *finding missing people. Intriguing.*

Chapter Six

THE WAY WE WERE

CLAIRE

Anastasia Datsyuk had a happy childhood in Moscow. Both her parents were physicians, staunch supporters of Russia, well respected, and earning a good living. They lived in an expansive and well-appointed apartment in the Basmanny neighborhood in Moscow, had access to all the best shopping and healthcare and adored their clever daughter. They believed everything they were told. All else was propaganda. Their life was good. Like the righteous born into any of the many religions in the world, Russians thought they were the chosen ones, and the rest were to be pitied or damned.

From a very early age, Anastasia read everything she could. She knew Russia's history and, for that matter, much of the history of the world. She closely observed the government's public presentations, listened to everything her friends whispered and questioned everything. Her parents were uncomfortable with the burgeoning critical thinker their young prodigy was becoming and would try and gently persuade her to keep her questions to herself. They heard uncomfortable things about dissidents. They weren't complete fools, just blindly content.

For the sake of this story, we'll call Anastasia by her American pseudonym, Claire.

Claire dreamed of leaving Russia and experiencing what was beyond the borders. She'd followed Putin's career. He'd apparently applied to be a spy when he was young and was told the best path to that career was to go to law school. That became Claire's goal. Get a specialist's law degree in computer science, become a spy for Russia and see the world.

It wasn't an easy straight line. Grades were vital to being selected. She had to be the most brilliant little Russian in the school.

Claire was all edges: tall, sharp nose, sharp chin, thin face, straight hair, thin all over. She didn't send out a welcome message. Over those long university years, a few somewhat unattractive nerds, thinking she was a kindred spirit, asked her out. She wasn't interested in awkward social outcasts. She preferred good-looking boys. The nerds weren't in her intellectual league, and the good-looking boys definitely weren't. She didn't feel she was missing anything. Her life was busy and challenging. She had a goal. She thought *I'll do men later. When I have the time and interest.* It never happened.

She spent seven years completing her computer science undergrad and law school courses. Nose to the grindstone, no fun, no alcohol, no boys, few friends. Studying and coursework filled her days and nights. When she finally graduated, she was exhausted, stressed, and uninterested in joining a law firm, although many vied for her. She was a catch. Practicing law was the last thing she wanted to do. However, she had to play the game and wait to achieve her goal. Russia's foreign intelligence agency, the SVR, was suspicious of applicants. They preferred to do the selection. They handled foreign intelligence operations and international counter-terrorism operations and conducted hacking abroad. Their US equivalent was the Central Intelligence Agency (CIA).

Claire took a job with a small legal firm and found herself with a desk full of other people's problems. She hated every moment of it. Her parents thought she'd come to her senses and stopped questioning the infallibility of the government. They were wrong, but she didn't discuss that with them anymore. Her well-placed father knew people who knew people, and finally, her name rose to the top of the SVR recruiters. They were looking for an expert hacker, and she was definitely that.

The call came, followed by a series of increasingly intense interviews and tests. Even with her impeccable family credentials, high grades, and specialist law and tech degree, they had to be sure. When she was finally accepted, she learned she would spend another three years learning the trade. She also had to refine her language skills to speak English, Spanish and French without a Russian accent. She groaned to herself. I'll be almost thirty before I get my first assignment.

The night before she left the country, her parents had her over for dinner. It was emotional. They were bursting with pride but knew they wouldn't see her again for a long time, let alone communicate. They didn't know where she was going. That was classified. They were losing each other. Years after, as the country's leadership tightened its grip, they began to wonder if losing her was worth the price. Claire tried not to think about it too much but knew she'd deeply miss them. Turning away from the two people you loved was a heavy price to pay for freedom. She hadn't looked hard at the danger she might put them in in the future.

The SVR wanted to position her in a well-known large Florida tech security company, MPLtech Corp. MPLtech had numerous large clients nationwide in many fields. A gold mine of tech to steal. First, she'd need a well-known American computer science college degree. Her Russian credentials wouldn't do. They'd given her a new identity. Anastasia was no more. She became Claire Richmond, who'd lived in Idaho all her life. Her backstory was she'd been homeschooled through high school, taken an interest in computer science, and completed several high-level online computer courses. Her parents needed care, so she didn't go to university as she was caring for them. When they died, she was finally able to apply to university. The SVR had prepared all her reference and support information for the application. Her SAT score was 1580. They had her placed in the University of Florida Gainesville for Computer Science. Going back to school for another four years seemed too much to bear. Once again, she buckled down and completed the degree in two years. She was now 30 years old. It had been a long haul, and she was tired.

She had one more hurdle. She had to actually get a job with MPLtech in Miami. She submitted her application and waited. Weeks went by. She called and got the "We're reviewing all applications. Thank you for your patience" telephone message. She couldn't even get through to a live operator. She started to think she might have wasted the last ten years of her life and she'd be sent back to Russia. After a month, she received a text asking her to come to an interview in one week. Claire was never nervous, but so much hung on her nailing this. She didn't sleep the night before, rehearsing every possible answer about her new fake life. She wasn't surprised it was a small committee interview team. They were interviewing for a position with one of their highest security levels. She'd have access to clients with exceptionally sensitive databases. She could shut down half the country if she went rogue. They liked that she was a small-town girl. They checked all her references. The SVR had the right people answering the questions at the other end of the phone. They were all agents and were well prepared with her back story. She was tested again and again, including thorough personality tests. She'd been taught how to fake her way through those, providing the answers they wanted. She was a complete fraud, and they loved her. She got the job.

She received a brief but satisfactory message from the SVR on her secure phone. Хорошая работа! It meant 'Great job!' High praise indeed. She deleted it immediately.

Claire was most at home with her nose and mind buried in a complex computer program. She was first assigned with minor system problems that needed fixing. This was simple but satisfactory work for her. She was fast and explained things very clearly. MPL quickly began receiving high praise for her work with the clients she'd serviced.

She enjoyed the Florida lifestyle. She had a nice little apartment with a view of a park. The weather was glorious year-round when it wasn't too muggy. A February in Miami was a far cry from a February in Moscow.

MPL stood for the company owner's name, an officious-sounding Montrose Phelan Lexington. MPL. They all called him Monty. He was anything but self-important. He was supportive and kind and the smartest person Claire had ever met. She would have had a crush on him if he weren't so old. She admired him so much that she almost hated what she would be doing to his clients. It was the first time she'd ever faced down her own morals. Not the last.

Monty liked Claire a lot. She wasn't antisocial, just not a joiner. She seemed happy enough. He saw his younger self in her before he started his business.

A quiet little techie. He felt fatherly toward her. More to the point, she was so talented. She could get past any firewall in minutes.

She had assignments in states nationwide, some of which she traveled to if the work required more time. Many just involved upgrading their security systems but a new problem was emerging. Someone was shutting down systems and demanding ransom. This person seemed to be targeting businesses with a religious or racial lean, Jews and blacks, primarily. This person didn't care whose lives or businesses were inconvenienced or, in some cases, endangered or lost. Claire knew his signature, found his online fingerprints, and shut him down when she found his work. Through her SVR contacts, she learned he was Malek Bouziane, an Algerian operating under the alias of Michael Robertson. Too many of their clients, worried about the bad press of having their security system compromised, paid up. They would then call in Claire to shut the door behind him.

Claire and Malek had been at war for years, but he had no idea who she was. He knew someone had his number. She was too good to leave a trace. That there was someone else better than him out there made him very nervous. He could end up in prison. It didn't stop him. He, too, had goals.

After several years working with Monty's company, Claire knew she'd probably mined most of the new tech Russia might be interested in. Monty's client base remained stable. She wondered if Russia had ever used what she'd passed on. Meanwhile, she quietly built her own escape fund. She only stole from large companies who could afford it. She would create an accounting entry in their books and send the money to a secure, untraceable offshore account. The company's auditors often didn't even notice or question it. She had fun making up fictional entries for her personal withdrawals. Advertising accounts had a broad brush that accountants didn't look too closely at in large companies. It had been approved by someone. The someone being Claire. Her offshore accounts were doing well. It would soon be time to put them into action.

Claire knew where Malek lived, and when he moved to a new condominium called Vanilla Palms just outside of Jacksonville, she decided to follow him. She was getting bored, and he intrigued her. She only went into the office once a month or so, so the commute to Miami wasn't an issue. She didn't tell them she'd moved, and she didn't tell Russia. She wanted to keep a close eye on Malek. She suspected he was up to more than his ransom gig and intended to find out what that was.

She also had a new goal: freedom at 40. She was 39 now. She had enough money to disappear forever.

She rented from a charming Jewish man at the Vanilla Palms condo. He owned several condos up and down the coast. This building was predominately occupied by retired New York Jews getting out of the bitter northern winter. They were attracted to the building mainly because of the low price; it was new, and maintenance costs were low. It was inland, away from the ocean and the storms. A safe haven. Not that Claire cared, but her rent was reasonable; the apartment was a nice size and had a distant view of the coast.

Her landlord's mother, Ida, lived on the same floor as she did, along with a couple of her friends, Liz and Jennie. The 'girls,' as they called themselves, spent a lot of time together. Two of them were widows. Liz hadn't been married but had quite the life, lots of men and stories. Claire knew Jewish history, but these women embraced life, despite that horror. They were always laughing.

Ida had a walker, but Liz and Jennie were still mobile. They were the tanners, lying out on their lounges in their bathing suits, crepey skin, dark spots and flappy arms be damned. In their younger days, they'd all lived near each other in the Bronx. They still spoke with that crazy nasal accent. Claire loved their accent. They all liked a cocktail.

They had families: kids, grandchildren, nieces, and nephews who loved their embrace of life. It was always fun spending time with the old girls. They bragged and teased and hugged and spoiled. The terrifying past hung on the periphery of their minds but was refused entrance. They only let in sunshine and love. These were the women who drew Claire into their fold.

They played cards in the afternoon and met for happy hour at their local hangout on Fridays. Saturday was dinner night. They took turns cooking for each other, trying new recipes. They went out to Jimmie's Lounge a couple of times a month for dinner. Jimmie's was an old Florida restaurant where the clientele was mostly over 80, and the men still wore sansabelt pants high over their expanded bellies. The women were too tanned, over-dressed, and dripped with jewelry, particularly rings, not all authentic. They all wore hearing aids, but you could tell by their pasted-on smiles they were still missing most of the table conversation in the noisy restaurant. They made an entrance, calling out to each other in their finery. Many had trouble walking a steady path, sitting down, or getting up. They ordered one fancy drink and took home most of their food in a box. They weren't de ad yet.

When Claire started joining them for Friday happy hour, they wanted to know more about her. They'd ask, "Do you have a boyfriend? What do you do? Are your parents still alive? Where do they live? What did your father do? Claire could skirt all this with, "No, I don't have a boyfriend, I work in tech, My parents are gone. I didn't know my father. I'm from the Midwest." Then she'd ask them about their lives, and they would move on, overtalking each other with their stories. They never seemed to notice their questions had been evaded. She would have loved to be able to say, "Actually, I'm a Russian spy here stealing tech secrets and millions of dollars from my company's clients." But that wouldn't do.

Claire had a new problem. The Russian SVR felt her usefulness in her current job was diminishing. She'd provided them with little new infor-mation for over a year. They wanted her to move into a government tech security job. They told her they were setting that up for her. She didn't have a choice. She had an interview with the CIA in a month. The CIA would already be checking her credentials. There was little time.

She hadn't ever believed in Russia, and all it stood for, as her parents had. She was too clever for that. In her opinion, all governments were corrupt, with some systems more appealing than others if they worked as they were meant to. Many didn't. You choose sides.

Claire had been given some cyanide pills before she left, just in case she ever got caught. She wasn't about to kill herself for these bastards. She thought I'd rather go to jail in the States. Hardly the gulag. Besides, eventually, I'd get out. It was plan B.

When Claire left in the night, leaving the girls behind without saying goodbye was hard. They'd be insulted, if not hurt. But, it was the path she'd chosen.

When she heard they were dead, her sadness was only exceeded by her anger. Her ladies had been so glad to be alive. She'd wanted to be like them. She hoped they'd had fun the night before. They'd taught her something about living.

Malek did this. She was sure of it. He was now a terrorist in her books.

RANDY

Randy was inconvenient, an unwelcome surprise. He arrived ten years after his sister and fifteen years after his brother. His mother was 46 and a busy paralegal. His father was 54 and had his own accounting firm. Neither of them wanted to do 'baby' again. They had careers and busy lives. They had no time to attend baseball games or whatever sport this child took to.

They were Jewish but mostly non-observant. Randy always thought being observant was like birdwatching, always watchful, staring into the trees with binoculars. He didn't really know much about being a Jew or what they would be looking for. In the early years, before Randy was born, his parents had attended temple on the high holidays. It was the thing to do. When Randy's older brother turned thirteen, they held a bar mitzvah. Nothing big or splashy. They skipped his sister's bat mitzvah. By the time Randy was twelve, they'd lost interest in keeping up the façade.

Randy was a sweet, affectionate, uncomplicated little guy. No trouble, no drama. Shy and introverted, he had few interests. He watched a lot of TV but didn't read books, even comic books. School was torture for him. He wasn't good at it, never did his homework and was always called out in class by the teachers. His older siblings had excelled in everything. Thinking he might have a learning or mental disability, his mother had him thoroughly tested. It turned out he was just naturally unremarkable. His father had no patience for him and showed him little love and attention. Randy didn't mind. His mother adored him. He was always her baby boy.

He did his time at school. That's how he saw it. He pulled through high school with low C's and some math tutoring. He was relieved to be finished and had no interest in college. His parents suggested trade schools, but he wasn't handy and couldn't see the point. He wasn't unhappy but didn't have any close friends. He quietly passed through his childhood and teen years. He didn't give much thought to things and couldn't be drawn into opinions. Certainly not debates. He just wasn't that interested. His parents tried to draw out a personality, to no avail. Randy was a blank slate.

He had one quirk. He was tidy. His room was clean, bed made, clothes hung up, and laundry in the hamper. He happily did the after-dinner cleanup and unloaded the dishwasher in the morning. He'd pull out the vacuum and do the hard parts like the stairs. He liked mowing the lawn. He wasn't obsessive, but he liked order.

In their bedroom at night, when parents whisper about their kids and their futures, they'd come up with few options for Randy. He needed a job.

He picked up work at gas stations, low-end retail, and things that required little skill or effort. The year he turned 20, he got a job in an Amazon distribution center. He did well there. No homework or thinking involved. Just move the inventory where he was told. It was easy, and he liked it. He began to relax with his life. He had a small apartment and rarely went home. No pleasure or reward there.

If you rode a drone across the top of an Amazon warehouse floor, you'd see acres of shelves, bins, boxes, and packages. You'd also see a hive of workers and floor bots buzzing around with purpose, spinning in the biggest, most crowded square dance. You could almost hear a country band and a caller saying, "Now, allemande left and docey-do." Everyone knew their job and their direction; no collisions. Organized chaos. Randy was mesmerized. He loved the hum and the rhythm. He was first assigned to a sorting conveyor belt. Handling 1,800 packages an hour didn't faze him. It was mindless, easy work; he was young, and it took no physical toll. As soon as he could, he got his forklift operator's license and became one of the busy drivers whizzing around the warehouse. He learned to operate all the equipment and became the 'go-to guy' when someone new needed training. He was not seen as having supervisor or management potential yet; too young. Still, he was a good worker, showed up on time every day, and worked overtime when needed. They liked him, and he liked them. He made friends. He had a future. He was happy.

When Randy's parents aged into their 70s, they reviewed their substantial assets. They decided to give some early estate money to their three kids, giving them each $100,000. Their stipulation was that each would include repayment of this money in their will should any of them predecease their parents. Randy used this money as a down payment on an inexpensive condo outside Jacksonville. That he ended up in a predominately Jewish building was a fluke. It was all about price. There was an industrial park in the back of the building, but Randy didn't care. The building was new, maintenance was low, and it was cheaper than rent, even with his mortgage. His parents were impressed. The son they thought had no future had a decent job, made sound financial decisions, owned property and was an upstanding citizen. They wouldn't know that part would soon change.

Randy didn't drink much, a beer now and then. He also didn't do drugs. Not for any moral reasons. Just not interested. A few of Randy's Amazon buddies did a little side dealing of drugs and were making some extra cash. Nobody was flush, but they drove better cars than him, and Randy needed a new car. He had his eye on a second-hand Jeep Gladiator. He could use some extra cash. He started to ask around. One of the guys tipped him in as to how it worked and passed his name along.

A week later, Randy got a call. A well-spoken male with a Spanish accent said, "Hello, my name is Miguel, and your friend gave me your name. I hear you're thinking about making some money." Randy said, "I only want to sell weed, none of the other stuff. Are you okay with that?" Miguel thought *he'll get used to the money and eventually want to make more. I'll humor him, but first, I have to meet him.* He said to Randy, "Sure, whatever you're comfortable with." Randy asked, "So, how do I start?" Miguel said, "First, we meet and talk. This is a business of trust. "Randy said, "Sure, okay, where?" Miguel asked, "Do you live alone? If so, how about your place? We can talk privately there." A few days later, Randy buzzed Miguel up to his apartment. He idly wondered how skanky this drug dealer was going to look and wondered if he should have let him into his building. He had every crazy, stoned cartel drug dealer image from 'Breaking Bad' in his head. The man who came through his door was tall, lean, and slightly muscled. He was in his late 40s. He wore his expensively cut black hair short, dressed well and didn't look at all like a drug dealer, more like a downtown Miami banker with a little spice in his dark eyes. He put out his hand and said, "Hi, I'm Miguel." Randy thought, *okay, so far so good.*

Miguel surveyed Randy's apartment. His furnishing choices indicated no imagination or taste, but everything was clean, neat and tidy. He asked Randy, "Do you always live like this?" Randy said, "Like what?" Miguel glided his finger across the coffee table, looked up at Randy, and said, "In a dust-free environment." Randy laughed, saying, "I just like to keep things clean." He offered Miguel a coffee, but he declined with a wave of his hand.

Miguel sat down elegantly, crossed his legs, pant creases intact, flicked a tiny bit of lint off his knee and said, "I have a few questions. First, the big one. How much money do you need to make?" He thought *that will tell me how hungry you are*. Randy said, "Not much. I thought it would be easy to pick up a few extra bucks. I need to replace my car in the next year or so." Miguel asked, "Wouldn't a part-time job be safer?" Randy said, "Doing what? Flipping burgers? Don't think so." He reiterated, "I don't need much; I just thought it might be an easy way to pick up a few extra bucks." Miguel thought *he might not be hungry enough to flip to selling harder stuff. He might be a waste of time.*

Miguel asked, "What are your politics?" Randy thought, odd question. He looked at him and asked, "What's that got to do with this?" Miguel shrugged and said, "Tells me a bit about you." Randy then said," I don't know what I am. They're all lying bastards. Who knows what's really going on? I don't always vote." He said to Miguel, "What about you?" Randy thought *I could give a shit, but he brought it up*. Miguel said, "I don't vote. I just watch." Randy thought to himself *probably an illegal immigrant and can't vote*. Miguel then asked, "Are you religious?" Randy was again surprised by this question and asked, "What's that got to do with selling weed?" Miguel smiled and said, "It just interests me." Randy didn't answer. Seemed like a stupid question to him.

Miguel said, "You can change your mind about what you want to sell. There's more money in the other products." Randy thought to himself, *nope, not getting into that. He thought Miguel wouldn't want to hear how firm he was about that. It was Miguel's business to grow his business.* Randy thought *I'll just pull out if he insists on me selling the hard stuff.* He then wondered if he'd be able to do that easily. His mind was racing.

Randy decided to answer the religious question: "I'm a Jew, but my parents weren't very serious about it when I was growing up." He said to Miguel, "What about you?" Miguel was not used to his prospective sellers asking him questions back. Miguel said, "Not into any of that." Randy thought *he's Mexican, probably raised Catholic.*

Miguel then asked, "So, did you wear that little beanie on the back of your head?" Randy answered, "A kippah? No, I didn't have one. Contrary to common belief, they're not a requirement when you're a Jew." He asked Miguel again, "Why did you ask me that?" Miguel said, "This is a dangerous business with people who'll kill us both if they don't trust us. I like to know who I'm dealing with. I don't trust political zealots or religious freaks. They can turn on you."

Miguel then said, "Let's talk about how this all works. First, the rules. You keep your mouth shut. Be careful who you're talking to. There are probably a bunch of underground narcs working at Amazon. When arranging a sale, you share only information about the product, the price and the point of exchange. You never tell them where you're getting it or my name and contact. Nothing. Don't become a hotshot and start bragging. It could get us both arrested or killed." He said, "You also need to protect your and your client's privacy and safety. Get a burner cell and only use that for your deals. Don't email, text, or communicate online. Leave no trail."

Miguel continued, "You probably already know who smokes up at work. Just quietly let them know you have a supply and mention the price. I have good stuff, and it won't take long for a little client base to build up. Then they tell someone, and they tell someone, and suddenly you have a nice little income stream."

He said, "Don't ever cheat or shortchange anyone." He gave him the scale brand to buy and said, "The weights you deliver must be exact." He continued, "Needless to say, it's all cash. They give you the cash. You give them the dope. Never the other way around."

Miguel looked at Randy and said, "Always obey my orders. Sell at the prices I tell you. Pull out of a deal if it stinks. Listen to me. I know what I'm doing and what's going on in the street."

He then said, "Be ready to disappear if you're found out by the police or another cartel. The rival cartels are unforgiving if they think you're selling on their turf. They are all addicted and have twitchy trigger fingers." Randy thought *and those are the Breaking Bad characters I was worried about.* He also thought *disappear? Seriously? Because of a little weed selling? Maybe I don't want to do this after all. What am I getting myself into?* What indeed.

Miguel said, "I'm worried you're too nice a guy. This is a dangerous business. You could get killed, shot or arrested. Do you still want to do this?" Randy thought *a drug dealer is trying to protect me, and it makes me feel like my mother's little boy.* He hadn't thought this through, but he didn't want to back down. He'd feel like a wuss.

Randy inhaled and said, "Let's start small and see how it goes." Miguel said, "Smart man." He said, "I'll bring you a small supply, and we'll talk again."

They shook hands, and Miguel left. Randy already felt like a bit of a small-time gangster and liked the feeling. He'd always been such a good boy.

A week later, Miguel dropped by with a small supply of marijuana. Randy had since bought the recommended scale. They reviewed weights and measures, not Randy's strong point. He didn't know a gram from a pound and had to learn. He did what he was told. Sure enough, he soon had a steady stream of small-time weed buyers. Many wanted other drugs, and he just said he didn't supply that stuff. Gave no excuses. He never brought the product to work or transported it in his car, always on his motorcycle. He kept his supplies in his motorcycle lock-up, never in his apartment. Most sales were done in large, busy mall parking lots. To be careful, he wore a Kevlar jacket to his exchanges. No sense dying from a bullet wound for an ounce of pot.

His job carried on, but his life was filled with a bit more excitement now, and the cash began to build.

A new girl started working at the warehouse on one of the service desks. Randy rode by her and scouted her out. She was almost too skinny, had long blonde hair tied back in a high ponytail, and loose strands always flew around her face. She wore no discernible makeup, but in Randy's mind, she was gorgeous. He learned her name was Mary. Randy developed his first big crush.

He stopped his forklift in front of her desk and said, "Hi." She looked up, smiled and answered in a questioning manner, "Hi?" She saw a guy in his early 20s, about 5'6", with a softish body, obviously not a muscle boy, going bald, not ugly, just not particularly attractive. He also looked harmless. She learned his name was Randy. Other than "hi" they'd never talked.

For several days after that, Randy drove by, waved, and said "hi." Soon, she was smiling back. Randy thought he was making headway. He wasn't. She wasn't even vaguely interested in him. She was just a polite, small-town girl. As the weeks passed, Randy noticed other warehouse guys hanging around her desk. Some she was laughing with, some she was doing work stuff with. *She just seems so damn nice*, thought Randy. He'd read her wrong.

One day as Randy approached Mary's desk, he noticed Tony Alhonde, a guy everybody thought of as an asshole, standing too close to Mary. Tony had a boxer's build, all shoulders. He always wore tight t-shirts and pants to show off his gym body. He was good-looking and strutted a bit when he walked. He was all machismo. Randy was anything but. Randy saw Mary step back from Tony with a frown on her face. Tony grabbed her arm and moved in close. Randy noticed Mary was not intimidated, just pissed. Randy pulled up and said "Hey Mary" to her, his intention being to break this up. Tony let her arm go, looked over his shoulder at Randy, and said, "Tell Mary she should go out with me." Mary shook her head behind Tony's back. Randy said, "That's up to her." Tony looked at Mary and said, "You'll go out with me. Just a matter of time." He leaned deep into her, grabbed her arm again, and twisted it, saying, "Isn't that right, Mary?" Mary said to Tony firmly, "If you ever touch me again, you pumped-up prick, I'll report you." Randy was sitting on his machine observing all this and thought, *Wow. Never thought I'd hear those words come out of her mouth.* He also thought *this guy is not only a jerk but probably dangerous.*

Tony realized Randy had seen this interaction and while looking straight at Randy, said to Mary, "Good luck with that girlie. Isn't that right, Randy?" A threat. Randy knew this guy could beat the crap out of him but said, "If she doesn't report you, I will." Tony laughed and said, "Let's see how that works out for you." Randy thought *Tony will be waiting for me in the parking lot if I report him.* He decided to do it anyway. Amazon had a 'no tolerance' policy for sexual abuse or harassment. Management confirmed the story with Mary, and Tony was walked out of the building and off the parking lot within hours. Randy thought *we'll both have to watch our asses.* Randy needn't have worried. Tony was only interested in Mary's ass.

Mary was a small-town girl from North Dakota. She grew up on a farm with five brothers. She was the oldest and in charge. Her mother was tough as nails, and Mary learned a lot from her. Her father was a pushover for his only little girl. When Mary finished college and turned 22, she moved to Florida to escape being a small-town girl and a big sister. It was smothering her. She didn't miss the North Dakota winters much, either.

A week after Tony was fired, Mary noticed a car following her closely. She knew immediately who it was. Mary was smart and had rear and front dash cams installed in her car soon after she moved to Florida. People got murdered here. Jacksonville was a big, crowded city, and she took precautions. As Tony cruised up about a foot off her rear fender, she snapped a dozen pictures of him and his license plate. She then drove straight to the police and reported him. She'd dealt with bullies before, and her brothers never pulled any crap with her. Turned out Tony had several priors of harassing women. The police were impressed with this angry little blonde, and two muscle-bound cops paid Tony a visit and laid a little fear in him. Tony knew if he got caught again, he was going to jail. He had priors. He decided Mary wasn't worth it. That was the last she saw of Tony.

Mary now had to deal with Randy. He obviously liked her. She thought *how do you get rid of a nice guy who did you a big favor?* He asked her out for coffee, and she went. She needed to let him know early this wasn't going anywhere. He disarmed her, saying, "Mary, I'm not looking for a girlfriend. I just thought we could be friends. No expectations." She thought *I only know a few people outside of work. Why not. He's a nice guy.* That was how they proceeded. He never came on to her or made any assumptions. He'd go for weeks and not call her. She could talk about guys she dated, and he'd listen. Randy had a keen sense of human observation and cracked her up describing the various characters they worked with. She was smarter than him, and he liked that. They talked a lot about subjects he'd never considered before. She forced him to think about things a bit more. She wasn't even aware she was giving him an education in life. They would get together for coffee or catch a movie or any new stuff in town worth checking out. She was completely relaxed with him. She didn't consider that Randy was waiting for his chance. Randy took his time. He knew he wasn't a prize, but hoped she'd come to see him differently if he hung in. He didn't tell her he was dealing dope. Didn't think she'd approve.

After the warehouse incident and the subsequent break-in of his apartment and car, he worried about Mary. If he was being watched, she might be too. He would never forgive himself if she was hurt because of him. As he prepared to leave town, he remembered his promise to his parents regarding the $100,000. loan. He went online, drew up a will bequeathing that money back to them, and left his condo to Mary. He had it witnessed at a local coffee shop he visited sometimes. Depending on what his condo might be worth, Mary would get some cash after the mortgage and his parents were paid off. It was a grand gesture. Randy hadn't considered he'd be a missing person and not declared dead for five years. He also didn't realize Mary or someone would have to keep up the mortgage, maintenance and utility payments for those five years.

He called his mother, telling her only that he had made a will as requested and that there was a copy in the filing cabinet in his den. She asked, "Is everything okay? You haven't been in touch?" He brushed her off and said, "All good, just taking care of our agreement. Gotta go. Love you, Mom."

It was the last time he got to say those words to her in person.

Mary did have a break-in, but she thought it was Tony and reported her suspicions to the police. It turned out Tony was doing a short stint in jail, so, not him. They fingerprinted her place, but whoever did it wore gloves. They put it down to a random break-in and told her to reinforce her locks. They said, "It's Florida, happens every day." When she told Randy, it only made him more certain of his decision to leave.

Randy only contacted his parents every month or so, so they wouldn't know he was gone for a while or be looking for him. He desperately wanted to say goodbye to his mother and Mary, but couldn't. He closed the door to his life and rode off into the night.

ANTONIO

Before he was born, Antonio's parents, Felipe and Violeta, had walked north through Mexico for days to meet their 'coyote,' their smuggler, in a dark parking lot in Tijuana. Life had become unbearable and dangerous; they were young and wanted something better in the States. They knew the risks. Their smuggler greeted them but did not introduce himself. He was wearing a full face mask. The pair did not know if they were being robbed or helped. The smuggler said, "Dónde está el dinero?" and Felipe handed the bundle of cash over. The smuggler opened the envelope, counted the cash, nodded at them and popped his trunk. He said, "Venir de prisa."

They could have said "no," but they'd come so far. They looked at each other, nodded, and climbed into the trunk, spooning together in the tight space. Violeta was shaking with fear, and Felipe tried to calm her by stroking her back, saying, "We'll be okay, we'll be okay, don't worry." They wondered if they would be too cramped to run when they got out on the other side. That's if they got to the other side. When the trunk lid snapped shut, they also both wondered if they would die there. The smuggler's fee was high, but family and friends helped, and they'd been able to raise the money. The worst case would be they would be found and sent back. No refunds. Actually, the worst case would be if they never got out of this trunk again. They bounced along, each thinking their dark thoughts. They traveled in January to avoid roasting in a hot trunk, but it was cold; they were shivering and terrified.

Their smuggler said the border wasn't far, and after an hour, the car slowed and pulled to a stop. Felipe and Violeta wondered if they'd reached the border and had been caught already. The smuggler had provided a blanket, and they pulled this over themselves so they wouldn't be immediately seen in the dark if the trunk was popped. It was a weak disguise, but it was all they had. It was two in the morning, and they hoped the border guard was tired and hopefully couldn't be bothered checking the trunk. A muffled conversation ensued. They didn't know it, but a small part of their payment had been handed to the border guard. He waved them on, and their smuggler drove into San Diego, California. The car came to a stop. They heard footsteps outside the car, and suddenly, the trunk opened.

Their smuggler said, "Eres libre de ir." You're free to go." They unfolded
their cramped bodies and climbed out. They were in the back of a large
dark building, which was well-lit at its front. It was a grocery store parking
lot. Without looking back, their smuggler drove off quickly, leaving them
there in the middle of the night. They were cold and stiff, and both jogged
on the spot and circulated their arms to get the kinks out. They had no
idea where they were but had a telephone number. The phone booth at
the corner of the store was too well-lit for their comfort. Two Mexicans
with little English, no money and no papers in the middle of the night. If
the police found them, it would all be in vain.

To their relief, Felipe's cousin Robert was waiting for their call, and within
an hour, they were safe in the back of his car. He dimmed his lights, drove
up to his house, and quietly let them in the side door in the garage. He was
legal but was risking that to hide them. They sat up the rest of the night,
making plans for the rest of their route. They had to cross seven states to get
to her mother in Miami. At dawn, they fell into a deep sleep on a mattress
in the basement. They had never been so grateful for a mattress. They still
had a long way to go.

Violeta's mother, Antonio's grandmother, gave birth to his mother at fifteen. His grandfather was murdered shortly after that for some unknown
offense. Antonio's grandmother heard she was next on the list. Her mother, Antonio's great-grandmother, told her to leave, save her life, and try and
get into the States. She said, "I'll take care of the baby, go." His grandmother left her baby daughter, Antonio's mother-to-be, got across the border,
and found work as a housekeeper for an older white man in Florida. He was
kind, they got along, and after some time, he offered to marry her to make
her legal. A little sex with an old man was a small price to pay to become a
permanent resident of the States. She had hopes of bringing her daughter
Violeta, Antonio's mother-to-be, into the States, but the immigration laws
kept changing, and it never happened. At last, her daughter was coming,
and her old husband wasn't happy about it. He hadn't signed on for a
basement full of illegal immigrants, even if it was his wife's daughter and
husband.

Felipe's cousin Robert thought the best plan was for him to drive them to
Miami. Their English was poor, and managing a four-day bus ride would

be challenging. Felipe and Robert had been like brothers before he moved to the States. Robert wanted them to have a chance here.

They made it to Miami and moved into Violeta's mother's basement. Through the underground network, they quickly found farming work. Violeta's stepfather was very unhappy with this arrangement. They could all be arrested. When Violeta became pregnant, he nagged away at her mother to get them out. It was too dangerous.

She had a healthy baby boy, Antonio. He spent his first six months crying with colic. His wails reached up through the air vents to his grandparents' ears. Antonio's grandmother took care of him while his parents worked at the farm. After a year, their farm was raided by the feds, and Violeta and Felipe were deported. They always assumed Violeta's stepfather had turned them in.

They never got a chance to say goodbye to their little boy. Violeta was inconsolable for months, but Felipe would remind her he was in a good place. He was safe in the land of honey. He would have citizenship. His grandmother loved him. He promised her they would see him again. It was not to be, but she clung to that promise.

Long-distance calls from Mexico cost money they didn't have. They didn't have a phone, so Antonio's grandmother couldn't phone her daughter. Antonio's mother wrote when she could afford stamps and envelopes. Always for his birthday and Xmas. His grandmother sent them pictures of him at every stage. Antonio had no idea what his parents looked like. They were like a fairy tale. Not quite real. His mother went on to have three more babies, and their daily survival took precedence over her first son. As Antonio's grandmother aged, communication with her daughter receded. Antonio had never known his parents other than through his mother's letters. One year, the letters stopped coming. He never heard from his mother again.

Antonio's step-grandfather hadn't bargained on the baby being left behind and complained incessantly. Antonio's crib was moved to the spare room, and his grandmother took over his care. He was a cute little boy and a handsome young man. He was good at sports, polite, charmed the ladies and kept his nose clean. As he grew, his reluctant grandfather stopped complaining. Never showed him any love but wasn't unkind. Antonio wasn't welcome, but life was okay.

After high school, he completed a two-year agricultural college diploma but realized he wasn't a farmer. He decided to join a large agricultural processing company. He had good pay, a decent health plan, and physical work, but he liked that. It left him free to play without a lot of responsibility. Antonio liked to play.

Since his penis first flickered with pleasure when he was ten, Antonio had wanted sex, and when he finally got it at fifteen, he wanted more. That first body rush was cocaine to him. He was an addict. He loved the excitement and anticipation of someone new. He was so charming that most of the girls he bedded, then discarded, still liked him.

Occasionally, barbecues were held for the staff where Antonio worked. Antonio enjoyed these; he got along well with everyone, and he could scope out the women. One day, he spotted a beauty. She had a cute ass and great tits, a prerequisite for Antonio. Most of all, she had a beautiful face. She was Mexican, with tanned clear skin and long black hair tied back off her face. Her lips were full, and when he smiled at her across the parkette, she returned his smile and looked away. A tease, he thought. Her name was Mira. That was the beginning of the dance. She was shy but not a fool and encouraged him, then turned him down. She was available to spend time with him, then not. She would not sleep with him. This went on for months. Antonio was used to the quick conquest, but this was a different quarry. He was falling for her. She was not sorry when she finally gave in to his gentle ways. Antonio knew a thing or two about pleasing women, and she was pleased. Two months later, she was pregnant.

His grandmother knew her family and heard about it before Antonio did. She called him and said, "Antonio, you have to marry the girl." Marriage had not been in his plans. Mira told him the next day, dead-eying him, daring him to abandon her. She didn't even give him the option. They married within two weeks, a quick city hall wedding and a small family celebration. He had been smitten with her, but marriage changed all that. She had severe morning sickness with her pregnancy and definitely wasn't interested in sex. His sex drive overwhelmed her. She was tired with the baby and her job all day. He would turn to her in the night, and she would accept him so she could get some sleep. Knowing his erection was waiting for her in the morning was too much. She couldn't get away from his hungry cock. He wasn't abusive, just too sexually needy. She started turning him down early in their marriage. He started going elsewhere. He managed to keep his extramarital flings quiet in the early years. She suspected, but it was easier to say nothing. He was a good father and kind to her. She loved him. They had two little girls within three years, and Antonio started to change. He adored his daughters, and they settled into a happier life together. He still strayed, but not as often. He tried to be discreet. Mira always knew.

He knew he shouldn't have favorites and loved both his girls dearly, but the oldest girl stole his heart. His younger daughter looked like her Mexican grandmother: short, squat, and thick around the middle. She'd not been easy to love. She was always angry, even at a young age. She'd been a difficult teenager. She hated Florida. She wanted to get away from her Mexican roots and the prejudice she experienced every day. She moved to England when she finished college and never looked back. She married a Kiwi who found her exotic. His oldest was a loving, happy delight. She could have passed for Italian and rarely mentioned her Mexican heritage to her friends. She lived her life as if all was rosy. She was popular and surrounded by friends. She didn't really feel the sting of prejudice her sister had. She didn't allow it in. She also had Antonio's heart in her hands.

Antonio's wife, Mira, remained a simple, naive girl. She didn't read much and didn't grow. She had no real interest in the world other than her own small one. Antonio read everything he could get his hands on. They had nothing to talk about. The girls were very protective of their sweet, innocent mother. All she wanted to do was care for her husband and raise babies. She loved Antonio to the end, even after she'd left him. He'd given her syphilis once. His oldest daughter told him with tears running down her face. She couldn't forgive him for that. That wasn't what killed her. A bad heart did that job.

After the accident at work, Antonio changed. He was addicted to his painkillers, but his back was still in constant agony. The man who had always been good-natured became angry and irritable. He couldn't work or play. He was bored and was always in pain. He had no patience with his daughters and took his disappointment in his life out on his wife. She couldn't do anything right, and they argued all the time. For all the rancor and heartbreak, she still received him when he turned to her in bed. She still loved him.

However, her patience wasn't infinite, and Mira tired of his self-pity. She couldn't help him. She had planned to leave him the week he came home with his insurance payout. The money would help her get on her feet, and he'd taken care of the girls. He left the house for a few days after he gave her the money. When he returned, the house was empty, stripped of all their personal things, hangers swinging in the closets, drawers emptied. No note. It was over. They'd left for an extended trip to Europe with Antonio's cash.

Antonio wasn't heartbroken. He hadn't loved Mira for a long time. He went upstairs, hauled down a suitcase and packed up what he could. He then got some boxes and boxed everything else he wanted to keep. It wasn't much for a lifetime of living with her. He packed up his car and drove away. He paid off the mortgage and left 5 years of cash payments covering all the utilities, the property tax and the various cell phone and cable services. He deposited another $500,000 into their joint bank account. Mira wondered how much that insurance settlement was actually for. Antonio was certainly flush with cash.

Within a year, Mira had a fatal heart attack. She never got over Antonio. His daughter sent him a letter with no return address. It said simply, "Momma died yesterday of a heart attack, but you broke her heart. Live with that." His girls were lost to him.

Antonio was living in a small apartment and needed a change. He started scouting out Jacksonville and, through a real estate agent, found the condo at Vanilla Palms. It was new, and the price was right. He paid cash.

Tired of fighting back pain, he finally went to a pain clinic and started physiotherapy. Slowly, his body settled back into itself, his spine lining up for the most part. The pain receded but still hurt when he was tired. He ditched the pain pills.

He missed his daughters and, some days, his quiet little wife. After much silence, he stopped trying to contact his girls. He was on his own, had a lot of money, and could do anything. He no longer really cared. He was comfortable living alone, but his life was quiet. He was in his mid-fifties but was feeling old.

Antonio began visiting his old haunts. The old chase didn't do much for him anymore. The fire in his pants had faded over the years. Marriage and kids and responsibility and the everydayness of life had dulled that.

It was early evening when he sat down at the end of the bar and ordered a beer. There weren't many customers, and the music wasn't as loud and pounding as usual. He settled in to watch the basketball game on the TV over the bar. He and the bartender were old friends and chatted idly about the game. The bartender knew way more about basketball than Antonio did. His night would get busier later, and there wouldn't be time for sports chatter with the customers.

From the corner of his eye, Antonio noticed movement at the other end of the bar. When he looked down the row of stools, he saw a small woman, probably in her late 30s, legs crossed, foot kicking to the music, flipping her backless shoes off and on her feet. From where he was sitting, she looked good. Her tits were burgeoning out of a too-tight top. Her dark hair was cropped short, but it looked good on her. She gave him a big smile and said, "Hi." Antonio said, "Hi yourself." The bartender said under his breath, "Careful, Antonio. She's a little viper." Antonio grinned at him and said, "I could use a little venom in my life." He moved down beside her. Up close, she had a slight Latino look, big dark eyes, full lips, and tanned skin. In Antonio's opinion, she wore too much make-up but was cute. He could swear he could hear electricity snapping around her. Danger. Don't put your finger in that socket. Their immediate flirtation made Antonio feel alive again. He still had it. He was being played but was blind to that in his vanity. That was the beginning of Lily.

Lily was fun at first. She was a racy little sportscar, lots of hot sex, tits, tight short skirts, and booze. She ran too fast for him, though. He wasn't much of a drinker or a partier. She would tell him how good-looking he was and how much she loved him. He was vain; he liked hearing the good-looking part. She always called him Tony. He hated that name, but it was her cajoling name. "Tony, I need new shoes. Tony, buy me this or that." She thought he had money. He did of course but he never shared that with her.

Lily was living in her mother's basement. Her mother had a boyfriend and spent most of her time at his place, which suited Lily. Lily paid her mother nothing because she rarely worked and had no money. When she felt like it, she worked a jewelry booth at a flea market for a guy she knew. He didn't pay her much but would give her a little more for special favors. Her mother threatened to throw her out regularly. She was living on the edge. She needed a change.

Antonio and Lily fought often. He would think *it's time to end it*. She always came back in tears, saying, "You don't love me. If you did, we could get married." Make-up sex was always good, and he would relent. She talked him into going to Vegas and, in a very weak moment, getting married. Antonio knew that even in Vegas, he could get a quick prenup made up. Lily balked at that, but he said, "No prenup, no marriage." She signed it. At least now she had a home. She didn't have to pay for rent, food, or utilities; Antonio paid for everything. She didn't have to work or give out favors. Antonio hoped his sparky little wife would settle down and stop the party. Lily thought he would keep her for life. She saw security, and he began to see disaster.

Lily soon figured out there wasn't a lot of money. None he was telling her about anyway. All she saw now was an aging, out-of-shape man who wasn't much fun and constantly criticized her. He was a clean freak. She was not. She started going out to bars with her girlfriends and, soon, staying out all night. He didn't care. He no longer liked her, let alone loved her. She was a slob. Her clothes were tossed wherever she stripped down. Make-up smeared on the bathroom counter. The toilet and bath didn't get cleaned, the sheets didn't get changed, and wet towels were dropped on the floor. Antonio did all the cleaning. He moved out to the den, ceding the bedroom to her. It became her personal sty.

When she came home drunk, often early in the morning, she was angry and cruel. She had come to despise Antonio. She hated watching him sleep on his back, snoring with his mouth open, big belly to the wind. She hated how he ate voraciously. Like it was his last meal. He was beginning to walk like an old man, his legs bowing. She thought, *when did he get a horse, and where is it now?*

He hated everything about her. After her nights out, she would struggle out of the bedroom midday with mascara all over her face, lipstick smeared, and hair wet with sweat. She stank of the street and period, and he didn't want to know what else.

Antonio was fastidious about his clothes, hair, mustache and home. She rarely bathed. He had stopped having sex with her after she gave him a dose. It was over.

One morning, after she staggered out of the bedroom, he said to her, "Let's talk." Lily had a moment of fear and then defiance. She knew he wanted her gone. He said, "If you're so unhappy, why don't you just leave? She looked at him and said, "I'm not moving. You leave." Antonio thought, *not happening, baby*. He knew she had nowhere else to go. He was her free ride. It wouldn't be easy getting her out of his life. He could change the locks but envisioned her screaming in the hallway. He could divorce her, but that would take forever. He could sell the condo, move all her stuff onto the street and walk away. That idea was beginning to look like an option, but again, he envisioned her in a tantrum on the street. Getting rid of Lily without a fight was going to be a problem.

The other option was to leave, disappear, change his identity and start over somewhere else. He started planning an escape.

ESTELLE

"Her mom's a whore." Estelle was six years old when she heard this whispered behind her back at school. First day in grade one. She'd been looking forward to school. It was the mid-eighties and constrained San Antonio, Texas, wasn't very forgiving of single, good-looking moms with lots of boyfriends. They didn't know the half of it. Little Estelle sat alone, eating her jam sandwich. No cute little lunch box with cartoons on it, no extra cookies, no fruit. She just had a plastic shopping bag. Tears rolled down her face. She was shamed and miserable. The whisperer just turned away. Didn't want to witness the damage.

Estelle always picked up a pack of cigarettes for her mother on the way home from school. Her mother had a running bill at the drugstore. Estelle loved this store with its aisles of colorful choices of seemingly everything. She'd walk them all and then liked to flip through the fashion magazines at the back of the store. The owner, Mr. Smithy, didn't mind. He felt sorry for her. She was a homely little creature. Always by herself. As Estelle left, she lifted a chocolate bar from the shelf. "See you, Mr. Smithy," she called out. "Yes, see you, Estelle," he responded. He called after her, and she froze. *He saw me,* she thought. Mr. Smith said, "Ask your mother to come in and pay her bill, will you?" Estelle said, "Will do." It was her first theft. She was buzzed, and she liked the feeling.

Her mother, Amy, was raised in a strict Baptist family. No sin, no fun, no freedom. At sixteen, she broke loose and never looked back. Her parents disowned her. Estelle had never met her grandparents. Didn't even know where they lived. They were never discussed. They'd turned their backs on Amy and didn't know they had a granddaughter. It didn't matter; they were dead to Amy. At eighteen, Amy conceived Estelle at a wild pool party and had no idea who the father might be. She woke up the next morning on a pool lounger in the heat of the sun, feeling like crap. The night before was gone from her memory. She didn't know any of the guys and never saw any of them again. She was completely honest with Estelle when she asked about her father. "I have no idea, honey. I was pretty drunk the night I got pregnant." That was it. No apologies.

Amy went through many disintegrating stages while her young daughter Estelle grew up alone. In the early years, Amy partied a lot, smoked a lot of dope and pretty much left Estelle to find food in a cupboard or fridge that was usually empty. There were always strangers around when Estelle came home; the music was loud, and the room was filled with drifting pot smoke.

Estelle started stealing from grocery stores to eat. She got caught with a box of cereal once, but the store supervisor took one look at the raggedy, homely little girl and said quietly, "Take it. Just don't do it again." Estelle moved to a different store. She'd soon sussed out the easy ones.

Her mother, Amy, moved on to heavier drugs and addiction. Estelle never really thought about where her mother was getting the money to buy these drugs or pay the rent, for that matter. Just as well. There were often strange, creepy guys in the apartment when Estelle came home from school. Amy sat in a thin grey lump at the end of the couch, usually unconscious, no longer fun to be with. Her dealer delivered. He was slimy, and Estelle avoided his greasy eyes when she answered the door. Amy and Estelle didn't communicate, and Estelle just stayed in her room with a heavy lock on the door. She had lifted a very sharp knife from a kitchen supply store and slept with it under her pillow. Fortunately, Amy's men weren't interested in her unappealing young daughter.

Estelle thought *I'll finish high school, and when I'm eighteen, I'm gone.* When she needed a lift, she went shoplifting. She always bought something small so she could produce a receipt if challenged.

Estelle's looks were a problem early on. The grade school mean girls were cruel, and the boys got meaner as she entered middle school. Her mother didn't help. She'd look at her and say, "You must take after your mystery father. Can't believe I would have screwed somebody that ugly." She destroyed her little girl.

Estelle receded into herself, staring at her image in the mirror in her bedroom. In her deepest thirteen-year-old depression, she had an eureka moment. If it ever gets too bad, I can always kill myself and end this misery. Oddly, this realization armed her for the future. It never got that bad, and she got through high school. She wasn't a stellar student, but she liked numbers. She got a part-time job working at an ice cream shop. It was mostly a cash business; lots of sales weren't rung up, and the teenage supervisor didn't pay much attention. It was easy to shift cash into her pocket unnoticed. She didn't tell her mother about this job. She'd want the money. Amy just assumed Estelle was out with friends after school. Estelle didn't have any friends, but Amy didn't register that. After high school, Estelle found a two-year bookkeeping diploma course at the local college and signed up. For the first time in her life, she excelled at something. She graduated with honors, turned eighteen, moved to Miami and got a job within a week. San Antonio had so many bad memories. She didn't even say goodbye to her mother. Amy barely noticed Estelle was gone.

Estelle didn't smoke, never had, but she had the look of a tough heavy smoker who'd spit in your eye if you pissed her off. Nobody insulted her to her face anymore. She met girls through work, and they went to bars and clubs together, but Estelle never got hit on. She was used to it. She thought of herself as the invisible woman. They set her up with a few guys over the years, but the dates were almost always over the minute the guys saw her. Her saving grace was she had a good body. This bought her a couple of one-night stands with sex, which was not as advertised. She wondered *what's the big deal with sex?*

Cosmetic surgery was out of her reach, but she put a little money aside when she could. She thought of it as her beauty bank. Someday, she'd fix her face and change her life.

She started taking on private bookkeeping clients outside of work and realized she could have a nice little business. At 32, she took the leap, put an ad in the local newspapers and was surprised at how quickly her client base grew. Lots of small businesses needed bookkeeping and didn't want to pay a full-fledged accountant for the privilege. She had a good reputation, and her clients trusted her. She had a personal rule to never steal from her clients. Most didn't have much extra money anyway. She still stole from stores, just not from her clients.

One of her first clients was Phil. He ran an animal rescue and adoption business and made a little money doing it. Not much, but enough that he needed a bookkeeper. Phil was Estelle's first male friend. He was also gay, but she'd never known him to have a boyfriend. He was a large, soft, overweight guy with folds of fat hanging over his pant waist and a puffy face with broken blood vessels all over his cheeks and nose. His hair was thin, and he moved with effort. He was only 42, but his diabetes gave him foot trouble, and he definitely wasn't watching his diet or his numbers. For all of that, Estelle liked him. He didn't judge her looks. They never talked about their early lives. There was a shared understanding that wasn't a place to revisit. Phil looked out on the world from his island of body weight with acuity and acidity. He was funny. They shared their failed romantic encounters and the sorry state of the world with a sense of resolution. Neither of them had ever had a relationship of worth.

The rest of her clients were all small businesses, many little charities, and single operators who knew nothing about money, taxes, or the IRS.

For years, she'd done income taxes for a wheelchair-bound client named George. He was in his late 80s and lived on his own. She only saw him twice a year, once to pick up his receipts and forms and again to deliver his tax return for signature. He was a sharp old guy and read every line of the return before signing it. They always had a drink together before she left and toasted the year to come. She liked his optimism, given his age. She'd been in his kitchen many times over the years, mixing their drinks. She was a snoop and knew he kept a gun at the back of his middle drawer with the frying pan flipper, the cheese grater and the oven mitts. None of which he used anymore. He had all of his food delivered. He also had a cleaner in weekly, and home care dropped in on him three or four times a week, doing welfare checks. Lots of different people passed through his apartment. Estelle had a gun, but she thought having one that couldn't be traced to her would be wise. She was always thinking ahead.

Every year, the gun was in the same place, and one year, she dropped it into her purse. If George caught her, she would say she'd taken it to protect him, didn't want him shooting himself. She thought *I'll come up with something*. He didn't notice the gun was gone for almost a year. He thought it could have been taken by anyone who passed through his apartment. Some of them were probably illegals. He could get into trouble if that was discovered. He didn't report it to the police. He never thought for a minute it could have been Estelle. Mislaid trust.

It was an old .380 Colt Mustang pocket pistol. It was loaded and probably hadn't been fired for decades. She brought it home and cleaned it, then went to a firing range to test it. Estelle was a good shot. Steady hands and nerves. Some might say she was nerveless. Not much fazed her. Good thing. Finding ammo without producing a firearms license would have been difficult. The gun worked fine. She thought I might have to rely on this someday. It has to work.

Estelle had been looking at small condos in Miami but couldn't afford anything she liked. Her real estate agent looked farther afield and came up with Vanilla Palms. It was just outside of Jacksonville, new, and at the right price. She moved. She did most of her client's bookkeeping online and only saw them every 3-4 months. The five-hour commute to Miami was doable. She would have dinner with Phil, sleep on his couch and go home the next day.

She placed ads in the small Jacksonville newspapers to pick up local clients. This was successful, and one of these new clients was Janie. She ran a one-woman hair salon. Janie was the same age as Estelle, and they hit it off. She was Estelle's bar buddy. Janie attracted men. Estelle did not. If the music was live, she enjoyed the nights out anyway. She'd used dating apps unsuccessfully. At least they knew what they were getting. She had taste, not desperation, and life went on. She'd long ago given up on men. It barely bothered her. Barely.

One night, Janie suggested they go to the Swinging Goose, a well-known black club on the outskirts of town. There had been a few gang shootings at this club, and Estelle thought it was too dangerous. Janie said, "The Soul Boys are playing tonight. I'd love to catch them." She told Estelle, "Don't believe everything you read in the news."

The club was dark and crowded and smelled like summer sweat and cologne. They were two white women in a sea of black faces. Heads turned, and Estelle swore the din of voices quieted for a moment. They sat down at the bar, and within minutes, they were swarmed with young black men.

Janie had the looks, but even Estelle was appreciated here. She might be homely, but she was tall, blonde and had a nice ass. The men checking her out thought *she's old and ugly, but she might be looking for a bit of strange, and she might have money.* Within a half hour, Estelle and Janie were inundated with black men, standing near them or off a bit, trying to get closer. Estelle had never had this kind of male attention in her life. She knew what a bitch in heat felt like. She reveled in it, standing with her shoulders back, breasts thrust forward, a big crooked smile on her homely face. She didn't realize it was a game. They'd seen their mark and moved in like hyenas, licking the ground around them. They were like wasps to late August wine.

The band started up, and the music had a slow, danceable beat. A tall, thin guy with too much gold jewelry asked Estelle to dance. She couldn't remember if she'd ever been asked to dance. He took her hand and led her out on the dance floor. He moved smoothly and expertly to the rhythm and started to draw her just a bit closer, their hips touching. She could feel his piece harden as it hit her thigh. It was foreplay on the dance floor. He returned her to the bar and said with a big smile, "I'm Rudy. Who are you?"

They flirted all night, with Rudy moving in closer to her and brushing his hand across her back or just touching her ass or a slight touch on her breast. He had a little thing he did with his mouth; he'd lick his lips, look away, and smile. It made him look like he was up to something. Estelle thought it was cute. When she asked him what he did, he said, "A little of this and a little of that." He didn't tell her it was a little dealing and a little stealing.

She'd never had anyone in her new apartment but took a wild risk and brought Rudy home that night. She had visions of hot, satisfying sex, something she'd never experienced. She hadn't had sex often. His dance floor talent indicated he might be a good lover. Estelle didn't have much money, but she had good taste and a certain style, and her apartment looked more high-end than it was. Rudy took it in and thought, *this old ugly broad's a gold mine.*

Sadly, the sex was hurried and slam bam. The song *"I want a lover with a slow hand"* ran through Estelle's mind as she lay there on her back while Rudy hurriedly bounced up and down on her, in a race to the end.

No tenderness there. Within minutes, he rolled off and was asleep. That enticing hard dance floor cock was now a dead blackbird, lifeless, small and soft.

She lay on her side and watched this strange, naked black man asleep in her bed. He mumbled in his sleep and cried out a couple of times. He tossed and turned and grimaced. He wasn't having a good night. Estelle didn't sleep at all that night. Rudy was up early and in her kitchen asking, "Got anything to eat?" She watched him wolf down a bowl of Cheerios. He was a bit twitchy and nervous. He said, "What the hell are you starin' at?" She just said, "Nothing." She didn't realize that he needed a hit. He was gone in a half hour. *That was interesting and disappointing*, she thought.

A week passed, and he called around midnight, wanting to come over. Estelle thought he was fun at the bar. *Maybe it was just a bad night for him. I'll give him another try.* She let him in and regretted it immediately. He didn't look well. His eyes were darting back and forth, and he said, "Baby, I'm not going to do you tonight, but I need some money." Estelle thought, so one lay, and now he wants to get paid. She said, "Sorry Rudy, I don't give money to anyone. I don't have enough to share." He ignored her, tried to put his arms around her, and said, "Come on, baby, just $100. That's all I need." She wriggled out of his arms and said, "I don't keep any cash here, and it's time for you to leave."

Rudy wasn't happy with that answer, spun around and smacked her hard. He was used to hitting women. Estelle's head rang with the force of the slap. She was in shock. No one had ever hit her in her life. "You're an ugly old cow," he spewed at her. Estelle held the door open and said, "Get out." She watched him walk down the hall to the stairs. He wasn't walking straight. He was on something. She turned off her lights, watched down at the parking lot and made sure he drove off. She had a bad feeling that wouldn't be the last she'd see of Rudy. She cried herself to sleep that night, thinking *now I'm sleeping with a drug addict who beats me.*

Rudy was a meth addict and needed a fix. He'd been sure he could cadge some cash from Estelle, but she wasn't the desperate pushover he'd imagined. She was a no-go. He drove into town and found a dealer who'd give him a hit on loan. It would cost him a lot when he finally got the cash. He wasn't done with Estelle. He was sure she had money.

The next time Estelle was in Miami, she met up with Phil and shared the Rudy story, including the shock of the slap. When she left in the morning, Phil said, "Be careful of that guy, Estelle. Drug addicts have no conscience."

It turned out he was right. While Estelle was in Miami, a very stoned and belligerent Rudy had gained entrance into her building; it wasn't hard. She hadn't been responding to his calls; she'd blocked him, making him even more furious. It was midnight, and he was kicking and banging at her apartment door. A neighbor called the police, and he was taken away. A note with the Jacksonville police department header was attached to her door when she got home. She called them, and they asked if she wanted to press charges. She said no, but she wanted a restraining order placed against him.

After that, Rudy wanted revenge. Estelle stopped going out unless necessary and imagined she was being followed when she did. She was stressed and exhausted. A couple of times after she had turned off her lights at night, she looked down into the parking lot, and his car would be there. She'd called the police, but he was always gone when they arrived. She was sure he'd eventually kill her.

She took a chance early one morning to run out for some milk. She figured he'd be flat out somewhere else at seven-thirty in the morning. Still, she always had George's old gun strapped to her calf under her pants. Estelle was returning to her car with the milk when a man came up behind her, stuck something hard in the middle of her back, and said, "Get in." It was Rudy. Estelle had underestimated his need for money.

He said, "You drive and don't try anything." He shoved her toward his car. The hard thing she'd felt in her back was a gun. Rudy looked sick. He was pale, sweating, breathing heavily, and very nervous. He had the gun stuck into her side now. She knew she had to proceed carefully, or he'd do something stupid. He said, "Drive to the nearest ATM. We're going to make a large withdrawal."

She pulled slowly out of the parking lot and drove down the road. There were lots of ATMs around but she wanted to get out into the country. She had a plan. Still, with the gun jammed in her side, Rudy actually nodded off at one point but then sat bolt-upright and said, "Where the hell are you going?" She said, "I thought I would go directly to my bank. Then I can take much more cash out and help you." She smiled at him. Rudy was confused and frantic. He needed a hit. His dealer had cut him off for non-payment. He had to get some money. His mind was racing along with his heartbeat. He'd lost control here.

Estelle turned off onto a country road. Rudy screamed at her, "Get me some money and stop fucking around." He jammed the gun hard into her ribs. She remained calm and said quietly, "If you shoot that thing, you won't get any money. We're on our way. It won't be long." Estelle was the essence of calm.

There were no cars on the road, and she slowed to a stop. She popped her seat belt. He yelled, "There's no fucking bank here. Don't fuck with me." Remaining calm, she said, "You've made me so nervous, I've got to pee. I'm sure you wouldn't want me to pee all over your car, would you?" She opened the door and stepped out. She was thinking, *steady, keep steady. Don't do anything fast.* He was out after her with his gun waving wildly. She dropped to a squat, looked up at him and said, "Do you want to watch?" He was going crazy. Rudy thought *she can't get away from me out here, so let her piss.* Estelle pulled Frank's pistol from her calf holster and stood up just as Rudy turned around. She shot him in the heart. He dropped hard. She checked his pulse. Yep, he was dead.

Was it self-defense? Estelle sure thought so. This guy was never going away and would eventually try and kill her. She didn't lose any sleep over that choice, just the possibility of getting caught.

The smell of shit filled the air. Rudy's body had convulsed as he died and evacuated his bowels. She had a small cross-body purse with her. She always carried a tube of hand cleaner and used it now to wipe down every surface she thought she might have touched in the car. She grabbed his cell phone. He'd called her on it. That was a connection straight back to her. It had to go. She'd already cleared all his call records on her phone, but the police could find them if they looked, so that phone had to go, too. She also had to get rid of the gun. She started the long hike back to her car in town. As she walked, she spotted a large swampy pond. She pitched the gun and the phones deep into its center. A couple of cars sped by. Just a crazy woman out for a speed walk in the morning before it got hot. Nobody remembered seeing her. She was soaking when she arrived back at her car. The milk she'd bought was warm. She quietly drove home. Her apartment was cool and safe for now. She thought *the police will be coming for me. They know Rudy was giving me trouble. I had a restraining order on him. I need to stay calm.* Estelle didn't know there was a sizeable list of women who had restraining orders against Rudy.

The flies had already gathered when Rudy's body was found days later. Dead bodies didn't do well in the Florida heat. He was already stinking. The police observed he was out of the car with a gun in his hand, and the closeness of the shot told them he probably knew who shot him. It was probably a messed up drug deal or a hit. He'd pissed someone off. They didn't bother to check the car for prints, assuming it had been a drive-by. He was carrying ID, and they looked up his priors. The Estelle interaction was there, but they didn't connect her at all. She wasn't a murderer, just a homely bookkeeper. More misplaced trust.

The coroner did a tox report and found several drugs in Rudy's system. The bullet that killed him came from an old gun, not what was running on the streets these days. Old stolen guns do find their way into the hands of gangs. The gun Rudy was carrying was also stolen. When they contacted his mother, she wasn't surprised. She didn't clasp her throat in shock or despair. She just looked down and shook her head. Rudy had been in trouble since he was twelve. She'd been almost expecting this. They told her it could be any number of people. She knew it wouldn't be followed up. When the police left, she went inside and pulled a picture from her shelf. It was Rudy at six; he'd just lost a baby tooth and was grinning. She remembered that day of innocence. So much had happened since, nothing good. Now, he was just another dead drug addict. No newspaper recorded his death. She held herself in her private grief and rocked back and forth.

Estelle waited for weeks for a knock on the door from the police but heard nothing. She was very nervous. She stopped going to clubs with Janie, thinking it was better to lay low. Rudy had friends. They might make the connection when he stopped showing up.

She got a burner phone and gave Phil the number, telling him she'd lost her phone somewhere. All her clients emailed her, so they didn't need the number. A month later, she came across the suitcase of money at Phil's place. That's when her life really changed. She was a murderer and a thief. She had to get out of town.

Chapter Seven

SECRETS AND LIES

Within two hours of the explosion and the news broadcast, Zenith's cell started ringing. He'd advised security downstairs to only let people up to his offices with his approval. The police, Carolyn's insurance company, and Zenith were under siege, and all three were only taking messages. "The accident is still being investigated. Please leave the name of the person you are enquiring about and your relationship, and someone will be in touch when more information is available." The calls were coming in from all corners; the press, lawyers, bereaved, or just plain nosy families and friends. It was an onslaught of grievances and threats. In Zenith and Billy's case, they called them back if they seemed to have information about one of their missing owners. If not, they left it to Caroline to respond. No one had anything pertinent to share so far. Carolyn's company held the policy for the dangerous goods handler. She was expecting a class action suit, but first, they had to figure out who was there and who was not. She'd sent out a blast email request to all Florida legal firms regarding the wills of the dead people. She thought, *you never know. Something might turn up*. Nothing did.

Billy and Joe worked through all the owners' emergency contact lists. They were successful with most of them and delivered the hard news of the deaths. Many already knew. They'd read the news, and their friend or loved one wasn't picking up. Billy thought they should go to people's homes to deliver the news, but Joe reminded him this wasn't the movies. It was impossible to visit everyone personally. Many lived out of state. Some of the contacts listed didn't exist or were false numbers. Some people said, "I hardly knew the guy; I don't know why he'd name me as a contact." When asked if they were willing to come and identify the body, a few flat-out refused. Nobody wanted to pick up the burial costs of someone they barely knew. Everybody had secrets, including the contacts.

Morty, the president of the condo, took his job seriously. The condo and its residents were his coop of chickens, pecking through their lives. He knew them all, or at least something about them. He certainly had his own opinions. He was 83 years old, and many owners had been his friends. He'd encouraged them away from the crumbling Miami beach condos and recommended they buy upstate in Vanilla Palms. Now, they were dead. Morty didn't know what to do with his guilt. He'd barely slept since the day of the explosion. His heart fluttered constantly, and he was sure his blood pressure was through the roof. He'd felt his face go numb a couple of times. He thought *I can't have a stroke now. The few people who weren't there and survived this horror might need me.*

It took several days to cycle the relatives and friends through the laid-out bodies. The sight of a room full of body bags was overwhelming. The unidentified bodies stayed partially unzipped, their dead faces waiting for recognition. The coroners had closed everyone's eyes and mouths out of respect. Someone had sprayed the room with a deodorizer that smelled like an old Miami cab. Time was running out. These bodies would start to decompose soon and needed to be moved on to their final stop. It was a horrible scene of sadness. People in such deep grief. A few of the apartments contained other people the family didn't know. They had IDs and were easily tracked back. Still, there were obviously a few surprises for some people. Strangers in their loved ones' lives they'd never heard of. There were four unidentified bodies, none of whom were the missing six people. These bodies were moved on to the local morgue, pictures taken for any later identification and moved onto the crematorium in due time.

It was the empty apartments that were the puzzle. Six people weren't there and had yet to check in. Billy said to Zenith, "Morty knew everyone in that building. We'll ask him what he knows about the missing people." He also said, "I do know that one of them, Randy Behrman, had a break-in about a month ago. There wasn't much damage, and he said nothing had been stolen. He had his door fixed and the locks changed."

When Billy checked in with Morty, Morty was almost grateful to be asked for help. He said, "Whatever I can do for you, Billy. I can see a lot from my windows; my apartment overlooks the parking lot, and I'm up early. I knew almost everyone in the building reasonably well. I rarely spoke with the missing people, though, and one of them, Michael Robertson, not at all. I didn't see them around the building very often. Most people just came in from the parking lot, checked their mail and disappeared into their apartments. We didn't have a social committee or anything like that.

He continued, "The young man in 502, Michael Robertson, was a tenant, not an owner, so you'll have to speak to the apartment owner. Michael had his food and groceries delivered. He didn't have a car and never went out." He was referring to Malek Bouziane but, of course, they didn't know that. Morty said again, "He's the one I never met."

He continued, "The couple in 907 were odd. His name was Antonio Cervantes. Mexican. Big, quiet guy. Seemed a bit sad. He often went out fishing very early in the morning, pre-dawn. I'd see him sometimes checking his fishing gear in his trunk when he returned and bringing in his catch. He never said much, but he at least smiled when greeted at the mailbox. Not one for small talk."

"The woman he lived with or was married to, I never knew their status; she was a hot little hornet. I think her name was Lily, but we were never introduced. She wasn't interested in the social niceties. She'd fall out of a cab in the middle of the night, often in the morning. Her makeup was always smeared, and her clothes were half on or off. She never wore much anyway. She looked and dressed like a prostitute. I found her once slumped on the floor in the entry. It was around six in the morning. I asked her if she needed help. Her response was, "Fuck you, old man." "I just left her there." Morty said, "Excuse the language, but that's what she said."

"They fought a lot, well, she did. She would scream at him, but he never raised his voice. I couldn't hear what she was yelling about. Some of the neighbors complained."

He continued, "Claire Richmond in 607 worked at home. Never knew what she actually did. I don't know what people are doing on their computers at home to make money anymore. It's all beyond me. She was also a tenant and seemed close to our building owner's mother and her friends. They were killed, but her son might have some insight." He gave the boys his telephone number.

He said, "Estelle Green in 208 also worked at home. She was very quiet. Every now and then, she'd be gone overnight. I don't think she had a boyfriend. I hate to say it, but she was homely. She was away one night, and a black man got into the building and was kicking and banging at her door, yelling for her. The police were called. I never heard who he was or what happened, but he never returned."

"The young man, Randy Behrman in 810 worked at Amazon in their warehouse, as far as I know. Billy, you'd remember he had a break-in a while back. I don't think anything was stolen. He fixed the door quickly. He was a nice, quiet kid who never said much. He did drive off late at night regularly. He was never gone long."

Billy said, "Thanks, Morty, that's a good start. We'll follow up on the contacts they provided in their files. We should be able to track them down."

He didn't know they were dust in the wind.

Phil hadn't heard from Estelle in weeks and was worried. She hadn't done his payroll, and he had to pay his two employees and himself by check. Estelle usually took care of that with automatic deposits. He kept thinking about that guy Rudy hitting her. Something was very wrong. He'd never been to her new condo and didn't have her address, but he thought, *how many new buildings outside of Jacksonville could there be?* There was a real estate office down the street from him, and he went in and asked. Three buildings had been built in the last five years in that area. They gave him the property managers' contacts. The agent said, "One of them just had a horrible incident." Phil had read about it but hadn't made the connection. The agent said, "All the occupants are dead." Phil's heart stopped. *That must be it.* Then he thought, *no, that doesn't make sense. She hadn't called or responded to his messages for three weeks. Well before the explosion.* He called that property management company first and got Zenith's phone message. Within ten minutes, Billy called him back. He said, "Phil, thanks for calling. We were just about to call you. Estelle had you as her emergency contact." Phil said, "So, she's dead?" Billy paused and said, "We don't think so; she wasn't there. We don't know where she is." Phil asked, "Have you been in her apartment?" Billy said, "No, we wanted to talk to you first in case you knew where she was." Billy said, "There are a few missing people, and I'm working with a detective to find them. We'd planned to check Estelle's apartment today." Phil said, "There's something you should know." He shared Rudy's story. He said, "I think she could be in danger." Billy said, "I'll tell the police, and we'll check it out. We'll get back to you when we know more. We appreciate you checking in."

Billy and Joe headed to the building to check the apartments of the missing people. They first went to Estelle's. Joe gave Billy some gloves and put on his own. He advised Billy not to touch or move anything. Walking into someone else's life felt invasive. It was as if Estelle, whoever she was, might burst in on them any minute and ask them what the hell they were doing there. They first noticed the spilled coffee and overturned chair in the kitchen. There'd been a tussle of some sort. They found her purse with all her ID hanging on her bedroom door. Her gun still sat in her bedroom side drawer, unused. Her bed was unmade. It appeared all of her makeup, toothbrush and toiletries were there. They thought *she wasn't planning to leave voluntarily.* Estelle's ruse had worked. Joe called in forensics to fingerprint the apartment and to check her laptop. They checked her drawers and the file cabinets in her office. There was nothing in there but client files and the usual stuff people file and never look at again. Joe did find one file named 'Will.' When they read it, they saw that Phil was the sole beneficiary of her estate. Now, he was also a suspect.

They wrote up their notes and moved on to Michael Robertson's apartment. When they contacted the owner, he told them Michael had paid a year's rent in advance, in cash. Joe and Billy both thought that was a lot of cash to lay out at one time. When Billy called Michael's emergency contact, the person didn't exist. When they asked the owner if Michael had provided references, he said, "Yes, his last apartment in Miami. It was a solid reference." Billy got that number, and the previous landlord had no complaints other than Michael had left the apartment filthy. The current owner said Michael had been quiet, and there'd been no complaints, but he hadn't been in the apartment since he'd rented it to him.

Michael's apartment looked like the worst college boy's digs, filthy. There was half-eaten food everywhere and greasy food boxes lying on every surface. The bed had no sheets, just a pillow and a duvet, and two dirty towels were thrown over the shower. Everything had a skim of grunge on it. T-shirts, sweatshirts, and a few jeans were in balls on the floor, along with dirty underwear. A wide circular desk sat in the living room with five computers and large screens. When Joe turned these on, they were all dead. Michael, whoever he was, had erased them and cleaned them. The guys looked at each other, and Joe said, "Something was going on here. I'll get computer forensics in to search the drives." There were no filing cabinets or boxes to search. This guy lived on his computers.

They moved on to Claire's apartment. Again, it seemed she may have just stepped out for a quart of milk at the corner store. Her purse was there and all her clothes and personal things. The apartment was messy but looked lived in. She hadn't made her bed. Her computer sat open on a small desk. The screen was locked, and Joe couldn't get in. Another job for forensics. Her contact was her boss, Monty, and he confirmed he had been waiting to hear from her for a few weeks. He briefly explained her employment role with his company, and Joe's alarm bells went off. He asked Monty if there had been any security breaches, and Monty said, "Absolutely not. Obviously, we're on top of that." Joe asked Monty for her computer access, and Monty said, "I'll provide that if necessary. It's a security issue. At this point, it's not a murder case, is it?" Joe said, "No sir, it's not." Claire didn't leave a gun in the apartment, and none were registered to her. If she had an illegal one, she'd taken it with her. Joe still had to talk to the owner of her apartment, her landlord. Maybe his now-dead mother had some insights into Claire she may have shared. All he could remember was his mother said Claire was very private.

They then moved on to Randy's. Billy said to Joe, "This is getting stranger and stranger." Joe said, "Yeah, wonder what we'll find here." They opened the door, and unlike Claire's, Randy's apartment looked unlived in. It was spotless. He had a small laptop lying on his living room coffee table. It was unlocked and didn't reveal anything remarkable. Still, they got forensics to look at it and see if he'd been searching for anything in particular. He'd meant to leave. His shaving gear and toothbrush were gone, and only a few pieces of underwear were left in his drawer. His car was still in the parking lot, so how did he leave? No guns were found, but he did have two registered to him. The guys wondered, where are they and where is he? Randy's emergency contact had been his mother. Her first response had been, "Thank god, then he must be alive." She said she'd been waiting to hear from him for a month. In a cleanly labeled filing cabinet, they found his will. He had left $100,000. to his parents and the condo to some female named Mary Johansen. Without giving away the contents of Randy's will, Joe asked Randy's mother if she knew Mary. She said she'd never heard of her, and as far as she knew, Randy didn't have a girlfriend. He'd never had a girlfriend. Joe thought *mothers never know their kids as well as they think*. Billy reminded Joe of the break-in, and Joe began to realize there may be more to Randy than this ultra-neat apartment indicated. He planned to follow up at Randy's workplace and see if he could find Mary.

When Randy's mother saw the apartment, she looked strange. "What's wrong," Joe asked. She said, "I bought him a very nice sofa and loveseat set. It was expensive. It's not here. Just this ratty two-seater."

They moved on to the last apartment, Antonio and Lily's. Antonio's car wasn't in the parking lot. The apartment was a paradox. Most of it was clean, neat, and well-maintained. The morning dishes were in the dishwasher, and the coffee pot, still partially full, sat waiting for a reheat. They noticed the den couch had a duvet and a pillow rolled up in the corner. Someone slept there regularly. They moved on to the master bedroom. When they opened the door, the smell hit them first. Perfume and sweat and dirty underwear and unclean things. The bed was a tossed mess. There were dirty women's clothes tossed all over the floor and flung over every surface. The bathroom counter was so covered with makeup and stains you could barely see through to the bottom. The clothes they could recognize all looked a bit tarty. This must be where Lily slept.

In the den, there was a small laptop on a desk that wasn't locked and didn't give up much. Pictures of two young Mexican-looking girls laughing together on the screen saver. Antonio's kids? There was some fishing gear in the hall closet but no file cabinet. If Antonio was keeping any files, they weren't here. Billy thought *everybody has some paperwork. Where are his tax files and condo purchase files?* All of his shaving gear, toothbrush, etc., were still there. It didn't look like he meant to leave and never come back. Again, Joe had forensics check his computer to see what he might have been looking up. Joe would discover Antonio was way ahead of them and never looked up anything about his planned escape on that laptop.

As for Lily, not much was known about her either. They found no purses other than ratty old used ones tossed about. As much as they could determine, she'd expected to come back. Morty had mentioned she took a lot of Ubers. Joe knew he'd have to follow that up and see if he could find some drivers who might have picked her up. Where did she go, and where was she returning from?

There weren't any cell phones in the apartment, so they must have had them with them. Joe thought *we could locate their last ping. That might tell us something.* The last ping on Antonio's cell just took them to the parking lot where they found his car. They didn't have a cell number for Lily to trace.

Meanwhile, Carolyn put on her insurance investigator hat. She had to consider a lot of angles with this explosion and related deaths next door in the condo. Several Jews were living in the building. Could it have been a hate crime? If so, did the person leave any clues, online diatribes, or anything? So far, nothing had surfaced in that corner. Nobody with an axe to grind. If the explosion next door was due to negligence, she'd have to prove it. If it was discovered the explosion was caused by a bomb, she could lean on the terrorist exclusion clause, but she knew how many lawsuits would follow that. Besides, she personally thought that clause was cruel. Insurance should cover all losses. Insured people don't invite terrorism through negligence.

She'd shared her concerns with Detective Joe Piccioni regarding the cause of the explosion. He reminded her that a bomb could have been laid by anyone, not necessarily a resident of the condo. He'd shared what he and Billy found in the empty apartments. There was still a lot of follow-up to be done to chase down leads. Joe said, "One of those empty apartments could very well lead us to the explosion. It's too early to say. Once forensics has looked at the computer drives and the fingerprints and I've talked to all the connections, we'll know more. Maybe one or all of them had a record or a beef."

When they got back into Billy's car and drove back to the office, Billy looked over at Joe and said, "Well, pal, you wanted to be a detective; you've got a shit load of detecting to do here." Joe grinned at Billy and said, "Not just me, Kemosabe, you're helping. We've got a lot of work to do."

In these darkest days of death and missing people, Billy had never felt more alive.

Chapter Eight

NEW LIVES

CLAIRE

The trouble with being a Russian spy was there was no retirement plan. You're a spy forever. Well, that's one problem; there are a few others. Claire had no intention of being a spy forever. She hadn't shared that with her parents. They were so proud of her getting this assignment.

Her parents were on her mind as she drove up the freeway to Chicago. Her decision to leave the SVR put them in grave danger. As soon as the SVR knew she was missing, they'd be interrogating them. She purposely hadn't contacted them for over a year to make it easier for them to say they hadn't heard from her. They had a way to message each other through a safe channel, but she couldn't even use that right now. They'd be watched.

On Claire's last night in Russia with her parents, she'd said, "I know you're proud of me and love Russia, but I'm going to be doing something dangerous. It could put you at risk. Do you understand?" She said, "If things change and the SVR loses trust in me or I need to leave the service, your lives could be in danger."

I'll get a message to you. I'll send a blank piece of paper. That will mean you need to leave the country immediately. You're in danger. I'll find a way to get in touch when it's safe. Do you understand?"

Her parents told her, "We're not fools. We know what could happen." Claire's parents couldn't imagine their wonderful daughter would ever fall in disfavor with the Russian government. She'd worked so hard for this job. Why would she want to abandon Russia? What they didn't realize was that was her goal. A ticket out of Russia and freedom. Claire thought *you are fools, but I can't seem to change you.*

For all of that, they'd discussed an escape plan. Claire's father, Andrej, had a friend he'd known since childhood, Mikael. Mikael left Russia decades ago. He was openly against the regime running the country, particularly Putin and his thugs. He'd had to leave, or he would have been arrested or killed. He now helped people get out of the country. He had a small private inn in a town up the coast of Azerbaijan. The town was big enough that Claire's parents wouldn't be noticed. They could always go there if it became necessary. Anastasia (Claire) would contact them through Mikael. He could be trusted.

Claire's father looked at her with love and said, "I'm sure it will never come to that. You'll work to a young retirement age and then return to us." Claire looked at her darling father, thinking him so naïve. She dead-eyed him and said, "I'm serious; if things go wrong with me, you're not safe. If I disappear, it's time to go. You have to leave immediately. It could mean your lives." He looked at her sternly and asked, "Are you planning to disappear?" Claire said, "Papa, I know you don't want to believe it, but this country is changing and not for the good. We may all have to disappear someday."

Claire's Russian minder had dropped the ball and didn't even know Claire had moved upstate months before, let alone disappeared altogether. He knew she continued to send in reports to Moscow regularly about her work at MPL, so no warning bells had gone off. Thinking she was still in Miami, he occasionally stopped by her old building to see if he could catch a glimpse of her coming and going. He hadn't seen her in some time. That didn't worry him. She worked at home and lived a quiet life. She was one of theirs and had never indicated she might stray. He'd never actually met her but knew her personnel file inside out. She was one of the good ones. He thought.

It didn't bode well for him when the SVR realized one of their best had jumped ship and disappeared on his watch. His instructions were to find her and kill her.

As Claire approached Chicago, she dropped down the I-90 and took West Harrison Street toward the lake. She wanted to live near the lake and the parks and started her apartment search there. She had some decisions to make. First, she wanted to park, walk around, breathe, and think. Her life had flipped upside down; she was in great danger but loved a challenge. Her life had been dull and predictable for a spy. That was all changed.

Chicago wouldn't be her last stop. She knew she'd probably have to move a few times. She knew she'd have to lay low for the rest of her life, raise no suspicions, keep contact with outsiders to a minimum, and become invisible. An exhausting thought.

Her main goal was to get out of the States and try to get her parents out of Russia safely. She'd thought a lot about how to do that, but she couldn't even contact them right now. She'd planned to get a message to them through Mikael, but he would also be being watched. She'd need to take her time.

She also wanted to find Malek. He'd gone quiet, but ransom requests rarely hit the news. She'd had access to him in her old job but was, of course, blocked now. Claire had other ways to track him. Malek's targets were always large Jewish organizations or organizations led by a Jew. She was sure he'd targeted her condo and was the cause of the explosion next door.

Malek, meanwhile, was hiding in plain sight. He'd changed his alias, cleaned up, and taken a short-term rental in a waterside condo in Miami. He never touched his computer. He dressed well, went out for dinner frequently, and had drinks at the bar, chatting casually with other tourists. He pretended to be an amiable visitor from New York catching some rays. He knew someone was on to him, and the CIA or at least the FBI, was coming for him. He didn't realize it was Claire, but the government also tracked his work. They wouldn't find him, but Claire would. They'd be looking for the old him.

Unbeknownst to Claire, a CIA agent had gone to the town listed on her fake ID to check out her background. He'd shown pictures of her around town. No one recognized her. There were no medical records in the system. She'd apparently never been to the hospital, a doctor's, a dentist's, the library, or the corner store. Her resume said she'd been home-schooled, so grade and high schools wouldn't remember her. They did discover a baby named Claire Richmond had died at birth and was buried in the Catholic graveyard. That baby's parents were also dead now. There was no record of siblings or any relatives. The neighbors of her old address hadn't lived there long. They knew nothing. The CIA no longer knew who Claire really was, other than a talented hacker. Someone had wanted her placed high up in their organization.

Now they were looking for Claire Richmond (whoever she was) and Michael Robertson (Malek) if he was who he said he was. They'd lived in the same condo and disappeared around the same time. There had to be a connection. The question was whether they had anything to do with the explosion next door.

Claire's father, Andrej, had been ignoring his friend Mikael's political warnings for years. Andrej took him with a grain of salt; he wasn't political, he and his wife had a thriving medical practice, and their daughter was successful. Their life wasn't affected. The rumors couldn't be true. All governments were a little corrupt. Still, years ago, as insurance, he'd quietly opened an offshore account in the Cook Islands and regularly transferred small amounts of money out of the country. Not enough to raise alarms, but he'd gathered over €200,000 Euros in his secret account. Money for a rainy day. He woke up and started paying attention after the Ukraine invasion and international drug companies cut Russia off from imports. Three of his patients died because they couldn't get their drugs.

Now, ten years after their daughter Anastasia (Claire) left Russia, an SVR agent was at their door. He was young, in his early 20s, and seemed nervous. He didn't tell them their daughter had disappeared. He asked them if they'd heard from her. Andrej was immediately alert and said, "No, we haven't received any contact from her for over a year. We were starting to worry. Why? Is something wrong? Has something happened to her?" The agent thought *they're genuinely concerned; she hasn't been in touch.* He said, "No, just following up. You know our rules about contact, only through our safe channels." Polina said, "Of course. Could you possibly ask her to check in? We'd like to hear from her." The agent smiled and said, "We'll get that message back to her." *If only we knew where she was,* he thought. Just as the agent stood to leave, Andrej said, "Oh, by the way, we're planning a short vacation; we'll be away for two weeks." *Andrej hoped he wasn't asked where they were going.* He said, "Hopefully, she doesn't try to contact us while we're away." The agent looked hard at the two of them. They were smiling and relaxed.

A warning bell was pinging in his head, but he had a friend waiting for him at his favorite bar. It had been a long day, and he wanted a drink. He shook off his doubts. They were staunch, loyal Russians, professionals; there was no reason to mistrust them. He thanked them for their time and left. He immediately forgot this nugget of information had been shared with him, and he did not tell his superiors he had been told this. When he learned they were missing several weeks later, he thought *I can't say they told me. I'd lose my job, maybe my life.*

After the agent left, Claire's parents looked at each other. Andrej gestured Polina into the bathroom and shut the door. He turned on the shower and the sink taps. Polina whispered, "That was quick thinking." Andrej whispered close in her ear, "Something's wrong. She's gone missing, and they don't know where she is. We've never had an agent at our door asking about her. They would know if we'd heard from her. She's either dead or left the SVR and gone underground. They'll be watching us now. Our phones are probably already tapped, and they probably have wires around the house and in our cars. We can only have free conversations outside where we can't be heard. It's probably not even safe in here. We need to leave now." Polina said, "We haven't received a blank paper from Claire." Andrej said, "She would know they'd be checking our mail and be very careful sending anything to us from abroad if she's gone to ground. Let's drive to Mikael's inn tonight. I don't dare phone him. He should have some advice, at least. Anastasia knows how to get in touch with us there. If we're questioned at the border, we'll say we're going on holiday. We might still have time. That agent won't be reporting in until tomorrow. He's probably at a bar right now getting drunk."

They packed as if for a short vacation and left within hours. Andrej had tucked away €20,000. Euros in the back of their bedroom closet. He hid this under the car carpet. If they got caught with that, it would be all over. He could access the rest of his money when they left Russia. He left a brief message with his office. "Please cancel and rebook all our appointments for the next two weeks. We've decided to take a holiday. Sorry for the trouble. See you in two weeks." It was a three-day drive to Mikael's in Azerbaijan, pushing hard. Miraculously, they had no trouble at the border. Just two married doctors taking a road trip. No alerts had been set up yet, watching for them. They watched any car coming up on their side, stomachs tightening every time a car followed them too closely. They had never been so terrified, and all they could think was, *is Anastasia (Claire) alive? Where is she.? What's happened?* They couldn't even imagine their own future. They desperately hoped there would be a message from Anastasia (Claire) when they got to Mikael's.

They slept in the car, picking up take-out food along the way. They had just left their entire lives and careers behind. Neither of them would probably ever be able to practice medicine again. They didn't know where they'd end up or if their daughter was alive or dead. They were numb. The enormity of their decision would hit them later. They were now refugees and targets. They couldn't stay long at Mikael's. The SVR knew he was a friend. They had to keep moving for his safety. If Anastasia (Claire) had gone rogue, the SVR would want to make her pay. Killing her parents would be a start.

Back in Chicago, Claire walked around the park at the lake and thought about Uruguay. According to her research, it was relatively easy to get into. Passing through airports with false ID was worrying. Getting her parents to make the leap would be more complicated. She couldn't fly out of a major airport now. Too much of a risk of facial recognition being used. She would have to consider using smaller airports and short hops to reach her destination. Doable but still a big risk. She hadn't ruled out cosmetic surgery to completely change her look. She would need complete discretion. Her face would need to be altered so that she was unrecognizable. There was a reconstruction plastic surgeon in the city who came with five-star reviews. She thought *I'll meet him first and see if he can be trusted. I'll tell him I need to hide out from an abusive husband.* She made an appointment from the hotel that afternoon. Claire never wasted time.

The surgeon's office was in a well-kept, small brick building on a quiet, leafy street. The cars parked on the street were expensive. There was no sign outside the door, just the street number on a soft bronze panel on the building. *So far, very discreet*, Claire thought. His name was Doctor Anthony Williams. He was in his early 50s, pleasant-looking but not pretty. He was slim, losing his hair and going gray. He wore his street clothes, no doctor's white jacket. He didn't look like he'd had any work done. There was no façade. She liked him immediately. She introduced herself as Sheila Sandstone, one of her many aliases, and wore her disguise: wig, false nose, mask. He smiled warmly at her and said, "You're safe here. You can take all that stuff off. He offered his hand and said, "Nice to meet you, Sheila; I'm Doctor Williams; what can I do for you."

For all of Claire's disguise, he noticed she kept her body erect and a bit stiff. She looked coiled to spring. She was thin but fit, with well-muscled arms, no makeup, and it didn't look like she'd ever worn it. Her eyebrows were tidy but not plucked. She wore her hair in a straight cut; he surmised she did it herself. It was a natural light brown with no streaks, roots, or hair dye. She didn't care about being pretty. She was all business.

She shared her lie about an abusive husband who wanted to kill her and her need to hide and completely change her look. She reassured him, "You'll be wondering. Money is not a problem." Doctor Williams didn't respond. It was her business, but he didn't believe her story. She didn't look or behave abused or terrorized. She apparently had unlimited cash, so he thought *she's either a thief or a crime wife wanting to escape the life.* He was betting on a thief. She'd do herself up if she was a rich man's crime wife. She was too confident to be a victim. He met all kinds of people with various backgrounds in his business. He observed, didn't judge, and asked no personal questions.

They discussed some options for her face. She told him she wanted to completely change her look and that beauty wasn't a necessity. He suggested a larger imperfect nose, more prominent cheekbones, a rounder chin, lowering her eyebrows and changing her eyelids to look ever so slightly Asian. She wouldn't be ugly, but she wouldn't be pretty either. She definitely wouldn't look like her old self. He said, "This will be expensive, extensive, and painful. Are you up for that?" She said," Yes. How long before I can go out into public and look normal?" He said, "It takes about six months for all the swelling to go down, but you'll look normal in about six weeks. No one will know but you. "Claire said, "I want to leave the country. Will the airport face rec. pick up on face reconstruction. Would I be recognized?" He laughed and said, "Not yet, but it's coming. He said, "Your eyes can be a giveaway, but we'll have changed yours considerably, and I'd suggest you get brown contact lenses. I won't even ask you about passports and IDs. It's not my business." She smiled at him and said, "Wise man." She trusted him. He would have loved to know her story. He never would.

She booked a surgery date and a private room while she healed. It took two months before she was ready to go public. The drains and dressings came off within days. She was swollen and bruised, but Claire already loved the results. She never thought much about her looks, but now she looked vaguely Mediterranean and exotic. No longer the vanilla girl from Russia. The facility was completely discreet. She paid a sizable fee with cash. After two months, she moved out of the clinic's room and into a hotel. She dyed her hair darker to accompany her new face and ordered brown contact lenses from an optometrist. She prepared three new identities with her new face, including passports. She was ready for the next chapter.

Claire had been using the clinic's internet to look at available apartments and found a ground-floor suite with a walkout to a small private garden that looked interesting. It was pricey, but money was not her issue. She got her backup story together and her next persona. She was Caroline Mitchell. She'd lived with her aunt in the Midwest all her life. The aunt had just died and left her a bit of money. She hadn't worked and couldn't provide references, but she could pay six months' cash in advance. The landlord said, "There must be someone I can call to check on you." Claire said, "I knew this would be a problem, and I'm afraid there isn't anyone to call. I'm trustworthy. I don't drink, do drugs, or smoke. I'm a reader and very quiet. I love the apartment and would take good care of it." The landlord looked hard at her. She was an interesting-looking woman, not pretty, but interesting. He thought he was a good judge of character. He said, "Okay, I'll take a chance this time. Don't let me down." She said, "I won't, I promise." She paid him the six months' rent in cash, and he gave her the keys.

As he turned to leave the apartment, he said, "Oh, by the way, your neighbor is a black man. Is that going to be a problem?" Claire had never had a racist thought in her life. She responded, "Only if he's noisy, is he noisy?"

The landlord smiled at her and said, "No, ma'am, he's a nice quiet guy. He has a dog, though."

She bought some simple furniture at a discount store and had it delivered the same day she moved in. She added a laptop, encrypted it, and locked it down. She used Starbucks WIFI when she needed to access the internet. *Don't leave a trace*, was always her mantra.

Claire went out early every morning for a run. It didn't take long before she met up with her neighbor, Sam. He was in his mid to late 70s, tall, carrying a bit too much weight and had a severe limp. He was black, as promised. He took his dog out to do his business early in the morning. He introduced himself and his dog, Cooper. Cooper looked like Tramp from Disney's Lady and the Tramp. All ears and whiskers and waggy tail. He was a mutt. She'd never been exposed to pets, but this dog took to her immediately. Sam was surprised and said, "He's usually pretty timid with strangers, but he likes you. Do you have cookies in your pocket?" She smiled and said, "No, no cookies." She picked some dog cookies up, though, and they quickly developed a morning routine of a simple "Good morning "and a cookie for Cooper. She liked Sam because he didn't press for more interaction, minded his own business and was always a smiling face to run into in the morning. His cheerful mood made her feel better.

Meanwhile, all that was on her mind was getting a message to her parents. She thought *they must be going mad with worry* and wondered if they were still in Russia. It had been almost three months since she'd left the condo and her job. She needed to get a message to Mikael without putting him in danger. She considered using some circuitous delivery so that the initial postmark wasn't hers. But that could still be traceable if anyone was really looking. A lucky opportunity presented itself.

One afternoon, she heard a light tap on her door. It was Sam. He said, "Sorry to bother you, but I have a huge favor to ask, and feel free to say no." Claire said, "What?" She immediately thought about everything she wasn't willing to do for anyone. He said, "My mother's in Jamaica and dying. I need to go see her. I have no one to take care of Cooper. I'd have to leave him at the pound. It should only be about two weeks. She's 97 and very close to the end." Claire didn't know what to say. She thought quickly. *This is a huge ask. What if he doesn't come back?* She weighed her own risks and thought *no one would be looking for me with a dog, that's for sure.* She also saw this as an opportunity to reach Mikael and her parents.

She said, "I'll do it, but I need you to do something for me too, no questions asked." He waited for her to continue, no expression on his face, wondering what was coming. Claire said, "I want you to mail a letter from Jamaica. There'll be no return address. You'll see it's going to Azerbaijan. Mail it regular mail, not airmail." He squinted at her and said, "Sounds like high dudgeon, but I won't ask. You're doing me a huge favor."

Sam was leaving in the morning and would drop off Cooper and his gear first thing. Claire got to work on her plan. At Dollarama, she found a card with palm trees on it. She handled this wearing disposable gloves. In the kids section, she found an invisible ink pen. An old trick that might work. She put a message on the card: "Hello from Jamaica. We'll be in touch about a booking at your inn. Or leaf a message with us". She signed it "The Smithsons." She had purposefully misspelled "leave" to leaf, hoping Mikael would pick up on it. Then, in tiny print, she wrote the phone number of one of her burner phones in invisible ink on the palm tree leaves. She was betting the reader wouldn't suspect invisible ink if the envelope was intercepted. It was such an old tool no one used any more. The message wouldn't be relevant to any of his clients, so he'd know it was her. It would take three weeks for the card to get there. At least her fingerprints wouldn't be on it. Now she had to wait for a call she hoped would come.

Claire dropped the card into an envelope. When Sam dropped Cooper off, she handed it to him, wearing disposable gloves. Sam looked at her hands with a question in his eyes. She said, "Oh these, I'm cleaning out the fridge." Sam said, "At six in the morning?" Claire said, "No time like the present."

That night, Claire did not sleep alone; she had a furry, shedding, snoring dog, four paws in the air, pressed against her side. The weight of his body against hers was somehow comforting. He wasn't stressed, but she was.

Claire and Cooper fell into an easy routine. They ran in the morning, took a long walk at noon and a shorter one in the evening. He loved the exercise, and she had to admit she enjoyed his company. He was an affectionate pup, intelligent and well-trained. She found herself talking to him throughout the day. When she was sitting, he always wanted to be beside her, bodies touching. Sam had been gone for over three weeks, and she began worrying. *If he doesn't come back, what will I do with Cooper?* She couldn't see herself dropping him off at the pound. She'd given Sam the number of one of her burner phones, but he didn't call. She had no way to contact him.

Finally, late in the evening, there was a tap at the door. Sam was back, and she had to give Cooper back. She was surprised at how much she missed him. She asked Sam how it went with his mother, and he said, "It was a happy death; all of us were there. She knew she was loved." Claire thought *not what my death will be like, I'll die alone.*

She told Sam she'd been running with Cooper in the morning, and he said, "If you want to continue doing that, I'm sure he'd love it. My running days are over." He said to her, "By the way, mission accomplished. I mailed your letter the first day I was back." He grinned and said, "Is my next assignment waiting for me in a phone booth?" Claire paused and said, "You've been watching too many old movies." Still, his reference to old spy tricks made her uncomfortable. She changed the subject and said, "What do I owe you?" He said, "Don't be silly, honey; you cared for Cooper. That's worth a million bucks to me."

What he didn't tell her was he was nosy. When he got to Jamaica, he steamed the envelope open and examined the postcard. He thought *this message must have a coded meaning, it doesn't make sense.* The misspelling of 'leaf' was also odd. Claire spoke almost too clearly, with no slang. There was the tiniest hint of an accent he couldn't place. He didn't think she'd make such a spelling error. He looked up the address of the inn it was addressed to on Google Maps. It looked like a tiny little inn, nothing special. There was no website. He checked out Caroline Mitchell, the name Claire was using. She had no social media, nothing. Sam was not a fool. He knew Azerbaijan was right next to Russia. He thought *there's more to this woman than what she's presenting.* He, of course, couldn't ask. He resealed the envelope and mailed it as she'd asked. He liked her; she was good for Cooper and wished her well. Everybody has secrets. He had his own.

They fell into a new routine, with Claire running with Cooper first thing in the morning. Besides that, Sam retreated to his privacy, and Claire retreated to hers.

Claire stared at her phone and thought, it's been too long. Mikael should have received the card by now. It's been intercepted. Something's gone wrong. I hope I haven't put him in danger. I've put my parents in danger. What the hell was I thinking?

Meanwhile, Mikael had received the card, but secure phones were hard to get in Azerbaijan. At least something he could really trust. He was being extremely cautious while he asked around with trusted friends.

Mikael knew things and knew people. He'd helped a lot of people move out of Russia. A lot of Russians had moved to Turkey or Syria, especially after the invasion of Ukraine. They were somewhat welcoming countries. 'Somewhat' being the operative word. He'd recommended that Claire's parents go to the French embassy in Baku to get a Schengen VISA for France and fly directly there. They'd need proof of travel and health insurance, proof of hotel bookings and a copy of their recent bank statement. He'd helped them arrange all that. That at least got them out of Eastern Europe, where the tentacles were too close. That would only allow them 90 days in the country, not that anyone in France would be looking for them. Once they were inside France, they could apply for a residence permit. If that was approved, it was good for a year but could be renewed. That gave them time to figure out next steps and where they wanted to end up. Given Claire's parents were doctors, they could get priority applying for refugee status, depending on which country they chose. They'd shown proof of a hotel booking for three months but stayed only two days. They needed to disappear. Mikael had arranged a small, damp basement apartment at the back of a house in a neighborhood outside of Paris. It had little light and low windows. It was a long way from their large, sunny apartment in Moscow, but for now, they were safe.

When Mikael finally secured a safe phone, he called Claire's parents first. They had worked out a simple message between them should anyone be listening in. They trusted no one. It gave nothing away, but it meant so much. "Your laundry is ready" was the message. It meant he'd heard from her and would get back to them. They embraced with relief. Their daughter was alive but obviously in hiding. Mikael would call them again once he had spoken with her.

Back in Miami, after Clair disappeared, a detective and a very serious CIA employee started asking her old boss Monty questions. Monty instructed his staff to provide no information. As a security company, they didn't want anyone to know she'd had high access to their computers and was a talented hacker.

Monty then started rechecking her personnel file and background. She'd supposedly been thoroughly vetted when she was hired as a junior. It had all checked out then, but the person who'd done that had since been fired for incompetence. No one had bothered to check her security file as she showed her skills and was allowed further access. Human mistakes. Monty wondered who she was and what she was doing with his client's files.? She'd been in charge of following up minor thefts. She was always able to block the offender and often identify them. They didn't know that she dipped herself before shutting down the security breach. The more significant thefts from the larger corporations weren't detected. They'd just written it off as an accounting error, barely noticed. Claire was a wealthy woman.

She'd copied all of the files from Malek's jobs. She'd traced his last job, shutting down a medical transport bus company that primarily served the black community in Flint, Michigan. It was a charity with no extra money. Monty had offered Claire's services pro bono. As it turned out, it was a coup. Malek was sloppy on that job and left more of a signature than he probably meant to. He hadn't checked in anywhere since she'd watched him leave the condo the night she also left. When he did, she would trace him and know his location.

In her Chicago apartment, Claire continued to stare at her phone. She worried the card she'd had Sam send had been intercepted. Maybe Mikael hadn't twigged to her 'leaf' message. Would he know to put heat on the invisible ink? Azerbaijan was nine hours ahead of Chicago. Had she slept through a call? Finally, late one night, her phone rang. She worried about answering it. What if it wasn't Mikael but an interceptor? It was him, though, and they quickly caught up, and he congratulated her on getting out. He said, "Putin is an evil bastard, along with all of his cronies. You did the right thing." He said, "Your parents are in France, safe for now." She said, "Mikael, we owe you so much. How will we ever repay you?" He said, "Let's get you all to safety. What are your plans?"

She told him about her face reconstruction. He laughed and said, "I can't wait to see that, but I probably never will." She said, "Someday, I'll send you a picture." She told him she was thinking of Uruguay as her final destination. He said, "Uruguay is more open. I presume you're using a false ID and passport. Getting those for your parents would be difficult, so they'd have to emigrate as themselves. Start looking into what that will involve in terms of paperwork." He told her he had let her parents know she'd been in touch. He said, "They're frightened and shell-shocked." He went on, "They're also resilient and have each other. Let's get them out of Europe." Claire said, "Tell them I love them and how sorry I am about ruining their lives." Mikael said, "They would have had to leave eventually. This just hurried it up a bit." Claire said, "After we hang up, Mikael, lose this telephone number. I'll destroy this phone after this call; I suggest you get rid of yours, too. She gave him a new number on a different phone. Call me in a week, and I'll tell you what I've learned about getting my parents into Uruguay. Then we can make plans.". She removed the SIM cards from all her phones and kept them in a Faraday bag so they couldn't be hacked.

She hated to hang up. Hearing Mikael's warm, familiar voice speaking Russian reminded her briefly of her childhood. It was the sound of home. Thomas Wolfe said it best, "You can't go home again." He was right. She signed off, "Please, please don't take any risks. Stay alive. Maybe we'll get you to Uruguay too." Mikael said, "Yes, I'm thinking about it."

Claire knocked on Sam's door a week later to get Cooper for their run. There was no answer, and she could hear Cooper barking inside. She returned several times during the morning with the same result. She called her landlord and asked him if he could do a health check on Sam. She was worried. They found Sam on his face on the bathroom floor, gray, dead. His large body was in an awkward slump. They straightened him up and rolled him over. His eyes were still open, as well as his mouth. Claire closed both and put a towel over his head. He was hard to look at. Cooper was upset, whining and bumping up against Claire's leg. She realized he probably needed to go out and hadn't been fed. She looked at her landlord and said, "Sorry about the garden, but the dog needs to do his business." She took Cooper out, where he promptly peed and pooped. Poor guy must have been busting. She then put some food down for him, which he walked away from. This never-stressed dog was stressed. No wonder.

Her landlord asked Claire if she knew Sam's relatives or friends. She told him about Sam going to Jamaica and having no one in Chicago to care for Cooper. His relatives were all in Jamaica. Claire checked Sam's phone and called the first person with the same last name as his. It was his brother. He went silent on the phone. "He was just here," he said. "We had a wonderful time together, even though it was my mother's funeral. How can this be?" Claire had no answers for him. People die. She said, "He told me what a great gathering the family had for your mother. I'm so sorry. He was a good man." Claire was curious to know if Sam was really a good man but it seemed the right thing to say. She asked, "How would you like us to deal with his body and belongings? What do you want to do about his dog?" The brother said, "I will arrange to bring him home. I'm sorry, I can't take the dog." Claire relayed all of this to their landlord. He said, "We'll have to call the police and get his body to a coroner and in a freezer in the meantime. It's summer."

He looked at her and asked, "What do you want to do with the dog?" Claire said, "I'll take him for now. Maybe I can get him adopted out through the humane society. Not sure how that works." She knew she now had a dog, and Cooper wasn't going anywhere. This complicated her escape plans. It was a long flight to Uruguay, and there were no nonstop flights, not that she'd want him in the hold for twelve hours anyway.

Claire did some research and found a company that moved pets safely internationally. You didn't have to travel with them. They advised her on all the paperwork required. She'd need someone on the other end to receive him until she arrived. She figured many dog rescue organizations would be happy to get him at the airport and keep him until she arrived. She'd provide a healthy donation. She found what sounded like the right organization, contacted them, and they said they'd be happy to do it. Claire said, "I'll send you the donation in the next few days." It was more than they got funded in a year. They were ecstatic.

Claire frequently did her research on her encrypted tablet using Starbucks WIFI. One particular morning, two men, decidedly not American, came into the Starbucks she frequented most, although she did move around. They ordered coffee and sat down. They spoke in Russian. A chill ran up Claire's spine. They were talking about her. They knew she was in the Chicago area, just not where. They were closing in.

Sam's fingerprints on her card to Mikael led them here. Sam got into some trouble with the law in his younger years. His fingerprints were on file. They were easy to match up. Finding people in the States was easy when they weren't hiding. The next day, they showed up at Claire's apartment building, and she heard them knocking on Sam's door. Of course, there was no answer. They went quiet, and she assumed they had let themselves in. Sam's brother had been there, boxed everything up and shipped it back to Jamaica for the family to go through. The apartment was stripped, the mattress bare, and the closets empty. No one lived there now. The Russians looked at each other and shrugged. They then knocked on Claire's door. She knew who it was but looked out the peephole to confirm. Cooper was barking and snarling. She'd never seen him act like this. He didn't like whoever was outside her door.

She thought *it's now or never, might as well try out my new face.* She opened the door with the chain still on and said, "Yes?" They said, "Sorry to bother you, but we're looking for the man who lives next door; we're old friends of his." Claire thought, *yeah right. Liars.* She said, "He died about a month ago." The men thought Anastasia (Claire) would not have opened the door, yet this woman did. Also, this woman's face didn't match their picture of the old Claire, and she wouldn't have a dog. She'd be on the run. This wasn't Anastasia (Claire). They asked, "Do you know if he was friends with any people in the building?" Claire said, "I don't know, he kept to himself. This is his dog. I'm taking care of him." They said, "Okay, thanks." She shut the door in a full-body sweat. It was time to get out of Dodge.

She thought I'll go to Uruguay first, find a place to live and get set up. Then I'll bring my parents in. She booked Cooper's flight and then called Mikael to fill him in on the Russians and her plans. He was in danger. They had intercepted her card, taken Sam's prints and let the card go on to Mikael.

They were setting a trap. Hoping to catch four birds. Mikael, a long-hated dissident, Claire's parents, and the prime target, runaway spy Anastasia (Claire.)

Claire and Mikael had a code. She'd call, let the phone ring three times and hang up. If it was safe, he would call her back at the last number she'd left with him. She hoped her parents were on board with the move. She couldn't discuss it with them. She had to take it on faith her parents would want to join her. She was all nerves.

Mikael didn't call for hours. Claire had a lot to do. She was impatient, and she had to warn him. When he finally called, he was quiet at the other end of the phone. Claire said, "Something's the matter. What's the matter?" In almost a whisper and choking while he spoke, Mikael said, "They got to your father. They poisoned him. I'm so sorry, Anastasia, he's dead."

RANDY

Both Randy and Pauly were fearful all the time, not sleeping well and sharing the same bad dream of the one-eyed dead guy on the warehouse floor. Sometimes, he moved; sometimes, he raised his gun and aimed at them. Most of the time he just lay there with his head blown off. It was the nightmare of nightmares. For the rest of their lives, the two of them were intrinsically linked through this nightmare of an experience.

Randy had five million cash in a storage unit in Hollywood. Pauly had five million worth of cocaine in his bedroom closet in Jacksonville, and he'd murdered three men. They didn't know who knew, if anyone, and who had seen either of them at the warehouse, if anyone. They weren't innocent anymore.

The police didn't know what had happened. The dead men were known to them, all dealers and suspected murderers. Maybe it was just a cartel meeting that went wrong. They couldn't find anyone who would talk. No loss. The cartel head, Cito Herrares, knew exactly what was missing and he was pissed. Someone would pay. As soon as he found them.

Young Paul Jacobson, nicknamed Pauly, was buying the weed from Randy for his boss. His boss was a big player in the Miami real estate game and wanted a steady supply of rolled joints for his parties on his large cruiser. Pauly now had to figure out how to turn the cocaine in his closet into money without tipping his hand and pissing off whichever cartel he'd stolen it from. He wasn't a dealer, had no connections on the street and had no idea where to start. There had only been a small line of news about the murders, nothing about the missing drugs. He hadn't seen the money Randy had taken. Pauly told his boss the deal with Randy for the large weed purchase fell through.

Randy worried, maybe Pauly and the guy from Amazon talked after the murders. Given human nature and the inability of anyone to keep a secret, the probability of more people knowing Randy was at the warehouse murders was high. That would be good gossip for the terminal. It would also be a dangerous connection to Randy if the police talked to the Amazon referral guy. There were too many loose threads that could lead back to Randy and Pauly, for that matter. "Oh, the evil web we weave, etc."

Randy's dealer, Miguel, knew Randy had a big sale of weed coming up, but in their last conversation, Randy hadn't told him where he was meeting up with the client. Pauly had chosen the site, thinking it was safer than a mall parking lot for the amount of weed he was buying.

Miguel considered Randy one of his 'baby' dealers and wouldn't see him involved in something like the warehouse murders. As far as Randy knew, Miguel had left town. Randy wondered, *where is Miguel now and was he connected? He sure was nervous about those murders. But then, maybe all the drug dealers in Florida were nervous.*

While Randy rode to his future in Hollywood, back in Florida, five men met. If you were a fly on the wall, it would have looked like a laughable casting call for drug dealers. Except they all really looked like that. Four late 30's Mexican men who had run out of options long ago and one man at the head of the table. All four sold their souls to drugs and money years ago. That they were still alive was miraculous. Their bodies were a writhing sea of bad tats with long-forgotten meaning.

The man at the head of the table's name was Cito Herreras, but he just went by Cito. A one-name wonder like 'Cher,' only not as good-looking. He had no conscience and was a murderous, drug kingpin. Cito was 5'8" and weighed about 310. Not all the way to Yabba the Hutt, but getting close. He dressed impeccably. His clothes were expensive and expansive to cover his girth. He wore Italian leather loafers at one end and lots of gold at the other. He was completely bald, and his face was round and tight with the fat. He didn't smile often, but when he did, it was slow, slid across his face like a snake, and was cold and cruel. His anger was quick, accusatory and often deadly. No excuses for sloppiness and these men weren't very disciplined. Anyone in his presence wondered if they'd come out of these meetings alive. For Cito, just cutting out a poor performer was too dangerous. They could turn into an informer. If you worked for Cito, you didn't get fired; you got fired at. You were Cito's for life, however short that was. But...the money was good and worth the risk...for men with no opt ions.

Cito had waited for the dust to die. The cops would be watching. They met to discuss the warehouse murders and, more importantly, the missing money and drugs. This hardly looked like a board meeting of suits. The room smelled like sweat and a sweet cologne. Cito's cologne. Sitting at the table were four nervous, tattooed, greasy-looking punks, one wearing an oily durag, one with his hair tied back in a tail, and two over-muscled gym rats, but not marathon runners. One looked like he'd never eaten, hooked on his own product. Cito didn't approve. His time was coming to an end. None of them smelled like they'd been near a bar of soap for a while. Except f or Cito.

Cito said, "There's five million in cash missing and an equal amount of cocaine evaporated. Who's got it?" The men shifted cheeks and looked at each other. They didn't know, and that was not going to go down well with Cito. Cito went on. "Two of our guys were shot along with the buyer. Someone else was there." In addition to Cito's gang, there were at least two other large rival cartels in Florida, along with a lot of smaller ones. Cito was betting it was one of them. No one on the street was talking, of course. He didn't realize it was because they didn't actually know anything.

He asked, "Anybody else missing in the chain? One of the guys said, "No one's seen Miguel in a long time. Rumor has it he cut town. He hasn't ordered any product for a while." Cito said, "I don't think he was connected, not his area and he doesn't do anything that big for us." He asked, "How many guys did he have working for him?" The man in the dew rag said, "There were about 20 guys, mostly small time." Cito said, "Make sure they find one of our dealers." He asked, "Where do you think Miguel would go?" The man said, "He could be anywhere; money wouldn't be a problem." Cito said, "Keep an eye out and let me know if he's working for the competition. He won't be for long." The men exchanged glances with a flicker. They all privately knew Miguel just wanted to get out from under Cito, and they'd never see him again. They also thought, *good riddance. He thought he was better than us.*

Meanwhile, Detective Joe Piccioni, and his assistant Billy Knudson started asking questions at Amazon about Randy. Lots of people knew him and knew he sold small amounts of marijuana. Not to them of course. No, definitely not. When pressed, they'd answer, "No, they didn't know who he got it from or why he disappeared." They said, "Guys leave the job all the time. What's the big deal?"

Joe and Billy found Mary, but she hadn't heard Randy was missing, nor did she seem to care. They asked her, "Did you know he was selling weed?" She said, "No he never talked about that to me. I find that hard to believe." Billy said, "You must have heard some gossip around the depot?" Mary said, "Nobody knew I hung out with him. He was kind of a quiet nerd. That never reached my ears."

When they told her she was in his will, she was genuinely surprised. She said, "Strange, we were just casual friends, not close at all. We hung out a few times. Nothing romantic. I wasn't into him that way. He was a nice guy though."

She then asked, "So, how does this inheritance thing work?" Joe and Billy told her, "We need a dead body first. We don't know where Randy is." Billy said, "I wouldn't count on taking possession anytime soon. You have to wait five years before you can declare a missing person dead and collect on any inheritance. He could just have disappeared for his own reasons." Mary asked, "Could I move in, and in five years, it's mine? Except if he comes back, of course," Billy said, "I'm not sure how that works. You'd have to speak to a lawyer about that." He said, "You'd have to keep up the mortgage, utility, property taxes and common area costs if you wanted to hold on to it."

She said, "So, meanwhile the bank could just repossess it for unpaid mortgage payments?" Billy said, "Ostensibly." She laughed and said, "Well, thanks for nothing, Randy. I presume someone will let me know if they find him." Billy said, "We will." After they left her, Joe said to Billy, "Talk about misplaced trust on this guy Randy's part. Mary could give a damn if he's alive or dead."

Cito didn't even know he should be looking for Randy or Pauly. He was following the wrong scent. The trail also went cold for Joe and Billy. Randy had vanished.

When Randy dropped onto the Santa Monica Boulevard in Hollywood, he rode the strip. It was sunny and hot, but not Florida hot. This was comfortable. He rode slowly around town to get a feel for it. He'd heard of most of the streets, mostly through TV shows. He found Melrose Ave, Fountain Avenue, Sunset Blvd. and Hollywood Blvd. Unlike Florida, there were tons of people walking the streets. Every race, country and stripe seemed to be comfortably represented here. Even talking to each other. He thought *I like what I'm seeing. I'm going to be okay here.*

Randy cut up to Forest Lawn Drive to check out the film studios. That was disheartening. Two miles of homeless people encamped along the road. *Poor bastards,* he thought. *Nowhere to go from here. So much for 'California Dreaming.'*

The first thing he had to do was find a secure storage unit for his money. He couldn't leave it in a motel or on his bike while he looked for an apartment. This was a transient town, and it turned out there were lots of storage units. He rented a small locker and tucked his money away in a large green garbage bag. He thought *I'll put it in something more secure later, at least it's off the bike and locked away.* He experienced an amazing feeling of lightness dropping off that money. It had weighed heavy on his bike and his psyche. The woman renting said, "You can store your bike safely here, too, if you ever need to." Randy had to get a car but didn't want to give up his bike. Storing it was a good option.

There were lots of motels to choose from, and he chose a central one. Nothing fancy but it looked clean. The hotel clerk was obviously gay and almost overly pleasant. Good looking, tanned, blonde, surfer boy look. He was wearing his motel's golf shirt and tight bermuda length shorts. Randy thought *they're 'check my ass out' shorts.* The guy seemed to be hairless other than his thick headful of scattered professionally streaked blonde hair. Randy thought *probably waxes everything. Ouch.* Having shaved his head, Randy now noticed hair.

When Randy asked if there was a secure place to park his bike, the clerk said, "I keep mine in a lock-up out back. You can lock yours in there, too. I'll give you a key." Randy asked, "How much?" The clerk, whose name was Gerald, laughed and said, "The least we can do is keep your bike from being stolen. There's no charge." Randy said, "Wow, thanks, man." Gerald grinned and said, "My pleasure, welcome to Hollywood."

Randy needed some new clothes next. He hadn't brought much with him, and his two pairs of jeans were scuzzy and well-lived in. On his ride around town, he'd spotted a discount clothing store. He needed everything, but for now, he just had to get through the week in some clean clothes. He picked up a few things and headed back to the motel for a shower and a change. Then it was time to eat.

Just up the street, he'd spied a bar called "Message at the Beep." There seemed to be a lot of theme bars in town. They looked expensive. He just wanted something to eat and some human contact. This bar looked a bit forgotten. When he walked in, it took him a few minutes to adjust his eyes from the sunny outside to the dark long bar inside. At the end of the bar, a faceless girl called out from the shadows, "Welcome to the Beep; what can I get you." Randy thought *safety, peace of mind, my old life back, but for now, a friendly face will do.* He'd been lonely these past weeks. Unlike Claire, Antonio and Estelle, he didn't enjoy his own company. The girl moved down the bar toward him with a menu.

She was short and had a tight little body. Looked like she spent some time in the gym. She had one tat of an eagle on her left upper arm. Her hair was dyed white blonde, short and punky and she had a big smile and a welcoming face. No tits to speak of but a good ass. Randy took all this in without her noticing.

Randy wasn't much of a drinker but a cold beer and a burger sounded just right to him now. "Yes, fries with that please." She said, "Hi, my name is Jules. I haven't seen you here before. Where did you blow in from?" He pulled up a vague version of his backup story. Up north, no town was named. She said, "What brings you here?" He said, "Looking for a change." She said, "Well, welcome to Hollywood. This town changes every five minutes."

There was a certain valley girl cadence in how some native Californians spoke. It was an affected way of talking. They all sounded a little stoned, and maybe they were. It was as if they'd never left the 70s even if they weren't even born then. This girl spoke with that kind of a surfer girl twist, but she didn't look like she'd ever ridden a wave.

He recognized a song playing by Amy Winehouse. He liked that there wasn't a throbbing beat playing in the music. The atmosphere was low-key and calm. A few screens were on over the bar with games going, but the sound was turned down. He liked this bar.

Jules read people pretty well. She had lots of male friends, but too many couldn't keep it that way. If a woman was being nice to them, that was an invitation. She didn't feel like she was being scoped for potential sex by this guy. He had a shy smile, and he was polite. He looked tired, and his shoulders were tense. Something was on his mind. Some men she immediately felt safe with. Randy was one.

She left him alone to eat, and when she came back for his plate, Randy said, "My name's Jake; I like your bar." She said, "Well, it's not mine. I just work here, but thanks. Nice to meet you, Jake." He said, "I'm looking for an apartment. Any ideas on the best place to look?"

She said, "Let me think about it." She went off to the end of the bar for a while and kibbitzed with a guy at the far stool. She came back and said, "If you're looking for work, every bar in town is looking for help." Randy hadn't thought of bar work, but he had to be paid cash only, and the bars would need to be legit. He said, "Not immediately but thanks for the tip". They chatted back and forth about Hollywood, L.A. traffic, tourists and general living. He knew she was assessing him.

After a while, she said "I know where there's a sublet coming up soon. It's my friend's, and he has to go home to take care of his sick mother." Randy said, "I could be an axe murderer." She put her weight on her forearms, leaned into him, looked him up and down and said, "Nope, not seein' an axe. Pen knife maybe". Randy laughed and said, "Don't know if I should be insulted or flattered."

She said, "There are lots of LGBTQIA+s living in the building." Randy said, "I should know what all those letters stand for, but it doesn't matter; it's not an issue with me." She said, "I'll call him."

Within two weeks, Randy moved into a fully furnished apartment in downtown Hollywood. Randy handed the apartment owner a year's rent in cash. The owner, his new landlord, said he hoped to be back in a year.

Randy said, "I'm a tidy freak; I'll take good care of your things while you're gone. You have great taste." He loved living in this man's apartment and taking on his life. He'd never had any style when decorating and hadn't really cared. This space was full of comfortable furniture, interesting lighting, colors, cushions, throws, area carpets and beautiful original art. He knew he'd do things differently when he got a place of his own. Next, he bought a 2022 Jeep Gladiator and paid cash for it, using his new Jake identity to get it licensed and insured. He could afford more, but he didn't want to draw attention to himself. He still needed to live quiet and low.

The apartment was in an end unit, and his next-door neighbor knocked on his door early and introduced himself. "Hi, thought I should say hello. I'm Kenneth. Welcome to the neighborhood." Randy introduced himself as Jake. Kenneth was a big guy, ebullient and hard to ignore. He was wearing scrubs and worked as a nurse at the hospital up the road. He had a streak of blue dyed into his hair and was wearing a very light touch of mascara. He launched into all the social things people in the building did together and said "There's a party at 420 on Saturday night. Feel free to drop in." Randy thought that unlikely but thanked him anyway. It was hard to close the door on this guy. He wanted to chat. Randy finally said, "Well, I'll let you get back to your day." Kenneth looked a little hurt.

He'd apparently been good friends with Randy's landlord and missed him. Randy envisioned himself going to a party of gay men and all the misunderstandings that would come out of that. Kenneth was relentless. The next afternoon he knocked on the door again. He said, "Look, I know you're not gay, and I'm a bit overbearing at times. I just love most people. Can't help myself. You seemed to be on your own, and I just thought you might like some human company. Don't worry, I have enough boyfriends." Randy laughed and invited him in. They soon became good friends.

The problem with Randy's new friends was they were all inquisitive. They couldn't leave Randy's past alone. Everyone in this town was friendly and open, but they wanted to know everything about you. Randy had to be careful with his story. He'd never had to be a liar, and he wasn't good at it. His inner dialogue was, *careful, don't say too much.* Also, someone always knows someone from somewhere. "My sister had a roommate from there."

Using the home-schooling story kept lots of that at bay. He'd explain he didn't go to college because his aunt got sick. He took care of her until she died. His parents died young. There were no siblings. Randy had studied his fake hometown and the area. He'd pulled it up on Google Maps and knew all the streets and places of note if challenged. Randy had to be firm and said, "Look, I don't talk about my past, so I need you to stop asking about it. Can you do that?" This, of course, conjured visions of old familial abuses and all kinds of nasty stories about Randy's past. But, they allowed him to remain a mystery man and accepted him at face value. A simple nice guy. Definitely not a run-away drug dealer and big-time drug cartel thief. Definitely not.

Randy did all the tourist sites available in L.A. and Hollywood that wouldn't likely involve cameras. That meant the movie studios were out. There'd be lots of cameras there and security. His days fell into a rhythm. The "Beep" became his local, and he stopped in there most afternoons for a beer or just a coke. He liked chatting with Jules and was always disappointed when she wasn't working. Kenneth dropped by after work most days and shared his hospital stories and tales of his very active love life. Randy didn't drink with him, but he always had a gin and tonic on hand for Kenneth. He started walking everywhere. His shoulders began to loosen. His fear began to fall away. The nightmares didn't stop, but they weren't nearly as frequent. He wondered if he'd ever feel truly safe again.

One morning, his world started to fall apart. He woke with a pain in his belly and started vomiting. He knew he was running a fever. He was soaked. He thought *this is more than the flu or food poisoning, but I'll ride it out. Kenneth will drop by later, and I can ask him about it.* He thought the day would never end. By the time Kenneth rapped on his door, he practically crawled over to open it. Kenneth said, "Oh Jesus, honey, what's wrong with you? Tell me your symptoms." Randy groaned out what he was experiencing. Kenneth said, "Right, sounds like appendicitis to me. I'm calling an ambulance. Do you have health insurance?" Randy said, "No, but I can pay for it." Kenneth said, "Are you sure? Surgery could be over $20,000." Randy said, "Don't worry, I've got it covered." Then he fainted with a new stab of pain in his gut. While waiting for the ambulance,

Kenneth applied a cold towel to Randy's face and mopped him down. "Don't worry, honey. Help is on the way."

Randy's appendix had burst, and he was on the verge of sepsis. He was in the hospital for weeks. It was touch and go, with Randy surfacing and then falling back into a deep sleep. Kenneth stopped in every day, not sure if he'd find him alive the next.

When Randy finally came to, still sick and weak, but on the mend, Kenneth told him he had been rambling in his sleep. He asked him, "Honey, what on earth did you do to your mother? You kept saying, I'm sorry Mom, over and over." He said, "I tried to check your phone for a number, but it was locked. If you're going to do this again, I need an emergency number to call." Randy said, "There's no one to call. If I die, donate my body to science. Kenneth said, "You need to fill out some paperwork for that; it's not that simple." Randy said, "Whatever, we'll figure it out when I'm home." He then held Kenneth's hand and looked at him. "Thank you for sticking by me. You are a true friend." Kenneth hugged him. He was a hugger. Randy was not, but he needed a hug from someone right now. Randy then looked at him and lied, sort of, "It was a long time ago, and I didn't hurt her if that's what you think. I just let her down." That's the most Randy had ever shared about his past, but it was a nugget for Kenneth he kept for later. "So, he did know his mother, and fairly well from the sound of thin gs."

When Randy finally got back to the apartment, he was down fifteen pounds he couldn't afford to lose, tired all the time, and feeling very homesick. He still felt frail. He missed his mom. Never his dad. His mom had always been in his corner, and now she probably thought he was dead. She was as good as dead for him. He couldn't contact her. Too dangerous. He sobbed into his pillow. He wanted to go back to his old life.

It took him a month to get back on his feet, but when he did, he was antsy to be doing something. He needed a job. There were a few notices tacked up on the bulletin board near the mailbox looking for housekeepers. He had an idea. He could run a small cash-based housekeeping business. He was one of the few people in the world who enjoyed cleaning. He was good at it. He contacted the three numbers on the bulletin board and set up meetings with each of them. He couldn't do it if they wanted him full-time. He'd be a drop-in maid, not a live-in maid. It turned out they were all in the building and only wanted him once a week. Perfect. He scheduled them in and went out and bought supplies. All three were ecstatic about his service. "My bathroom grout is white again," one said. "He cleaned out my fridge, and I didn't even ask him to," another said. "He got my stained carpet clean. The cat had peed on it, and that stain was always there," another said. Referrals started pouring in. He stuck to the apartment buildings in the area. Lots of people just couldn't keep up with cleaning. Randy did it for them. He insisted on cash up front; he was reasonable, reliable, and honest. He was good, and he was busy.

Randy started enjoying his new life. He was beginning to think he'd gotten away with his escape from Florida and the men who could kill him. He was about to learn life had a way of smacking you when you got too cocky.

He dropped into the Beep one afternoon for a beer. There were a few guys at the other end of the bar watching a baseball game. As usual, the bar was dark. Jules skimmed by to say hello and ask him how his business was doing. She teased him about being so good at housekeeping. As they laughed back and forth, one of the guys further down the bar leaned back on his stool and looked long at him. Randy looked back and froze. It was a ghost from the past. Even Randy knew that old Bogart line from Casablanca. "Of all the gin joints in all the towns of the world, she walks into mine." Except it wasn't Isla (Ingrid Bergman), it was his ex-drug dealer, Miguel. *What the hell was he doing here at the Beep?*

ANTONIO

When Antonio arrived in Seattle, the sky was gray, and the rain drizzled on his windshield. He had his wipers on low and listened to their slow beat, thumping back and forth just enough to remove the water beads before the blades swung back. Some welcome, Seattle, he thought. His drive past harborside Seattle revealed no street life. A few tourists bundled up in rain gear circled around the Pike Place Market area. People who lived here were dry inside, wrapped in sweaters. It was mid-July. He thought *this is going to take some getting used to.*

He looked at the gray, cold, choppy waters of Elliot Bay and thought *won't be swimming in that any time soon.* No more dawn fishing in the warm blue ocean off the coast of Jacksonville, wearing just a t-shirt and shorts. He still wanted to fish and had decided the Bellevue side would give him good access to fishing in Lake Washington. He'd have to dress warmer and get some rain gear. Or, find a new hobby.

First, he had to store his money and found a high-security vault. He wasn't crazy about the security iris scan. Still, he thought *they're my irises, and I'm the only one using them to gain access.* Dropping that bag off gave him the first relief he'd felt since leaving the Jacksonville dock and walking up the road that steamy dawn. Antonio sat in his car in the parking lot, staring bleakly out the window. The downpour continued, no let up. Antonio never got depressed, but he sure wasn't happy.

He wanted an apartment in a rental building. More privacy. Condominium owners would want to know who's living next to them. Renters don't care as long as you're not annoying. He contacted Apartment Finder, spoke with an agent and laid down his fake story of taking care of a sick mother for years, no rental references, blah, blah. She was working on commission and didn't care about his record. He had a year's cash for the rent. She'd get a piece of that, and he wasn't looking for a bargain. She found him a roomy, modern apartment overlooking the lake, move-in ready. He ordered furniture and some decorative touches from his motel, and in two days, he was in. That day, he breathed another sigh of relief, thinking *now my new life starts, whatever that turns out to be.*

He watched the daily news for reports on his old condo and the dead occupants. The news cycle about the explosion had lasted about a week and faded. The juicy bit had been all the mysteriously dead people. Nothing was reported about anybody missing from the building. Antonio remembered many people were never found in Lahaina after the fire. They weren't named either. He wondered how many had taken their chance and slipped into the mists of the Pacific. It wouldn't be that hard to get off the island unnoticed if you had fake ID.

There'd been one small article about him in the Jacksonville Daily Record. "Missing Occupant of Vanilla Palms is believed to have drowned. Antonio Cervates' boat washed up on shore. A wallet, keys and a cell phone were found in a compartment on board. He apparently wasn't wearing a life jacket, as it was found tied to the boat. His locked car was found earlier. His body has not been found." Antonio thought, good, that ruse worked. Thankfully, his picture wasn't included, although the only one they'd have would be his driver's license. He had thick black hair and a mustache in that one. The article wasn't picked up by any big newspapers or the Florida Times. He thought it was odd there was no mention of his wife Lily missing at all. Public interest had moved on. Replaced by the next mass shooting or churning tornado moving up somebody's coast and just about to make landfall. The public's attention span was tickled by a splash of disaster and death, but tickles that go on too long become annoying. Next disaster, please.

Antonio's fake backstory was a single white woman named Sarah Caldwell had adopted him from an orphanage on the Texas border. They'd lived out in the country on the outskirts of Des Moines, Iowa. The fake Sarah had home-schooled him, worried about the prejudice a little Mexican boy would experience in Des Moines. He completed high school online and then audited agriculture university courses. She'd given him a lot of love and a good childhood. When she got sick, he cared for her until she died. She'd left him well off. He didn't know where the money came from.

Antonio stood in his jockey's and stared at himself in the mirror. He was a hairy guy, an aging mid-fifties overweight man. When he turned sideways, he had a growing gut, and as he exhaled, it got worse. His arms, once strong, were no longer muscled. His ass was flattening. He continued to shave his head, but his face showed his age. He noticed some white threading through the black if he let his head go too long without shaving. His back had been bothering him a lot. Although he still had a supply, he no longer took his heavy-duty pain meds, just the drugstore variety. On bad days, they didn't touch the pain.

On another dreary day, he went to the nearest dock to check out boat and fishing gear rentals. He looked at what the other men wore on wet days and discovered that few went out fishing on those days. No one was sailing out at dawn. It was too damned cold and damp. He started to think he may need to find something else to do. He was miserable and bored.

He scouted the internet for nearby gyms, thinking he'd start working out and rebuild his body. Gyms and workout facilities were everywhere in Seattle. It was a young city, and everybody was into fitness. Just down the street, in a small strip mall, there was a clean, modern-looking place called Syd's Whole Body. The reviews were exemplary, and he dropped by.

The woman at the desk was about 5'11", mid-fifties, his age. Her hair was long, thick, a little wild and totally gray. She had a kind of 'no bullshit' face. She wasn't thin but solid and strong-looking. Not his type. He liked small women. She introduced herself as Syd, and he introduced himself as John. He asked the obvious, "Is this your place?" She said, "Yessir, all mine." She didn't share any additional information. He told her he was looking for a place to tone up and get advice on using the equipment. She looked him up and down and said, "We have some good kinesiology students working for us. If you like, I could match you up, and one of them will put a program together for you. Fix what's ailing you." He said, "Who says anything's ailing me." She said, "You're here, aren't you? You want to change something."

Syd was a straight shooter, and Antonio laughed. He said, "I do have a back problem, an old injury. I need to stretch it out, but I need to be careful." She said, "I have just the guy for you. His name is Andrew. I'll show you around and introduce you to him. You can take it from there or not."

Andrew was about nineteen, with wire glasses and really pale, slightly pimpled skin. He was short and skinny and had very thin arms. Not a muscle to be seen. Antonio wondered what this kid could possibly do for him. He quickly realized how smart he was. Andrew knew his stuff. He was more interested in the physiology of bodies than weight lifting. He was studying to be an R.N. He thoroughly interviewed Antonio and asked to feel his spine. He said, "You broke it some time ago." Antonio said, "You can tell?" Andrew said, "Of course. I would love to get an X-ray to see what I was feeling. We have equipment on site if you're up for it." Antonio said, "Sure." Andrew said, "Let's take your blood pressure first." He did this several times, telling Antonio he wanted to ensure he got a good reading. He frowned at Antonio and said, "Your blood pressure is pretty high." He ran him by all the symptoms of heart failure. Antonio had none of these but knew nothing of his family's health record. For all he knew, both of his parents could be dead of heart disease. His grandmother died of a heart attack in her early 70s.

Andrew suggested he set up some tests with a cardiologist. Antonio asked, "Can you do that?" Andrew said, "Nope, you've seen the limits of my expertise. I can connect you with my GP and he'll refer you on. Do you have health insurance?" Antonio said, "No, but I've got it covered." Andrew said, "Heart surgery could bankrupt you." Antonio said, "Whatever, might as well find out the worst. Andrew said, "Meanwhile, we can help a lot with a change in diet. You'll be doing all the right things exercise-wise. Just be aware of breathlessness on the treadmill. Back off if you start breathing too heavily.

Antonio was getting better attention than he'd ever received from his doctors. Andrew said, "We'll start you on a few light exercises. I want you to go easy. I guarantee you will feel some back relief pretty quickly." Antonio started going to the gym every day following Andrew's workout program. It was his new religion, not that he'd had an old one. He began losing weight and building muscle in his arms and shoulders, and his gut hollowed out. He stood taller and no longer winced when he stood up from a seated position. Andrew gave him some diet advice, nothing drastic. Antonio wasn't a dieter, but he stuck to it. He hadn't felt like anyone had cared so much for him in a long time. Best of all, his back hadn't bothered him in weeks. His heavy pain meds weren't calling to him from the bathroom cabinet anymore.

It wasn't good news when he finally got through testing with the cardiologist. There were some blockages. He didn't need stents or surgery yet, but would eventually. Meanwhile, he was prescribed a regime of heart drugs that pissed him off. He didn't want to die, so he took them. He hated taking drugs. At least they weren't narcotics.

The gym began to feel like the song from the old Cheers sitcom, "Where Everybody Knows Your Name." Whoever was at the front desk greeted him every day. "Good morning, John." If it was Syd, she'd always say, "Good morning John, how's it shaking?" He'd banter back, "Still rising with the sun, darlin'." She'd grin.

The gym was like a small family. The same people came every day, first names were exchanged, and everybody greeted each other.

Syd told Antonio about an upcoming Thanksgiving party for regulars she was holding at a restaurant downtown. Antonio was not much of a joiner, but he liked these people. They minded their own business but had become familiar friendly faces. He needed that. He went to the party.

Turned out it was no small party. There were well over 150 people all talking to each other. A small trio played in the corner, not that you could hear it over the din of voices. Food and drinks were laid out at several stations. All the gym usuals from his workout time were there, but Antonio didn't know anyone else. Syd was way over on the other side of the room, talking to some people. He didn't want to bother her. He regretted coming immediately and decided to make a quiet exit. This wasn't his scene. The last company party he went to was a lifetime ago. He'd met his first wife there. That hadn't gone well.

Jane had been watching Antonio since he came through the door. A tall bald man, probably Mexican, standing on the sidelines. She thought, *if he was invited here, he's been well vetted by Syd*. She thought he was good-looking. She'd watched him exchange hellos with a few people, but he was obviously uncomfortable. Within a half hour, she noticed him move to the hallway exit, preparing to leave. She caught up with him. "Sneaking out?" she asked. Antonio looked over his shoulder at a pleasant-looking woman standing just behind him. She said, "Hi, I'm Jane. I've never met you at the gym before. Are you new?" As one does, Antonio quickly assessed her looks. He thought *late forties, medium height, pleasant face, good lips, not much makeup, dyes her hair, respectable body. Loose shirt, but it looks like she's got decent tits under it*. He did this in a nanosecond without her noticing she'd been evaluated. He introduced himself as John and said, "Yeah, I've been coming for a while. I've never seen you there." Jane said, "I come for an hour before closing." Antonio said, "I'm there first thing in the morning. Ships in the night." She said, "I've always loved that expression. It brings up a vision of two dark shapes passing each other under the moonlight." He said, "I always thought of it as missed opportunities. There's no moonlight in my understanding of the phrase." She laughed and said, "Yeah, maybe a bit too girly, romantic." He smiled at her and said, "Nothing wrong with romance." A flirtation started. Antonio couldn't help himself. He missed the game.

Antonio said, "I thought it would just be a few people. I'm not a crowd fan." Jane said, "Not my thing either. Do you feel like grabbing a coffee? There's a spot just down the street."

They talked for hours like hungry old friends who hadn't seen each other in a long while. They also did the dance of early courtship. Humor tried on, a tease of a side remark, seeing what made the other smile. He learned she was a professor at the University of Washington. Jane said, "I'm teaching two courses this year; one is called "Trust in the Age of Liars." A loud warning bell pinged in Antonio's mind, given his whole persona was a lie. He thought *keep her at arm's length. Don't get involved. She'll be questioning everything I tell her*. He said, "Let me guess, it's about fake news?" She said, "More than that, everybody lies a little, more than they think. It's a venial sin and very human. Everybody has secrets." Antonio thought *yeah, I've got some beauties*. She said, "Obviously, fake news is huge, but it's been going on for centuries. That's my other course this year, Herod the Great. It's part of a series of the history of the Roman Empire. Lots of lies there." Antonio said, "Aaah, yes, Herod, the evil monster of the Bible." She said, "Yes, and there's no mention of anybody named Jesus in Herod's recorded history. Everybody's understanding of history is up for interpretation based on the story they've heard." She said, "The first course is more about deciding what you're willing to accept or challenge." Antonio said, "Yes, critical thinking is a must these days. Believe nothing."

He said, "I'm working through various U.S. Presidents' biographies. There are some dandies in there. Garfield and Van Buren were flawed men. I've always wondered how well Harry Truman slept when he retired in Independence, Missouri. Did he have nightmares about the Enola Gay?"

As they grazed over an open plain of topics, Jane realized there was little Antonio couldn't bring an informed insight to. She liked his intelligence and sensitive way of thinking.

Antonio looked at his watch, lied, as she'd predicted, and said, "I've gotta go, but this has been pleasant. She said, "I enjoyed it too. Nice to meet you." He didn't ask for her number. She thought *so much for him. He's not interested*. But he was.

He went home that night and thought *I look better than I did six months ago, but I'm still a late middle-aged man.* He'd always been so sure of his looks and attraction to women. Not so much now. He thought *I haven't taken my shirt off in front of a woman for a while, let alone my pants.* He decided not to pursue Jane. He didn't want anyone questioning his past. He also wasn't ready to take his shirt off.

Antonio returned to the gym the next morning. Three women in their late seventies, obviously old friends, also worked out in the morning. They would do a few pulls on this and a few knee bends on that and maybe ten minutes on the treadmill, going really slow. Mostly, they talked. Antonio introduced himself as the fake John and asked them their names. Now, they all said hello to each other. The women were a bit more careful with their makeup before they came in now and started sneaking peaks at this young, fifty-six-year-old Spanish Adonis as he worked out. He was to them anyway. That would have amused him if he'd known. He started teasing them as he passed, saying things like, "Jeannie, do five more lifts. You'll notice a difference." Or "Barb, try putting the treadmill on a slight incline for five minutes. You'll notice a difference." They liked the extra attention and started to get a little competitive, upping their workouts. They would brag to him about their new achievements. "John, I lifted the five lb. weights fifteen times today." He'd say, "Wow, that's great. I can see a change already." They'd go home, check themselves in the mirror, and swear they could see a difference, too. Syd observed this banter as she walked her gym. Too many of her older male and female clients dropped off quickly after a few weeks. Not these three. They wanted to please John.

There was a young disabled kid who came in alone on crutches two or three times a week. He was in his early twenties and pretty frail. Someone dropped him off at the door but didn't come in with him. His independence mattered to him. His name was Jack, and he'd work his way slowly to the back of the gym where the equipment was. No one looked directly at him, but everyone held their breath, hoping he wouldn't fall. Andrew had given him a workout program he could manage, and he was determined to work through it. Antonio kept a side eye on him and saw him watching the weightlifters. He said, "If you want to try the weights, I'll spot you." He didn't compliment Jack as he worked out. He just said, "One more lift, and then you can go home and get drunk." Jack thought this was hilarious." Antonio knew Jack didn't want to be the sad cripple in the gym, just one of the guys. When Jack had enough, Antonio didn't make a fuss, just said, "Good workout. See you next time." Jack would grin and say, "Yeah, next time, thanks John." Then he'd slowly peg his way out, pole in front of pole, one floppy foot down and then the other. His head was not steady on his shoulders, but there was pride in his eyes. As he pegged by Syd at the front desk, she asked, "Good workout?" Jack said, "Yeah, but I'll do better tomorrow. John's awesome. See ya."

Syd had been watching Antonio (John) helping various people over the past few months. He had a light hand, not too invasive. He seemed to know when someone needed encouragement or a pat on the back. Ever the businesswoman, she thought about her clients' needs. She needed to keep her clients returning. When John walked past the front desk that morning to leave, she called him over. She said, "I've been watching you. You've been very helpful with a lot of people. I was wondering if you'd consider working here. You'd have to take a certified personal trainer course. I can recommend a good online course. It would be part-time, and I can't pay you much money. How's that for a crappy offer?" She laughed.

Antonio was taken by surprise. He hadn't thought that kindness was a marketable skill. Neither was he looking for a job. He said, "Syd, you don't have to pay me. I enjoy helping these people. I wouldn't mind taking that course, though." She said, "I think you and a small team could be ambassadors for the gym without being a pain. You could help me put the program together, even if you ultimately decide not to work with me. Would you at least consider it?" Antonio said, "Can I think about it? I'm not looking for work or responsibility. I'm retired." Syd said, "Of course, my friend. We can talk about it later and bounce around some ideas." She wasn't going to let him off the hook.

He chewed on it for a few days. Antonio didn't have a history of being a nice, thoughtful guy. He'd been selfish rather than generous most of his life. He hadn't cared much about what was happening in other people's lives or his effect on them. This was a brand new Antonio. He regretted so many things he couldn't change now.

As the song went, he was *"looking at the man in the mirror."*

He liked this new him, and he liked Syd. He came back to her with a counteroffer. He said, "Okay, I've thought about it, and I think you're onto something, but it has to be handled very casually. Lots of people don't want someone nosing into their workout routine. How about I take the course? Maybe I'll learn something, and then we can sit down and talk about the job. I have some thoughts about how to approach this."

She said, "What about money?" He said, "I'm okay for money. I don't need to be paid, but I'm happy to help." She said, "I'll find a way to reward you." Antonio thought *put me back on my fishing boat on a warm Florida morning*. Then he put that faded dream behind him. Syd set him up for the course.

Antonio got his personal trainer certificate, and he and Syd started planning how to approach the gym ambassador project. She said, "We need someone on the floor throughout the opening times. Someone who works out here already. Do you have any recommendations? Are there any other nice guys like you back there?" Antonio didn't know anyone well enough, so they posted the job. Syd knew all her clients and knew what she was looking for. Within a week, they had a small team. Syd's client turnover decreased, they felt good about themselves, and referrals increased. Business was booming. Antonio just kept on doing what he'd been doing.

Meanwhile, Jane thought *it's been over a month and John (Antonio) hasn't contacted me. He could find me through the gym if he wanted to.* She had thought a lot about him and decided to take one more crack at it. She thought *if he doesn't bite, then he's definitely not interested.* She'd checked him out, of course. He'd shared part of his fake back story. It sounded too pat to her. He'd rattled it off fairly quickly and then changed the subject. He was an enigma. No social media presence at all, but that's not unusual for guys his age. Many didn't bother getting into Facebook and all of that. She wondered if he'd had any friends in his old life. People he'd worked with on the farms. It seemed he'd started anew here in Seattle. She was trained to question everything and taught the subject. Her mind flipped a lot of questions over.

She left a note at the gym's front desk, asking him to contact her. Now he had her telephone number and her email. She wondered if he'd respond or completely ghost her. A day and a night went by with no contact. She thought *so that's it. He's not interested.*

When Antonio got the note, he wasn't sure what to do. This woman wanted more, and that was risky. He had thought a lot about her, though, and after sleeping on it, he thought *I could approach it honestly. I'll say, "I'm not looking for a relationship, but I'd enjoy having dinner occasionally." We'll see how that goes.* He phoned her.

Jane said, "Dinner? Sure. How about my place this Friday night?" Antonio thought *her place? Be careful.*

Jane's apartment was a warm home, not a box of rooms. It was painted in soft colors, she had a view of the water, and a gas fireplace was going. The lighting was subdued; some light jazz played, and everything looked inviting. It was the kind of place you could easily curl up on the sofa under a blanket and read a book.

She asked, "Wine, beer, a soft drink?" Antonio said, "A soft drink, thanks." Thinking *have to keep my head straight here."* She said, "I should have asked. I hope you're not a vegan." He said, "Nope, meat and potatoes guy." She said, "Good, that's exactly what you're getting tonight." She was a good cook and served a lightly grilled steak, some interesting potatoes and asparagus. A simple meal. He liked the idea that she wasn't showing off with anything fancy. She was relaxed and at ease as she moved back and forth between the kitchen. They chatted about the gym and the new ambassador program, and she talked about some of her students. It was like being with a comfortable old friend. He said, "I'll make some coffee if you show me where it is. As she stood at the sink, he reached over her head to get the coffee from the cupboard. She turned, facing him as she tried to move out of his way. They looked long at each other. Antonio had no trouble taking his pants off.

She discovered he was a good lover. He knew his way around a woman's body. He'd had a lot of practice. Now, they were both in trouble.

They'd find themselves in each other's beds on Wednesdays, not just the weekend. He'd wanted to keep it loose, but the sex and the easy familiarity were so comfortable. Jane was wary. John's past seemed to be wrapped up into a bow, not to be untied. She had a friend in the police force. She asked him if he could check John out. Her friend didn't look that deeply but came back to her and said, "He is who he says he is. He has no record."

Still, her new lover was a mystery. He was tuned out but very tuned in. He only had a flip phone. John (Antonio) said, "I don't need to be on call 24/7. I'm not a doctor." She noticed his laptop on the floor of his apartment, under a stack of books. He didn't seem to ever use it. He always phoned, never emailed. She didn't know that he spent a lot of time at the library using their computers and WIFI to research his old life or watch his daughter and grandchildren on Facebook. Obviously, he couldn't 'friend' his daughter, but she still left lots of pictures on her site he could look at. He was cautious and took few risks. His relationship with Jane was a risk. She asked a lot of questions.

Lying lazily in bed one Saturday morning, she asked him, "Do you regret not having children? His mind flashed to his two daughters. Then he lied again. "Not at all. I don't think this country wants more Mexicans in it." She said, "What about more Johns? I think that would be a valuable contribution." He didn't answer and got up to pee. End of subject. He didn't ask her about her childbearing hopes. He didn't want to know.

Another time, she asked him if he'd ever considered trying to find his parents or siblings through a DNA match. He said, "Nope, that book's closed." She asked him if that had to do with his Mexican heritage. He looked at her, kissed her quickly and said, "Jane, leave it alone." She assumed it was about being Mexican, but she was wrong. The last thing he needed was to be found by some Mexican relative looking for a reunion. He just wanted her to stop asking questions.

They'd become used to each other's mature bodies. Antonio lay beside her, his hand idly stroking her soft belly or her breasts. He was a big, hairy guy, and she liked running her fingers through his chest hair or down his arms. She asked him, "Why do you shave your head? It looks like you've got a full head of hair. I imagine you with long, thick hair with a streak of gray. Kind of a mad artist look." He said, "I prefer a clean look." She started to say, "But it's probably gorgeous; it could be magnificent." He kissed her and said, "This is what you get." Antonio was thinking *I'm going to have to end this. I don't want to, but the closer we get, the more she wants to know. It's not safe.* The thought of breaking up with her made him very sad. His future years looked lonely.

Antonio wasn't sleeping well. Too many images flashed up in his brain. He kept remembering the last time he saw his second wife, Lily.

She'd come into the kitchen, showered, in a decent pair of shorts and top, not much makeup. She usually rolled in about this time, looking like she'd slept in a dumpster. She was never up this early or this clean. Antonio looked her up and down. His bullshit antenna was up. Without saying anything, she poured herself a coffee and sat at the table. She put her head on the table with her arms crossed and said, "Tony, I know you want me out. I get it. I'll go if it makes you happy. I just don't want you to hate me. We used to be in love. We had so much fun. Let's part friends." Antonio mistrusted this new contrite Lily. She was a schemer, and she was up to something. He said, "Lily, you know this can't be fixed. It's over."

She held her hands up and said, "I know, I know, but let's just go for one last boat ride for old time's sake, and then I'll leave." He said, "You always hated the boat. You said you got seasick. What are you playing at?" She looked up at him, big eyes full of tears. She said, "The ocean is calm. It's a beautiful day. We can let the sea breeze blow away our hate. Let's part with a good memory."

Lily didn't tell Antonio she had no options. She had nowhere to go. Her mother had moved. She had a few couches she could sleep on for a while, but after that, she had nothing. She'd be on the street. She despised Antonio and wanted him dead. Then the condo would be hers, and her troubles would be over. She had a plan.

She didn't know Antonio had mailed a copy of his will and prenup to his daughter. The condo would go to his two daughters if he died.

Antonio mistrusted this new Lily, but he was a sucker for tears. He said, "Alright, let's go for a short boat ride, then I'll help you pack up your stuff." He thought *she's almost gone; I can do this one last thing if it gets her out of my life.*

When they got out onto the water, Lily settled herself at the back of the boat, face to the sun, a slight smug smile on her face. *It'll be over soon*, she thought. Antonio looked at her and thought humorously *bloody queen of the sea*. They got pretty far out, and it was getting choppy, so he decided to turn around and end this. He didn't want her getting sick on his boat.

As he brought the boat around, he thought he heard her say, "Bye, bye Tony." He had his back to her, looked over his shoulder, and asked, "Did you say something?" She said it again. "So long, Tony." He turned around quickly to see she had a gun trained on him. His heart quickened, but he said, "You don't have the guts." He wished he was sure of that. Unmanned, the boat continued to motor forward and lurched on a small wave. It was enough to jar her arm. She shot wildly in his direction, aimed too high, and missed him. Lily was sweating and lost her grip on the gun. It rattled to the bottom of the boat. Her face said it all. She knew he'd turn her in. Her mind was going wild. *I can't do jail again*, she thought, *not for years for an attempted murder charge.* Lily had done a little time in the past.

She reached forward and grabbed the gun off the boat floor, losing her balance as the boat bounced around. As she fell halfway out of the boat, she tried one more time to shoot. The boat pitched sideways, and as she reached for the side of the boat to steady herself, the gun went off. A large red splotch was spreading on her chest. Antonio checked her pulse. She'd shot herself, and she was gone.

Antonio panicked. *Fuck*, he said to himself. He'd be blamed for this, probably charged with her murder. He was innocent, but he'd never be able to prove it. They had a history of arguing. Her friends would know they hated each other. He was Mexican. It was Florida. Not a good combination.

He couldn't see any blood on the boat, but gunshots spattered. If someone was looking, they'd find it. He threw the gun over the side. It wasn't one of his. Small mercies. Then he moved Lily's body over the side and watched her sink. Face up to the sky. Queen of the seas. Then he vomited his guts out off the side. He couldn't stop shaking.

The dock was busy that day but he never talked to anyone there because he fished so early. His slip was at the end of the line beside a large cruiser that never left the dock. He worried that someone would have noticed he was returning without his wife. He needn't have worried. Nobody noticed him go out or come back. He was well hidden behind the larger boat.

He couldn't lose the image of Lily's dead, dark eyes staring at the sky as she sank.

It was early December in Seattle. Cold and damp, still. Antonio hated the weather here. He was at the library, skimming the Florida news, particularly Jacksonville, to see if anything new had been reported about the explosion, the condo and any missing occupants.

His heart skipped a beat. The Jacksonville paper reported, "A woman's skull washed up on Ponte Vedro Beach. It's believed to be Lily Cervantes, Antonio Cervantes's missing wife. Mr. and Mrs. Cervantes lived at Vanilla Palms, the condo with multiple deaths due to an adjacent explosion. Mr. Cervantes was believed to have drowned around the time of the explosion. Police are now investigating a possible murder-suicide." There was no other information about her other than she was his wife. It was a short news item but now, their pictures were at the top of the article.

Now, he's a murderer.

He stared out the window. A light snow had started to drift slowly to the ground.

ESTELLE

Estelle's first night in the New York hotel she'd booked near the bus station wasn't as breezy as she'd thought. It was dirty; it stank of old cigarettes, a cheap deodorizer, and life. A suspicious-looking, short, black, curly hair was in the bathtub. She had to move. She thought, *hell, I've got some money, why not treat myself?* She researched a number of the upper-scale hotels in Manhattan and settled on one called The Big City. It looked pretty cushy. She liked the name. Said it all. She booked in for a month with cash. From here, she could get to know the city, find an apartment, and figure out what she'd do with the rest of her life.

She was observant. She didn't look like a New Yorker. Too Florida touristy, too casual. The women who walked these streets had a lot of style. She needed new clothes. She'd read about a few places to go shopping. There was a fashion district, of course. Why wouldn't there be? That felt too daunting. Her first stop was Orchard Street on the Lower East Side. Interesting clothes in the windows. A young girl with long hair and a nose ring approached her. Estelle said, I've just moved here, and I'm out of touch. I need some help putting a Manhattan look together. The girl was thrilled and started having fun. She pulled outfits off the racks Estelle would have never put together. The girl knew what she was doing. Estelle loved everything she chose. She looked back at herself in the mirror and thought, *I look fabulous!*

She walked miles exploring and figuring out the train and bus systems. She rode out to the outer boroughs to see what the Bronx, Queens, and Brooklyn neighborhoods looked like. She spent many days walking Harlem, the Theater District, SOHO, Greenwich Village, China Town, the Theater District and the Fashion District. She explored every corner she had ever heard of or hadn't heard of. Estelle would stand at the edge of Central Park and look up at the surrounding towers of buildings. She'd heard the wealthiest women in the world lived there. The empresses who'd inherited old money and big corporations from their grandfathers. Divas before the word was invented. She envisioned thin, crepey, powerful women in their eighties, running the world. The city was like a theme park, only it was real. The streets were covered with gum, grot, spit, stains, and the smells of humanity. There were rats and shootings, crazy people screaming on the corner and horns honking. The city was beautiful and ugly, with unique pockets of architecture, surprise graphics, street art, and artistry. Every street was a kaleidoscope of surprises.

Eight million people live in New York City. In a city like New York, you could be from anywhere. Everyone was. They were all aliens. New Yorkers are talkers and will stop and share their opinions with anyone. But if you're in trouble, they'll step right over you.

Estelle loved every inch of New York City.

In her apartment search, she'd stipulated to the agent it had to be below 23rd Street, 1,000 plus square feet, one bedroom, lots of light, sizable closets, a view, an elevator, and ensuite laundry. She wasn't about to start doing her laundry in some old brownstone's dingy, musty basement. She gave the agent a light version of her back story: she'd lived at home, never rented, her mother died, and now she was starting over. Therefore, no previous references. She had cash and wasn't too worried about the rental price. The agent thought *my ideal customer*.

Estelle stopped into the hotel's lobby bar every night for a drink after her city explorations. The people-watching was delicious from this vantage point. Every night, the bar was filled with well-dressed people who looked like they had money and were very busy doing unusual and important things. No shorts and sneakers here. The waiter came to know her and brought her the white wine spritzer she always ordered without being asked. According to his name tag, he was Dieter, and she'd thank him, using his name. He never asked for hers. She thought *probably hotel protocol*.

The person who fascinated her the most was Donald, the concierge. He worked directly across from the bar, and she could watch him in action. He was in his early thirties and always wore a well-cut sports jacket and an open-necked shirt. He looked professional but friendly and casual. His clothes weren't cheap. He was a redhead and wore his hair short. He was a laugher and a bit of a tease. His clients always seemed to be having a good time engaging with him. He greeted everyone with the same big, welcoming smile. He would spend some time questioning them and then go to work. He didn't wear a headphone, possibly too impersonal. She'd watch him switch his phone from ear to ear as he asked his clients more questions and made calls. His clients always seemed to walk away thrilled with whatever and wherever he had found bookings and reservations and tickets for them. No one ever left disappointed. Estelle loved watching his performance.

Estelle had a eureka moment. She could do that. She just needed the connections. She approached him one night, introduced herself with her fake name, Sharon Branson, and said, "Donald, I've been watching you from the bar. You have an interesting job, and you're obviously good at it. Everybody leaves your desk smiling." He smiled and said, "Thanks, I enjoy it." He then said, "Can I help you book something?" Estelle smiled and said, "Not right now," then pushed on. She said, "This will sound strange, but I want to buy some of your time. I'm new to the city and want to learn how to do your job." He laughed and said, "You mean steal my job?" She said, "God, no, that's not what I meant. I would apply elsewhere once I knew what I was doing." He looked her up and down. She was well dressed. No jewelry. Simple, classic. She looked as if she had a bit of money. He liked simple style on a woman. She was older than him, well-spoken, and seemingly sane. He wondered what she was up to, but she seemed sincere. He said, "You do realize we make no money, just above minimum wage. You can't live on what I make in Manhattan." Estelle said, "That doesn't bother me." He said, "Really? It bothers me." He gave it a minute and then said, "I'm not sure if I want to share any trade secrets with a complete stranger. There aren't that many of us in this business." He said, "Do you have a resume?" She said, "No, but don't worry, I have lots of life experience." He wondered what that meant, and his imagination examined some ideas. He didn't come close to reality. He said, "Let me think about it. I'll give you my answer tomorrow."

He slept on it and ultimately decided it wouldn't hurt to have an apprentice. Someone he could trust to fill in for him if he needed it. He decided to take her up on the offer. He could use the extra cash. He thought *we'll see if it's too steep for her. My experience is worth something*. When she showed up at his desk the next night with a hopeful smile, he said, "Tell you what, for $5,000. I'll introduce you around and connect you to all the places you need to go and know about. I haven't got time to take you all over Manhattan, but I'll tell you what to look for and who to watch out for." He continued, "I get Mondays and Tuesdays off. We can start then." Estelle said, "Tell you what. When I get a job, I'll double that $5,000." He said, "Sounds great. It's a deal." Donald didn't believe for a minute he'd ever see that second $5,000. He couldn't believe she'd agreed to the first payment. Didn't even wince. He thought *maybe I should have asked for more.* He said, "I don't want to waste my time; I want the money upfront." Estelle said, "Of course. I know you doubt it, but you will get the second half." He said, "We'll see. There aren't many of us, and we don't move around much." Estelle said, "People's lives change." She thought, *look at mine*. They planned a place to meet on the following Monday and got started.

Estelle wore a slightly edgier outfit when they next met, but it looked good. She also wore sneakers. Donald noticed and said, "Smart girl." He asked, "First of all, how familiar are you with the city?" Estelle rattled off all the places she'd been. He looked impressed and said, "I haven't even been to half those places. That's great. You have a general idea where things are." He said, "There are several categories, for lack of a better term, you'll need to get familiar with. The two biggies are the theatres and the restaurants. With the theatres, you need to know what's on, what it's about, who's in it, when it stops running, times, ticket cost, seating, ticket availability, accessibility, location, and how to best get there. I try to get to all the matinees, so I know what I'm talking about. After a while, they'll comp you tickets. Playbill wil l be your bible."

Restaurants are a category unto themselves because menu and diet restrictions are essential, reviews are important, and there are four levels: ultra high end, high end, medium for the regular people, and bargains for families and young couples, usually. Accessibility is a big issue. Lots of people can't climb stairs." He said, "Then there are all the tourist sites and places people have heard of and just want to walk by." Estelle said, "Times Square being the obvious one." Donald said, "You'll need to know every museum and gallery in town. People are eclectic. Someone will want to see the blue widget museum, and you have to be able to speak a little intelligently about it. Have you been on the Staten Island Ferry? Estelle said, "I have." She said, "And... I've ridden most of the trains and buses and can whistle up a cab." He laughed out loud. She loved that laugh. "You're a natural," he said.

Donald said, "Knowing who to ask for to break through the front line of reservations is important." Estelle asked, "And do you know who to ask for?" He said, "I do, but that'll cost you a bit more." She lifted her eyebrows at him with a grin. She admired his nerve. He was right, though; his knowledge had a price.

And so they started. They worked their way through all the theatres first. Donald seemed to know everybody, and they just waved him in. He walked her through the good and bad seating, washrooms, wheelchair access, exits and some history of each building. Donald knew everything. He knew which buildings had lousy air conditioning or heating. He said, "You need to tell women if they might need a sweater."

That took two full days, and she was exhausted at the end of it. She'd taken notes on her tablet and wanted to retreat to her hotel room and digest it all. She said, "Can I buy you a drink?" Donald declined with a smile. "Thanks, but places to be." She thought, *of course, this charming guy has a life*. He said, "Next, we'll start on restaurants. We won't be eating, just observing, and we'll be out late."

In one very high-end spot, Donald waved at a man in his late sixties sitting in the corner. He was a small man, partially bald and was dressed smartly. Estelle noticed his nails were manicured and polished a very pale pink. She found that a bit creepy. She thought he looked like a mobster. The man beckoned them over, and Donald introduced him as Oscar, the restaurant owner. Oscar eyed Estelle up and down like she was a dripping cold popsicle on a hot day. He reached out to her and clasped her arm. He asked Donald, "Who've you got here?" Donald explained what they were doing. Oscar smiled slyly at Estelle. He was now running his hands up and down her bare arm. He was snake slimy. Oscar said to Estelle, "Let's have dinner, and we can talk. I might be able to help you." Estelle and Donald flickered glances at each other. Estelle said, "Tell you what, I've got a lot going on right now, but I'll give you a call. Do you have a card?" Oscar knew he'd been dismissed and lost interest immediately. He said, "Your loss."

Estelle extricated her arm from Oscar's roaming hands. Estelle thought *I'll definitely remember you, buddy.*

When they got outside, Estelle said to Donald, "I hadn't imagined there'd be a casting couch for this job. What a creep." Donald said, "That creep owns a lot of restaurants in town. If he blackballs you, you're dead. You'll never be able to get a reservation in any of his restaurants." Estelle said, "What did you do to get on his good side? Besides sleeping with him, I mean?" Donald laughed his crazy laugh. "I'm extremely obsequious with him. Yes sir, no sir, you're looking particularly good today, sir, etc.. He's so vain, he eats it up." Estelle said, "I'll remember that. Hopefully, I won't have to surrender my arm or any other body part the next time I meet him."

It took them a month to work through all the places he wanted to show her. On the third week, he suggested she tart herself up a little because they were going clubbing. They worked through all the clubs for five nights in a row, including the better strip clubs. He knew all the guys working the ropes and the lineups and introduced her. He asked if they minded sharing their cell numbers. They looked Estelle up and down, deemed her club material and said sure. She was starting to build a list of contacts. They only stayed at the clubs long enough to get the tour of entrances, exits, washrooms, wheelchair access and what the club offered. New York was a big city to cover. He said, "There's always a new club or restaurant opening or closing, and you need to stay on top of it. He gave her all the social media feeds that provided that.

Meanwhile, Estelle's real estate agent had lined up several apartments for her to look at. Many were just too much money, even though she had lots. Finally, the perfect space came up in a highrise, in the right neighborhood, and had everything she'd asked for. The view wasn't of anything in particular, just the big city. But it was a view. She took it and began ordering furniture. She would move in on the first of the month. Of course, the building had a name. The Arrow.

Estelle wondered if Donald might be gay. He never mentioned any women in his life. He never mentioned any men in his life, for that matter. They often stopped for coffee, and their conversations related to what they'd seen that day and stories he would share about the various locations. After the first week of relentless touring of sites, she looked hard at him and asked, "Who are you really? You don't talk about your personal life. You're all business. Who's the guy underneath all this perfection?" She thought *I've got a lot of nerve asking him that, given I'm a complete fake.* Donald laughed, "Hardly perfect." He said, "I'm married. Her name is Marie, and she's an actress. She's in "Hot Takes" on Broadway right now and working every night." Estelle had fitted in a "Hot Takes" matinee, and it was good. She said, "I've seen that show. Which one is she?" He said, "The lead." She remembered Marie had the stage most of the time and took down the house with her performance. She said, "Lucky man, she's beautiful and talented." He said, "Yes, life is good with Marie."

Estelle wanted to know more, but he was a private guy and pleasantly changed the subject when she brought up Marie again. In fact, he didn't want to talk about where he was from or where he went to school; none of it. New Yorkers like to probe. They're always interested in what college you went to. Then they can place you. It's their silent caste system. Donald hadn't asked and hadn't shared. She thought *he's not a true New Yorker. He's from somewhere else he's not proud of or needed to escape. Or, he could be that rare New Yorker who minds his own business.* She began to wonder if he, too, was on the run. Everybody has secrets.

At one coffee stop, he looked at her and said, "It's none of my business, but you don't seem to be hurting for money. Are you sure you want a job, particularly one where you'll be making crappy money, even with tips?"

Estelle said, "Let's just say I'd go nuts without something interesting to do. Being a concierge is unique, and I think I can do it."

After week four, Donald looked at her and said, "You've done well. I'm impressed. I think you'll be a great concierge." He then said, "We're finished, but you're not. You still need to see all the sports stadiums, a selection of spas, just those that advertise on the internet, concert halls, music venues, ballet, opera, and orchestras. Think of everything someone might want to do in this city and go there." She thanked him profusely for his time. They shook hands, and Estelle took another month to finish off his suggestions.

It was coming up on September, and Estelle thought *I'm ready. Time to get to work.* She'd asked Donald if she could use him as a reference since he'd trained her. He was okay with that.

She called the personnel offices of every hotel in town using a concierge and asked for an appointment. She was offering her services as a temporary concierge. A fill-in. She polished up a resume about her concierge skills with her picture attached. She offered her services on a contract, flat fee basis, with no benefits expected. She didn't say it but she thought, tips are mine. Some agreed to see her and thought it was an interesting concept, even if she had no real experience. Some turned her down flat, so she just dropped off her flier. As it turned out, the Big City Hotel, Donald's, was the first hotel that needed a fill-in. He was taking a few days off and referred her in. Now, she had some real experience.

When she handed him the final $5,000 cash in an envelope, he said, "I would have recommended you even if you hadn't made that offer. Are you sure you can afford it?" Estelle gave his arm a pat. She wasn't a hugger, and you didn't hug Donald. He definitely had a *don't enter my personal space* vibe about him. She said, "I'm sure, do something fun with it." He grinned, "Don't do too good a job. I want my job back." Estelle said, "Are you kidding? I can add this to my resume. I'm a real concierge, thanks to y ou."

Her shift started at 9:00 AM. The early morning clients were looking for lunch spots and things to do the rest of the day. Too many were last-minute artists wanting the best at the latest hour. She found it more challenging than she'd thought it would be. Staying pleasant and calm when people were disorganized and hadn't planned took patience. Not her strength. Estelle deduced the best approach was to assume they were all idiots, and her job was to guide them to satisfaction. It became a game.

Estelle took a page from Donald's book and kidded them about their indecision rather than chastised them. Still, she had to bite her tongue a lot.

Too many visitors would say, "We don't know, we've never been here before. What do you recommend?" Then, she'd start a general interview.

"What brought you to New York? Are you into a Broadway show, a mu-
sical, or any performance? Sports? What about food, restaurants, sightseeing?" She'd use her fallback list of the 20 best things to do in New
York City and start there. Donald had a diary of contacts to refer to,
and she'd work her way through the client's plans, making bookings and
reservations. Invariably, there'd be something someone wanted to see they
hadn't mentioned to their partner or their traveling companions. They'd
then take up her time discussing choices while other clients shifted their
feet impatiently behind them. She'd often send them over to the bar to
figure out their choices and return when they knew what they wanted to
do. It was a balancing act, keeping them all happy and the lineup behind
them satisfied.

She updated her resume with the three days of experience and recirculated
it. Soon, the calls started coming in. "We have a few days next week we need
covered. Are you free?" "Our concierge will be off for a couple of weeks.
Can you cover it?" She was busy, and she was having fun.

Most hotels paid her by check. She'd wanted to avoid banks but figured
if she kept the deposits and withdrawals small, she wouldn't attract the
attention of the IRS. She opened a no-interest checking account, so she
didn't have to claim that. She thought *I'll just set up a small business account
for tax purposes next year, report the income and some tips, and stay honest.
That will keep the IRS eyes off of Sharon Branson.*

She'd return to her apartment at night, pour herself a glass of wine and take
the elevator up to the roof garden. The city would be a sea of lights. She'd
think, *I love my new life.*

Estelle slogged through her first winter. She loved her work but hated
this weather. Slushy, dirty, freezing New York streets weren't the streets of
summer. You learned to stay away from the corners of buildings. Those
winds were bitter and could take you down on an icy day.

Now that she could have any man she wanted, Estelle found she didn't
want any of them. She'd had a lifetime of bad treatment from men and
didn't trust the new interest her pretty face attracted. Besides, dating complicated things. A boyfriend would want to know who she was, where she

was from, her family history, and always, always...where she went to college. She couldn't take that risk.

Still, one guy broke through her wall of resistance. Dieter, the bartender at the lobby bar at the Big City Hotel spotted her when she first started coming in. He was from a small town in Germany, just outside of Nuremberg. He'd come to the States years ago, managed to get his green card, and worked in restaurants and bars ever since. He liked working the bar scene. He thought *you get to see a snapshot of the world in big city bars.*

When Estelle started doing shifts at the concierge desk, he introduced himself and welcomed her to the hotel. Estelle didn't feel like he was flirting or checking her out. It seemed like a genuine gesture of welcome. She didn't realize he'd checked her out months ago and thought she was an interesting-looking woman with a lot on her mind. He'd watched her face change constantly as she eavesdropped on the bar customers. He could also tell by her face some of her concierge clients were pissing her off. He thought that was amusing being in the customer service business himself. You did have to stay contained.

When she'd finish up with a group and send them off happy, he'd cruise by her desk and say, "A glass of wine is only two hours away." He was a tease, and she liked him. He was about forty-six, not great looking, shorter than her by an inch, almost bald, and with the beginning of a belly. His whole look really was non-threatening. He was always smiling. They started getting together for a drink now and then. He never pushed for more. He'd been divorced for eleven years and liked his single life. She liked that because she liked hers too. He was funny. She hadn't laughed much in her life, and he amused her. She always went home feeling good after a few hours with him.

She'd been invited to a special screening of a new movie and had been comped two tickets. It was a hot show, and she got brave and asked Dieter if he'd like to join her. He said, "Sure. But let's have dinner before or after. I know a great place I bet you've never heard of." That was the beginning for them. He kissed her on the hand when he walked her to her cab. She thought *very old world and weird of him to do that. Maybe it's a German thing.* It would be a long time before he got to kiss any other parts of her.

It was a slow courtship. Weeks would go by, and she wouldn't see him. She liked that. He didn't crowd her or expect anything from her. He was also testing the water. *Was she going to be a clingy pain in the ass?*

On the contrary, she was indifferent to his calling or not calling. Sometimes, she'd call him up and suggest a drink. If he couldn't make it, she'd give him a light-hearted "another time." She treated him like a friend, not a potential husband. He wondered if she was even interested in him romantically. They did this easy circle dance for months.

They hadn't been in each other's apartments. Dieter would have liked to at least have moved on to some sex by now, but he wasn't getting an invitation from Estelle. She liked the casual friendship with a nice guy she felt safe with. That's where she would have preferred to leave it. She wondered if the cosmetic surgeon had also removed her sex drive. She wasn't feeling it.

One night, after dinner, she decided to deal with their non-relationship. She liked him and didn't want to hurt him. She came at it sideways and said, "I'm really enjoying our friendship. I'm sure you have some actual romances going on somewhere. I want you to know If our friendship ever seems to bother anyone you're involved with, some women don't like their lovers having female friends; I'll step back; give me the word."

He looked at her and laughed. "Catch anything with that long fish pole of a story there?" Then he said, "I'm not seeing anyone." He went back to his dinner and changed the subject. Estelle was surprised; she felt some relief.

She'd tipped her hand. Dieter now knew she was interested.

About a week later, he decided to jump into the deep end. He invited her to his place for dinner. Estelle asked, "You can cook?" Dieter said, "I won't poison you." She said, "Can I think about it?" He said, "Sharon, I have no sexual designs on you if that's what you're worried about." Estelle wasn't used to him calling her by her fake name. He'd called her bluff; she had no excuses. She said, "Of course not, me either." He said. "Good. Then, we're both saved from the den of sin. It's just dinner."

His apartment was what she thought of as 'very male.' Like most Manhattan apartments, it was small but had a good layout. His dark leather furniture was too big for the space. She thought, *what's with guys and leather furniture?* He had a few good pieces of art, a well-stocked bookcase of mysteries and a big screen TV taking up too much of a wall. A few of his surfaces could have used a dusting, but overall, the apartment was tidy. Like her apartment, he had a view of the city but nothing recognizable. He poured some wine, turned on some easy music and returned to his cooking. She sat at the bar watching him. He was comfortable in the kitchen. She hadn't known this about him. She wondered what else she didn't know. He had a couple of frying pans sizzling something and at least two other steaming pots of something.

He served up a delicious schnitzel, which they ate together in silence. He said, "I was going to suggest we go down to the corner to the bakery for dessert." Estelle said, "I'm stuffed, Dieter. I couldn't eat another thing." He then said something that really amazed her. He said, "I was never a good dancer, and I've been taking dance lessons over the past couple of months. Do you care to risk it and do a few spins around the floor? We could work off dinner." Estelle laughed out loud. She said, "How many more secrets do you have, a cook and now a dancer?" He said, "That's it, you've seen all my surprises." She said, "I'm not much of a dancer myself. Are you sure you want to risk it?" He changed the music to some old eighties ballads and offered his hand to her. She kicked off her shoes and joined him. His hand was firm across her back as he guided her through a slow dance. They were almost even with her shoes off, and their cheeks were together while they moved slowly to the music. He moved her around the small apartment floor space with a slow rhythm. She relaxed into it. He was easy to dance with. After about twenty minutes, he leaned back, looked at her, and asked, "May I?" She didn't say no, or anything for that matter, but his kiss was long, warm, and tender. She didn't regret it.

After she'd gone to sleep, he lay beside her, watching her. She twitched in her sleep, never seeming to relax. Her makeup had come away a bit, and he noticed the very fine white scars around the perimeter of her face. He thought *she's had a major overhaul. Strange for such a young woman. She wouldn't have needed anything done yet.* Then he thought *maybe another reason, an accident, abuse? She doesn't talk about her past at all. Shuts it down if I ask anything*. He also thought *she'll tell me in time. It's none of my business.*

At about four in the morning, Estelle sat up straight in bed with a night-mare memory of Rudy's murder in her head. Dieter woke and said, "Are you okay?" She said, "Yeah, yeah, go back to sleep, just a bad dream." He was aware of her awake for another hour, staring at the ceiling, her hands knotted tight on the duvet. He thought *this girl has secrets.*

Estelle woke in his bed the next morning and thought, *now what?*

Dieter came bouncing in, dressed only in his jockeys and offered her a cup of coffee. He was not self-conscious about his body. Completely comfortable. He said, "I suspect you'll want to escape." He said, "I'd love for you to stay, but it's up to you." She said, "Thanks, Dieter, but I've got things to do, and I need to shower, change, do my hair, powder my nose." He said, "It's winter. Nobody's going to see what you've got on. I've got clothes that will fit you with a belt. You can wash your face, put on some lipstick and be good to go. Estelle thought *I've got a bit more to hide than lipstick will take care of.*

Dieter said, "I go roller skating on Saturday afternoons. Come with me." She said, "You are full of surprises. How did cooking, dancing, and roller skating never come up in our conversations over the past six months?" He said, "I like to be active." She said, "Besides, I don't know how to roller skate." He said, "You must have had a deprived childhood." Estelle thought *you don't know the half of it.* He said, "I just learned last year. I'll teach you. It's easy. It's fun." She said, "Dieter, I've got three concierge bookings in the next two weeks. I can't do them in a cast." He said, "I'll be there. You won't fall." His words carried more meaning than roller skating. This guy was so light-hearted and fun, he was hard to resist. She kept thinking *trouble, trouble, don't get too close.* She did take a pass on the roller skating.

Estelle was getting a lot of work and had to turn down offers because she was totally booked. At the same time, she was enjoying the work less and less. Her patience for some of the clients was running thin. For someone who'd had her unfortunate looks judged all her life, Estelle was very judgmental.

At one hotel, there was a demanding client who stayed often. The woman had a large head with oversized features, nose, eyes, and lips. She wore exaggerated eye makeup on those big eyes, very red lipstick, and had a mass of messy, thick dark hair, barely confined in a top knot. She was big, loud and demanding. This woman brought out the bitch in Estelle, and she'd think, I bet she spends a fortune waxing her mustache and legs. The woman was never satisfied.

At another hotel, there was Squeaky Fromme. Obviously, not the real Squeaky. That Squeaky was out of jail and living somewhere in Syracuse. Estelle had never heard the actual 'Squeaky' speak, but it was how she imagined she'd sound. This woman looked like her voice, high and nasal, very pale with a sharp, thin nose over nonexistent lips. Exactly the noise one would expect from that face. This woman could never decide what to do and wasted Estelle's time.

Then there were the talkers. People who tripped over their words trying to vomit all of their racing thoughts out at one time. They were martyrs to their flapping mouths, unaware and unable to control the spew of disconnected thoughts they desperately needed to share or would die. Or so it seemed. They were also time wasters. Estelle had a tactic of visually drawing her hand in front of the person's face to break their stream and saying firmly, "Let's get back to your bookings."

Conversely, there were the unresponsive men. They looked startled when you asked them what they wanted to do. Estelle would think *where did you think you were going when you got in your car, or the bus or the plane?* Then there were the sports nuts. They just wanted to go to a game. She knew when they returned to their hotel rooms they'd turn the TV to a game somewhere and tune out their partner. They hadn't bought into this trip. Everybody has their own addiction.

Estelle started to think maybe it was time to consider other work.

Estelle hadn't forgotten the so-called all-powerful Oscar, the restaurant owner. Unless you knew someone inside, you had to book into his high-end restaurants months ahead. The midrange restaurants were relatively easy, but you needed to know someone. When Estelle was working,

she never booked any of them. She pretended to check if they were requested and said, "Sorry, they're totally booked; how about..., and she would
provide another recommendation." It was a small thing, but she enjoyed
boycotting Oscar's restaurant emporium. She remembered his tight grasp
on her arm while he stroked it. He was predatory, and she wasn't going to
help his business.

Oscar kept close tabs on his bookings and knew what to expect from all the
city hotels. He started to notice some minor blips. There'd be a two-day
freeze from a usually reliable hotel, then a one-week freeze from another.
It would be brief, and then bookings would pick up again. Oscar didn't
know Estelle was boycotting him, and he couldn't nail it down because she
moved around.

He sent in a plant, one of his friends, to one of the larger hotels he was
losing bookings at. Estelle happened to be working that day. Oscar's friend
specifically asked for one of Oscar's restaurants. Estelle pretended to call,
acted out a false conversation and turned to the person and said, "I'm
so sorry, they're totally booked that night. I have several other excellent
recommendations though." The fake client reported back to Oscar.

Later that week, Estelle was working a shift at the same hotel. She felt
someone looking at her from across the hall. She looked up and recognized
Oscar immediately. He smiled coldly at her and pretended to shoot a gun
at her with his hand and fingers. Then he left. She wondered if that was a
threat? Oscar looked like he could be dangerous. She started watching her
back when she walked home and more often grabbed a cab so she couldn't
be followed. It was a big city, and bad things could happen. She bought a
gun. Life and her false sense of safety had subtly changed.

She spoke with Donald about it. He said, "Why don't you just throw him
a bone with some bookings, get him off your tail." She said, "Because he's a
bully and a slimeball and doesn't deserve it." Donald said, "Be careful. He
knows everybody. He could cut off your concierge bookings."

Over the spring, Estelle noticed her phone was ringing less often. Her
bookings had dropped off considerably. She'd been hit with the Oscar

curse. He'd murdered her new career, not her. She'd tired of it anyway. It didn't hurt a bit. Time for a change.

She and Dieter had agreed to proceed very slowly and keep it cool. She loved being with him but couldn't afford to start loving him. That wasn't in the cards. He was okay with that. He thought *at least she doesn't want to get married. I'm done with marriage.* Once they both understood this wasn't going anywhere, it was easier. No expectations. She never invited him to her place, and he never asked her why. Again, he thought *her business. She must have her reasons. Maybe it's a crummy apartment.* She didn't want him to see she was living in a more expensive place than his and wonder where the money came from.

Then she'd have to make up another lie, and they were piling up.

Back in Miami, Phil had received bad news. He had stage four kidney cancer and had been given a few months. He was on dialysis but had a few days off between treatments. He'd always wanted to visit New York City, see a Broadway show, and stand in Times Square. He loaded himself up with painkillers and flew up, checking himself into The Big City Hotel. He liked the name. It turned out to be an interesting few days. He wasn't supposed to drink, but he thought, *screw it, I'm dying* and headed down to the lobby bar.

He gazed across at the female concierge. She had lifted her head to look at her clients. Estelle had always had a quirky lip turn up on the left side when she smiled. The surgeon hadn't changed that. Phil thought *can't be, that woman doesn't look like Estelle, other than that little lip thing. Probably a coincidence.* Then Phil heard her voice.

Estelle was working on some paperwork and had her head down. She became aware of someone standing quietly in front of her desk. She put a smile on her face, lifted her head, and got ready for the next client. She really wasn't in the mood today. Standing there was a thin, pale, sickly man staring hard at her. There was some malice in those eyes. It made her uneasy. Estelle didn't recognize him until he spoke.

PHIL

Before Phil came to New York, he'd been sitting at his desk in Miami thinking about Mike the Spike. The million bucks Mike left him was sitting nicely in a T-bill, less the purchase of his new car. He didn't need much, and the money was good security for later. He wasn't fool enough to blow it all. He didn't have health insurance, and he might need it someday. His curiosity was getting the better of him. He wanted to know more about this kind man, this cat lover, this reputed mobster. Phil thought, *what was his real story? How dirty was this money he'd left him?*

The only person who might have inside information about Mike would be the woman who'd worked for him. There'd been a brief note about the housekeeper in Mikes's death notice, but her name wasn't mentioned. He knew the neighborhood Mike had lived in, but not his address. He decided to look her up. When he drove there he found a walled neighborhood, lots of security, very private. The houses you could see behind the walls screamed, "We've got a lot of money." A few gardening companies were working around, and he thought if anybody knew where Mike had lived, one of these guys would know. Phil was wearing his large, loose shorts and shirt. He was obviously not carrying a gun. He didn't look dangerous. The Mexican guy he stopped and asked looked him up and down and quickly decided that dead Mike the Spike's security wasn't his business. He directed Phil down the street to Mike's old house. Phil drove up to a twelve-foot brick wall dripping with ivy, a locked drive-through double oak gate, and a security system. He got out of the car, spoke into the box and said who he was. There was a good chance the housekeeper didn't live here, or the place had been sold, and he'd never find her. No one answered. He suspected someone was watching him through the camera. It could just be the new housekeeper.

He drove home and left it for a week, thinking maybe no one was there. When he returned and spoke into the box again, a female voice said, "You're a persistent fuck, aren't you?" Phil laughed and said, "Sorry to bother you. I'll go away if you'd prefer." He then stood there and waited for a response. The gates slowly opened, and he drove up a long lane through waving palms and heavy gardens. It was a private park. When he walked up to the house door, it opened a slice and a short woman in her sixties stood there. She had cropped dark dyed hair, a bit too much makeup, and was wearing black tights with a floral shirt over top. She was thick through the middle and sported a dark tan. Her nails were daggers, painted an ungodly shade of purple. She was a woman who'd come into a lot of money, but it hadn't changed the housekeeper.

Phil stood in the doorway, hot and sweating. He wore a loose sky-blue nylon shirt over his big belly, and his patterned shorts looked like he'd been in them for days. He had. Phil didn't pay much attention to his appearance. Jo, the now-retired housekeeper, looked him up and down and said, "Well, you don't look like a millionaire." Phil didn't think she did either but decided to keep his mouth shut. He offered his hand and said, "Hi, I'm Phil from the Dog Shelter." She wasn't used to shaking hands and offered the ends of her fingers. She said, "I'm Josephine, but my friends call me Jo." Phil said, "I'll make no assumptions. We've just met."

She brought him into a beautiful large living room. The whole house was stunning. Phil took some time and looked around. "This place is fabulous. Are you enjoying it?" He asked. She said, "Yes, but it's not the same without Mike. I miss him. He was my boss, but we were friends for years." Phil said, "I miss him too. He loved my old cats."

She said, "You do look like you need a cold beer. Any preference?" Phil said, "Amstel?" She said, "Aren't you fancy?" She then said, "How about a Coors?" Phil said, "Whatever you've got." She disappeared into another room that housed a giant cooler. Phil thought *she could keep a body in there.* She said, "Have a look around. This is all Mike's taste, but I like it." Phil stuck to the massive living room and went onto the deck. It looked down over an expansive manicured lawn that ran down to the water. A ten-foot security fence surrounded the property, and cameras were everywhere. He said, "How are you maintaining all this?" She said, "Mike took care of all that before he died. I have no expenses, property taxes, groundskeeping or security costs. All paid for in perpetuity by Mike's estate." Phil said, "I'm surprised the feds didn't seize it all." She tapped her nose and said, "Mike gave me good advice. He left enough money in my name to pay for all this, and the feds don't know where the rest of the money is". Phil said, "And you're not sharing." She said nothing, just smiled.

They settled in two lounge chairs on the deck. Jo looked at Phil and said, "Well, why are you here, really?" Phil said, "Mike was very generous to me. I just wanted to know more about him. I guess I kind of want to know whether that was blood money of some sort." She laughed out loud and said, "Well, if it was, you couldn't give it back now, could you?" He said, "No, but I might think differently about how to use it." She said, "Six million is a lot of money. No reason you couldn't put it to some good use." Phil coughed and had a hard time not showing his surprise. He thought *six million, not one million. Did someone get to that bag before he did? It was sitting outside. Anybody could have gone through it?"* She said, "I helped him pack it up in that bag."

Phil said, "So, he was obviously a mobster; that was in the paper, but he got off. What happened there?" She said, "People got paid off, and the charges went away." He said, "What did 'the spike' refer to in his nickname, dare I ask." She laughed and said, "He was a golfer and loved spiked golf shoes. He collected them. He never 'spiked' anyone that I'm aware of." He said, "That's a relief; how did he make all his money?" She said, "He had his hands in various sources." He wasn't killing anyone or selling drugs. It was all 'white collar crimes,' as they say. He stole from the rich." Phil said, "and gave to the poor?" Jo said, "He spread it around to some good causes before dying. You were one of them." Phil said, "So, Robin Hood, in the end?" She said, "Well, hood, at least."

They sat together quietly, drinking, staring out at the water, out of things they wanted to share. Phil rose to leave. He had what he came for and then some. He thanked her for filling him on Mike and wished her well in her new life. She said, "You too. Splurge and get some new clothes, why don't you?"

He drove home thinking *six million? Where's the other five?"*

Joe, the detective, had asked him the last time he'd seen Estelle. Phil had to think about it. She was in town at least once monthly to see her clients, although he didn't know if she always saw him. They'd had dinner together the last time he saw her, but she hadn't stayed over. Then she went quiet. She'd stopped answering her texts or her phone. He didn't have Janie's number. He started thinking about her Rudy story with him hitting her.

He began to worry. He'd found her building and the property management contact and heard about the explosion. Except her body wasn't there.
Now he was really worried. They'd been friends for so long he'd forgotten
she'd picked up his accounting information the night the money bag was
probably dropped off. He thought she might be murdered. He did not put
her together with the missing money. She wasn't a thief. She was his friend.
He was so naive.

When they found her apartment tumbled with all her stuff still there, he
was sure Rudy had killed her. It had been too long. His old friend was gone.
It was easy to dispose of a body in the Florida swamps. Nothing lasted long
out there. Lots of hungry creatures ready to feast.

After a while, Phil stopped worrying about the missing five million. The
money was gone, probably to some street person who put it up his veins. It
had never been his. He could hardly report it to the police. His remaining
nest egg was growing slowly, and he enjoyed reading his bank statements.
As for Estelle, he missed her.

About a year later, Phil woke up one morning and vomited up his guts. He
was so shaky he could hardly stand. He let it go for a day and felt worse. Sick
as the proverbial dog. By day three, he called 911. Something was seriously
wrong with him.

Chapter Nine

SNAKES AND LADDERS

Eight months after the explosion, the Vanilla Palms condo sat alone in the Florida heat in silence, blinds drawn, windows dark. It was a graveyard. The nosy 'lookie-loos' had long given up. Nothing to see. Just an empty building with a terrible story.

Its almost new white stucco exterior was still pristine, reflecting the sun. Billy had pulled the shades in each apartment to protect the contents from sun bleaching. It still gave him the creeps entering all these people's former lives. Zenith had kept on the grounds workers. The grass was mowed, and the shrubbery clipped. Cicadas sang with the birds, and the three large palm trees trucked in when the building was constructed waved in the breeze. At night, the building sat there, dark and unwelcoming.

Because of the risk of poisoned air from the explosion, no one but the professionals were let into the Industrial Park for weeks after the explosion. Once the air was considered safe, only the other industrial businesses were allowed to return to their sites. They were told to bring in bottled water to drink. They weren't sure of the groundwater.

Twenty-three owners and renters were away when the explosion happened. Most had returned to their apartments and moved their things out entirely. They couldn't fathom living there again with the ghosts in the hallways.

Morty, the condo board chair and his wife had moved into their daughter's back bedroom. It was uncomfortable. None of them wanted to live that close to each other.

Six people were still missing. Billie and Joe had been working hard to find Estelle, Randy, Claire, Antonio and his wife, Lily, and Michael. Only Claire and now the FBI and CIA knew Michael's real name. They still didn't know who Claire was. Certainly not who she really worked for. She was under suspicion.

The cause of the explosion next door had still not been determined. Class action lawsuits were launched, lawyers were making money, realtors were contacted, and banks examined their mortgages. The banks placed liens on the condos with unpaid mortgage payments, and the utility companies and city did the same for their missing payments. Zenith did not place liens for missing condo payments. He had another plan. The power stayed on for now. Many estate inheritors had initially kept up the payments to maintain the value, thinking they'd sell when the dust settled.

As the months went by, and it was taking forever for lawsuits and insurance payments to be settled, most of the remaining owners and heirs to the dead owners just wanted the building to come down. A town hall meeting was called. It was a mad Jerry Springer show. Grief and anger and yelling. Most were willing to take the land value of the condo and call it a day. Some of the owners wanted to take their chances and sell. They came to no agreement.

Billy, Joe and Zenith attended all the meetings. The boys thought someone might have an idea where the missing people were. Other than Morty, the condo president, none of the surviving owners remembered the missing people. No one recognized their driver's license pictures. "Did they live here?" They'd ask. "I don't remember them."

At the last meeting, the owners and the inheritors decided to strike a committee to decide what to do. Zenith had other ideas. He walked to the front of the room and took the microphone. He said, "Hello, my name is Zenith Bachman. I own the property management company that manages Vanilla Palms, among many other condos in Florida. Let me first extend my condolences on your great loss. This is a tragedy beyond comprehension, and I know you are all in pain." The room was silent. Most were thinking *who is this guy with the accent, and what does he want?*

Zenith went on, "I've been attending these meetings to hear what you all had to say and to get a feel for how you want to proceed with your condos or inheritances. You should know that your land value would be maybe $50,000 or $100,000 in an equal location without soil contamination. Here, it will be next to nothing. No developer will rebuild and take on the cleanup costs. Now, they say the soil isn't contaminated. If you were buying in here, would you believe them? If you tear the building down and try to get land value, you'll get next to nothing. I also believe selling these condos in the short term will be very difficult. Not many people will want to buy into a building where so many people died.

Zenith paused, looked down, and then looked straight at the audience. "I'm offering to buy your condos at a flat rate. The price I would be offering would be better than land value, but not what they would have been valued at before the explosion. A woman shouted out, "Many of our insurance companies won't pay until they know if it was a bomb that blew the depot up. Terrorism notwithstanding clauses." Zenith said, "That's something each of you must work out with your insurance carriers. That's out of my hands. I'm just offering you a way out without losing everything."

A man stood up and asked, "What's in it for you?" Zenith answered, "Good question. It's a big financial gamble. In the long term, people will always be looking for a bargain in Florida real estate. I have deeper pockets and resources many of you don't have. I can afford to wait for the market to return. For those of you who don't have the resources or interest to hold onto your condos and carry the expenses, I can help.

Another male stood up and yelled, "And make a lot of money later." Zenith stayed calm, as he always did. He said, "Yes, I'm hoping to make a little money, eventually. You're right. But if I can't sell the condos later, I also stand to lose a lot of money.

Meanwhile, if I'm the owner, I'm covering the ongoing utility and property tax expenses, not you. I'm making an offer. I'll leave it with you for a week. The owners present will know Billy, our property manager. He'll leave his number, and you can get in touch if you want to arrange this." He thanked them for their time, exited the podium and left the room. Brief and to the po int.

Billy was floored. He thought *Zenith has that kind of money? Must be his silent partner.* Once again, he wondered who that might be.

The meeting adjourned right after that, and people lined up to leave their information with Billy. It appeared most of them wanted to take Zenith up on his offer. They wanted to sell. Billy said he would get back to them and make appointments with their lawyer.

Morty stood at the back of the room and started to think. He wanted his old life back. He walked over to Billie and said, "Let's talk."

Florida continued to tick over through its various tourist seasons. Snowbirds came for the winter, and young families visited for a week in the summer for Disney and a cheap summer holiday. Fried tourists lay on the beach destined to remove moles and crusty bits later in life, many too late to save them.

Billy and Joe continued their search for the missing people.

ANTONIO AND LILY

With Antonio and Lily, the boys first went through everything in their apartment and car. Antonio's car had been found down at the docks where Antonio fished. Antonio's laptop didn't yield much. His utility bills and property taxes were emailed to him, but there was no evidence of a bank account. The bills were all paid on time, so he must have been using money orders or going to the offices and paying cash. His internet searches were limited to food deliveries and sites about fishing. He wasn't on any social media other than Facebook and Instagram, but he hadn't posted anything. He didn't read any news feeds. They noted he'd been following his Vancouver daughter. He'd used a fake name and a dog picture as his ID. *Antonio was a dull boy*, Joe thought, *or a very careful boy*. His phone had no calls to Lily, which they found strange. Did they not communicate? Morty had said they fought a lot.

His storage locker contained some fishing gear but little else. There was a gun in Antonio's car and one in a locked cabinet in the den where he seemed to have been sleeping. Neither had been fired.

They found Lily's cell phone stuck in the bedding on the bed. That was valuable because she'd called a lot of people, and it led them to the people she hung out with. There were several men's names. When called, they were all cautious, asking, "Where did you get my number?" When Joe would say it had been found on Lily's phone, many said, "You must have got the number wrong; I've never heard of this Lily." Joe would say, "Well, she called you at this number over a dozen times in the last year. I think you did know her." Some would say, "Look, my wife can't find out about this. It's my business. Don't call me again." A few would say, 'Yeah, I knew Lily. We hooked up now and then." Apparently, Lily had been selling her favors. More interesting was she'd also been researching how to buy a gun on the black market, how to kill someone and get away with it, how to move a large body and how to get rid of a body. The boys thought she was planning to kill Antonio. They wondered if that was what really happened. He didn't accidentally drown?

Lily also had a couple of regular people she knew at a bar she frequented, but they couldn't remember the last time they'd seen her, and it had been a while. These people were in bad shape, and it was a miracle they could remember anything. The boys deduced Lily had been living on the edge even while married to Antonio.

In the same locked cabinet with the gun, they'd found Antonio's will, leaving everything to his daughters, along with a copy of his prenup from when he married Lily in Vegas. There was only one contact for one of the daughters. She lived in Vancouver, Canada. When they called her, she wasn't very receptive. Billy introduced himself and told him about the explosion. He said, "However, your father didn't die there. He is missing, and it's believed he might have drowned in a boating accident the morning of the explosion. Just a bad coincidence. He's left the condo to you and your sister." She was quick to answer." I don't want his condo. He was a bastard to my mother. My sister can make her own mind up. She can have my share." She neglected to say she'd already accepted a half million from her dad before her parents split, not to mention her half of her mother's million-dollar inheritance. The boys got the U.K. sister's contact. She was more receptive to the money. She said, "I hated him, but I'll take his money. There must be more somewhere. He was living on something. He received a big insurance payout for his accident, and he gave my mother and us more than two million between us."

This daughter was also clever. She said, "There must be a big lawsuit around the explosion. Was the condo insured? My dad's estate would get a piece of that, right?" Billy said, "We couldn't find any paperwork regarding insurance, banking or anything else for that matter." He then said, "You're right about lawsuits. A class action suit against the chemical depot is going on, and it could be worth a few million. Given your father didn't actually die because of it and doesn't appear to have been there, he might not be eligible." He went on, "You might want to speak to your sister again about sharing.". Billy took the time to tell her that in Florida, her father had to be missing for five years before she could claim her share of the estate. She said, "So, the condo sits vacant until then?" Billy said, there's a possible buyer if you want to sell. You wouldn't get much, but you'd probably get more than land value if the building was torn down. I can arrange a Zoom appointment if you'd like." Antonio's youngest thought *it will take time, but I'm coming into a lot of money. Thanks, you old bastard.* She said, "Have that buyer call me." Joe reminded her again she couldn't touch anything for five years.

Antonio's disability insurance payout seemed like it might be a fruitful lead. They started with disability claims lawyers in Florida. No one was talking or admitting they'd done business with Antonio. The boys figured he must have placed a non-disclosure on the business being awarded. More secrets. They thought he may have a large bank or investment account somewhere, but banks and investment companies don't talk either. His old employer claimed they had no record of him ever working there. Joe and Billy laughed about that lie. "Our insurance company paid out a whopping sum to him, but we've never heard of him." They thought, *sure*. They'd reached another dead end.

Joe told Billy, "Other than that hideous bedroom where Lily must have slept, Antonio's life was too tidy. It looked intentional. No discernible records in his apartment, and then he drowns? Like he didn't want anyone checking him out. Something doesn't feel right. He must have been using another phone and/or laptop where his real life was recorded."

Joe called the daughter in Vancouver again and mentioned the potential lawsuit payout in case the U.K. sister decided not to share. It might be a lot of money she was turning down. He also had a tug in the back of his mind and asked her, "If your father just wanted to disappear, any idea where he might go?" She said, "Do you mean he didn't drown?" Joe said, "Without a body, we can't be sure." She said, "I haven't seen him in years. He married that cheap broad Lily in Vegas and sent me a copy of the will and the prenup, so I knew that existed. He obviously didn't want to leave anything to her." She went on, "I have no idea where he'd go. He liked to fish and screw around. That's all I can tell you."

Then Lily's skull rolled up on the beach, and the game changed. Another coincidence? She traveled with a rough crowd and could have been murdered by anyone. Some 'John' who just wanted to shut her up. Had she killed Antonio, or had she hired someone to kill him, then they killed her? Too many questions and no proof. However, Antonio was now under suspicion of murder, and so were all the 'John's' in her contact list. If they could only find Antonio or at least his body.

Joe talked to his chief about going after the men on Lily's contact list. He asked, "Should we chase this down? If so, I've got a lot of in-depth interviewing to do with a lot of men who won't want to talk to the police." The chief said, "Let me think about it. You don't have a lot to go on other than a skull. You don't know how she died. She could have been drunk or stoned and just fell in the water. You don't even know if she was murdered. You have a possible motive but no murder weapon. It would be a hard case to build and prove against any of them." Joe said, "I agree, but I didn't want to just leave her dead without anyone looking into it." His chief said, "We may have to. We have too many murders to follow up on as it is. Leave it with me for a few days."

ESTELLE

Joe and Billy scouted Estelle's apartment and deduced she'd left quickly. All her personal things were still there, including her toothbrush, makeup, pots and potions, underwear, purse with cash, and laptop. An older cell phone sat on her desk with nothing questionable on it. There were a few calls to clients and to Phil, but her records didn't go back far. Phil told them she'd lost her phone recently and replaced it with a new one. Joe and Billy wondered if she'd ditched the previous phone for some reason. *Was there something incriminating on it?*

Her laptop held all her client files, locked down, but forensics found them. They were all straight bookkeeping files. They followed up with all her clients. All confirmed they hadn't heard from her in a long time. She'd disappeared and cut off all contact without any warning or notice. She wasn't on any social media, which they found odd. There were old emails and texts back and forth between clients and also with Phil. They matched dates he'd said he'd seen her last. The overturned chair and coffee cup in the kitchen meant something. They just weren't sure what. They only found Estelle and Rudy's fingerprints when they fingerprinted the apartment. Rudy's fingerprints were all over the kitchen, so he'd definitely been there. Her car was still parked outside.

When Joe followed up the Rudy lead and discovered he'd been found murdered weeks before the explosion, that elevated their interest. They checked with Estelle's old bar-hopping buddy, Janie, for more information on Rudy. Janie remembered the night they'd met and that Rudy had been all over Estelle. Rudy had a long sheet of charges, mostly drugs, a few break-ins and some violent attacks on women. He wasn't a nice guy. When they questioned his bar friends, they clammed up. The bartender said he was often buzzed but not on booze. He said Rudy didn't actually drink that much. Rudy's killer had never been found. It was assumed it was another drug deal gone wrong or a payback. There hadn't been a lot of follow-up. The lives of addicts and small-time drug dealers were cheap in Florida. There were bigger fish to fry.

When they sat down to look at the security tapes of the building's entrances, they realized the door to the parking lot had no active security cameras. They sat through a month of tapes for the lobby and saw nothing out of the ordinary. People coming and going, checking their mail, minding their own business. No sign of Rudy coming or going, so he must have entered through the parking lot door. People still had to be buzzed up, but there was no record of that. When the tape flipped over to the month prior to that one, it gave them no new information. They brought Morty in to identify their missing people. Now, they had visuals of Estelle, Antonio, and Randy checking their mailboxes. Not Michael. He obviously wasn't expecting mail. They all used the parking lot door rather than the front door, so there was no record of their comings and goings. Tapes older than three months had been automatically erased.

There was something about the previous month's tape that was bugging Billy. In the first one, one of the owners wore a bright orange shirt. A memorable shirt. He'd stopped at his mailbox, dropped an envelope on the floor and stooped to pick it up. He said, "Joe, play back the previous month again. I want to check something." Joe pressed rewind, and fifteen minutes into it, Billy said, "There, that guy appears doing the same thing in the first month's video." They realized they'd been watching a loop of the previous month. Someone had messed with the video, and it was someone who knew what they were doing to change the daily date and time to match the current one. Joe slapped Billy on the back and said, "You really should think about becoming a detective."

The security company manned 20 screens for different properties and barely glanced at the Vanilla Palms screen. Just a bunch of old people salted with a few younger ones checking their mail. Nothing to see here.

CLAIRE

Of the missing people, Claire and Michael were the only ones they'd identified with any technical skills. Enough to know how to change the security video camera.

Claire also left her apartment in a hurry, leaving her toothbrush, underwear and clothes behind. There was no evidence of makeup in her bathroom at all. Probably didn't wear any. There was a wallet with about $50. cash in it, no cell phone, no gun. Her laptop was locked entirely. When forensics finally cracked into it, which took some time, they only found connections to her work files, nothing out of the ordinary. Another person with no social media connections. Another missing person who didn't want to share her life with anyone snooping around.

Like Antonio, she'd left no paperwork, receipts, proof of rent payments, or bank statements. She was receiving a pay cheque. She must have been depositing it somewhere. But where?

Joe said, "I think we have another one using alternative cells and laptops that she didn't want anyone to see." Billy said, "And probably an exterior hard drive she took with her."

Joe and Billie met with Claire's boss, Monty. He was very worried about his favorite girl. Claire hadn't checked in for a month, and her work logs were inactive. *Where was she?* Next to Monty, she had the highest security access in the company. She could get into every one of his clients' accounts. *Had she been kidnapped? Would he get a ransom request?* He checked all her reports for the past year. She'd followed company security protocol criteria obsessively.

He didn't know she'd covered up Malek's tracks. Catching him had become a game of chess for her. She'd shut him down. Then he'd pop up again. Monty also didn't know she'd moved out of Miami and was now living in this condo hours away from the office. *What was she doing up there?*

Monty wondered if she'd been murdered in some random hold-up. Joe said, "We don't have any unidentified murder victims that match her pro-file. We have no proof she's been murdered. She could have just disap-peared on her own. People do that all the time. We don't know anything yet." Joe went on. He said, "No gun was registered to her." Monty said, "That doesn't surprise me; she was pretty quiet and peace-loving." Or so Monty thought. He was cautious about what he shared with these two guys; they didn't learn much. The day after Joe and Billy visited him, he was visited by one agent each of the FBI and the CIA. They said, "We have reason to believe your employee Claire was with the Russian SVR. In case you weren't aware, that's their version of the CIA."

Monty was shocked. He thought *Claire was a Russian spy? What was she doing with his client files all these years? What had she shared?* His whole business reputation was at stake if this got out. The CIA would want to interview his clients, especially the big ones that might have something of interest to Russia. Many of his clients were tech companies, continually developing new technology. They also handled big contracts for foreign countries. That information would be valuable to an enemy country.

When Joe and Billy left Monty's office, Joe said, "I have a feeling about this woman. She was a senior hacker with a big security firm. She had access to a lot of cash and a lot of secrets. Now she's missing." Let's dig a little deeper. Where was she from again?" Billy said, "Idaho."

Joe looked at Billy. He said, "It's a big state. Do you want to take a crack at finding out anything you can about Claire Richmond from Idaho? Billy said, "Way ahead of you. I've checked all the schools in every city in Idaho she might have attended. No record. She may have been homeschooled. I also checked the obits, looking for her parents, siblings, and grandparents. No luck. I did find one little item. A baby named Claire Elizabeth Rich-mond was born and died around the time that would match Clair's age. It looked like she only lived a week." Joe said, "Wow, good work. She must have been operating with a fake ID all these years."

RANDY

Joe and Billy had done quite a bit of checking at Randy's old Amazon depot. They now knew he was a small-time marijuana dealer. Joe's police street contacts had a pretty good idea of who would have been at the next level, dealing with Randy. There were a bunch of cartel guys; some they could find, and some they couldn't. The ones they could find didn't know Randy or didn't want to say they knew him. The ones that were missing could be dead or just disappeared into the night. Just like Randy. More dead ends.

Randy had planned his departure. His bank account had been cleared out, and he'd left a will leaving explicit amounts to his parents and Mary. He'd taken his shaving gear, toothbrush and personal products. He'd apparently had an e-bike, but he must have left with it, or it was stored somewhere. He'd left his old car in the parking lot. He had two guns registered to him, but they weren't found in his apartment or his car, so he must have them with him. Mary didn't even know he was gone, and his mother was distraught. She'd said to Joe and Billy, "Find him, please. He's my baby."

Figuring out why he would disappear was the puzzle. Randy's missing furniture and ripped-out car upholstery told them someone thought he had something they wanted. They suspected his furniture had also been ripped apart during the break-in, and he'd just had it removed. Joe thought he pissed someone off or he was suspected of something. Maybe his life was in danger. These cartels are merciless. Or maybe he was just scared shitless and decided to disappear.

Joe had heard about the murders down at the wharf. A rumored drug deal gone wrong. He made no connection to Randy. He was small change in the drug dealing world.

MICHAEL (MALEK)

Other than him being a slob, Joe and Billy had very little information about Michael Robertson (Malek.) His apartment looked like the back dumpster area of a fast food joint. Pizza boxes, food boxes, and wrappers were tossed all over the floor. At least 100 empty Coke cans lay around. There were no sheets on his bed or pillow slips on the pillows. Just a duvet tossed on the floor.

The emergency contact he'd had in his condo files did not exist. No one knew where he was from. His landlord said he'd paid his rent a year ahead in cash. He'd never had any complaints about him. His references on his previous apartment in Miami had been checked out.

They'd found five laptops on a long desk, with one wheely office chair. They were all open, all stripped and erased. Forensics could find nothing on them. Michael Robertson definitely had something to hide. But what?

Malek Bouziane, also known as Michael Robertson, was Algerian. His past was intrinsically tied to his family and his country's antisemitic history. His hatred of Jews was inbred and embraced by his family and everyone he knew. He hadn't examined it. It was like a religion to him, almost more than being Muslim.

He'd come to the States on a student visa, done one term and disappeared, going underground as Michael Robertson.

His family had no money, and he had no job prospects back in Algeria. Algeria changed leaders but was still under military rule and the site of political repression and injustice. He wasn't going back.

Malek knew there were easier ways to make money. The rush he felt when he shut down a Jewish business and was paid his ransom was as addictive as heroin. He knew his work was being followed by somebody better than him. Whoever it was never left any clues behind, but they shut him down regularly. That person would let him play his hand, then pounce. He didn't think it was the CIA. They'd have found him and arrested him. He'd never heard of Claire. Still, he couldn't stop.

When he moved into Vanilla Palms and realized how many Jews lived there, his whole being recoiled in disgust. His apartment overlooked the pool. He rarely went out on his balcony, but when he did and looked down on the people enjoying the sun, something curdled in him. He was sure they were all Jews. Something had to be done.

He'd formed a plan of destruction, after which he'd disappear again. He had sourced the kit of death; he just had to set it in place when the winds were right. It would be undetectable.

Chapter Ten

LETTING GO

Joe reported to work, and his chief signaled him to come into his office. Joe thought *now what?* The chief said, "How's that condo thing going? You haven't said much?" Joe said," Because we still don't know much. Six people are still missing, dead or maybe dead. Lily, Antonio's wife, is dead; Antonio could have murdered her, or not. Antonio could have drowned, or not. Estelle could have been murdered by a drug addict who has since been found murdered. Randy seemed in danger; someone was tracking him, and Claire and Michael did not exist, probably living under fake IDs. We have no proof of anything, and we're running out of leads."

The chief said, "Well, the FBI and the CIA just made your job easier. We've been told to back off on looking into Claire Richmond and Michael Robertson." Joe asked, "Why, what's going on?" His chief said, "I'm not at liberty to say, and I don't know much anyway, but you have your orders, step back from those two." Joe said, "Does this have anything to do with the explosion and poison gas? The number of Jews in the building? A bomb? Possible terrorism?" The chief said, "They're not sharing their secrets. Shut it down. Understood?" Joe said, "Yes, sir."

The chief then said, "With regard to chasing up that woman Lily's cause of death and possible murder, I think it's a waste of time. Drop that too." Joe wasn't surprised at that directive.

The chief asked him how much more time he thought he needed to provide his final report on the case. Joe said, "I need to talk to Billie, Zenith and the fire chief to find out probable cause, if they even know anything yet. Also, the insurance woman. Then I think we can wrap it up." He went on, "It's so strange. These people all disappeared into the night, like hundreds of thousands of people before them in this country. We have no idea where they are. People walk out of their lives into different ones. It's not hard to get a fake ID in this country. They could be anywhere."

He stood and said, "I'll write up my report in the next few days and have it on your desk." The chief said, "Good lad." Then he stood, and Joe knew he was excused.

When Joe got back to Billy to tell him they had to back off on Claire and Michael and the potential Lily murder, Billy said, "Those are your orders, not mine." Joe said, "I admire your diligence, Billy, but seriously, we've run out of options with those three anyway. Claire's boss has been told not to talk to us. We have no idea who this Michael guy was or what he was up to with all those computers. Claire was a professional hacker. There's probably a connection between the two, but we aren't to know. We have no proof Lily was murdered by anyone, let alone Antonio, or if she murdered Antonio. The chief has asked me to wrap it up. We need to meet with the fire chief, Jack Silvester, to see what they know about the cause and that insurance woman, Carolyn Sweeney. Can you set something up with Zenith and those folks?" Billy said, "Sure, but I feel like we might get a break and hear something on at least one of them." Joe said, "Maybe we will. Doesn't look like it right now. It's time to move on, buddy." He looked at Billy and said, "You've been a great partner. You really should think about joining the force." Billy said, "Yeah, I've been thinking about it a lot. I'm not sure about having to do years as a state trooper. It would take me a long time to get to detective status." Joe said, "If you don't start, you'll never get there." Billy said, "Still thinking. No decision."

Billy talked to Zenith, and they set up a meeting with all parties, including Zenith's lawyer, Doug McPherson. They wanted to hear from Jack Silvester, the fire chief. If they'd found the source of the explosion, many things could be moved along, including insurance claims and lawsuits.

Jack came in, shook hands all around and stayed standing. He said, "We have yet to issue our final report, but our people have found no obvious accelerant or source for the explosion. It blew up the terminal, but there was no evidence of a bomb. Some chemicals may have been released into the air and interacted, creating the explosion, but we have no proof. The other strange thing is that all of the chemicals being handled at the depot were researched thoroughly. We went over all their shipping records. Nothing in the depot we're familiar with could have moved in a cloud over that condo and killed all those people. We've all heard of biowarfare and undetectable bombs. This could have been something like that, but we need proof. The CIA and FBI have been in touch with us and are also investigating two of the missing tenants. There could be a connection, or it could be a coincidence. We've been told we cannot include that biowarfare supposition in our report. Carolyn asked, "Where does that leave the terrorism clause in some insurance policies?" Jack said, "There's no definitive proof it was terrorism and we will be reporting the cause could not be identified." I think your company and everybody else's will have to honor the insurance claims." He said, "It's key that this does not hit the media. Speculation will go wild. If it is leaked, I'll know one of you leaked it. This does not go outside of this room, understood?" He looked directly at Carolyn, and she shifted in her seat.

As Fire Chief, Jack knew a thing or two about undetectable bombs and what was being used secretively by various countries. The latest was called a Bleeder. It did just what it was meant to do. Created a diversion explosion in one place and spread a lethal undetectable gas in another. The wind had to be right if you were targeting something. Whoever laid it knew what they were doing. The wind had been right that morning. He couldn't prove it so it couldn't be reported.

Carolyn was thinking about the massive payout to the Surfside families, the condo that had imploded over on the coast. Her company represented the depot and would be on the hook now to the families of the Vanilla Palms people who'd died.

Zenith said, well, that doesn't change anything for us. I will continue to offer to buy any of the condos any of them want to sell.

After they all left, Billie, Joe, and Doug, the lawyer, stayed with Zenith. Joe told Zenith he'd been asked to close the case by his chief and was about to write his final report. Billie had been keeping Zenith up to speed about what they were finding out about the missing people. Zenith said, "You two did an exhaustive job. I know it's frustrating that you could not find these final missing people, but you did everything you could. It's out of your hands now. They could be anywhere." It does leave me with three unoccupied condos, though. That's unfortunate. Billy thought *business first with Zenith*.

Zenith said, "Billie, I want you and Doug to work full-time on arranging the purchases of the condos people want to sell. You'll be busy for a while. Joe, I guess you get back to other cases. Thank you for everything."

Joe said, "Thank you, sir, it was an interesting opportunity." He looked at Billy and said, "How about a beer after work?" Billy said, "Yes, that would be good, we can talk."

Billy had made his decision.

Meanwhile, the runaways also had decisions to make. It was far from over.

Chapter Eleven

YOU CAN RUN BUT YOU CAN'T HIDE

CLAIRE

During Claire's spy training, she'd been taught to never show a reaction or emotions. If she was caught and interrogated, she had to keep her head and respond without giving anything away. This was rehearsed every week. She could create a facial reaction to anything required. She was a talented actress.

Hearing Mikael whisper her father had been murdered by the Russians took her breath away. She didn't know what to do with the onslaught of grief, guilt, anger and fear. She hadn't had to use any of those emotions. Her father was dead because of her. She'd warned him but didn't believe the Russians would take it this far. She said to Mikael, "No. No. No!" Mikael said, "I am so sorry, Anastasia; I thought I had them in a safe place. Your father simply went out for a short walk. He was feeling trapped in the little apartment they were in." Claire said, "How did they find him?" Mikael said, "I'm not sure. They must have been closing in and were in the area. He fell into their hands, and they rubbed that hideous poison on his neck. He was dead in a day." Claire said, "Where's my mother, and where are you?" He said, "I'm in Paris with your mother. I moved her again overnight. We'll move every few days." She said, "How is she?" He said, "heartbroken, scared, and very angry." Mikael said, "Anastasia, your mother believes you did the right thing leaving those murderous bastards. She doesn't blame you." Claire said, "Please tell her how proud I am of her, that I love her and how very sorry I am." Mikael said, "These are dangerous times, she knows that."

Claire was in a panic. She said, "You need to get out of the country." She asked him, "Can you get new IDs and passports for the two of you somewhere?" He said, "I've already arranged that." Claire said, "Excellent. I have an idea. I am leaving for Uruguay within the next few weeks. There are two Russians here too close on my tail. I have to get going. I have a stop before I leave. I'm leaving the apartment within the hour with the dog. I'm shipping him out." Mikael said, "Are you sure that's smart? You don't need your exit complicated by a dog." Claire said, "I'm not leaving him behind." She thought, *besides, he's the only male I've ever slept with. I like having him beside me.* She didn't share that thought with Mikael.

She said, "There's a cruise ship, the SmoothSeas Cruise line, leaving for Rio de Janeiro out of Marseille in two days. I've been watching; they still had staterooms available last week. Book the two of you into the same room as man and wife. The cruise takes 18 days, and I'll meet you in Rio, and we'll fly down the coast to Montevideo. I'll have a place for us by then." I'm betting they won't think you'd be on that boat.

She said, "I'm sorry, Mikael, I'm asking you to change your life." He said, "It's okay. They would have tried to kill me sooner or later. It's time for me to get the hell out." She said, "What did you do about your inn? He said, "I signed it over to a friend. It's his now."

She said, "We've talked too long already. I'm ditching this phone now." She gave him her next contact number. She said, "Be on alert."

Claire set the apartment up with timed lights and left the TV on. She'd left her car in the underground parking. She rarely used it anyway, so they wouldn't be watching for it.

She packed Cooper's favorite chew toys and left the apartment on the auspices of a simple dog walk. She walked about a mile to a quiet residential neighborhood. There, she called a cab, telling them she had a dog with her, got the okay, and they picked her up. She went straight to the International pet shipping depot she'd prearranged. She had all the paperwork, proof of shots, and customs information. She hated doing this to him, but she'd been assured he'd be safe, well taken care of, and arrive safely in Uruguay in roughly two days. They'd split up his flights so they could get him off the plane briefly, lightly feed and water him and give him a chance to pee and poop. She'd already arranged the pickup at the other end. She looked at him. He was her dog now. He'd become an anchor for her. She didn't want him to see her upset. He walked off with the handler, tail high, and she watched him disappear around the corner. She felt a pull at her gut. *Arrive alive, my boy*, she thought, *see you on the other side.*

Then, she had the cab drop her off at a hotel near the airport. She was highly watchful of everyone, wondering if the two Russian men had picked up she'd left the apartment. They'd never figured out who this Caroline Mitchell woman was, but they thought she might have known Anastasia/Claire. In their minds, both women had known the now-dead Sam; otherwise, how did he get his hands on the message Anastasia sent to Mikael? They wondered if Anastasia/Claire was in Jamaica. Right now, this woman, Caroline Mitchell, was their only lead. They watched her take the dog for a walk. She was acting normally. They didn't see her return with him but didn't think much of it. It was dark. Besides, they wanted Anastasia/Claire, not this Caroline Mitchell woman.

For a week, they watched her apartment lights come on and off. They thought *she must be using the back garden for the dog. She hadn't walked him in days.* They couldn't see the garden from the street. They were bored and thought this was a waste of time, but they had their orders. Find Claire (Anastasia) and kill her. It dawned on them this Caroline Mitchell woman had given them the slip. They knocked on her door. No answer, no dog barking. They let themselves in, and it was clear she was gone. They exchanged looks. Their superiors wouldn't be happy when they heard they'd lost this woman, too. *They now wondered where this Caroline Mitchell woman fit into the puzzle. Did she know Anastasia? Why did she disappear? What was she hiding?* It never occurred to them she might be Anastasia.

Claire did not fly directly to Uruguay. She had something else she needed to do first. While waiting for Mikael to call, she'd tracked down Malek in Los Angeles. He was now living in a highrise and returning to his old habits.

She'd discovered he'd just blocked all the computers in a large temple in San Francisco. She could fix that, but first, she had a blind date with Malek.

She flew into L.A. using a new ID. She didn't need a passport for this flight. She'd hacked into his account and had his new name and address. From her rental car, she watched the building for several days. Very little fast food was delivered in any branded vehicles. Still, she watched several drivers get buzzed up with food delivery bags. That could be going to any of the apartments. She assumed he was having his food delivered by Uber. She had a plan. Order a pizza, buzz herself up and deliver it to him. If he came to the door, big if, he'd say, "I didn't order a pizza." She would then say, "I'm sorry, I must have the wrong apartment number. I can't take it back. Do you want it anyway?" She hoped he'd say yes.

She arrived in the lobby with the pizza. She used her master key and let herself in. A tool of the trade. Arriving at the eighth floor where he lived, her heart was in her throat. Now was the time to do some acting. She rapped on his door. No answer. She rapped again, calling out, "I have a pizza delivery." She watched a shadow pass in front of the peephole. She was surprised when he actually opened the door. She could have been 'anybody'. Well, she was 'anybody'.

Her nemesis stood in front of her. He was in a stained sweatshirt, baggy jeans, and bare feet. He was younger than she'd thought. He was unshaven. She had to quell the desire to slap his face.

She went into her spiel. "Hi, did you order a pizza?" Malek said, "No, not me. You've got the wrong apartment." Claire looked up and down the hall. She said, "There must have been a mistake back at the order center, and I've got the wrong apartment number. Claire pretended to look confused and worried. Now, I don't know where it was going; I'll get them to resend the order. Do you want this? It's free." Malek looked at her, thought briefly, and said, "Yeah, sure. He fished in his jeans pocket. Here, take $20." He took the box from her and closed the door. Malek didn't know there was an extra topping on his pie.

Claire watched his account for three days. It went dead the night she delivered the pizza. She thought, hope you're dead too, you bastard. She then called 911, pretending to be another tenant, and said she was worried about the tenant down the hall. He hadn't answered his door for days. Within an hour, the police showed up, then an ambulance. She watched as a fully sheeted body was wheeled out on a gurney. She smiled to herself *must have been something he ate.*

Claire thought about her Jewish ladies and said to herself *that was for you, girls.*

Meanwhile, she'd unblocked the San Francisco temple's computers. They came in the following day and everything was back to normal. They'd been considering paying the ransom. They thought *thank God, prayer works.*

Claire had no moral code that kept her up at night. Malek's demise was earned in her books. She had no quarrel with thieves. She was one. Racists were another thing. She truly believed everyone was equal.

Back in Chicago, the two Russian men didn't know where to start looking for the missing Caroline Mitchell and her dog. *Where would she go with a dog? Did she give the dog to someone? Leave him at the pound?* They started there, checking all the pounds and dog rescues in the city. Nobody had dropped off a dog like Cooper. They couldn't know that Cooper was winging his way to Uruguay. They checked all the airport passenger lists they could access, and neither Caroline nor Claire were listed. Caroline's car was still in the underground parking lot. Now, both women had vanished. They still hadn't realized they were one and the same, but they were still gone.

Now in L.A., Claire checked online, and there were no direct flights from Los Angeles to Montevideo. Most had two stops. She didn't want to have to stop anywhere in the States after she left. Too much exposure. She found a flight that did just one stop in Panama City, but it didn't fly every day. She had to wait. Having a couple of days to kill, she drove around L.A., recognizing the names of streets she'd read about. She had to find a place to stay for two nights and drove into Hollywood. She found a decent motel on the strip and booked in. She was starved. Normally, she'd never go near a bar, particularly in a strange city. When she asked the desk clerk for some fast food restaurant suggestions, he recommended she try the bar across the street. He said, "It's friendly, and the food is good." She decided to take him up on his suggestion. It was still very sunny, even though it was late in the day, so when she entered, she could only see a long, dark bar with a few people sitting on the stools. Three guys were watching a basketball game, not speaking to each other, and a single woman was perched on a stool scrolling through her phone. The woman looked up and smiled, and they nodded at each other. Nothing was said. Claire sat down, and the server came up to her and said, "Hi there, welcome to the Beep. Do you need a men u.?

Life is full of coincidences.

The next day at the airport, she wore a mask and tinted glasses and kept her head down. She stayed as far away as she could from groups of people and stiffened if someone walked quickly toward her. She thought a Russian was around every corner. She was sure men were suspiciously glancing at her from behind their magazines. It was so easy to transfer that murderous poison onto someone without them even knowing. She had come so far. She couldn't let that happen to her.

She boarded with a small carry-on and another new ID with a passport. She was going to be Joanne Filbert in her new life. It was going to be a long, tiresome flight getting there.

She had not heard from Mikael or her mother and wondered if they'd made it on board the cruise ship. She heard from her dog care contact in Montevideo. Cooper arrived safe and happy and was already stealing hearts.

Claire thought, at least one piece of good news.

She felt the plane accelerate and lift. She stared out the window at the fast-receding tarmac. Few people were flying out of Los Angeles to Montevideo. She was seated alone. She finally allowed herself to think of her sweet, lost father. Tears rolled down her face, and she began to quietly sob. Unbearable sadness was an unfamiliar emotion.

RANDY

Miguel, Randy's ex-drug dealer, sat at the other end of the long bar, looking straight at him with a quizzical smile. Randy gestured toward the door, and Miguel, still slick, well-dressed, and confident, sauntered out behind him onto the street. The sun blinded them both, and they squinted into each other's faces. Randy spoke quietly, not looking directly at Miguel and said, "Let's talk down the street, away from the bar." He didn't want anyone to hear Miguel use his real name. Miguel spread his hands in a gesture of whatever, and they walked together silently. Randy was trying to control the panic in his head and was thinking, *fuck, fuck, fuck."* Miguel had a slight smirk on his face but said nothing.

He thought *the boy looks different. He's lost a lot of weight but tightened up.* He noticed Randy shaved his head now and wore a three-day growth beard. He seemed to be dressing better. That was courtesy of his gay neighbor. Miguel thought *he's an adult in control of his life now. Not the scared, inexperienced kid I first met.*

They got to the end of the block, and Miguel looked at him and said, "So, what's up? Are we going to walk forever?" Randy stopped, turned, looked at Miguel, and said, "Look, I'm living under a new identity here, and I want to keep it that way." Miguel laughed and said, "Hey, me too, mi amigo. Don't worry, I won't blow your cover if you don't blow mine." He then frowned at Randy and said, "You seemed to have a good life, decent job. W hy this?"

They continued walking side by side. Randy said, "Not long after you signed off, some greaser was waiting for me in a parking lot. He said he was looking for you and asked if I knew where you were. I told him no, 'cause I didn't. He said that from now on, he'd be my dealer. I told him I didn't know you and I didn't know what he was talking about. He didn't like that answer and shoved me up against my car, putting his stinking mouth way too close to mine. He threatened me with a gun if I talked. Then he got in his car and peeled off. That alone scared the crap out of me. Two weeks later, I came home, and my apartment and car had been ransacked. I'm talking ripped apart. My friend Mary's apartment was also ransacked.

When I started with you, you said I might have to disappear someday. I thought you were trying to scare me. I didn't believe you. Then I did. I was scared for my life.

Miguel thought Randy had overreacted after a simple rough-up and break-in, but he didn't know the whole story. Randy said, "Maybe you're used to threats to your life. I'm not." Miguel asked, "What do you think they were looking for?" Randy straight-faced lied and said, "No idea. I didn't keep any stock or cash in my apartment or car. I had practically no stock left anyway after you left."

Miguel knew what they were looking for. He'd left town the day after the warehouse murders. Cito would have been suspicious of everyone and might have thought he was connected and stashed either the money, the drugs or both with one of his junior clients. His boys were leaving no stone unturned. He said, "My boss' guys would have been shaking down my client list making sure they didn't go to the competition." Randy asked, "How did they get my name, address, and Mary's?" Miguel said, "It's business, buddy. They know everyone who's dealing their stuff." Randy said, "Mary wasn't connected at all. Why did they break into her place?" Miguel said, "First of all, you don't know who broke in, could have just been a coincidental random robbery." Randy said, "It was within a couple of days." Miguel said, "I don't know, maybe they thought she knew something, or you'd hidden something there." Then he looked hard at Randy and asked, "Are you telling me everything? Did you know something you shouldn't have?" Randy said, "Like what?" Miguel said, "I don't know, maybe saw somebody killed or something?" The whole warehouse scene flashed in front of Randy's eyes. The three dead guys, particularly the one on the floor staring at him with that dead eye, the money. He looked back at Miguel and lied again, saying, "Nope, didn't see anything." Miguel was looking closely at Randy. He read people well and was pretty sure Randy was lying.

Randt turned it around on Miguel and said, "You were pretty nervous the last time we talked. Enough that you needed to disappear. Did you do something I got connected with?" Miguel said, "No, but that was just after those murders down on the docks. Word on the street was there was five million cash and an equal amount of coke missing from the scene. My boss thought either the cops or another cartel had it. But everybody was under suspicion. If the cartel ever figured out who had it, they'd be a dead man walking." Miguel said, "Before you ask, I had nothing to do with it. I didn't want to get connected to it either. I wanted out. I was done with the trade. Too dangerous." Randy said, "Fuck, that's a lot of money and dope." He was becoming a pretty good liar. Miguel said, "Yeah if the cops don't have it, someone's going to show their hand when they try to sell the stuff. The money's long gone. They'll never see that again." Randy thought of his five-million-dollar stash stored just up the street. He was also thinking about his invisible client, Pauly. *Did he murder the men and take the drugs?*

Randy changed the subject. He didn't want to show too much interest in the warehouse murders and thefts. He said, "Look, Miguel, or whatever your name is now, I've got a nice quiet life here. I've got a little cleaning business that's doing okay. I don't want to have to leave it because you showed up. Are you planning to hang around here? Why this bar? Miguel said, "Relax." He drew out the "relax" as he said it. "I just stopped for a beer. Pure coincidence you were in there. I was as surprised as you were to see you sitting there." He said, "My new name is Pedro. What's yours?" Randy said, "Jake." Miguel said, "Well, Jake, I won't be screwing up your little cleaning business and quiet life. I'm heading down to Mexico City. I've got some business ideas. I'm going legit. Don't worry, I'm leaving." Randy said, "Not that it wasn't good to see you, and it wasn't, but that's a relief." Miguel laughed and said, "I like the new you, Jake." He offered his hand in one of those complicated black handshakes Randy had never mastered. He fumbled his way through it, and Miguel laughed again and slapped Randy's arm. He said, "You'd never make it in the hood, mi amigo." Randy said, "Doing okay cleaning other people's floors." Miguel looked at him and said, "Adios, and good luck." Randy said, "Same to you, stay alive." He said to himself *and away from me.*

Miguel turned and sauntered away into the sunny afternoon, ever cool. Randy watched him walk away and thought again *fuck, fuck, fuck. That was too close.*

He decided not to go back to the bar that day. Someone might have picked up the quick communication between him and Miguel before they left. If it came up later, he'd act puzzled. "Can't think who you're talking about."

He'd say. He realized how precarious his new life really was. Anybody from his old life could walk into that bar and recognize him. He started being more watchful of who was around him. It wasn't an easy way to live life.

Randy continued his cleaning business, and his cell phone kept on ringing. He was almost at the point where he'd have to turn down clients. As had become their ritual, he and his neighbor Kenneth were sitting on Randy's balcony sharing their after-work drink when Kenneth looked at him and said, "Jakey, honey. None of my business, but it looks like you're making some real cash. It's not smart to hide it from the IRS. I like you too much to see you hauled off to jail for tax evasion. I use a bookkeeper who could make you legal. I can give you her name." Randy didn't want to involve his fake ID with the IRS but thought it could be worse if he didn't and got caught. He said, "You're right. I need to look into that." He thought, *but not from anybody you know. Everybody gossips here. There are no secrets.*

He started looking for a bookkeeper who could handle a cash-only business. He connected with a woman who sounded promising. On the phone, she said, "Wow, your little cleaning business sounds great. Do you like doing that kind of work?" Randy said, "As a matter of fact, I do; I'm a bit weird that way." "She said, "I like weird. I can do your bookkeeping for you. I've got a lot of clients who only deal in cash. Why pay those bloody credit card fees if you don't have to, huh?" They then chatted about a bunch of random things. She was funny and seemed to have a casual approach to life. Her name was Emily, and they set up a meeting in a local coffee shop.

A woman in her late 20s walked in carrying a small laptop and looked around. Randy took her in. She was taller than him and had short dark hair cut in a bob. She wasn't pretty in a classic way; her features were unremarkable, but she wasn't ugly either. An average but pleasant-looking woman. She was wearing a short tent dress that skimmed her body. She was slim, not a workout queen. He raised a hand and waved at her. She sat down and ordered a latte.

She told him what she'd need from him, and he asked, "What if I don't tell you about everything I've received?" She said, "Your business, your receipts, I'm just the bookkeeper." He liked that answer. Truth was, he was scrupulously honest about his cash intake and reported it all. An old habit of being a 'good boy.' Strange, given he was actually a big-time thief. In his mind, that theft was in another compartment. Somehow, not really a theft. More like an insurance policy.

He hired her, and with business out of the way, they talked for hours, or rather, Emily did. Randy didn't share much, and she didn't ask. She seemed to have a lifetime of her own she wanted to share. She was a yakker, but he liked that. She made it easy.

He invited her to meet him for a beer at the Beep about a week later, and that was the beginning of Randy's romance with Emily, the bookkeeper.

PAULY

Meanwhile, back in Jacksonville, Pauly Jacobson, Randy's last client, the one he'd never met, was having bloody nightmares about three dead men. One of them looked at him with one eye. The other eye was gone with the rest of his head.

He thought *I had a nice, quiet little life, and now I'm a triple murderer and a drug thief. I had to shoot them; there was no choice there. Me or them. Wrong place, wrong time.* Then he'd think, *why'd you have to take the damn dope, you asshole?*

He had to ditch it but had no idea how. He was smart enough not to try and sell it. That would put him on someone's radar, and he sure didn't want to be there.

The guy from Amazon who'd referred Pauly to Randy told him the police had been asking around about Randy. Apparently, he was missing. That made Pauly even more nervous. *Where'd he go? Had someone killed him?* The Amazon guy said, "Don't worry, I didn't mention your name." Pauly said, "Good because I never met the guy; he no-showed." He thought *the last thing I need is to be connected to a missing drug dealer.* Pauly knew he had to lose the drugs fast.

There wasn't really anywhere Pauly could carry a large cardboard box of cocaine in Jacksonville and secretly drop it into the water. He'd be spotted. Instead, he broke up the contents. The drugs were wrapped in small plastic packages, so that made that easy. There was a construction site just down the road. Randy stopped by at night and picked up a bunch of bricks to give the packages some weight so they'd sink. Over a week, he drove around to several docks, waited until dark and quietly dropped the packages taped to the bricks into the water. He'd watch them sink, ensuring they were gone. With each drop, his stress lifted just a bit. He'd think *at least this shit will never hit the streets.*

He still had about a dozen packages left to get rid of. One night, he was down on a dock, dropping yet another bundle into the ocean, when a male voice said, "Hope you're not throwing anything nasty into the ocean. That would be illegal." Pauly turned around and was relieved the man speaking to him wasn't in uniform. He didn't answer him. He thought, *who's this busybody?* Then the guy flashed his badge and asked, "What did you throw in there?" Pauly quickly broke into a sweat, thought quickly and said, "Just a stale loaf of bread. Thought the fish could eat it." The cop said, "Looked like it was wrapped up tight in plastic." Pauly said, "Yeah, but it was open at one end." Then he asked, "Is feeding the fish illegal?" The cop said, "Depends what you're feeding them."

The cop identified himself as Officer Finley and looked hard at Pauly. Pauly was shifting his feet nervously and looking around. *All the physical signs of deception*, the officer thought. *He's up to something.*

He asked Pauly where he lived. Pauly sure didn't want to give this cop his address. Half the drugs were still there, with three bricks of it under his car seat. Reluctantly, he told him where he lived, thinking, *please don't follow me home.* The cop asked Pauly for some ID. Pauly said, "Sure, but am I under arrest for something?" Pauly's voice cracked as he said again, "I was simply throwing some bread into the ocean." Officer Finley said, "You see, I don't believe you. I think you might have been throwing something illegal in there." He checked Pauly's license and asked him where he was parked. He said, "I'll walk you to your car." Once they got there, he phoned in Pauly's info, and his car license only to discover Pauly was completely clean. No arrests, no record of any kind. He didn't have probable cause to search Pauly's car. He looked at Pauly and said, "Hit the road and stop feeding the fish." The next morning he called in a diver to retrieve the package.

Pauly knew he had to lose the drugs immediately. On the way home, he stopped at a convenience store and bought some green garbage bags. He drove around downtown Jacksonville several times to ensure he wasn't being followed. Then, he dropped the three packages in his car into city garbage cans, one by one. Then he went home, constantly checking his mirrors, and retrieved the rest of the supply. He continued to drive around, finding city garbage pails and dumping the remaining drugs individually into the cans. His fingerprints were all over the bags, but he hoped they'd get deposited, still wrapped in their garbage bags, into the garbage pit on the edge of town. He doubted any garbage guys would be picking through small green garbage bags in their public bins. He slept better that night.

The next day, two large cops showed up at Pauly's door. He thought *I'm fucked*.

They showed their badges, gave their names and said, "Can we come in?" Pauly thought *glad I got rid of that dope last night*. Pauly said, "Sure," and stepped aside. They quickly looked around but needed a search warrant, so couldn't take it much further. Yet. One of them said, "We'd like you to come down to the station with us and answer a few questions." Pauly thought compliance was his best approach right now. He said, "What about?" They said, "Officer Finley will talk to you." Pauly said, "Am I in trouble for something?" They weren't talking. They just ignored him. Pauly rode along in the back of the squad car, shaking.

They brought him into an interview room at the station and left him alone. He assumed he was being watched. He'd watched a lot of cop programs on TV. They probably wanted to see how nervous he was. Hell, he was nervous. After an interminable 20 minutes, Officer Finley came in carrying the drug package Pauly had dumped. Pauly hoped the salt water had eliminated his fingerprints, but he had no idea how that particular forensic science worked. Finley said, "We're checking for prints." As it turned out, they couldn't lift any clear prints off the bag, but Finley didn't share that with Pauly. Pauly looked at the package and pulled himself together. He thought *I'm not going down for this. I was just trying to dump the drugs, and the murders were self-defense. If he even knows about the murders.* Officer Finley made no connection between Pauly and the warehouse murders, but Pauly would never know that.

Pauly asked innocently, "What's that?" Officer Finley said, "I was hoping you'd tell me." Then he said, "We both know it's the package you dumped off the end of the pier last night." Pauly said, "I threw a loaf of bread to the fish. I don't know what that is. What is it?" Officer Finley said, "It's a package of cocaine. But you know that, Paul." Pauly said, "Are you trying to hang me with some crap you found in the water off the end of a dock that I had nothing to do with?" Officer Finley said, "Just quite a coincidence; it was in the exact same spot you said you dropped the bread." Pauly asked, "Did you look for the bread bag?" Officer Finley knew the diver had not, in fact, looked for a bread bag.

Finley then asked, "Was this someone else's coke? Were you protecting somebody?" Pauly said, "I've never seen that package before. I know you don't believe me, but I was really feeding the fish. I feel like I'm being framed here. What's really going on?" Officer Finley ignored this answer and said, "You see, I find it interesting that you don't do drugs, and you don't sell drugs. I think this is someone else's package. Maybe you disapproved and just wanted to get rid of it? You seem like a nice kid. Did you find it at your boss' apartment or on his boat? He sure thinks highly of you."

Finley had interviewed Pauly's boss, Frank Kingsly, that morning. Frank was skeptical. "Pauly? Are you sure you've got the right guy? He doesn't touch drugs." He thought, *except for the weed, he gets somewhere for my parties*. He never asked him where he got it. Didn't want to know. Finley asked, "Could he have found it on your property?" Frank said, "I don't associate with drug people." The cop said, "Maybe someone's trying to set you up. Paul found it and disposed of it to protect you?" Frank said, "He would have told me that." Officer Finley said, "Well, in my business, people lie constantly." Frank said, "I'll ask him, but I just can't believe it." Finley said, "Let me know what he says."

Pauly didn't want to drag his boss into this, even though he'd been down on the docks because of him. This wasn't his fault. Pauly stuck to his story. Lying came easy when there was so much at stake. When Officer Finley realized he wouldn't get anything out of him, he said to Pauly, "Listen son, this is dangerous stuff. I don't know what you were doing with it, but you were obviously getting rid of it. It would be wise to stay away from all of that." Pauly held his hands up in protest, "He said, seriously, I've never seen that package before, and I was feeding the fish. I promise I'll stop feeding the damn fish." Officer Finley thought *the boy's scared and lying, but he sure has balls*.

He didn't have a case against Pauly. He couldn't prove anything. Pauly was clean as a whistle, had no priors, and had good references from a reputable employer. He had to let him go.

He said I'll have someone drop you off at home. Pauly said, "Don't bother, I'll get a cab home. That's the last time I want to be in the back of a squad car." Officer Finley said, "I hope for your sake it was."

And that was the end of that. Pauly went home, shat his brains out, then vomited up everything he ate that day. He sobbed for hours. Scared and lonely, he had a rough night.

He woke up the next day feeling weak but somehow freer. He had to start thinking about his future. He dreaded the day when his boss would want him to buy some weed again. He didn't want to be connected with any of that. He called his boss and told him he had some family issues to take care of and that he'd be leaving. He thanked him for his generosity and said goodbye. His boss waited for him to tell him about the drugs and the police encounter. Pauly didn't bring it up, so he assumed nothing had come of it. He sure didn't want to be pulled into an employee's drug problem, so decided not to ask.

Then Pauly packed up and headed as far away from Jacksonville as possible. He thought he might start over in L.A. and pick up some stagehand work in the movie industry. He drove for days until he ended up in a motel in Hollywood. There was a cool little bar across the street called "Message at the Beep." He decided to drop in for a beer and a burger. He was tired and hungry.

Some guys were sitting at the bar watching a basketball game on the screen but weren't together. One was an older, bald, Mexican-looking guy, and the other was smaller and bald but about the same age as Pauly. He sat beside the younger bald guy and asked, "Who's winning?" The guy said, "Nobody yet, they're tied." Pauly ordered a beer and a burger and sat silently beside the bald guy while he ate. When he was finished, he looked over at him and said. "I just got here and I'll be looking for work; any leads?" The bald guy, Randy, said, "I think there's a lot of bar and restaurant work, and there's always the movie lots." Pauly said, "Yeah, I was thinking about the movie lots. Any idea where you apply?" Randy said, "Sorry, I don't. Why don't you go to one and ask." Pauly then offered his hand and said, "Paul. My friends call me Pauly." Randy shook his hand and said, "Jake." Then he said, "Welcome to Hollywood. Where are you coming from?" Pauly said, "Jacksonville." Randy froze thinking *it can't be.*

Life's funny with its coincidences. So funny.

ANTONIO

...."Well, I'm a-runnin' down the road tryna loosen my load.
Got a world of trouble on my mind.
Lookin' for a lover who won't blow my cover
She's so hard to find."
Take it Easy, The Eagles, 1972

Jane couldn't help herself. She'd kept questioning Antonio, "So tell me about your mother. Was she funny? What was Xmas like? Did you have any pets?" And on and on. The more he shut her down, the more she asked. She'd see the cloud draw over his face when she pushed; still, she couldn't stop herself. Antonio felt he was having to build lie upon lie. He hated it. He was done. One day he said sharply, "Jane, I don't give a damn about your childhood. Why are you so interested in mine?"

It wasn't just Antonio. She did it with everyone. Her need to ask questions was charming at first. People felt her interest in them. They had her full attention. Over time it became annoying and then invasive. She couldn't help herself. She needed to lift every rock.

Incessant questions hadn't endeared her to previous lovers either.

Antonio knew he had to disengage with Jane. If he was ever discovered and it was thought she'd been sleeping with a wife murderer, it could ruin her career. He also had to get himself out from under her interminable questions.

They were together for coffee. Antonio said, "I want to talk to you about us. I think we should step back a bit. Slow down." She looked at him for a long time and said, "So, just stop seeing each other?" Antonio said, "Yes, I think that would be the right thing to do." This wasn't the first time she'd heard a version of this from a guy she was seeing. She asked, "What did I do?" He thought, *asked too many damned questions*. He lied again and said, "You didn't do anything wrong. I like you too much to ever want to hurt you." She'd heard that before too. "It's not you, it's me." *What a load*, she thought. *It is me.* As she pushed back her chair, it screeched and stuck. She leaned over and pushed it in, looking at him. She said, "Too late."

She gathered her things and walked out of the coffee shop, back straight. She didn't say goodbye. She'd been dismissed by too many men over the years. She'd had hope for Antonio. Not to be. He watched her go. He was sad but relieved. He knew he couldn't take that risk again. Too painful.

Antonio thought *that's two wives and a girlfriend down, 0 for 3 in my relationships. I'm a wrecking ball.*

Over the winter, he spent a lot of time at the main library. He liked it there. Big comfortable reading chairs, good light, people coming and going but everybody minding their business. Interesting sense of privacy in a public place. He used their computers every day to search the Florida papers for news about Lily, the condo payouts, the missing people, and him being a murder suspect. He would also search Google for line items to see if anything was being picked up there. There was always some sensationalist weaving lies. Not in his case. He obviously wasn't that interesting.

It appeared the lawsuit against the dangerous goods site would be settled quickly. An estimated two million would be paid to each of the dead people's estates. His daughters would miss out on that. He wasn't a corpse from that particular occurrence. He knew the law and that one or both of his daughters would have to apply for conservatorship to be able to take over the condo until he was considered missing for five years. That meant one of them would have to have the interest to submit the paperwork. He didn't think his daughter living in Vancouver would care, but his daughter living in the U.K. might. One of them would have to keep paying the expenses to hold onto it. He had read that the Property Manager, Zenith Bachman was buying up the condos from anyone who wanted to get out. He thought, *smart move, Zenith. If the price is right, people will forget it's the building of death.*

Zenith had, in fact, advised Antonio's U.K. daughter to apply for the conservatorship and rent out the condo. He said he'd manage the rental for her, for a small fee, of course. He said, "If you wait out the five years and have your father declared dead, it'll be worth a lot more."

Over the months, all the news about the explosion had gone quiet. There was only one line item about Lily's skull showing up and Antonio being suspected of murder. They'd published his driver's license picture with that article. That made him nervous. He didn't look that different, even with his shaved head. Then, all went silent. If her body had shown up before the fish nibbled her up, they would have seen the gunshot wound, but that still wouldn't have been tied to either of his guns.

When Antonio purposefully sank his boat, it drifted to the bottom of the bay and landed on a hill of sand. There it sat, salt water eating away at it, metal rusting, rocking back and forth with the tides. A hurricane roared up the coast in December, creating a reverse undertow in the water. His little motorboat broke loose from the grip of the sand and washed up on the beach. Miraculously, the dashboard cabinet door was still intact. Behind it was the waterproof bag holding Antonio's keys, wallet and cell phone. When Joe, the detective, checked the cell phone, nothing was incriminating on it. If anything, it seemed underused. He still wasn't convinced Antonio had drowned. His computer, his files and now his phone were too cleanly curated. Joe couldn't prove anything. His boss told him to stop chasing phantoms and let the case go.

Antonio would never know the case had been dropped. He did know they had no proof of anything. Still, he wasn't about to march back into his old life to find out.

Antonio hated the wet slushy winter in Seattle. The damp cold got into his broken back and reignited the ache. No amount of gym exercise relieved it. He started looking around for a warmer option to live out his life.

There were 16 million Latinos living in California, more Mexicans than Caucasians. Antonio thought *sounds like a good place for a Mexican guy to get lost*. He thought it would be best if he changed his ID again. He didn't want any Seattle people following him. He ordered up his new ID. He'd now be Cedro Escareno. His old fake name, John Caldwell, had never fit his Mexican face. He sold his car and bought another, almost like it, in Cedro's name. He didn't have much to pack up. He told Syd he was leaving, had some business to take care of and thanked her for everything. She gave him a long hug, then stood back from him and said, "I hope your secrets don't eat you alive, John." She knew he was hiding something. She'd always thought he might tell her someday. Not today. Antonio stopped on the sidewalk and looked back at the gym. He'd been happy here. He hadn't felt that sense of satisfaction for a long time. He had an idea for his new life.

It was late February when he headed down the coast to California. He was less concerned about being seen this time, and the drive was easier. The first night, he stopped in Crescent City, Oregon and found a hotel on the beach. He had his money in a locked case where the spare tire usually lived. The tire was now sitting in the trunk. He had a steering wheel lock on, took a risk, and walked the beach. The surf was high and dramatic this time of year. The fresh, blowing ocean air filled his lungs and released a lot of tension. He slept like a man with a clear conscience that night. The next day, as he closed in on San Francisco, winter finally released its chokehold on him. The air was spring-like, and he was overdressed in his parka. His lungs opened up, his shoulders relaxed away from his ears, and his back relaxed. His reflection in the car mirror wasn't as pasty and puffy. His whole body said, "Aaaaahhh." He'd made the right decision to move on.

He drove down to Hollywood and rented a storage unit for the money. He had to get it out of the car. He found a hotel on the strip. He'd been thinking during the drive about possibly buying a small gym. He thought he'd model it after Syd's. He had deep pockets and could afford to take a risk. There were hundreds of them for sale in California. It had to be just right. That was tomorrow's project.

He was exhausted and wanted something light, a beer and a burger. He headed to the bar across the street and grabbed a stool at the bar. There were a couple of young guys watching a basketball game a few stools down and two single women, who weren't sitting together. One's nose was buried in her phone. The server approached him and said, "Welcome to the Beep. What can I get you?"

ESTELLE

Phil said, "Hello, Estelle." She knew that voice. *Damn*, she thought. Phil was a big boy the last time she'd seen him. No more. All his weight had melted away. His eyes were watery, and his skin was gray. He looked so sick.

Phil stood there quietly, waiting for Estelle to respond. She thought *no sense pretending*. She lifted her head, looked at him and said. "Hi Phil, you look like shit." Phil smiled and said, "You, on the other hand, look like a million bucks, or is it five million? I forget how that goes." She heard him and guessed he suspected her of taking the money. She chose to ignore the comment. She lowered her voice and said, "Phil, I have a new identity. My new name is Sharon. Please don't blow my cover. My life could be in danger." Phil's eyebrows raised as he looked at her. He said, 'I'm dying to he ar *that* story." Estelle said, "Give me your room number. I'll come up when I finish my shift. I work until eight." Phil said, "How do I know you won't disappear again." Estelle said, "I won't. See you at eight."

At 8:10, she took a deep breath and rapped on Phil's hotel room door. Her first impression when she came in was the room smelled like fever and vomit. Phil was in a sweat. Estelle asked, "What's wrong with you? You look like death." Phil said, "Not surprising; it's around the corner." She asked again, "What's wrong?" He said, "Kidney cancer. I've only got a few months left." She stepped forward with her hand out to touch him, but he recoiled. He said, "I thought you were dead, murdered. For a while, the police thought it was me." He looked at her and asked, "What the hell ha ppened?"

Estelle asked, "Do you have anything in that bar fridge we can drink?" He looked at the fridge and said, "Help yourself." She pulled out the small bottle of white and held it up to see if he wanted some, but he shook her off. She poured herself a glass, took a deep drink and looked at him." She then shared the whole Rudy murder story. Phil said, "You could have just called the police and reported it. It was self-defense." She said, "First of all, I shot him with a stolen gun." She then said, "Don't ask." Phil said dramatically, "Oh, I'm asking."

Estelle ignored that. She said, "If I'd reported it to the police, I would have had to prove it was self-defense. I did murder him, in cold blood, as they say in murder mysteries. Rudy had a gun on me, but he didn't when I shot him. His friends were all drug addicts, thieves and punks and would have quickly known it was me who shot him if the media got a hold of that. They would have killed me." She continued, "I had to disappear." He said, "And the new face? When did you have that done?" She said, "Before I came to New York." He said, "Nice job, by the way. Must have cost a bundle. Where'd you get the money for that?" She said, "I always hated my looks. I had some money saved up. I thought, now or never." Phil thought that's easily $50,000 worth of plastic surgery. She wouldn't have had that kind of extra money lying around. He said, "I won't even ask where you got the new ID." She shrugged and said, "That's pretty easy these days." He said, "I wouldn't know." He thought *stolen gun, murder, new face, fake ID from who knows where. What else don't I know about this woman?*

Phil stood up, said, "Excuse me," and ran to the bathroom. He left the door open, and she heard him retching." She went in to ask if she could help. He'd spewed vomit all over the bathroom. He came back, wiping his face with a towel. Estelle said, "Shouldn't you be in the hospital or something? What are you doing here?" He said, "I'd never been to New York and always wanted to see it. I was between dialysis treatments and thought I'd fly up for two days, catch a Broadway show, take a tour bus, see the sights and fly back." She asked, "Is anybody looking in on you back in Miami?" He said, "No, I've been mostly okay so far." She said, "Well, pack up your stuff; you're coming home with me tonight. I left you once, and I'm sorry. It was necessary. I'm not leaving you in a hotel room to die."

Phil didn't argue. He was feeling worse and wasn't sure he could make it back to the airport and home again. When they got to her place, Phil looked around and said, "Nice digs. Must cost a fortune in this city." Estelle lied, saying, "I make good money and great tips. It's affordable, barely, but I make it work. I don't eat out, that's for sure."

Phil rolled this over and thought *she's working, so she needs money. Maybe she doesn't have my missing five million.* He was not a fool, though, and thought again *that face would have cost a bundle. It's a work of art.*

Phil sank into the sofa, exhausted, looking gray. Estelle asked, "What can I do for you? Are you in any pain? Do you have meds you should be taking?" He said, "Don't worry, I'm on it. Good pain drugs, just can't keep anything down." She said, "I have a pull-out couch in the den. I'll make you up a bed. Stay as long as you want." She asked, "What can you eat?" He said, "I'm craving a pizza." She ordered one in, loaded, and he wolfed down two slices. He looked up, gave her a weak grin, and said, "The fat boy's still in here." Then he rushed to the bathroom and chucked it all up.

Phil spent the night vomiting. She had a large bowl beside the bed. She said, "Should I call an ambulance?" He said, "This usually passes. I ate and drank the wrong stuff. It looked so good, but I can't eat or drink what I used to." He whispered this in the voice of a man in misery. Estelle got up with him every time she heard him getting sick, wiped his mouth and face with a hot towel and sat with him until he fell asleep again.

She knew she couldn't leave him alone like this. The next morning she cancelled her shift. She didn't have anything booked for a week after that. For once, a relief.

She said to Phil the next day, "You must have a dialysis treatment due. I'll fly back with you if you want." He said, "Don't worry, it's not due until next week. She knew he was lying. She asked, "Are you giving up?" He said, "Hey, I found my old friend. You're not dead. I'm tired of feeling like shit, it's only going to get worse, and then I'll die." He looked at her and said, "Estelle, I don't want to die alone." She put her hand on his and said, "You don't have to. I'll be here with you. I'll help you do whatever you choose." Phil said, "I choose to stop treatment."

Estelle had no idea how to be the angel of death and usher someone out.

There was a drop-in clinic just down the block, and while Phil was sleeping, she ducked out and asked to see a doctor. She explained the situation and asked him what she should expect and how to care for him. He was most helpful and recommended she get a supply of adult diapers first. Estelle hadn't thought about having to clean Phil's shitty ass as part of what she was taking on. The doctor said, "If he's immobile or unconscious, there's a way to move him around to change his diaper and clean him up. He gave her the website. She thought *it's just piss and poop. It's the least I can do.*

She'd made a list of Phil's drugs, and the doctor told her what to give him. He already had a good supply of morphine. He said, "He probably won't need that. He actually won't be in much pain." He said, "He'll lose his appetite and sleep most of the day. He might be restless, and he might have visions of people who don't exist. He may be disoriented, confused and may no longer recognize you. His breathing and skin color and temperature will change as he gets close to the end." He said, "He'll be gone in a week or less." He then told her who to call when he did die and how to deal with that. She wondered if she would have gotten the same helpful response with her old face.

When she returned to her apartment, Phil was awake and sitting up. She told him what the doctor had told her. She thought *it's his death; he should know what's coming.* Phil said, "Well, that doesn't sound too bad. Trippy if I have hallucinations. I always wanted to try LSD." Estelle looked at him and asked, "Are you scared?" Phil said, "Of what, ending this? Nope. I've enjoyed my life. I think I did some good work with the animal shelter." He said, "By the way, I'm leaving my estate to the shelter. I've got a will, and my lawyer has it. You can find his card in my wallet. Call him when I'm dead. He has the keys to my apartment. He's my executor and knows what to do. There's an expensive SUV he'll have to sell as well." Estelle knew he had a million bucks, less the expensive car purchase. She didn't ask him what he had, and he didn't tell her.

He said, "I want to be fried, so you'll need to make arrangements with a crematorium." She said, "Any special requests with your ashes?" He said, "Shake me out somewhere warm. Your choice." Estelle wondered where that might be. She made some calls and prearranged his cremation, telling them it would be soon.

Phil slept through most of the next five days. The first morning, Estelle came into the den with a bowl of warm, soapy water and a clean diaper. He was out cold, so that part wasn't hard. She followed all the instructions, rolling him to one side and the other. She prayed he wouldn't wake up when she was soaping his parts. She looked down at him when she was done with the first change. He was completely unaware. She wondered *how do people do this for years?*

In the evening of what would be his last day, he surfaced. He smiled at her and said, "You've been a good friend." Then he drifted off again. She dimmed the lights and sat beside him, watching his face and chest, still lifting and breathing. He surfaced again, looked long at her, and said, "I need to know something, Estelle. Did you take the money?" Estelle knew this question would come. She thought about honesty and how overrated it was. He trusted her; she was seeing him out, and he did not need a final betrayal. She said, "What money?"

It wouldn't have saved his life anyway.

Phil smiled and fell back to sleep. She woke in the morning and went in to change him. He'd gone in the night. A quiet death. She called the doctor at the clinic, but he wasn't in. The front desk girl said she would call the coroner. Someone would come, pronounce him dead, and move his body to wherever she wanted it to go. Estelle said, "That's all arranged."

Phil's ashes sat on her kitchen counter. She didn't know where to keep them. The closet shelf seemed disrespectful, but she didn't want them on her mantel either. The bag greeted her every morning, saying silently, *"Take me somewhere warm."*

She had some unfinished business. It had been three weeks since she'd spoken with Dieter. He hadn't called, and she hadn't called him. She knew that was ending, too. She texted him and said, "Let's talk."

Dieter couldn't unsee Estelle's facial scars. The more he'd slept beside her, the more he'd noticed them. He began to imagine an entirely different woman living under that fake face. It became difficult to kiss her. Who was she? Other than her concierge profile, she wasn't on any social media. When he Googled her name, Sharon Branson, it produced nothing. She never referred to any friends or family. It was like she'd landed in New York from another planet. It tugged at him, and he started to pull away after a while. Something didn't feel right. She never took her makeup off at night. This left residue on his pillow slips. He hadn't appreciated that.

When Estelle got to Dieter's apartment, they were stiff with each other. Their old intimate camaraderie was gone. They made polite inquiries as to what each had been up to. They didn't touch. She didn't mention having Phil with her, let alone his death.

She smiled at him and said, "It's okay, Dieter. It was fun. Not everything goes on forever." He nodded and said, "It was fun." She asked him suddenly, "Do you have any Cohen music?" He said, "Yeah, pretty much everything he did; I love Leonard's stuff." She said, "Can you find 'Dance Me to the End of Love'?" He looked at her, moved over to his player, flipped through some selections, and chose one. When Leonard's raspy voice came on, Dieter offered his hand, drawing her up to him to dance. He moved her slowly around his living room to the music. Unlike the first time, there was no sexual innuendo or kiss at the end. There hadn't ever been love. When the music stopped, she looked long at him with an affectionate smile. Then she said, "It's been great, but I gotta go." Dieter didn't stop her. They both knew it was time.

She looked back at him from the open door as she left. Dieter said, "I would have loved to have known your secrets." She said, "My secrets?" He said, "Yeah. Your nightmares and those tiny white surgical scars circling your face." She left him with one last lie. "I have no secrets. The scars were a medical necessity. No drama." She returned to him, kissed him on his nose and left. When she got down to the street, her heart was racing. She thought *the surgery scars will stop me from doing that again. Too close for comfort.*

It was icy cold and windy standing there. Estelle watched garbage blow down the street and out under the roving taxi wheels. Never roving when you wanted one, mind you. February winds off the Hudson were brutal. A used coffee cup tumbled past her feet followed by a plastic bag that spread itself against a chain link fence like a crook with his hands up. It would live on forever in its non-degradable war. Plastic bags win.

Estelle's concierge work was done, and the city had turned ugly. She thought *Phil wanted his ashes spread somewhere warm. I can do that. It's time for a change.*

Estelle had grown up with winter. She didn't like it, but she thought she could put up with it. She realized she didn't have to. She started researching California. She thought, *L.A.'s a big city. I can get lost there. I'll figure out what to do when I get there.*

She thought *before I leave, I'll get a new identity. A brand new me. I don't want anyone from Manhattan following me.* She only took a few things with her. Some of her favorite casual pieces. She knew her wardrobe would change again.

She'd flown down, feeling braver about her face being recognized. Phil had said the police thought she was dead. No one would be looking for her. She'd packed all her money in a carry-on. That had to travel with her. She looked out the window at the tarmac. The wind was whipping the snow around in whirlwinds, leaving beaded sleet on her window. A blizzard had blown in, and the ground crew was de-icing the wings. She thought *I'm not going back. I'll stay at the airport until this blows over.* After two hours, her plane started to move, lifted and took off for the coast. She looked down at the outskirts of New York City. She thought *goodbye New York. You were great. Thank you. Off to a new adventure.*

When she disembarked at LAX, the air was warm on her face, and everyone in the airport was wearing summer clothes. She rented a car, picked up a map of L.A. and started driving around, exploring. She had yet to learn which were good or bad neighborhoods and thought *I'll do what I did in New York, hire an agent who knows the areas.* It was a big city, and she'd need to find somewhere safe. At the end of the day, she drove into Hollywood, checking out all the familiar street names, thinking, this looks more manageable. She pulled into a motel and booked a room for a week. She wanted some time to get a feel for the area. She hadn't eaten all day and spotted a funky bar across the street. It looked safe. She went in, sat on a bar stool and waited for the server. A few guys were down the bar from her watching a basketball game, but they didn't even look at her. They didn't seem to be together. Just men in a bar watching a game. A single woman came in after her and sat a few stools down from her. Estelle smiled at her, but she was busy looking at apartments on her phone and didn't want girl chat. The server showed up. She had short white blonde hair and an eagle tat on her left upper arm. She said," Hi, my name is Jules, welcome to the Beep. What can I get you?"

The last time these four were together in the same place, they'd lived in the Vanilla Palms condo outside of Jacksonville. They probably wouldn't have recognized each other even without the facial surgery and shaved heads. They were still strangers on the run.

Chapter Twelve

ENDINGS AND BEGINNINGS

CLAIRE

Sixteen hours on a plane in the cheap seats was a hard haul. Claire could have flown first class but didn't want to draw attention to herself. She flexed her body in her seat, trying to stay moving and not stiffen up. She went to the washroom and ran on the spot until someone knocked. She hadn't loaded anything to read so she watched movies, four in a row. She thought, now I know why I never watched movies. As the plane approached Carrasco International in Montevideo, she looked down at the vast blue expanse of the Atlantic. The city had a population of around 1,800,000, big enough for her, her mother, and Mikael to live quiet, private lives in safety and hopefully disappear.

Claire had been on the run for over a week in high-stress mode. She was exhausted. She rented an SUV at the airport and booked into the first decent-looking hotel she came across. She was desperate for sleep. She hung the "do not disturb" sign on her door, climbed under the comforter and slept for twelve hours.

She woke in the middle of the night, startled. It took her a minute to remember where she was. She was still on L.A. time. She thought, *If Mikael and my mother boarded the cruise ship to Rio, I only have about two weeks to find us a spot to live. We'll need a two-step arrangement, a short-term and final rental.* She'd studied city maps and had a pretty good idea which neighborhoods were good. She found a sizeable vacation rental on the ocean for the short term. She thought it would be better if the other two had some input into the long-term rental.

She would have been amused to watch Mikael and her mother, Polina, dance around each other in the small stateroom on the ship. They at least had two single beds, but privacy was limited to the tiny bathroom. Eighteen days was a long time for a new grieving widow who couldn't stop crying and a somewhat unsympathetic bachelor to spend together. They didn't go down for the joint dinners. There would be too many questions from friendly strangers. They did take the shore tours. That provided them with some variety and a break.

In their stateroom, they'd talked about the future. Claire's mother was still shell-shocked by the murder of her husband and the end of her life as she'd known it. They used the ship's WIFI to research Montevideo and get an idea of where they were headed. Claire's mother was worried Claire wouldn't be there at the other end. She thought she'd either be murdered by the Russians or unable to get there for some reason. Then they wouldn't be able to find each other. She worried a lot. Mikael told her they had several ways worked out to get messages to each other. It was going to be okay. He reminded her Anastasia had a lot of training and would know how to avoid trouble. He said, "If she's not there and we can't contact her immediately, we'll go ourselves. We'll figure it out. That was too many unknowns for Claire's mother.

Claire had left Cooper with his caretakers for now. No need to upset him by picking him up and leaving him again. She flew up to Rio a day ahead of her mother and Mikael's arrival date. She didn't want to take any chances and didn't know the city. She rented an SUV at the airport and made her way over to the dock. Parking was tight. It was steaming hot with a cloudless sky and no shade relief where she stood. Two other cruise ships had just docked, and thousands had disembarked. Cabs and tour buses were lined up. A freeway ran right beside the docks. It was chaos with horns honking, thousands of conversations going on, and harbor boat horns tooting. Crowds made her very nervous. She could see another liner approaching. She thought, what if they aren't on it? She knew they wouldn't recognize her new face and would be wary of a stranger approaching them in a crowd. As the big ship approached, she saw the name banner, the 'SmoothSeas.' *Please be on it* she pleaded with the universe.

It took another hour before the gangplank dropped and people started walking off the ship. She scoured every face as they appeared at the opening. They'd booked late so possibly would be last off. Another hour went by with no Mikael or mother. The disembarkers had dribbled down to a few people in wheelchairs and walkers. Claire was worried. *They missed it*, she thought.

Then suddenly, they were at the top of the gangplank, squinting down at the crowd in the sun. Hesitant. She moved forward through the crowd, got as close to the gangplank as possible, raised her hand and waved frantically, jumping up and down. They stared at this strange woman waving at them. She yelled up at them. "It's me!" They looked at each other, smiled, and moved toward her in the crowd. As they approached, Mikael was careful. He said in Spanish, "Where's Cooper?" If this woman wasn't Anastasia, she couldn't answer that. Claire laughed and said, "Smart, you were always smart." She said, "Cooper's getting his belly tickled and being spoiled by his caretakers. Thanks for asking." Mikael looked over Claire's new face, and she said, "I know, I know, not pretty." He laughed out loud and said, "Not ugly, exotic. I like your new look." She turned to her mother with her arms open and said, "Mama." Her mother embraced her tight, held her back, looked at her face, and said, "I don't like this new Anastasia. Where's my daughter?" Claire said, "Don't worry mama, I'm still in here under this n ose."

Claire said, "We're going to fly back down to Montevideo. It's too far to drive. We'll get tickets at the airport. I didn't know your new names. I've rented a temporary vacation home in Montevideo until we find something permanent. I wanted to wait for you two to be part of that choice."

On the way to the airport, they chatted about the cruise, their staying away from the dinner crowd, and the shore stops they'd made. They stayed away from the elephant in the room, her dead father. Lots of time to talk about that.

All three of them unwound at the vacation rental the first week. It felt like a resort. They ate and drank and talked and talked and talked. Claire had picked up Cooper, and he wandered around this new space, leaving his coat behind. Claire resumed running with him. Mikael and her mother weren't dog people, Claire realized. He didn't get much attention from them, but he moved back into Claire's bed. Claire's house rental agent came up with several good properties, and they decided on a large four-bedroom, triple-bath. It was set back from the road and very private. Then they had to buy furniture. Claire footed the bill for everything. Rather, the U.S. clients she'd stolen from did.

For the next month, life was rather dull. None of them had much to do. Mikael was on his laptop constantly. Safe, in Eden. After living on the edge for months, they were all becoming bored.

Their differences surfaced. Polina, Claire's mother, was tidy, almost anal. Claire was not. She didn't make her bed, pick up her clothes or see dirty dishes in the sink. Then there was the shedding dog who tracked in wet and dirty paw prints and left his dog hair everywhere. Claire didn't seem to notice. They were mother and daughter living together again after too many years and driving each other nuts. Mikael also left his personal stuff lying around. It didn't bother Claire, but it sure bothered Polina. Although Mikael had spent a lifetime helping people get out of Russia, on a one-on-one basis, he wasn't a very sympathetic guy. Polina's constant crying was getting to him. He thought it was time for her to get over it. He was also pissed at Claire's dad, Andrej. He'd been telling him for years what was really going on in Russia. He'd particularly warned him of the danger of going out in Paris. But he wouldn't listen. Didn't want his perfect life disturbed. Now he was dead.

Claire came home with Cooper one afternoon to find her mother crying. She sat beside her and patted her back. Claire's mother said, "I miss your father. I miss my practice. I miss my life. I feel like a fool that we did not see Putin for what he was. I have no meaning here. I don't know what to do with myself. I feel useless. I'll never feel safe again."

Claire was feeling rather useless herself.

Claire offered her mother some tissues and said to her. "Mama, you have to straighten your shoulders and find some way to step back into life. Papa would have wanted you to be strong and march on." She said, "First you have to be fluent in Spanish. You and Mikael need to take accelerated classes, and we'll only speak Spanish at home. Let's start there."

Claire added, "Start thinking about your skills and how they might be used. You won't be able to practice medicine. That's a given. But there's a lot of other things you could do."

Claire's mother looked at her, wiped her eyes and said, "Perhaps I should give you the same advice. You're too young to retire and not use your many talents."

Mikael had a bit of Spanish, and he and Claire's mother, Polina, actually started having some fun learning the language. With Claire's assistance, they were both very fluent in six months.

Polina had been checking around to see who was doing what medically in the city. She found a doctor with a geriatric practice, her specialty, and made an appointment to see him. His name was Strom Kubista, and he was a Czech. Polina wasn't a good liar, but she introduced herself as Sofia Marchenko. She said she'd just emigrated from Ukraine and was looking for work. She said she'd volunteered with seniors and thought she might have something to offer. She was a proud woman and hated presenting herself this way. They were about the same age, early 60s. He looked long at her and asked her to take a seat. This woman carried herself with confidence, intelligence and authority. She wasn't going to be anybody's front office clerk.

He said, "I'm also an immigrant and had to escape under risky circumstances. I was in my early 30s, just out of med school. I had to rewrite all my exams to practice here." He asked her, "Do you have any official medical training?" She stayed very quiet, looked down at her hands and said, "None I can speak of." He looked at her again and said, "Telling answer." He then asked her a simple question. It was about memory loss and a recent study that had just been published. She said, "Yes, I read about that." She then gave him a detailed opinion of the study, disagreeing with some findings. She spoke in the language of a specialist. He smiled slowly at her. Given her answer, he suspected she was also a doctor. He said, "Let's try this. You sit in on my appointments with me today. I've got a full schedule.

You can share your thoughts." We'll see where we go after that. She spent a packed day with him and gave him a thorough prognosis of each patient. She was uncanny in observing the patients' responses and asking inciteful and telling questions.

After the last patient left the office, he said, "Let's talk." He said, "My wife used to be my assistant, but I lost her to cancer five years ago." She said, "I'm so sorry." He said, "It was hard, but I had my work." He then said, "My practice is exploding. All the aging boomers are showing up. I still need a medical assistant. It's obvious you're a trained geriatric doctor. I understand why you can't say so. That's your business. Would you be interested in coming in to do the preliminary meetings and workups with the patients?"

Polina smiled broadly and said, "Yes, I would love to do that, Dr. Kubista. He said, "Please, between you and me, I'm just Strom." He said, "We'd better get you a work permit." He also grinned at her and said, "You speak Spanish with a Russian accent, by the way." She smiled back at him and lied, "It must be Ukrainian you're hearing; I'm not Russian."

That was the beginning of a relationship that gave them both work satisfaction and led to love. They were married in a year.

Mikael also moved on. He'd been dedicated to helping people find new lives all of his life. There was no one to save in Montevideo. He'd been following all of the political upheaval and immigration problems in Argentina. He contacted a few of the larger organizations that were helping or at least were involved. He offered his services, saying he'd had some international experience. They told him to get there as fast as he could. They needed all the help they could get. He had no money and went to Claire. He said, 'I'd ask for a loan, but I'd never be able to repay you." She said, "After all you've done for us? I'll transfer $500,000 U.S. to an offshore account in your name today. They'll fly a debit card here within days. You can draw on it at will in Argentina." She said, "Watch out for the bank withdrawal limits. I'm not sure what they are there. You don't want to come this far and get arrested for money laundering or something." She said, "When you need more, let me know." He looked at her incredulously and said, "I'm not even going to ask where you got all that money." She just said, "Nobody died."

Claire had also been looking around for work options. On a volunteer listing, she found a small school looking for people who knew a bit about computers to teach part-time. She talked to them and was told the students were made up of adults and kids from all corners of the city. Most of them were struggling financially. The first day she went in, she looked around. There were old laptops on about 20 desks. Before starting the class, she updated them all.

Her first class was made up of 12 people. There was a mix of ages and sexes. The oldest was a man in his late 70s who wanted to "keep up." The youngest were a pair of brothers, seven and eight years old. They were Soren and Silas. She wondered why they weren't in regular school. The administrator said they wanted to give them a leg up and were really only missing a couple of gym classes. None of them had computers at home. She prepared a very simple program to familiarize them with the basics. She introduced them to Google, email and basic word processing. She had them do searches for all kinds of topics on Google. She wanted to get them excited about the machines they were playing with. She showed them YouTube and found some concerts of bands they'd all be interested in. She'd loaded a couple of games they could play. That was day one. They left talking and laughing with each other. She overheard one woman in her 50s say to her daughter, "This is going to be fun."

The administrator had said, don't expect much. Only half of them will show up for the second class. The next class, they were all there, big smiles on their faces. She said, "Let's review what we learned last week." It was a ten-week course, and she was proud of them all. They were all very proficient at the end. As a graduation present, she bought them all laptops to take home. They were cheap; she could afford them, and they were thrilled. She reminded them they needed WIFI or a paid provider to access the internet and told them about a few of the café's around town that offered it free. She also suggested getting a library card and using their computers. A few of them asked if she would offer an advanced class, and she said, "No, unfortunately not, but if you keep working with it, you'll learn a lot on your own."

In the next round, she found the two boys in her class again. They had both been naturals, as kids are, and she asked them, "Why are you here? You don't need me anymore?" The older brother Soren said, "We thought we could help show people what to do. Be your sort of class assistants." After that, the boys became a fixture in her classes, moving around to desks when people were stuck and helping them out. She asked them if their mom would mind if she invited them out to eat after the second class. They both shook their heads, "No." They weren't familiar with ordering in a restaurant, and she helped them out. When their food came, it disappeared fast. They were starving. She asked them what their parents did. The younger one, Silas, said, "My mama cleans houses." He then volunteered, "We don't have a dad. He died." She said, "I'm so sorry, what happened?" He said matter of factly, "Car accident." She asked, "Was this recent? Soren said, "No, a long time ago. He wasn't living with us when it happened." Cl aire thought *whatever a long time ago could possibly mean to these two little kids.*

Claire said, "I have a dog. His name is Cooper. I'm going to ask the ad-ministrator if I can bring him to class next time." They both thought that would be great. They'd never known anyone with a dog.

The administrator was okay with Cooper being there as long as Claire checked with the class first. A lot of people don't like dogs. As it turned out, they were all okay with it, and Cooper became a fixture in her classes, wandering about and getting spoiled. She and the boys would walk him after class and then stop to get something to eat.

Claire taught this class for years, introducing new things as they came up. The boys stayed in her classes until they hit high school and couldn't get away. They still met once a week after school, walked Cooper and got something to eat. She listened to all their chatter about their classes, sports, and friends. She watched them grow tall and smart. They became the nephews she would never have. She hadn't ever met their mother, but Soren brought Claire a card one day. It was written in an awkward hand and said, "Thank you for being so kind to my boys. They are becoming good men because of you." She didn't sign it with her name, just Soren and Silas' mama. Claire sent her back a note saying, "You should be very proud of your boys. They will go far. It has been my pleasure being their friend."

To get citizenship, Claire bought a house. It had a view of the ocean and a fenced yard for Cooper. She had dinner often with her mother and Strom. As the boys moved on to university, they often visited Claire with their friends and girlfriends. They found conversations with this experienced American woman interesting. They would never know she was actually Russian. She had a bigger view of life and its opportunities than they had dared dream about as little guys. They'd become family. Claire lived an ordinary life.

Did Claire pay for her crimes? Because of her career choice and decision to leave, her father was murdered, and she put her mother in mortal danger. Her mother had to leave her medical practice, comfortable life, and country. Mikael had lost his inn. Their lives had moved on. Maybe they would have anyway. Claire had done the world a favor by killing Malek. So that was something.

Claire sat on her balcony and looked out onto the water, idly scratching Cooper's head. His eyes were half closed in pleasure. His muzzle and floppy ears had gone gray, and he'd rather sleep than run these days. He was almost fifteen. Over the next six months, she watched him weaken. She was losing him. Her vet said, "He's struggling to breathe. I think it's time." Claire said, "I'll bring him in tomorrow." She wanted to feel him sleeping up against her one more time. He spared her having to put him down and died quietly in the night, snuggled up against her. Not even a whimper. Losing Cooper was the biggest heartbreak she'd ever felt, including that of her father's murder. Cooper was her boy.

About a year later, she drove by one of the local animal shelters. On a whim, she went in. A scared dog, no discernible breed, was huddled in the corner of its cage, looking out at the noisy world. Claire had them bring her out. The dog was terrified. Claire just sat with her for a while, letting her get used to her presence and smell. After a while, the dog, named Mel, decided Claire was okay. She had cookies and hadn't raised her hand at her. She moved in closer to this kind human. Claire took her home that day and Mel moved into Cooper's spot beside her in bed. Claire knew she couldn't live without a dog. She continued her computer classes well into her 70s.

She'd never be out of danger and would be looking over her shoulder for the rest of her life. As time separated her from the old days, she thought *the Russians would have murdered me, and the Americans would have put me in prison for spying. I'm alive. Malek is dead. That's good enough.*

Meanwhile, Ivan Nechayev arrived in Rio de Janeiro from Moscow. It was hot, and he was wearing a wool sports jacket. He'd needed it when he flew out from Moscow. Sweat soaked his forehead and his shirt. He carried a small vile of Novichok in his breast pocket. It was well sealed. It could kill him. He thought *Anastasia's down here somewhere.* He had his orders. Russians never forget.

RANDY

Cito Herraras' guys searched all of Miguel's dealers' homes and cars, thinking the missing dope and cash might be stashed there. They came up with nothing. He knew Miguel left town and heard one of his small-time dealers, Randy, had also gone missing. Coincidence? He wondered. But only briefly. People go missing all the time. He still didn't think Miguel was involved. It wasn't his kind of thing. As far as he knew, he'd never murdered anyone. Cito was still convinced one of the other cartels had the money and the drugs. He'd never be able to prove it unless someone talked. The street was silent.

Less than a year later, Cito came out of a Miami club around one in the morning. Music pounded out the door behind him. The lineup had disappeared. All the good-looking girls were inside. He stepped forward ahead of his boys, belly out, picking his teeth, confident, ever the leader. "I'm the man." Big mistake. A male in a black hoodie and mask stepped out of the dark and called out his name. "Hey Cito, Tony says hello." It was the last time Cito would look up. A single gunshot in his lung dropped him to the ground. He gurgled blood onto the pavement. The shooter had used a silencer, and by the time the two men who usually guarded Cito got to him, the shooter had hopped into a car and peeled away. Cito died there on the pavement. A stolen car, presumably the getaway car, was found by police a few blocks down. None of it was caught on camera. No one was talking. Tony, the gang leader who'd ordered the hit, thought *good riddance, Cito.*

The police were left with another unsolved murder case of the many they had in Jacksonville. The three murders in the warehouse district last year were almost a distant memory. They hadn't been looking hard at it anyway. Thought it was gang-related. All the dead guys were known to them, but that didn't give them much to go on. Gangsters killing gangsters. Four fewer on the street, including Cito.

Neither Randy nor Pauly would ever know they were off the hook. No one would be looking for either of them.

After Pauly introduced himself to Randy at the Beep, saying he was from Jacksonville, he started dropping into the bar regularly. Randy was the first friendly face he'd seen when he got to Hollywood, and he anchored onto him. This made Randy very nervous. He kept thinking *fuck, what if this guy Paul is the client I was supposed to meet.* Then he'd think *lots of people are called Paul, and lots of people are from Jacksonville. It's probably just a coincidence.* He thought again, *whatever it is, I don't want the guy hanging on to me.* He envisioned Pauly getting visitors from Jacksonville, maybe someone who knew Randy back at the Amazon warehouse. He didn't like this but didn't know what to do about it.

He stopped his regular visits to the Beep, dropping to a few times a month rather than a few times a week. The last time he was in, Jules said, "Where you been Jakey, we haven't seen much of you lately?" Randy said, "Working mostly. I've got a lot of contracts I've got to service." She said, "Your new bestie Pauly has been in a bunch of times asking for you." Randy said, "Jesus, what's with that guy? I met him once and had a ten-minute conversation about work in Hollywood, and he's glommed on to me. Honestly, he's another reason I haven't been in lately. I'm trying to lose him." Jules said, "I can handle that for you if you want. I'm real good at getting rid of pain in the ass guys." Randy asked, "What would you do?" She said, "The next time he comes in asking for you, I'll tell him you're not a regular, and we rarely see you. I'll also tell him you're an asshole and should be avoided." Randy laughed and said, "Thanks Jules, I think." She came around to his side of the bar and hugged his back. "I don't think you're an asshole, honey. We just want him to think so." Randy smiled over his shoulder at her and said, "Hope it works."

It did. Randy never saw Pauly again. Pauly found work on one of the movie lots and started hanging out with a few of the lot guys. They had their own bar. Besides which, Jules had told him that guy Jake at the Beep was an asshole.

Meanwhile, Randy and his bookkeeper, now girlfriend, Emily, were having problems. Randy ran on a low hum and didn't get excited about much. Emily was high maintenance. She needed attention, even if it was negative, and spent a lot of time niggling him. "We never do anything," she'd whine. Randy would say, "What do you want to do?" She'd say, "Take some day trips, go out to dinner, catch a movie or some theatre, go to a bar with a live band." Randy would say, "I'm too busy to get away, and I'm not really into clubs." She said, "Well, what about a movie? We live in Movieland?" He asked, "What do you want to see?" She'd list a few romcoms mostly, none of which interested him. Then they'd do nothing, stay at home, order in food and on a Friday night, maybe have a beer at the Beep.

Randy was content and oblivious to her boredom. He was getting laid regularly. That was kind of good. He wasn't a lover though, and it wasn't good for her. She often had to initiate sex.

After a year, she'd had enough. One Friday night at the Beep, she said, "I think you should find another bookkeeper." Randy wasn't surprised. He said, "Do you have anyone in mind?" He thought to himself *that was cold. I should have given her a kinder reaction.* But, it was out. She got up from her stool, grabbed her purse and said, "Anyone but me." She walked out quickly. The fact he'd barely reacted was the finishing touch for her. As she marched down the street, she thought *he wasn't even a bastard. He was just nothing, dull. He didn't care.* She was right about that. He was happy she'd broken it off. She had started to bug him, but he didn't know how to end it. He did have to find another bookkeeper, though.

After she left, he felt lighter, free of needy Emily. He thought *maybe I'm just not the kind of guy who does well with girls.* He'd never had a high sex drive. He thought about Mary for the first time in a long time. He remembered her long blonde hair blowing in the hot Florida breeze as she crossed the parking lot at Amazon. He would have loved to have had a chance with Mary, but he would have bored her, too. She hadn't been interested. He wondered if she knew he'd willed her his condo yet. It wouldn't do her any good anyway, as long as they thought he was still alive. He couldn't be declared dead for five years. She didn't have the cash to cover the condo expenses if she waited.

The next day, he made up another list of potential bookkeepers and interviewed them on the phone. He hired a guy this time. That was the end of Emily. No muss, no fuss.

Randy's cleaning business continued to grow, and he thought about bringing on a helper for some of the smaller contracts. It would have to be someone as meticulous as he was. He posted a listing around some of the laundromats and corner stores to see who applied. This turned out to be a disappointing introduction to the rough side of Hollywood. He'd just left his email and got over 100 inquiries within a week. He knew if he was going to have someone working for him, he'd have to like them, and there'd have to be a basic intelligence there. They'd also have to be able to spell, even if that had nothing to do with cleaning. The applications were comical. "I can start today. Call me." "As long as I don't have to do toilets, I'm interested." "Would I be cleaning any of those big houses on the hill?" He smelled lazy, thief and just plain stupid on most of them.

One application stood out. It was from a woman, Chevelle Robinson. She spelled out her experience, her expectations and her standards. She provided five references, some of whom she was currently doing work for. At the end of it, she said, "I have a Jamaican mother, and I was taught how to clean by the best." He called her up and arranged a meeting in a local coffee shop that had a quiet section. She was dressed smartly and carried herself well. He liked her before even talking to her. She was around 30, sporting a short afro, a pretty face and a huge smile. Her handshake was firm and confident. So far, so good. He explained his business, and she said she'd been doing the same for a few years around Hollywood. She told him she'd come in behind other cleaners and had to start from scratch in many people's homes because the previous cleaner's work had been so sloppy. He liked what he was hearing. He told her he was also fussy and had built his business by going the extra mile. He said, "If the fridge needs cleaning, and they haven't asked, do it anyway." They talked about products and tricks of the trade. In fact, they had so much in common they spent two hours talking just about cleaning. He hired her, paying her an above-average hourly wage. That impressed her.

He learned she had a daughter, Francie, five years old, who stayed with her sister when she was working. She said, "Don't ask; her daddy's long gone, and good riddance." She went on, "She's a good girl."

Chevelle started picking up work from Randy two days a week. He would check with the owners after she'd cleaned there. They loved her. It was a match.

Randy's business continued to grow.

Just before his apartment rental year was up, his landlord paid him a visit. He looked around his old apartment and said, I never kept it this tidy. It looks great. He sat on one of his sofas and said, "I've got an offer for you." He said, "My mother died and left me her house up in Connecticut. I've decided to stay there. It was my home." He continued, "Would you be interested in buying this condo and the contents? Not the art, that comes with me." Randy hadn't thought about owning. He loved this apartment and his life in this building. His landlord said, "Let's get a realtor to estimate value." When the appraisal came in, Randy told his landlord, "I can pay you cash, we won't need a realtor, and you won't have to pay commission." His landlord looked at him and said, "You've done well. Good for you!" He dropped the price much lower than the appraisal and said, "It's yours." Randy retrieved the cash from his locker and handed it to his lawyer, who said, "Wow, you weren't kidding. I thought you'd do it through a money transfer or something." Within a week, Randy was the proud owner of his own condo. The apartment looked naked without the wall art.

Randy and Chevelle became good friends, and she and her daughter Francie joined Randy and Kenneth regularly for dinner. Francie was a good girl, as advertised, and seemed to enjoy these visits; she liked to help out in the kitchen.

Randy got Kenneth and Chevelle to help him choose replacement art for his bare walls. Randy laughed and said, "I'm not rich; these have to be affordable and something I will want to look at every day. Kenneth said, "You were rich enough to pay cash for this place." I heard you drove a pick-up truck of $5.00 bills up to the lawyers'. Randy laughed and said, that's not how it went, and where did you hear that bullshit? Kenneth smiled, "Oh around, you know what it's like here." Randy said, "My landlord was exaggerating. It was only an SUV, and it was ones, not fives." Randy was rarely funny, but this made them laugh. Kenneth said, "You do have your secrets." Randy thought, *you don't know half of it.*

Randy's life had turned out well. He had his cache of stolen money in his storage locker. His business was doing so well he never had to draw on it, other than to buy the condo and his car. He didn't feel guilty about it. He thought of himself as an honest, hardworking thief. He still looked at the remaining money as insurance.

The only thing Randy missed about his old life now was his mom. She, in turn, thought about him every day. She'd think *he wasn't street-smart; at least, I didn't think so.* She couldn't imagine her son selling drugs, let alone putting together a disappearance. She clung to that. He may be out there somewhere and would get in touch. Joe, the detective suggested Randy might have gotten into some trouble with the drug cartel. She couldn't believe these words were being used about her son. She said, "What you're not saying is he could also be dead." Joe kindly said, "No, I'm *not* saying that." Randy's father was sure the fool was dead. He was disgusted

Randy drove into Arizona one weekend and mailed his mother a short letter. It was a small risk. If she told the police, they would know he wasn't dead, but they wouldn't know where to find him. He'd still be just another missing person. He wrote, "Dear Mom, I'm safe and doing well. I'm sorry for scaring you, but my life was in danger, and I had to disappear.". He wrote, "Thank you for all your support over the years. I know I wasn't the star child you wanted, and now this. You'll be relieved to know I'm not a complete failure. I have a small, successful business. I think you'd be proud of me. I have good friends, and I'm okay. I think of you every day, and I hope everything is okay at your end. Mom, it would probably be safer for me if you didn't tell anyone you've heard from me, not Dad and not the police. I'll write again. Much love...Randy."

She wept hard when she received this, holding it to her heart. Randy wrote every month after that, and she tucked his letters away in a secret place and told no one. Her baby was alive out there somewhere, and he missed her. That was something.

Randy felt better writing his mother, even though it was a one-sided communication. A few years went by. Randy was feeling cocky and safe. He thought *I'll take a few days, fly back and see if I can see her. I'll call her when I get there. Maybe we can have a secret meeting.* When he landed at Jacksonville International, he looked around and moved quickly. He didn't want to run into anyone he'd known in his past life. He rented a car and booked a hotel near his parent's place. He took a deep breath and called her. The phone rang out with no message prompt. Odd, he thought. He wore a baseball cap and sunglasses and drove slowly by his old house. There was only one car in the driveway. His mother had liked small cars.

This was a large SUV. He started to get a sick feeling in his stomach. *Did she tell his dad he'd been writing? Had they split up? Where was she?*

Randy drove by several more times over the next few days. There was no change. One SUV was parked in the driveway. One afternoon, a man came out and got into the SUV when he drove by. It wasn't his father. He realized they'd probably sold and moved. He looked up the address, and sure enough, the house had been up for sale a year ago. He didn't know why it hadn't occurred to him earlier, but it suddenly hit him. Maybe his mother was dead. Maybe both his parents were dead. He looked up the Jacksonville obits, and there it was. She'd been gone for a couple of years. His father had died just after he left town. He choked on his grief, sobbing all night. He was also thinking, *what happened to my letters?*

The next night, Randy went to a small restaurant down the street for a burger. He was flying home to Hollywood in the morning. He was the only one in the restaurant. He was feeling pretty down. A young, skinny kid about 17 came in. He was moving strangely, looking all around him. Randy had a bad feeling. The kid approached the counter and pulled out a gun. He ordered the young girl at the counter to give him the money in the till. She was wide-eyed, frozen with terror, and didn't move. He screamed at her, "Hurry up!" He looked around the restaurant while he waited for her to give him the cash. His eyes were not focused. Randy was watching all of this from his table by the window. He didn't know what to do. It was all happening very fast, and there was nowhere to hide. The kid took the money, stuffed it into his pockets and decided robbing the place wasn't enough. Whatever was in his veins gave him a false sense of power. He started shooting. He shot the girl in the chest and circled around, the gun going off randomly. A bullet found its way into Randy.

When the police searched his body and found his ID and his cleaning business cards, they called that number. They just got Randy's voicemail. Randy wasn't home. *Wonder what he was doing here?* The cops asked each other. They contacted the Hollywood police, who followed up, and eventually, Chevelle and Kenneth were notified.

Randy had done one thing right. Before he left for Jacksonville, he'd thought *anything could happen in Jacksonville*. He'd made up a will and left his condo and his business to Chevelle. In a file folder in his apartment that said "For Chevelle and Kenneth," he enclosed the will, told them about the money in storage and left the padlock key. The note said, "Thank you for being such good friends. Split the money and enjoy." When they found the stacks of cash and counted it, they looked at each other in shock. Kenneth said, "Jesus, I always guessed he had secrets, but wow. Do you think he stole it?" Chevelle said, "I can't believe the Jake we know would do that. He was so honest." Kenneth said, "Should we tell the police?" Chevelle said, "And what, have it confiscated while they investigate forever?" She said, "We should take it, keep our mouths shut and enjoy it, just like Jake suggested." That's just what they did.

After their parents died, Randy's sister cleaned out the house and got it ready to sell. She found Randy's letters tucked into the back of their mother's closet and read them. She thought *he was always a strange kid. It's better to leave it alone; nothing can be done now. He doesn't want to be found.* She tossed the letters and didn't think to tell the police. She wondered what he could have done to cause his life to be threatened. She would never know. Randy wasn't talking.

ANTONIO

Antonio ate supper at the Beep every night for the next two weeks. He usually sat on the last bar stool before the door and didn't talk to anyone. Randy noticed him but didn't think much of it. Guys came and went all the time at this bar. It was central. He didn't remember him from the Vanilla Palms condo back in Jacksonville.

Antonio contacted a real estate agent to find him a good rental. He figured it would be better if the first contact the potential renter got wasn't from a Mexican, especially one with no references. When he told the agent he could pay a year's rent in advance for the right place, the agent thought *yeah, right, drug money*. Antonio made it clear he didn't do drugs, had the odd beer, didn't smoke and was a very quiet tenant. He'd given him his story of caring for an old aunt up north for years. He didn't think the agent ever bought his story, but the agent did find him a nice place. Fifth floor, good size, very modern, two bedrooms, lots of light and a sizeable balcony overlooking a park. Of course it was pricey. He went shopping for furnishings and had it all delivered on the day he moved in. The weather was warm and sunny. *So far, so good*, he thought.

While he waited for his apartment, he'd checked out fishing spots. Most of it was pier fishing, which didn't appeal to him. If he wanted to get out on the water, he'd need a more powerful boat than he was used to. The Pacific off the California coast was a very different ocean than the warm Atlantic off the Florida coast. This water was cold. He thought *maybe my fishing days are over*.

He also started looking at listings for gyms for sale in L.A. The list was long. That told him most had failed for various reasons, but probably not enough money in it. He wasn't looking to get rich; he just wanted to run a little gym. He made some calls and had a short list of places to drop into. He decided to stick to the Hollywood area for now. He had a list of requirements, one being the gym was still open and operating. The equipment had to be relatively new and recently serviced. It had to be safe so women would feel comfortable coming. He ticked off several other requirements on his list as he visited each gym. One gym stood out. It was called "Movement." There wasn't much movement going on there though. He dropped by around ten in the morning, and the woman sitting at the front desk looked up from her phone but said nothing. She was in her late 40s, a bit ropey, almost too thin. She had very dark hair tied back in a low nape knot. She had a strong, almost angry face. At first glance, Antonio got a Spanish dancer vibe from her looks, stern demeanor, largish nose, dark darting eyes, and dark skin. He had a quick flash of her with castanets, flipping the skirt of a tight red dress around, clicking the floor hard with her heels. He blinked again and saw a bored woman wearing a black leotard and sneakers, not a Spanish dancer.

He introduced himself and asked if she was the owner. She didn't smile and said, "Yes, and whatever you're selling, I'm not interested." Antonio put both hands up in a mock hold-up position and said, "Not selling anything; I'm looking around town for a gym." Still not smiling, she said flatly, "Well, you've found one," Antonio thought *no welcome here.* He said, "You misunderstand me. I'm thinking of buying a gym. I saw your listing." She looked him up and down and thought *great, he's a damned Mexican, this will be a waste of time.* Antonio knew he'd just been assessed and came up short.

He ignored that and asked her, "Why are you selling?" She said, "It's not easy running a gym with only a few staff. I'm here all the time, and I'm tired." She didn't want to say, "and I'm running out of money." She thought, *who knows, he might be the next sucker to buy this place, even if it's not making any money.* Antonio asked, "Do you mind if I have a look around?" She said, "Sure, go ahead. There's no one here right now." She added, "I get busy later." That was a lie. Antonio went into the gym. It was a fair size, and the equipment was in good shape. He got on each of the treadmills and ran them through the levels. He did the same with the bikes. The TV screens were all working. The exercise machines all did what they were supposed to do. The weight room was well equipped. The showers could have used a cleaning, but the lockers all had well-fitted doors. Everything worked. Given her attitude, he was surprised the place was in such good shape. When he returned to the front he asked her, "How long have you had the business?" She said, "Less than a year. I bought it off a young guy whose daddy paid for the whole setup, brand new everything. He found out he would rather play than hang out here." She said, "I've discovered I prefer having a life than being here all the time. It was a mistake." He said, "Can I ask what you paid for it? She said, "Only my life savings."

Antonio said, "I might get back to you. Thanks for your time." She thought *fucking waste of time. Doesn't have any money but acts like he does. Next.* She went back to scrolling through her phone. Antonio walked up and down the street. It was a wide, busy street, with parking and a parking lot just a few buildings away. There was a medical center across the street. That interested him. He went into a coffee shop across the way, sat near the window, and watched people passing by the gym. The windows were blocked with signs with cartoon images of a man and a woman in gym gear. You couldn't see inside, so you wouldn't know what you would run into if you went inside. The overhead sign was small, unlit and disappeared in the street signage noise. Hollywood street signage was colorful and visually no isy.

He slept on it and came back to it the next day. It was overcast and raining. The gym storefront just disappeared into the stream of stores and services on the street. Nothing stood out. He thought, "Her asking price is prob-ably more than she paid. I doubt she's got much of a client base to sell." He decided to take the leap and crossed the street. The gym was closed. No signage, nothing. *No wonder she's losing her shirt*, he thought. He went back the next day but she didn't open until noon. When she finally opened, he went in and she said, "You again. What do you want?" He thought *so pleasant, this woman.* He said, "I want to buy your gym. I'll pay you $30,000 cash for everything, equipment included. She said, "I'm asking $50,000." He said, "Take it or leave it." $30,000 was exactly what she'd paid for it ten months ago. She was thinking *better move on this before he changes his mind.* She said, "You're getting a deal, but okay. Let's do it." Antonio said, "I'll contact a lawyer and get the papers drawn up. I'll be in touch."

Within a week, it was his. He took down the old window signs and put plain brown paper on the windows for the interim. He bought a ladder, climbed up and took down the sign. There was a small graphic design shop down the street. Antonio dropped in. A young blonde guy sitting at a computer stood immediately, smiled, and said, "Hello, what brings you in here?" Antonio introduced himself, told him what he was doing, and said he needed help with sign design. The guy put out his hand and said, "Well, my name is David, and I really like your concept. Maybe I can help you put it together." They went over some ideas, and he quickly came up with some designs Antonio liked. He sketched up a large window sign, saying, "Coming soon STRETCH, a gym for every body. No contracts, competitive rates. You're going to love this gym."

David said, "I've always wanted to see the inside of that place. Can you give me a tour?" When he walked in, he said, "I think people should be able to see in, to start with, and the front lobby should have color and plants and couches and carpets and some decent posters. Maybe even a gurgling fountain. I'm thinking zenny California here. There should be some good music playing. The entrance should say, "Come in, you'll be welcomed here." When they went back to the back, he had several great gym decor ideas. Antonio said, "Are you interested in doing this?" David said, "I'd love to. I can also do your website and social media advertising for you." Antonio hired him to put it together. David created a design for a large backlit sign that said simply STRETCH. The word "Stretch" leaned to the right, in a long stretch. Antonio found a company that could make the sign and install it.

He went to the medical drop-in clinic, introduced himself to a young doctor working that day, and told him about his concept. He asked if any of the doctors on staff might want to be the doctor of record he would recommend to clients who could use medical care. The doctor said, "Sure, great idea. You can refer me. As long as they have medical insurance, of course." He laughed. Antonio said, "Of course." He then did the same with the physiotherapist, the chiropractor and the massage therapist.

He checked out which local colleges ran kinesiology programs, found one and visited their admin office. They suggested he post on the student board, explaining what he was looking for. They were sure he'd be inundated with applications. It was coming together. Antonio was busy, and he was having fun.

Antonio hired and coached all his staff and trainers on his welcoming approach. His front desk people were all mature with average everyday looks and bodies. The idea was to welcome, not intimidate. He held an all-day open house for his grand opening. He had it catered with light snacks, a juice bar and soft reggae played in the background. David had suggested the reggae, saying it always made people want to sway with the rhythm. It felt like a happening place. Antonio had a list of offerings, classes, personal trainers, individually designed programs, clean premises, and, most of all, no judgment. He signed up over 50 new clients within a week. He was immediately swamped.

He knew the business had to be legit with the IRS. He'd have to risk his new identity and get a bookkeeper to set him up legally. He took a deep breath and hired a woman to do this.

On the other coast, the phone rang back in the Miami Lucerne Property Management head office. Billy took the call. A woman with a deep, raspy, smokers' voice asked, "Are you the people taking care of the Vanilla Palms property?" Billy said, "Yes, can I help you?" She coughed and said, "I heard my daughter Lily was murdered by that bastard Mexican husband of hers, and he's dead too. I'm her next of kin. That condo's mine." Billy said, "You might want to verify that information with the police. What did you say your name was?" She said, "Maria Losa, I'm Lily's mother." Billy said, "I'm sorry for your loss, Mrs. Losa." She went into an extended coughing session and said, "We weren't close."

Billy thought, *go carefully here. This could be somebody from the media looking for a story.* He said, "I can put you in touch with the detective who looked into your daughter's death." Billy was careful not to call it a murder. He said, "He'll verify your relationship and tell you anything they know." Maria said, "I'm her damned mother, I don't need to talk to no cops." Billy said, "Well, I can tell you the condo was willed to Mr. Cervantes' daughters." Maria said, "That's bullshit, Lily was his wife, she should have got everything." Billy said, "There was a prenup filed with Mr. Cervantes' will. Everything went to his daughters. I'm sorry." Maria said again, "That's bullshit. I'll get my lawyer to look at that. I bet he made it up." Billy prejudged but doubted this woman even knew a lawyer, let alone had the means to hire one. He said, "Might be a waste of money. It was all legal, registered in the court." He asked her again, "Would you like the detective's number?" She said angrily, "No, I told you, I'm not talking to a damn cop." Billie wondered what Maria had been up to that made her so adverse to speaking with the police. Her daughter Lily was hooking even while living with and married to Antonio. *Nice family*, he thought.

He asked, "Is there anything else I can help you with?" She said, "My lawyer will be in touch." and abruptly hung up. Billy thought *don't think we'll hear from her lawyer soon.* He did share the call with Zenith and their lawyer, Doug MacPherson, all the same. Doug said, "We had nothing to do with it." Billie said, "Yeah, but the condo is under his daughter's conservatorship right now, and we're renting it out for her and making a bit of money; that might not look good should her mother really try to look into it." Doug said, "His will and prenup were all legally prepared. We're fi ne."

Back in Hollywood, Antonio's little gym was buzzing every day. His clients were happy, his staff were happy, and finally, he was happy.

He'd stored his money with another high-security storage company. This one didn't need his iris imprint, but it was still very protected. They insisted on being paid monthly. Their reasoning was as long as you were paying your monthly fee, you were alive. If you stopped, they had a reason to contact you. If they could not contact you, they could access the vault after six months. They still had to wait two years before claiming whatever was in your locker. In his locker, Antonio had left sealed letters for each of his daughters, along with detailed instructions on contacting his Vancouver daughter. If they couldn't find her, there were instructions as to how to track down his U.K. daughter. He also left a sealed letter for the Jacksonville police saying, "To be forwarded only upon my death." It contained the explanation of what had happened with him and Lily. He left the same instructions regarding his daughters and where the money was in his apartment.

He'd long abandoned the thought of ever reconciling with his daughters. To them, he was a dead man. Drowned in the Atlantic. He couldn't take the risk of coming back from the dead and attracting a murder investigation.

Antonio ran out of his heart drugs when he left Seattle and hadn't plugged himself into the walk-in clinic and had them replenished. He felt fine and thought *I'm fit, at a good weight. I don't need them*. He'd always hated taking drugs.

About a year after he opened the gym, Antonio was working out on the treadmill and had worked up to a slow, steady jog. He suddenly felt lightheaded and was hit with a stabbing pain in his shoulder. He didn't remember anything else. He woke up in the hospital in the cardiac unit. The doctor said, Mr. Escarino, you've had a massive heart attack. We barely saved you. You need a quadruple bypass immediately. Everything is blocked. Do you have health insurance? Antonio said, "How much?" the doctor said, "Could top $250,000 when all is said and done." Antonio said, "I've got it covered, don't worry." The doctor said, "So, we have your permission to proceed?" Antonio said, "It's either that or die. Get it done."

Antonio was only in the hospital for four days, and his staff visited when they could. He and the graphic designer David had become friends, occasionally seeing each other for dinner and talking about their businesses. He dropped in on Antonio on the day of the surgery when he was still plugged and wired. The scar down the middle of Antonio's chest was puckered and angry with stitches, as was the one down his leg. He had tubes all over. David thought *he looks so rough. He might not make it*. Between them all, they arranged home care and physio programs to get Antonio back on his feet. It was weeks before he could walk from one end of his apartment to the other and months before he returned to the gym. He appointed one of his more mature staff to be acting manager in his absence. His team held up, and the business moved along. They gossiped among themselves about the fact he had no one to call. No family, no friends. It was strange.

Antonio had a lot of time on his hands to ponder his life and his death. He realized he needed a backup plan for the gym, just in case. He wanted to protect the staff and his clients. He had a long talk with David and asked if he'd be interested in taking over the business should something happen to him. David was taken aback by the offer and said, "You're going to be fine; you'll get back on your feet." Antonio said, "I think so too, but just in case, is it something you'd want to take on?" David said, "I could try, but that business has you all over it. It would never be the same." Antonio said, "It could have you all over it, too. You have a good business head." David said, "Just to put your mind at ease, I accept your offer."

Antonio made up an online will in his new ID name, left the gym to David, and gave him a copy. He also tucked $500,000 in a small box at the bottom of his bedroom closet. He told David about the box but not what was in it. He said, "I've also left you a good luck charm in a box in my bedroom closet. If I die. It might help." David frowned at him and said, "I would have never guessed you to be superstitious." Antonio said, "Sometimes it helps." He said nothing more. David forgot about it.

While off, Antonio stopped shaving his head and grew a beard. He'd noticed his eyebrows getting grayer but was very surprised when his thick hair grew back almost white. His beard was a bit darker but still had a lot of gray. He didn't look like his old self or his new self anymore. The man looking back at him in the mirror looked old and frail. The day he returned to his gym, he didn't announce it, just dropped back in. The front staff initially didn't recognize him with his full head of hair and beard. He still had the same big smile and caring way, but his vigor was gone. Antonio was beginning to look like an old man.

He tired quickly and often left mid-afternoon. He was no longer there seven days a week. His lack of energy was getting him down. He hadn't been the same since the surgery.

One quiet day at the gym, he decided to play hooky. He waved over the back of his head as he passed the front desk. "See you tomorrow." His staff could manage without him. It was a sunny, warm day, and he needed an ocean hit. He drove down to El Segundo. It was a long beach and pretty deserted midweek. He walked about a mile and realized he still had to walk back. It was warm, and he was breathing heavily. The sun shimmered on the sea, creating small pockets of light between the gray ripples. He breathed in the sea air and thought, *give it time, I'll get better.*

A small plane droned above him, cruising lazily through the clear blue sky. He heard a dog bark way down the beach. The plane and the dog were the last sounds Antonio would hear. His heart stopped beating.

Antonio's Vancouver daughter didn't recognize the U.S. telephone number on her phone. She waited for the message to beep. She was astounded to learn her father had recently died. She'd thought he was already dead.

She also learned she and her sister were over seven million dollars richer. Antonio had left a note for them saying, "I always loved you. I'm so sorry to have let you and your mother down. I've thought of you every day. I was a selfish bastard and hurt some people along the way. Most of all, your wonderful mother. She didn't deserve my deplorable behavior. I hope this makes up for it a little. Split it with your sister. Give it to your children if you don't want it. Have good happy lives. Again, I'm so sorry."

When David heard that Cedro/Antonio had died, he almost had a heart attack himself. Now, he had two businesses to run and wasn't sure he could do both and do them justice. David had keys to Cedro's apartment because he'd been checking on him daily to ensure all was okay. He went in and looked around. Cedro/Antonio had always been tidy. An organized man. David went into the den and opened the file cabinet. He found the file with the note regarding the money. When he went there, he and the security guard opened it together. There was about seven million dollars in one hundred dollar bills in a large box. On top was a note that said, "For my daughters." They saw the other envelopes addressed to his daughters and the Jacksonville police. David was dying to open them. The security guard took the envelopes and said, I'll take care of these. We honor our client's privacy and requests, dead or alive. We'll make sure his daughters get every cen t.

David went back to the apartment with more questions than answers. Where would Cedro have gotten that amount of money? Why was he writing the Jacksonville police department? Did he steal the money? Not knowing Cedro was actually Antonio, he would never find out.

He remembered a conversation he and Cedro/Antonio had about super-stition and the good luck box. He searched the apartment, and right at the back of Antonio's closet, he found it. In it was a note. "David, thank you for all your kindness. Keep my baby business alive if you can. If you can't, I know you will have tried. Here's something to help you along the way. David couldn't believe his eyes.

ESTELLE

Estelle got in touch with an apartment realtor the next day. She gave her the new fake backup story and the cash upfront offer and told her what she was looking for. Once again, cash up front dispensed with the need for references. The realtor didn't disappoint and found a big, spacious apartment on the tenth floor of a Hollywood condo. Estelle moved in.

She looked out at her view from her balcony. Pricey-looking ranch houses with big yards and pools were scattered below. Turquoise squares and ovals of chlorinated liquid twinkling in the sun. No one was doing the backstroke in those pools. No one in them at all. She thought of the pool back at the Vanilla Palms. It had always been busy with over-tanned seniors dog paddling and breast stroking around the water, calling out to each other. Nobody did the crawl. Exercise wasn't the point. *At least it got used*, she thought. *Who's using it now?*

Phil's ashes sat on her kitchen island. Estelle thought *I don't want to drop him off some dock. I need to find a sandy beach where I can shake him out inconspicuously and let him get washed out to sea*. She drove up toward Malibu and stopped at Topanga Beach. No one was there, and the setting sun was on the horizon's edge, spreading orange across the sky. *Perfect*, she thought. She waded out among the rocks and sprinkled him around the water eddies. The water was freezing. Her feet looked blue under the surface. She thought *Toto, I've a feeling we're not in Kansas anymore. I miss the warm Florida seawater*. The tide was receding, and it took Phil's ashes with it. Estelle called out to him in her head *safe travels, old friend*. She didn't apologize for cheating him out of five million dollars.

Estelle started looking for a car. Los Angeles was not short of car deal-erships. A sleek silver Honda Accord spoke to her. She retrieved enough cash from her storage locker and laid it on the sales manager's desk. He just stared at it, then looked up at her and said, "Haven't you ever heard of e-transfers or checks?" Estelle said, "Don't need them, do I?" The boys on the lot talked about that for the rest of the day.

Next, she took a week and did all the tourist things, avoiding Disney. A big, crowded theme park wasn't her thing. She updated her wardrobe to match what she saw on women on the L.A. streets. Light and cool but never cheap. The clothes on the street weren't Florida casual. Only tourists wore shorts and flip-flops. Looking in the mirror at her pretty face and short hair, she thought *I'm looking too buttoned down, too New York*. She'd noticed some gray in her roots. She decided to let her hair grow out. In a year, it was long, wavy, and gray. The result was quite earthy, loose and attractive. Estelle had transformed herself again. She looked kind of artsy.

After three weeks in her new digs, Estelle was bored. When in Florida, she'd sporadically gone to a local gym. She'd done nothing in New York. *I can at least get fit*, she thought. She'd noticed a gym one street over called STRETCH that looked interesting. She dropped by and was warmly greeted by a lovely woman about her age who explained what they had to offer and the fees. The welcoming front lobby felt like the entrance to a spa. Estelle did a short tour and liked what she saw. People were talking to each other, laughing, having fun. In the weight corner, the usual meatball weight lifters were missing. It was now occupied by women and men of all ages, all in fair shape, a few lifting heavy loads. She was impressed. She went back to the front and paid for her first month. An older man walked by behind her while she paid. He had a thick head of almost white hair and a full beard. The woman at the front desk said, "Good morning Cedro. How you feelin' today?" Cedro said, "Better than yesterday but not as good as tomorrow." The front desk woman laughed, and Cedro went back to the gym. A flicker of recognition flashed through Estelle's brain. She said to the front desk woman, "Another happy client?" The woman said, "Oh, that's Cedro Escarino. He's the owner."

There had been a brief news article about a year ago when Antonio's wife Lily's skull washed up on the Florida beach. Antonio had been listed as a potential murder suspect, and his driver's license picture was shown. Estelle vaguely remembered him from the condo. She'd seen him at the mailbox a few times. She didn't even know why she was so sure, but she thought Cedro looked like Antonio, just whiter and bearded.

Estelle googled it, but nothing came up, not even the old news article and picture. Nothing more had been written. If Antonio's wife was murdered, no one was apparently interested. When she learned Cedro was new to Hollywood, her suspicions increased. This man Cedro had no online presence other than his website relating to the gym. He didn't exist outside of the gym.

Estelle had her identity secrets and wasn't about to out Antonio. She started going to the gym most days. She'd see the fake Cedro come and go, and he checked in on her workout progress and chatted her up pleasantly many times. She thought *if he's a murderer, he's a very nice one.* His staff and clients loved him. *Sleeping dogs*, she thought. *His business. I've got my own dark secrets.*

Estelle had enough money to see her through to the end of her life, but she didn't feel rich. That money was locked up in storage. She thought *it pays my rent and living expenses but I still need to be careful.* She didn't have health insurance and knew if something went wrong, particularly as she got older, she'd need that money. She still thought like a low-rent bookkeeper.

On a warm Friday, Estelle felt pleasantly exercised after a good workout at the gym. She stopped at a Starbucks, got an iced tea and went onto the patio to enjoy the sun and the view. An exciting selection of people always wandered by here. It wasn't the South Beach carnival you'd see on Ocean Drive in Miami. No people carrying costumed iguanas, barely clad roller skaters or performance art restaurant street hawkers luring people into their spot. Still, clothing choices were always imaginative. An inappropriate mink vest could be paired with old jeans and work boots. On a pretty young girl with salon-streaked hair, it worked. The more dressed down people were, the more likely they were famous. Estelle recognized a few actors and one aging rock star. Nobody bothered them. Street people also struggled with their life's belongings in their precious shopping carts. Way too many struggling people. Nobody bothered them either. It did not occur to Estelle that she could help. In her head, she still had barely enough to live on. Certainly not enough to share.

The patio was packed, and people were waiting for seats. Estelle was sitting at a small two-seater table back in the corner. A man she immediately thought of as an old silver-haired fox came out with a tray, looked around, saw there was no seating, and looked toward her. He mouthed, "Do you mind?" She extended her hand to the spare chair, and he joined her. Estelle thought, *what the hell, why not?* As he approached, she took in a man in his late sixties, tanned and in good shape. No middle age paunch. As told by his freckled, wrinkled face, he'd been a blonde as a younger man. *Too much sun,* she thought. He wore a well-cut pale blue sports jacket with a darker shirt, close-fitting pants, and white sneakers. His hair was thick, a little too long, and white as snow. As he arrived at her table, he said, "Thanks, I'll just eat and run." Estelle said, "Take your time. Relax. Enjoy your lunch."

He said, "Thanks, I will, I'm starving" and took a bite of his sandwich. He offered his free left hand and said, "Ralph Jamieson, thanks for sharing your table." Estelle smiled and said, "No problem." She didn't introduce herself. She watched him meticulously wipe his mouth and hands as he worked through the rest of the drippy sandwich. She said, "Now you're making me hungry. That looked good." He said, "Yeah, that was the grilled cheese, but their ham and swiss is also one of my favorites." She asked, "Do you eat here often?" He said, "Unfortunately. I work over at McGills and it's hard to get away. I should be smart and make a lunch, but these are so much better than anything I'd ever make." Estelle glanced over at McGills to see what it was. The signage was generic and didn't actually say what they did. She asked, "What goes on at McGills?" He laughed, took a drink of his coffee, and said, "Yeah, the sign doesn't say much, does it?" She waited. He said, "We set up marketing, websites, media management, P.R., brand management, product development, stylists and anything else a client needs to get and stay noticed." Estelle said, "Wow, like the Kardashians?" He laughed again. She liked watching him laugh. His eyes crinkled up, and his smile was broad and genuine. He had even expensive capped teeth. He said, "Yeah, like them. If only they were my clients." Estelle said, "Well, this is Hollywood. Everybody wants to be famous." He said, "Thank God. Those fame chasers are my bread and butter."

Estelle decided to jump in and introduce herself. She said, "I'm Danielle Wilson. Nice to meet you." He nodded and said, "Danielle," and continued eating. She hadn't heard too many people actually say her fake name. She thought, better get used to that. Estelle said, "I never thought about the mechanics behind stardom and here you are, the star mechanic." He said, "Hey, good marketing line, I think I'll steal it." She said, "I've got a million of 'em." She didn't, but it was fun saying that. He smiled and said, "Well,

Danielle, I've gotta run; Zoom meeting at 1:15. Maybe I'll see you again here." Estelle said, "Yeah, you never know. It's a small town."

She forgot about that chance meeting, but the following Friday, she was again sitting on the Starbucks patio, enjoying her iced tea. She had her head down, reading the news on her phone. *Always bad news, I don't know why I bother*, she thought. A familiar voice was suddenly at her side, saying, "Here you are again. Can I intrude?" Ralph was in a dark green golf shirt and cream pants. Estelle thought *this old guy always looks like a million bucks*. She looked up, smiled, spread out her hand, and said, "Mi table su table." She said, "I have no idea what the Spanish word for table is." Ralph said, "Mesa, but table works for me." Estelle said, "All this and bilingual too." He said, "Just Spanish and French. It comes in handy in my business. Almost sixteen million Hispanics live in California. Lots of them want to be famous."

This time, he wanted to know more about her. He said, "So you know what I do. Do you still work, or are you retired, like half the state?" Estelle thought, *here I go, building my litany of lies*. She said simply, "Retired." He said, "You must have done something along the way. Are you from here?" Estelle sketched out some of her fake background, partially true, mostly not. She didn't mention Florida. She said, "I was a concierge in Manhattan for a while." He said, "Really, that must have been interesting. You must have some great stories."

Estelle said, "The lineup of vacuous people who show up at your desk every day, having no idea about the city, let alone what they might want to do, got tiresome." She said, "I discovered I'm not very kind." He laughed out loud and said, "Honest of you. I think that about myself every day. Customers are a pain." He said, "How did you end up doing that?" She said, "Oh, you know, never did much when I was younger, stuck at home with my mother. I always wanted to live in New York. I just fell into the job." Ralph took that in and didn't question it. He said, "And what brought you to California?" She said, "The weather. I was tired of winter." She thought *so far so good, not too many lies*.

Estelle had checked his finger. No wedding ring, no tan line. After that, they ran into each other at Starbucks off and on for about two months and had brief but good conversations about many things. They were brave and discussed all the supposed no-go topics: politics, religion, and money. Turned out they agreed with each other on a lot of tricky subjects. He was also quick-witted, and his sarcasm made her laugh. She began looking forward to seeing him, saving up interesting things to share. One day, he said, "I have a friend who just opened a new restaurant. I'd like to try it out. Would you care to join me?" Estelle looked at him and said, "I dunno. Let's start with, are you married?" He said, "Good question. An old single guy hitting on a young, beautiful woman in Starbucks. What's his status?" Estelle said," Not young, but thanks for the compliment. What *is* your status?" He said, "Lost my wife to breast cancer eight years ago. We didn't have kids." She said, "I'm so sorry, devastating for you both." He said, "Yes, it was tough." She could tell that was the end of that conversation thread. He didn't elaborate. Estelle said, "In light of your bad, sad news, I will have dinner with you." Ralph said, "I'll see your pity and raise you one dinner." Then he laughed.

That was the beginning of the Ralph and fake Danielle romance.

Ralph had an expansive ranch-style house up in the hills. He wasn't a zillionaire, but he was doing very well. He was dedicated to his clients and always had his laptop and phone at his side. He got calls at all times of the day and night. His clients were very needy. Sometimes, they just wanted to share news of an audition going right or wrong. If it went wrong, he'd calm them down. He wasn't their agent; that was someone else's job. He just made them look good. He was everybody's mother in a way, except they paid him for the mothering. Estelle didn't mind the interruptions. It was his work, and he was good at it. It was fun to hear him encourage people. He was sincere and kind. She liked him more and more as time went on.

The first night Ralph asked her to stay over, Estelle looked at him and said, "I knew we'd get here sooner or later. I'm really sorry, but sex is off the table." She went on, "I really, really like you, but we won't be having sex." She continued, "I'll get out of your hair." She stood up and began gathering her things. She thought *I'm not going to have a Dieter repeat, with Ralph looking at my facial scars and wondering what monster lived under them.* She also thought, *what a shame. This will end our pleasant little reverie.*

Ralph smiled at her and said, "Interesting, that's exactly what I was about to say to you."

He watched her face for a reaction. Estelle thought *he's going to tell me he's gay. How could I have missed that?* She said, "I hope you're not going to say, it's not you, it's me?" He said, "Not if you don't say it." She laughed, and he said, "Seriously, I have a reason." Estelle said, "Okay, give it to me." He said, "That's just it. I can't." She said, "I don't know what you're talking about." He said, "Prostate cancer. I had mine removed. I'm cured, but the old boy doesn't care. He left the building." Estelle said, "Jesus, first you lose your wife and then your erection? Life ain't fair." Ralph said, "Actually, it was the other way around." Estelle thought, aaah, there was trouble in paradise.

Ralph said, "I'm alive and here to tell the tale. I love my work. I live in a beautiful place, and right now, I have a gorgeous girl sitting across from me. Life's pretty good." He took a sip of his wine, got up, walked around the pool, came back, sat down, and said, "I can't do much for you sexually, but tell me, are you just not interested generally, or is it me?" He said, "You can also tell me it's none of my business. It isn't." Estelle said, "It's okay. My reason sounds pretty shallow compared to yours." He said, "Share." She said, "I had some facial work done a while back, quite a bit, in fact. I still have the tiny white scars around the edge of my face. I didn't want to creep you out." He laughed out loud, stood up, walked over to her chair, and squatted down in front of it. He said, "Honey, half the state of California has had work done. I've had work done." She said, "Really, what?" he said, "Nose, eyes, chin implant. I had no chin." She exclaimed, almost with pleasure, "Me neither!" He showed her his scars. She showed him hers. It was the most intimate thing she'd done with a man ever.

He said, "I have a sexy idea that doesn't involve sex." She said, "What?" He said, "Let's skinny dip in the pool." She felt braver and freer than she'd felt in a long time. She stripped down and yelled over her shoulder, "Last one in's a rotten egg." He said, "Haven't heard that one in a long time. He stripped down and cannonballed her.

That night, she took her makeup off before coming to bed. They cuddled up together, and she learned he didn't need the old man to make her feel good.

She woke in the night and thought, *could I ever trust him with all the truth?*
She then thought *don't rush this. You have the rest of your life. Things could
change.*

Estelle still needed something to do. After the fake Cedro (Antonio) died
and David took over the gym, she got to know him better. She'd seen
him around, and he was always pleasant, but they hadn't talked much.
He didn't have the same relaxed approach Cedro/Antonio had. Antonio
had felt like a kind old dad, walking by you, encouraging you. David was
in his early 30s and seemed strained and over his head. One day, he was
sitting alone at the front desk when she came in, head down, staring at his
laptop. He looked up, smiled, and asked her how she was doing. She said,
"I'm fine, but more important, how are you doing?" He said, "Honestly,
I'm drowning. I have two businesses, both of them pretty busy. My graphic
design business was doing really well before I took this over. It's a one-man
shop, but I'm not always there now. I'm losing clients." She said, "Can I
help?" He said, "What did you have in mind?" She said, "What about I
manage the gym for you, reporting to you, of course, and you manage your
graphic design business? I'm not doing anything, and I'd do it for free.
I'm volunteering my services. I think I have a pretty good idea of Cedro's
approach to this place." He said, "I really appreciate your offer, but with all
due respect, I have no idea who you are or your background. Do you have
any experience running a place like this?" Estelle laughed and asked, "Do
you?" David said, "Good point." She said, "Like you, I don't have a scrap
of experience running a place like this." She said, "Why don't we do a trial
run for a month? You can tell me to get lost any time."

David was tired and stressed, and his gut said *go for it. Nothing ventured*. He
said, "Okay, let's give it a try. I'll run all the specifics by you. The front desk
staff know what they're doing, but you should know what they're doing.
Start there. Work beside them for a week. Then we'll see."

Estelle already knew and got along well with the three people at the front
desk. David told them he was training a backup. It went well, and Estelle
got to know more of the clients as they passed by. Occasionally, she'd go
back to the gym, wander through, and see how everyone was doing. Just
like Antonio/Cedro used to do. Positive reports got back to David. After a
week, he said, "You're hired." She said, "Contract only, and you have to pay

me in cash." David said, "I claim it as an expense to the IRS, so I need you to claim it as income." She said, "Hey, I used to be a bookkeeper. I know all that. Don't worry."

Estelle was now as buried running the gym as Ralph was in his work. They got together as often as time allowed but did not move in together. Ralph, of course, checked Estelle (Danielle) out. No social media, no history at all. He thought *this woman is not telling me everything.* One night, over dinner, he asked her about it. Estelle had her pat answer to that question. It was actually the truth. "I've never been comfortable with the lack of privacy on social media. Having a bunch of advertisers follow my account would creep me out. I never needed it. I'm old-fashioned. I phone. She said, "I'm not a Neanderthal; I Google and text. It's the only way to get through to you. You never answer the phone." Ralph laughed, "I always answer my clients' calls." Estelle said, "Exactly."

Another night, she turned the questioning around and said, "You never talk about your wife. You have no pictures of her around the house. What's that all about?"

Ralph said, "I like to live in the moment and look forward, not back. Looking back is a waste of time. You can't change the past." Estelle thought *an evasive answer. I wonder if your marriage was in trouble before your wife died.*

Estelle kept her personal life to herself. The only one who knew she was seeing Ralph was David because he did some website work for him.

Not long after asking Ralph about his wife, Estelle and one of the gym clients, Carol, were walking on the treadmills slowly side by side, warming up. Carol looked at Estelle and said, "So Danielle, are you seeing anyone?" Estelle (Danielle) was taken aback and said, "No, why?" Carol said, "I was just wondering. I saw you in Starbucks with Ralph Jamieson last week." Estelle wanted to shut this down fast and said, "We're just friends." Carol said, "You're new to Hollywood, right?" Estelle said, "Yes, why?" She thought *this is going somewhere. Where's it going?* Carol said, "You probably don't know this, but Ralph killed his wife about eight years ago."

Estelle's heart skipped a beat. She thought, *don't give her a reaction. That's what she wants.* Estelle acted disinterested and said, "Really? What happened?" Carol said, "I heard his wife was having an affair with their divorce lawyer, and he caught them together. They had a house down on the beach then. I think he shot her, or someone did." Estelle asked, "Why isn't he in jail?" Carol said, "I was never sure of all the details. He got off. It wasn't his gun that killed her, and he apparently said he wasn't there." She went on, "I guess they couldn't prove anything." Estelle didn't want to seem interested, so she turned up her treadmill to a faster pace and started a slow jog. Carol said, "Well, that's me for today. I'm done. See you tomorrow." Estelle said, "Yeah, see you, Carol."

Estelle didn't know what to do with this information, but she wanted to see if there was anything online about the trial. As soon as Carol left, she shut down her workout and left for the day. At home, she Googled it. There was a brief article about the murder and the trial, mainly about Ralph getting off. It didn't get into any salacious details. She thought *so; he's maybe a murderer, and he's definitely a liar. How about that? Almost as bad as me.*

She decided to keep her new knowledge to herself for now. She thought he could be innocent. The lie about the breast cancer was understandable. You can hardly lay that little tidbit out to a new woman in your life. "Hi, I'm Ralph, and I murdered my wife." She then thought, *who knows, maybe she did have breast cancer. She just didn't die from it.*

The following weekend, she drove up to his place. They'd ordered in, and he was laying out the plates. Estelle asked casually, "Ralph, do you have a gun?" He paused for a long time, kept on laying out the food, and poured each of them a glass of wine. He then said, "Yes, don't you?" Estelle said, "Yes, of course." In fact, since the Rudy incident and depending on her outfit, Estelle often had a small gun strapped to her calf. She also carried one in her bag. It had saved her life once.

Ralph said, "Why do you ask?" Estelle said, "Just wanted to be sure you had protection. You're alone up here in the hills." Ralph sensed she'd heard about the murder. He thought *maybe she's worried I might shoot her.* He sure wasn't going to talk about it with her. He thought *I'll wait and see how she plays this.* He just looked at her. She was pretending to look out at the pool. She was so transparent. Estelle thought *if he did it, he's cool as a cucumber. I don't see any guilty ticks in his behavior.*

He actually had three guns on the property and two at the office. Accessible and loaded. The house itself was well secured, with lots of cameras. He thought *yes Danielle, I have protection. You never know who might sneak up on you in the night.* He often worried about his wife's lawyer boyfriend. He'd been a suspect and could want revenge. Ralph kept his eyes open and his property protected.

Estelle and Ralph's relationship got even better after that. Estelle didn't feel so guilty about her lies and her past. She wasn't about to share that with him, but in her mind, they had a new alliance.

Estelle thought *Ralph had motive and means. His wife's killer had never been caught. Ralph didn't miss her or mourn her.* Estelle was sure he'd killed her.

Although Raph said he didn't think about the past, he did that night. He remembered the scare of having just gone through prostate surgery and been turned into a eunuch. His wife had made it clear he was no good to her anymore, and she was not kind. She'd humiliated him. Their divorce wasn't amicable. She wanted way more than she deserved, and she lied about everything. Her lawyer was younger than her and probably saw a cash cow. His lawyer didn't seem to be rising to the challenge. He could see himself losing a lot of money and his pride.

When he learned about her affair with her lawyer, Ralph went cold. He decided she wasn't getting anything. He was going to put an end to this.

He'd planned it meticulously. He'd set up his office as if he were working on a client's media plan with the plans on the work table. He knew his computer might be checked for operating time and turned it off early in the day. He did the same with his cell. His story would be that he did that when working up a program for a client. He didn't want to be disturbed. He left his car at the office and the lights on as if he was still working. He often worked late. He didn't turn the alarm on when he left. He grabbed an Uber and had him drop him off a mile from their house on the beach. Ralph had long moved out, but he still thought of it as their house. *And it will be again*, he thought. Earlier that week, he'd bought a gun and a silencer online using a burner phone.

They had home security cameras, but he knew where they were directed and how to avoid them. He dressed in black and wore a balaclava, gloves, and a bulletproof vest. His wife had a gun, too. He needed to be careful. He walked the mile to the house, avoiding headlights on the road. Using their shrubbery to hide himself, he snuck up just off the back patio and waited. He heard a male voice in the house. He assumed it was her lawyer. Ralph knew she swam in the pool every night. It was her exercise routine, and she was religious about it. After waiting for a couple of hours, she came out onto the pool deck by herself. He thought *you've got one chance; get it right*. He took aim, and she fell with the first shot. One problem, he couldn't be sure she was dead.

Ralph couldn't wait to find out. He stayed low while he walked slowly out of the neighborhood, keeping to the trees and the bushes. The street was quiet. He had to lose the gun, the mask and the gloves. Their neighbor three properties down was rarely there, and Ralph went down to the end of his dock and dropped everything over into the sea. He figured his wife's lawyer hadn't found her yet because there was no sound of sirens. Still using the burner phone, he called another Uber, returned to his office, ditched the phone in a garbage can way up the street and waited for the police to call. He was surprised that it took them so long. When the call came in, an officer said, "Mr. Jamieson?" Ralph said, "Yes." The officer introduced himself and said, "May I ask where you are?" Ralph said, "At m y office, why? What's going on?" He remained calm.

The officer said, "Sir, I'm sorry to tell you your wife has been found dead at your home. We're going to need to talk to you." Ralph smiled to himself. *Mission accomplished.* He feigned shock. "Dead? What happened?" The officer said, "She was shot." Ralph asked, "By whom?" The officer said, "That's what we intend to find out. We're sending a patrol car to your office. Can you give me the address? Ralph thought *stay cool, compliant, shocked. They can't prove anything*. Ralph said, "Of course, I'll be outside waiting for you."

And they couldn't prove anything. Ralph walked free.

Given Estelle's past and after much thought, she decided to leave the murder of Ralph's wife to him. She'd become a great believer in minding one's own business. They continued on with their part-time relationship over the next nine years, and the murder never came up.

After the first year of Estelle managing the gym, David approached her. He asked her if she wanted to own the business outright. Estelle said, "Interesting. What do you want for it?" David said, "It didn't cost me anything; Cedro gave it to me in his will. You are doing a great job with it and running it just like he would have wanted. I'm really not interested. It's yours. A gift from Cedro." Estelle said, "Wow, that's some gift. My own business." She said, "I'm not poor. There must be something you could use." David laughed and said, "I'm not into things. I can't think of anything I need or want. My business is doing well. I'm fine." He didn't tell her about the cash Cedro had also left him. They did the paperwork, and she was the proud owner of Stretch. Estelle didn't think David needed to know Cedro was actually the missing Antonio from Florida, a possible wife murderer. In her head, she said *thanks, Antonio.*

The year Ralph turned 77, he started to feel unwell. Follow-up revealed his cancer was back, and it was everywhere. He had months to live. He sold his business to his long-time assistant. She knew all their clients and was the natural successor. He got the rest of his affairs in order and rewrote his will.

As the end drew near, he was bedridden and miserable. He called his doctor and arranged for the End of Life option. He didn't want anyone changing his diapers. He thought *I'm dying anyway, why prolong it?* He asked Estelle to be with him when he got the final shot. She kissed his hand and said, "Of course, my darling man, whatever you want." She cupped his gaunt old face and said, "You're breaking my heart. I will miss you every day." They had never said, "I love you," and they didn't now. It didn't need to be said. He looked at her for a long time. He said, "Danielle, I did it. I killed the little bitch." Estelle took that in. She wasn't surprised. She said, "Now that you've got that off your chest, can you die peacefully?" Ralph said, "Don't get me wrong, I'm not sorry. I just wanted you to know that about me." He laughed weakly and said, "I'm not as nice as you think." Estelle said, "You're the nicest person I've ever known. Remember your mantra. The past is gone. You can't change it." Estelle wasn't about to confess anything. She'd live with her secrets. Besides, he could rally.

Ralph didn't rally. His was the third death Estelle had witnessed. Rudy, then Phil and now Ralph. It was another beautiful California day, and Ralph wanted to be wheeled out by the pool in the sunshine. The doctor came out with the apparatus and set up Ralph's arm for the final injection. They all sat together for a while, then he asked Ralph, "Are you ready?" Ralph said, "Yep, beam me up, Scotty." He looked into Estelle's face with a smile and squeezed her hand. He said, "Thanks, honey." The fluid entered his arm, and his body fell into itself. It was over. The doctor gently closed his eyes and said, "He wanted to donate his body to science, so we need to prepare him for that. You don't need to stay." Estelle said, "No, of course not. He's not in there anymore. Good for him." She leaned down and kissed him goodbye.

The following week was hard. Estelle couldn't stop crying. She couldn't remember the last time she'd cried. Maybe when she was a very little girl. She remembered Ralph's words about putting the past behind you. She straightened her shoulders and started over alone.

When the will was read, Estelle learned he'd left his house to her. It was worth well over ten million. She didn't want to live there. Too many memories. Combined with her stored cash, she was now a wealthy woman.

She sold the house and bought a large beachside townhouse in Laguna Beach. She kept her apartment in town and continued running the gym well into her early 80s. The club was so popular she had to limit membership and take waitlists. She was making money.

In Laguna Beach, she donated a lot of money to the community, particularly the animal shelter, in honor of Phil. The elegant silver-haired old lady named Danielle was invited to everything.

Estelle, perhaps the most duplicitous of them all, had a very good life.

LOOSE ENDS

Back in Miami at Zenith's office, Billy Knudson and lawyer Doug MacPherson continued to work on the Vanilla Palms condo sales and purchases. It was a lot of work.

Insurance claims had all been resolved, and the heirs and surviving owners received sizeable payouts that made their lives much more comfortable. The old saying, "It's an ill wind that blows no good," seemed applicable.

Roughly eighty of the heirs and surviving owners wanted to sell. That was the easy part. The more complicated part was that each apartment was fully furnished, with clothes, personal objects, and paperwork. Too many of the older folks were pack rats, having saved every piece of string they'd encountered since 1940.

Before selling the apartments to Zenith, the heirs and remaining owners needed to clear them out. Many heirs didn't even live in Florida, and many of the ones that did were very uncomfortable going into the apartments. Some said it felt like entering a crypt without the bodies.

Ever practical and expedient, Zenith told Billy to let them know there would be a sizeable clean-out fee if his company had to do it and gave them a deadline to get the apartments emptied. Otherwise, everything would be going out in one big truckload. Zenith thought *money and deadlines are always good motivators*. The feet draggers stepped up and cleared their apartments, and within two months, Billy and Doug were down to about ten apartments that hadn't been touched. Included in these were four of the five missing people's condos. Estelle's, Claire's, Randy's and Michael/Malek's. Antonio's daughter was renting out her father's apartment. Estelle's friend Phil was dead and wouldn't be taking Estelle's place. Randy's friend Mary didn't want his condo. It was too much hassle. Claire and Michael/Malek had no will and no heirs. Zenith had Doug apply for conservatorship so they could at least rent and maintain them and pay the property taxes until the Florida government allowed them to do the five-year paperwork stating these people were missing and presumed dead. It was all a bit messy.

All the remaining furniture, clothes and kitchen supplies were donated. Once the apartments were stripped, they needed to be cleaned, painted, repaired and readied for sale.

Zenith waited a year to finish all this, then put together a billboard advertising campaign offering the resales below market prices but way more than he'd paid. When people called, no mention was made of the explosion and the deaths in the condos. Surprisingly, very few people from outside Jacksonville had even heard about it. No one from out of state had. Zenith had been right; it wasn't an issue, and he would make a lot of money.

Nine owners who hadn't been there the morning of the explosion decided to stay. They had nowhere to go. Zenith assured them the value would return in a few years. Morty moved back in and resumed his position as condo president until a new board could be established and elections held. Zenith liked the continuity of Morty being there.

Meanwhile, Billy also worked hard at night, completing his Criminal Justice degree. He hadn't forgotten his plan to become a detective. He and Joe Piccioni were good friends and often got together for a beer. Joe reminded Billy he'd have to do years as a state trooper and get a few promotions under his belt before he could even consider applying for a detective's position. He told Billy, "Working with the underbelly of society can get you down. I almost walked away a few times." He'd ask Billy, "Are you sure you're up for this? The early years aren't fun." Billy said, "I have a goal. I'll be a good cop. I'll get there." Joe said, "It's not like in the movies. People you'll encounter every day, every hour of your shift, are usually nasty and angry. They hate cops and want to kill them. It's dangerous." Billy looked at Joe and said, "And...you're still here." Joe laughed. Billy said, "Just tell me one thing: does your job as a detective satisfy you, give you pleasure?" Joe smiled and said, "Every day." Billy said, "Then that's what I want too."

They'd long stopped investigating the missing people. They were gone. Joe and Billy never found out why the FBI and CIA took over the missing Claire Richmond and Michael Robertson investigations. Joe theorized one or both of them had something to do with the explosion. He was right, but it went way beyond that. They never heard that story.

One day, Joe called Billy and said, "Hey buddy, I've got some news. We got a letter from our missing Antonio Cervantes." Billy said, "No shit, what did he say?" Joe said, "He wrote we'd only get the letter if he was dead, so I guess he's dead." Joe read out Antonio's letter, which detailed Antonio and Lily fighting all the time, her agreement to leave, and the boat ride. Then, she pulled a gun on Antonio and accidentally shot herself. Joe said, "He figured because he was a Mexican, he wouldn't get a fair shake, and he would be charged with her murder. That's why he decided to disappear." Joe said, "It was an accident that saved his life but not hers." Billy asked, "Where'd he end up?" Joe said, "The letter was postmarked from Los Angeles. No return address." Billy said to Joe, "He faked his drowning, made sure his computer and phone were clean, planned his escape carefully, and his wife showed up dead. Sounds like a premeditated crime to me." Joe said, "I think his escape was premeditated, not his wife's accidental death. He wanted to ditch her, but I don't think he wanted to murder her."

"So, you believe him? Billy asked. Joe said, "Yeah, I do. He didn't need to write that letter, but he did. I think he's telling the truth. He didn't want his daughters to think he was a murderer. They already hated him." Billy asked, "Would he have been charged?" Joe said, "Probably. More because he was her husband than because he was Mexican. The legal system isn't that bent here."

Billy asked, "Have you told his daughters?" Joe said, "I thought I'd leave that to you. You guys are renting Antonio's apartment for one of the daughters, and you have the other one's number in Vancouver. They hated him, but this might vindicate him a little. I feel sorry for the guy."

When Billy called up Antonio's daughters, he learned they'd also received letters, but they hadn't contained any information about Lily or their father's disappearance. Neither of the women mentioned how much money Antonio had left them. The oldest daughter in Vancouver thanked Billy for calling and for the information and quietly hung up. She stared out her window at the mountains. She thought, *Daddy, you were a flawed, complicated, and unhappy man. I hope you found some peace in your new life.* Her hatred for him had been replaced with a bit of pity. The younger daughter renting out his Vanilla Palms apartment saw it differently and thought *yeah, Daddy, I totally get the Mexican thing; you would have been charged for sure. Smart move to get out of town. Thanks for the money.* She was always the realistic one.

A year later, Billy gave Zenith notice and joined the Miami Police Department. Zenith offered him a junior partnership to stay. Billy had become the son he'd never had. Billy said, "Zenith, I learned so much from you. You've been an amazing boss, and I'll be forever grateful. But we're different people. I don't really care about making a lot of money. I think I'll eventually be able to help people. I really want to do this." Zenith said, "We all have to make our own choices." He hugged him and said, "Stay safe, son. It's a dangerous world out there." He never really understood why Billy turned him down. Making money was so much more enjoyable than operating a speed radar gun out on some Florida freeway.

For Antonio, Estelle, Claire and Randy, having money, whether theirs or not, gave them options and allowed them to start over. None of them felt rich or lived rich, other than Estelle in her very senior years. She ended up with the best life and started giving back. Claire lived well but not extravagantly. She never stopped worrying about the fact that someone in Russia wanted her dead.

As their lives moved on and the chance of discovery became more remote, their burning secrets lost their heat. They stopped looking over their shoulders.

None of the four were spared life's challenges or grief. You can't run away from living, and death finds us all.

Does crime pay?

Sometimes.

Manufactured by Amazon.ca
Bolton, ON

39806267R00157